PRAISE FOR DiANN MILLS

TRACE OF DOUBT

"A well-researched and intimate story with some surprising twists along the way. In *Trace of Doubt*, Mills weaves together a tale of faith, intrigue, and suspense that her fans are sure to enjoy."

STEVEN JAMES, award-winning author of *Synapse* and *Every Wicked Man*

"DiAnn Mills took me on a wild ride with *Trace of Doubt*. . . . Filled with high stakes, high emotion, and high intrigue, *Trace of Doubt* will keep you guessing until the thrilling and satisfying conclusion."

LYNN H. BLACKBURN, award-winning author of the Dive Team Investigations series

"DiAnn Mills serves up a perfect blend of action, grit, and hear with characters so real they leap off the page. *Trace of Doubt* ta romantic suspense to a whole new level."

JAMES R. HANNIBAL, award-winning author of *The Paris Betray*

"*Trace of Doubt* is a suspense reader's best friend. From page on until the end, the action is intense and the story line keeps yo guessing."

EVA MARIE EVERSON, bestselling author of *Five Brides* and *Dus*

AIRBORNE

"When DiAnn Mills started writing suspense novels, she found her niche. They are strong stories that keep the reader guessing. *Airborne* was filled with twists and turns."

LENA NELSON DOOLEY, bestselling, award-winning author of the Love's Road Home series

"Mills keeps getting better with each novel."

LAURAINE SNELLING, bestselling, award-winning author of *A Blessing to Cherish* and the Home to Blessing series

FATAL STRIKE

"DiAnn Mills has done it again! *Fatal Strike* captivates the reader from the first to last page. Deliciously detailed, this fast-paced romantic suspense novel creates an emotional roller coaster that keeps the pages turning as quickly as they can be read."

REBECCA McLAFFERTY, author of *Intentional Heirs*

"*Fatal Strike* is a fascinating and page-turning suspense novel with fabulous characters and a touch of romance. Five stars from me! . . . The plot was full of suspense and plot twists and I was left guessing at every turn!"

SARAH GRACE GRZY, author of *Never Say Goodbye*

BURDEN OF PROOF

"DiAnn Mills never disappoints. . . . Put on a fresh pot of coffee before you start this one because you're not going to want to sleep until the suspense ride is over. You might want to grab a safety harness while you're at it—you're going to need it!"

LYNETTE EASON, bestselling, award-winning author of the Elite Guardians and Blue Justice series

"Taking her readers on a veritable roller-coaster ride of unexpected plot twists and turns, *Burden of Proof* is an inherently riveting read from beginning to end."

MIDWEST BOOK REVIEW

"Mills has added yet another winner to her growing roster of romantic thrillers, perhaps the best one yet."

THE SUSPENSE ZONE

HIGH TREASON

"In this third book in Mills's action-packed FBI Task Force series, the stakes are higher than ever. . . . Readers can count on being glued to the pages late into the night—as 'just one more chapter' turns into 'can't stop now.'"

ROMANTIC TIMES

"This suspenseful novel will appeal to Christian readers looking for a tidy, uplifting tale."

PUBLISHERS WEEKLY

DEEP EXTRACTION

"A harrowing police procedural [that] . . . Mills's many fans will devour."

LIBRARY JOURNAL

"Few characters in Mills's latest novel are who they appear to be at first glance. . . . Combined with intense action and stunning twists, this search for the truth keeps readers on the edges of their favorite reading chairs. . . . The crime is tightly plotted, and the message of faith is authentic and sincere."

ROMANTIC TIMES, 4½-star review, Top Pick

DEADLY ENCOUNTER

"Crackling dialogue and heart-stopping plotlines are the hallmarks of Mills's thrillers, and this series launch won't disappoint her many fans. Dealing with issues of murder, domestic terrorism, and airport security, it eerily echoes current events."

LIBRARY JOURNAL

"From the first paragraph until the last, this story is a nail-biter, promising to delight readers who enjoy a well-written adventure."

CHRISTIAN MARKET MAGAZINE

DEADLOCK

"DiAnn Mills brings us another magnificent, inspirational thriller in her FBI: Houston series. *Deadlock* is a riveting, fast-paced adventure that will hold you captive from the opening pages to the closing epilogue."

FRESH FICTION

"Mills does a superb job building the relationship between the two polar opposite detectives. With some faith overtones, *Deadlock* is an excellent police drama that even mainstream readers would enjoy."

ROMANTIC TIMES

DOUBLE CROSS

"DiAnn Mills always gives us a good thriller, filled with inspirational thoughts, and *Double Cross* is another great one!"

FRESH FICTION

"For the romantic suspense fan, there is plenty of action and twists present. For the inspirational reader, the faith elements fit nicely into the context of the story. . . . The romance is tenderly beautiful, and the ending bittersweet."

ROMANTIC TIMES

FIREWALL

"Mills takes readers on an explosive ride. . . . A story as romantic as it is exciting, *Firewall* will appeal to fans of Dee Henderson's romantic suspense stories."

BOOKLIST

"With an intricate plot involving domestic terrorism that could have been ripped from the headlines, Mills's romantic thriller makes for compelling reading."

LIBRARY JOURNAL

CONCRETE EVIDENCE

★ ★ ★

DiANN MILLS

Tyndale House Publishers
Carol Stream, Illinois

Visit Tyndale online at tyndale.com.

Visit DiAnn Mills's website at diannmills.com.

Tyndale and Tyndale's quill logo are registered trademarks of Tyndale House Ministries.

Concrete Evidence

Designed by Dean H. Renninger

Published in association with the literary agency of Books & Such Literary Management, 52 Mission Circle, Suite 122, PBM 170, Santa Rosa, CA 95409.

Concrete Evidence is a work of fiction. Where real people, events, establishments, organizations, or locales appear, they are used fictitiously. All other elements of the novel are drawn from the author's imagination.

For information about special discounts for bulk purchases, please contact Tyndale House Publishers at csresponse@tyndale.com, or call 1-855-277-9400.

Library of Congress Cataloging-in-Publication Data

A catalog record for this book is available from the Library of Congress.

ISBN 978-1-4964-5189-7 (HC)
ISBN 978-1-4964-5190-3 (SC)

Printed in the United States of America

28	27	26	25	24	23	22
7	6	5	4	3	2	1

Dedicated to Grace, Lane, and Ruby—

the best grands on the planet.

✮　✮　✮

AVERY ELLIOTT SPURRED HER HORSE across one of the thirty-five
thousand rolling acres of the Brazos River Ranch in the blazing heat.
The sultry August wind blew through her hair, bathing her damp face
and shoving aside her pensive mood. Granddad had told her once
that if he could lasso the wind, he'd ride that bronc to eternity. She'd
framed the saying and placed it in the reception area of their office.

Granddad had left at dawn to ride fence and enjoy some solitude
and think time. His work habits overruled his stomach, which meant
he wouldn't stop to eat until he'd inspected a recently repaired stretch.
Then the Internet had gone down ending her morning's work. A
good excuse for her to get away from the office and spend special
time with him.

She lightly grasped the reins of the most wonderful quarter horse on the planet and the perfect cure-all for the morning's

frustration. Closing her eyes, Avery allowed Darcy's rhythmic gallop to soothe her.

Avery slowed the mare to a walk and twisted her phone from her jeans pocket. Pressing on Granddad's name in Favorites, she breathed in the sweltering heat and envisioned him fumbling for his phone.

"Mornin', sweet girl."

"Can I treat you to a five-star restaurant for lunch?"

He chuckled. "You'll have to fly in the prime rib."

"I've packed us a picnic, and I'm on my way to meet you. Just say where."

"Drivin' or ridin'?"

"You've hurt Darcy's feelings."

"Give her my apologies. I'm west of the river about a mile from the family cemetery. Should be a nice breeze there this morning. We could talk and have lunch with your grandma."

"Good. I'd planned to stop at her grave while I was out." The oaks bordering the family plots would offer relief from the hundred-degree temps. With the abundance of summer rain, the area brimmed with green and vibrant wildflowers. "I'll make sure she has flowers on her grave."

"Not a day goes by that I don't think about her. Guess I'm a sentimental old man who never got over his first love."

Someday Avery wanted the same kind of love. She remembered the woman with warm brown eyes and a loving touch who fell prey to a stroke nearly fifteen years ago and never recovered. "You're not a sentimental old man but one who misses his wife and best friend."

"I see her in you." He sighed. "You have a spirit of strength deep in your heart. Others think you're quiet—until you're riled. Then you'd give the devil a run for his money."

"I hope I can always live up to that strength."

"You already have. One day you'll make the right man proud."

"Haven't found him yet."

"Time's just not right. So when will you get here?"

Avery studied the familiar landmarks—thoroughbred horses grazing to the south and cattle taking advantage of the Brazos River. Why anyone would choose to live away from nature's beauty made little sense to her. "About thirty minutes."

"You didn't bring tofu and carrot sticks? Mia's new diet is killing me. The doctor doesn't need to worry about my cholesterol or weight because she's starving me."

Avery laughed. "No. I packed ham and cheese, jalapeño-bacon potato salad, fresh tomatoes, cucumbers, and apple pie. You can eat light this evening."

"I have a political dinner at six o'clock and a deacon meeting at seven thirty. Hey, how did you get the forbidden food past Mia?"

"She was upstairs while I hurried in the kitchen." Their housekeeper and cook had entered the back side of her sixties and refused to slow down, but Granddad and Avery kept trying. Both knew better than to tell Mia to cut back on her pace unless they were looking to be chased down the road with buckshot in their rears. Granddad had no room to talk. He faced the big seven-oh in October, and he'd made no plans to ease back.

She slipped the phone back into her jeans pocket and hurried Darcy on. Avery wanted to arrive at the picnic site well before Granddad and have lunch set out for him.

Her thoughts crept back to the accounting issue from this morning. A work problem had made another moment at the ranch office torture, and getting away from the computer served as the perfect antidote. In examining Elliott Commercial Construction's records before the auditors arrived next week, she'd found a discrepancy. A paid bill for materials was much lower than it should have been. Why hadn't she seen this weeks ago at the completion of the Lago de Cobre Dam? The original bid for the project included the cost to supply additional rock and expand the footprint, footers, and other foundational elements to compensate for the soft ground. Those materials were ordered, canceled, and still the specs showed the work had been completed per the contract.

She'd contacted the material's supply company, and the accounting manager confirmed they'd invoiced what they supplied. Yet Avery's files didn't reflect a different supplier for the required foundation, as though Granddad had substituted inferior materials or hadn't followed the specs. He'd never sacrifice safety. Even the idea scraped raw against her conscience.

A call had gone to Craig, the foreman, but only voice mail greeted her. The accounting mess would drive her nuts until she resolved it, but she'd have to wait. Granddad would laugh at her fears about the dam's potentially faulty construction and explain the discrepancy. Accurate details ruled her thoughts, and perfectionism had a way of eating at her logic. A lot of good her Ivy League education accomplished when the numbers didn't add up.

Granddad said Avery shared his insight and discernment. The ability took practice, prayer, and purpose—his favorite three *p*'s as though he'd outlined a sermon. But Granddad was wrong. She must have made a mistake, and the error warred within her.

Avery rode the path to the family cemetery. Elliotts had owned this property and been buried there before Texas became a state. Irish, English, and Scottish heritage—hard workers and fighters for faith, family, and freedom. Which had a lot to do with Granddad's name, Dad's, and hers—Avery Quinn Elliott, respectively Senior, Junior, and whatever that made her. Fortunately, Granddad went by Quinn or Senator, Dad went by Buddy, and she was simply Avery. Proud family and heritage, although Dad and Mom slipped in applying all three traits of being an Elliott.

Not going there today. After spending time with Granddad and finding out the source of her accounting problem, she—

A shot rang out from the direction of the cemetery.

She dug her heels into Darcy's side and bolted ahead. Had Granddad met up with a wild pig, a rattler, or even a two-legged varmint? The latter caused her to slow the mare and circle a grove of trees. If she needed her Sig, the firearm rested in a saddlebag beside the packed lunch. Granddad wasn't in sight. Only his stallion.

She dismounted and grabbed her gun. Tying Darcy to a slender oak, Avery moved closer to the iron gate of the cemetery entrance and prayed he hadn't been hurt. How had he been a mile west of here when she called him?

Hesitant to call out for him and draw the shooter's attention to her, she hid behind an oak. A riderless motorcycle—a shiny, blue Yamaha Tracer 9 GT—had parked in the shadow of more trees outside the far edge of the iron fence, a few yards from a worn path leading to the main road.

On the opposite side of the cemetery, Granddad bent over a man, whose blood stained his chest and pooled on the ground. He felt for a pulse and lifted his head to the cloudless sky. In Granddad's gloved right hand rested a gun. He shoved the weapon into his front belt and lifted his phone to his ear.

"He's dead. This has to end." Granddad scanned the area, no doubt searching for someone. "I want Avery kept out of this, but I'm expecting her in the next twenty minutes." He kicked the dirt with the toe of his boot. "He parked on the road and walked back. She isn't to know about any of it. I'll handle the situation on my end. . . . Yes, I'll be careful and not let the authorities know what happened. Look, I need to move his body out of sight. He was a friend, one of the best. I despise where this has gone." Granddad waved his hand. "I told you Avery won't be a problem."

AVERY SWALLOWED THE ACID rising in her throat. Her head spun as though she'd stepped out of reality into a realm of horror, a nightmare of hallucinate proportions. What should she do? Ride in like she hadn't seen or heard anything? Call Granddad as though she were at a distance? Confront him?

She stole back to Darcy, glanced at the motorcycle, then rode back to the ranch. What had she seen and overheard?

Impossible.

The gunfire. Seeing Granddad bent over the body with his gun in hand. The call to someone . . .

"She isn't to know about any of it. I'll handle the situation on my end."

Granddad had made enemies in his political career, and while serving two terms as state senator, he'd been threatened. Many of those in the media referred to him as the Texas Peacock, but to those who valued his dogged ways to pursue justice, Granddad held the respectable title of Senator Elliott. His lucrative commercial construction business paved the way for enemies too. No one could make millions and not expect others to want him destroyed.

But the questions continued to plague her. A man lay dead, a man whom Granddad referred to as a friend.

Her phone alerted her to Granddad's call, the beat of a marching drum signaling he awaited her. He'd tried to reach her twice in the past ten minutes. No point avoiding him any longer.

"Hey, Granddad."

"Are you all right?"

"Not really. I was about to call. My stomach's upset, and I can't tell if the heat's getting to me or if I'm coming down with something. Hot and cold at the same time."

"You need to be inside with air-conditioning. I heard gunfire earlier, and when you didn't ride in, I tried to contact you. Scared silly, then I realized you might be in the no-tower zone."

"I'm sorry. Didn't mean to worry you. I heard gunfire too and thought you were target practicing." Avery despised liars, and she'd dropped into the same cowardice hole.

"Not me. I'll talk to the ranch hands when I get back."

"I'll put your lunch in the office fridge. That'll keep Mia from finding it."

"Thanks, sweet girl. You always have my back."

She loved the way his nickname for her rolled off his tongue, but today his deep voice sounded menacing. "We always have each other's back. Drink lots of water. This heat is the worst, so be careful."

"True. Are you going to lie down? I can take you to see the doc. I planned to be back in about two hours, but I can ride in now."

"Let me nap first. Note, I'm a grown woman."

"Even grown women need extra care. Love you to the moon and back."

Avery repeated the phrase, like they'd done since she was a toddler. Her heart ached for what she feared her hero might have done. *Think.* What had she witnessed?

She checked her texts. Craig had responded to her voice mail about the last construction project.

We used materials in the warehouse for the foundation.

The morning's uneasiness seemed like a cakewalk compared to now. His explanation made sense, and she thanked him in a voice text. If the auditors questioned the invoice, she'd point to the warehouse records. It seemed meaningless now.

Who was the dead man, and why had he been shot?

"Sweet girl, never pull a gun unless you or someone you love is in danger. Then don't hesitate."

3

THE LARGEST POPULATION IN PINE, TEXAS, shared the same address—the cemetery. Today a fresh grave added one more resident to the plot records. The sun exploded across the fiery Texas sky. Probably not a good sign for FBI Special Agent Marc Wilkins's dead father. The man had deserted Marc and his mother too many years to count, leaving them to survive on food stamps and a pitiful child-support check.

Marc placed his arm around his mother's thin waist, damp from her black dress in the blistering heat. She laid her head on his shoulder, and her quiet sobs mystified him. She still loved his father despite the wasted years between them. The best thing his father had ever done was to pack up and never return.

Marc kissed her cheek. Perhaps her tears were regret for what she'd dreamed her marriage might have been.

He turned his attention to the committal service. The military chaplain recited a list of Colonel Abbott Wilkins's achievements and commended his exemplary career. All that led to his appointment in the US Army Corps of Engineers. Many people gathered to honor a man who was married to the Army before he said, "I do" to Marc's mother.

Mom flinched at the sound of each volley salute from the rifle party. At his father's level, he could have been buried with all the military honors due his rank, but his instructions were to provide only the basic elements due every veteran who had served their country faithfully. After the playing of taps, the honor guard ceremoniously inserted three spent shells—symbolizing duty, honor, and country—into the flag and presented it to his mother, whom his father had never divorced.

"On behalf of the president of the United States, the United States Army, and a grateful nation, please accept this flag as a symbol of our appreciation for your loved one's honorable and faithful service."

Mom took the flag, and the ceremony ended soon afterward. Marc stood by her while the attendants offered polite condolences, supporting her as he'd always done in his father's absence. When the last vehicle drove away, he escorted her to his car.

"I'm right here with you." He wanted to add "unlike your husband," but Marc needed to harness his bitterness. A lump rose in his throat. Where did that come from? He opened the passenger door, and she slid in. Even the click of the seat belt signified finality.

He drove toward her small subdivision north of Houston. At least Mom was accustomed to living alone.

"How long can you stay?" She choked out the words.

"I took the rest of the week off."

She arched her shoulders. "Your father's heart was in excellent condition. Someone killed him."

"Oh, Mom. I know you're grieving. But he died of a heart attack."

She moistened her lips as though gaining courage to speak. "Two weeks ago, he forwarded me his yearly checkup. Blood work. Heart tests. Everything. Nothing indicated any health issues."

"Why send it to you?"

Mom stiffened. "Marc, you won't like what I'm about to say."

He gripped the steering wheel. Would she claim his father had been misunderstood? "Go ahead."

"Your father and I had been talking. He regretted all the years his career came before me, before his family. He asked for another chance."

Ironically, his father realized at age sixty-eight that he needed to settle down with the beautiful woman he'd married forty years ago while on military leave. "You agreed?"

"If we attended marriage counseling and proceeded slowly."

"Okay. I'm glad for your sake he made an initiative to rectify his mistakes."

"Don't talk professional jargon to me. I'm not finished."

He swung her a compassionate look. "Go on. Sorry to sound callous."

"He called this past Thursday, and we talked. He texted me a few hours before he planned to meet with a friend regarding a work project and promised to call later. He never did. Early the next morning, a three-star general and a military chaplain arrived in a limo to notify me of his death."

His father always kept his word, except with his wedding vows. "Because of meeting with friends, you believe someone murdered him?"

"I believe someone made Abbott's death look like a heart attack. And his cell phone is missing. You have the experience and resources to find answers to my questions."

Marc wanted to leave the past behind. His father's country honored him, and rightfully so, even if the sacrifices came at his wife's and son's expense. He didn't dislike his father—not really. How could he despise someone he didn't know? For years he'd hoped one day his father would figure out that adherence to responsibility included his family. Then Marc grew up and decided the man used his career as an excuse to avoid responsibility for his family.

"What are you thinking?" Mom's matter-of-fact tone made him feel like he was under interrogation.

"I suggest taking your suspicions to the Army's Criminal Investigation Division. They're equipped to make proper inquiries."

"Why would the CID take the case when the medical examiner's report said he died due to natural causes? I should have insisted upon an autopsy. And I know if his death fell under suspicious circumstances, they'd investigate it. All I'm asking is for you to talk to those at the Army Corps office who worked with him, like you were investigating a homicide. Afterward, if you're convinced Abbott died of natural causes, I'll accept it."

Investigate his death like a homicide? "I have work piling up on my desk. And I couldn't get involved unless CID requested FBI assistance. Besides, I'd not be permitted since he's family."

"He's your father." She punched each word and blinked back the tears. "If you refuse, I'll hire a private investigator."

Marc wanted to groan. The circumstances surrounding his father's heart attack weren't unusual. Yet Mom was adamant about her suspicions. "All right. I'll look into it."

"Son, there's one more thing."

4

MARC JUSTIFIED HIS MOTHER'S irrational response to her emotional state. Dealing with his father's unexpected death when she longed for a better life had crushed her. The man had disappointed her so many times that she should be relieved.

Dwelling on the past solved nothing. Some people changed when confronted with their mistakes, except he sincerely doubted his father had any of those inclinations. Marc would help her through the grief and hope he could find a logical explanation to ease her heart and mind. Right now, talking to her face-to-face instead of on the passenger side of his car would help the communication.

"Mom, what haven't you told me?" Silence invaded their conversation while he assumed she formed her words. "Take your time. I'm right here."

"Thanks, Son. The last time Abbott and I were together, he said he feared for a friend who was investigating a federal crime. The two talked privately for over an hour while I waited on the porch." Mom held up a palm. "I don't have a name. I've racked my brain trying to remember if Abbott even mentioned it. But he believed both of them were in danger since they'd uncovered incriminating evidence. I don't know if he met with the same friend on Thursday when he died."

Resentment toward his father had dug a deep trench, but Marc believed in guarding his mother's welfare. Burying his father must have hit him a little harder than he wanted to admit. "But you weren't in danger?"

She shook her head. "I asked him, and he said, 'Donita, absolutely not.' If he felt I was in a perilous position, he'd have asked me to stay with you until they completed the investigation."

"You believed him?"

"I had no reason not to."

How could she trust him? "Do you have anything for me to go on?"

"I might have taught kindergarten for thirty years, but I am perceptive."

"Yes, ma'am. A lead would help."

"Your father gave me the friend's phone number in case the threats were legitimate. I tried calling the friend several times to tell him about Abbott's passing, but the calls went to voice mail, and I wasn't able to leave a message."

"What did the voice mail say?"

"A woman said to 'Leave a number and a brief message, and I'll return your call.' She sounded computer generated." Mom reached into her purse and pulled out a slip of paper. "You will need this."

Marc took the paper and tucked it into his pant pocket. "I'll run the number when I'm back at the office. Did you call the Army Corps of Engineers? If the two men were investigating a case, the corps would have documentation."

"I contacted the Fort Worth office and spoke to Lieutenant Nick Shipley. In fact, he attended today's service. He offered condolences, but he couldn't help me without a name. He also said Abbott oversaw many projects, and all of them involved classified information."

Marc understood protocol to protect sensitive data. "On Wednesday I'll leave you alone for a few hours and drive into the FBI office. I need to wrap up some paperwork on my desk. While there, I'll contact the corps office in Fort Worth. Had Abbott mentioned the names of other friends?"

"Not during that conversation. I've thought about googling Abbott to see if he's pictured with anyone or mentioned in connection with others who could help. But why would I put others in danger?"

"Good call, Mom. You must be related to the FBI."

She gave him a thin smile. "I have a wonderful son who means everything to me. He's smart, hot—as the girls say—and loves his mother."

How could Marc refuse anything she asked?

"Son, will you tell me everything you find out and hold nothing back?"

"I'll do my best." He took her hand into his. "I see how the circumstances surrounding my father's death have upset you. I'll do some probing to ease your mind. Be patient, answers may take a few days. I'd like his cardiologist's information and the medical examiner's name who signed his death certificate."

"I have those at the house."

"Did Dad reference anything or anyone else? An identifying factor about his friend?"

"Nothing I can recall. Can you search Abbott's office and records?"

He continued to hold her hand. "Not the FBI's jurisdiction. If the corps suspects foul play and requests assistance from the FBI, then I might learn more. But with a medical examiner referring to his death as natural causes, I don't see any reason for them to spend extra money on—"

"A grieving wife insisting her husband had a healthy heart per a cardiologist?"

"Honestly, you hit the nail straight on. I'll do all I can. No promises."

"I understand. But you are his son. Surely you have a little clout. Can you arrange for the corps to send me his personal effects? I have his house key."

Marc chose not to dive into how or why she had the key. "I'll request those things when I contact them. At some point we'll want to go through his home. Unless he has a will, his estate will be tied up in probate."

She stared out the windshield. "Thank you. I'd also like for you to talk to his regular GP. Abbott could have forged his health report for some unknown reason. But I doubt it. He's guilty of a lot of things, hard to forgive things, but lying wasn't one of them."

How well Marc remembered the man's bluntness. Truth came before sparing feelings, whether the information was needed or not.

"You're a disappointment, kid. Life isn't about books. It's about being a man, playing sports, and moving toward a career in the military. And your mother encourages your behavior. That's why I'm outta here."

His father had loaded up the trunk of his car and driven off, leaving a brokenhearted wife and eight-year-old son.

"The harsh look on your face tells me you're holding a grudge against your father. Gracious, Marc. Leave the past behind you. Forgive him because bitterness will only eat you alive. I should know." Mom sighed and released her hand from his to dab her eyes. "Your dad's gone, and in the end, he made amends with me and wanted to do the same with you."

Why? They had nothing in common. "For your sake, I'm glad you have peace."

"Peace is finding out who and why your father is dead." She rubbed her forehead.

"What aren't you telling me? I feel like I'm prying a splinter out of a rock."

"I have a copy of his will."

"What? Have you read it?"

"Yes, and a few things will shock you."

Marc neither wanted to hear this nor deal with any issues regarding his father.

"You look angry," she said.

He leaned his head back and searched his vault of mom responses. "I've given my word to help. Is this the last bomb?"

"Yes."

"I'm ready."

"As I said, Abbott gave me a copy. He left me 40 percent of his estate and his home. You receive 30 percent, and . . . your fifteen-year-old half sister will receive the other 30 percent."

5

SLEEP EVADED AVERY, but not nausea and tears. She had this link connecting her emotions to her stomach, and when disturbing things happened, she kissed the porcelain rim. When the worst of the vomiting had passed and her body wrung weak, she grabbed her phone and checked local news for a possible murder. The local, county, and state law enforcement had nothing to report. Granddad had either not contacted the authorities about the body, or he'd followed through and had the body removed. Neither option measured up to the man she loved. Prayer didn't ease the fear and concern stalking her like a hungry lion.

Only a few hours had gone by since she'd seen the victim from a distance, but not his face. Notifying next of kin explained the news delay. She needed her laptop in the office to check Granddad's calendar . . . to find a possible indication of what had happened this morning.

At straight-up 5:30 p.m., Granddad's diesel truck roared to life. He sped down the mile-long driveway for his dinner and meeting, as punctual as the rooster ushering in sunrise. Avery waited fifteen minutes before creeping down the back stairway. The door near the bottom opened onto a stone walkway that led to the office 1,250 feet from the house. As one hand wrapped around the doorknob in her best attempt to keep quiet, Mia's voice met her ears. Avery cringed.

"Are you feeling better?" the older woman said. "Senator Elliott said you were feeling poorly."

She slowly faced Mia. "I think so. Haven't vomited in the past hour. Temp's down."

"You're white as flour. Shouldn't you be in bed?" Her gentle tone laced her words in love.

"I thought a little fresh air might do me good."

"At the office?" Mia knew her all too well. She crossed thin arms over her chest. "How about a few crackers and ginger ale to settle your stomach?"

"Maybe later. I need to check on a project from this morning. It's been bothering me."

"You and the senator are chiseled from the same piece of granite. He was preoccupied with something and didn't want to talk much."

Avery caught her breath. "I won't be long. I promise. Then back to bed." She gave Mia a reassuring smile and walked outside into the suffocating heat.

After entering the numbers to disarm the office alarm, she stepped inside and locked the door behind her. She didn't want any surprises. Elliott Commercial Construction's filing systems were her design after she'd complained to Granddad about how nothing could be found. He'd agreed, and she organized easy access to all the documents and paperwork for each building project. Her stomach protested her efforts to stay calm, and she made two trips to the bathroom. Oh, how she hated this weak side of her. Shouldn't prayer and determination be enough?

Someone knocked on the office door. She expected Mia to have brought crackers and ginger ale. The dear woman took her role of caring for the Elliotts seriously. When she opened the door, Craig greeted her, a rugged-looking man in his midthirties who'd received a generous portion of looks and charm. Thick, nearly black hair and blue-green eyes under a cowboy hat caused the women to beg for his attention. Craig hadn't married, probably because his expectations were too high.

"The senator said you weren't feeling well, and now you're working."

She forced pleasantry into her words. None of this was Craig's fault. "I needed a change of scenery and thought this might help."

He crammed his hands into his jean pockets. "You look awful. I suggest hightailing it back inside the house."

"I will. Just need to spend five minutes with work from today, and I want my laptop to catch up since the Internet is working again."

"Anything I can do?"

"No. I want to finish up before Granddad returns tonight." More truth there than she cared to explore. "I appreciate your getting back to me about the warehouse materials."

"No problem. We have the approved inspection report from the state, and there haven't been any issues with the reservoir since it filled."

"Perfect." She should verify the materials used and update her records. But not tonight.

"Want me to stay and lock up?"

"Thanks, but I'm good."

"All right. Text if you change your mind. By the way, did you hear a gunshot while you were out riding?"

Avery toyed with how to answer. "Yes, but no idea who did it or where it originated."

"The senator asked me about it. Probably some yahoo ignoring the No Trespassing or Hunting signs."

"Have you ridden out to where Granddad heard the shot?"

"Heading there now. One of the hands claimed to have seen a motorcycle on Oak Valley Road arrive at the ranch property this morning."

Avery's stomach threatened to empty again. "Let me know what you find."

"Sure." He leaned on one leg. "Why weren't you in choir Sunday?"

There he was, flashing the born-again badge like a Puritan. "I preferred sitting with Granddad. He had a headache, and I wanted to be with him."

"Are you okay? Struggling with your faith? Do you need to talk?"

"You're sweet, Craig. If I want to talk, you're at the top of my list."

"Hey, I'm your brother-friend. Let me know."

"Thanks." He left and she locked the door. Craig had been attending cowboy church with Granddad and her for the past year. He meant well, and he had their respect and trust, but a few things hadn't clicked yet. She and Granddad called him their personal Jesus project.

Avery slumped into her chair. Craig mentioned the motorcycle. It must belong to the dead man. What happened to it? Still at the cemetery? Should she check? She'd raced Darcy back to the ranch, but it was doubtful she'd have heard a motorcycle from that distance.

An hour later, she powered down her laptop. Nothing surfaced on the news or on Granddad's calendar, and he wrote down every phone call and appointment. She found no answers to the questions pressing her, and that meant a sleepless night with a churning stomach.

6

MARC WRESTLED WITH THE REALITY of having a sister—one he never knew existed. He stretched out on the spare bed in Mom's craft room and imagined what the teen looked like. In the darkness of night and the darker depths of his soul, anger surfaced from the heartache his father had inflicted on his mother . . . and him. The boy in Marc shouted "abandonment" and "not good enough" to the man who'd fathered him. Didn't help that those who had attended the funeral stated one accolade after another.

His father had found a replacement family. Had they measured up to his sky-high expectations? His critical tongue? His feigned affection in public? If that were the case, why hadn't he divorced Mom? Guilt must have caught up with him to seek her out.

Marc's mind bolted with all the events of the day, and the same mental overload also denied him sleep. He'd buried his father and learned of a fifteen-year-old sister. Sounded like the basis for a reality

TV program. Mom said her name was Tessa Elizabeth Wilkins, and she lived with her grandmother in Fort Worth. Logic told him his father had indulged in an affair and got hit with a paternity suit. Although his father hadn't married the woman, why give the girl his last name? And why did she live with her grandmother instead of her mother? Did Marc even want to know why?

How sad if his sister had been discarded like he had. Tough on a boy. Most likely worse for a girl.

Was Marc angry or jealous? Or both?

Mom stood in the craft room doorway, the shadowed figure of inconsolable sorrow.

"Can't sleep?" he said.

"No. The memories, good and bad, keep replaying in my mind. What could I have done differently to make our marriage work and Abbott a better father?"

"Mom, we went to church, and I heard you pray. I remember your tears when special occasions came and went without him contacting us."

"God was my husband and comfort."

Marc had become a Christian at a junior high church camp, and his faith stayed intact—except when it came to his father. He'd kept God off-limits there. A man was entitled to one stain on his heart.

He swung his legs over the bed and patted the empty spot beside him. "Talk to me. Tell me everything you're thinking. I'll listen, and we'll figure it out together."

She eased beside him and laid her head on his shoulder. So frail. Vulnerable. Wounded. "Thank you."

He wrapped his arm around her waist. "First of all, from all my recollections, you did more than anyone to placate my father. You'd teach school, come home, clean, and cook an incredible dinner."

"The man I married made me feel like I held his heart in my hand. The first eight years we shared laughter and so much love.

We traveled with the Army and planned a future with a houseful of kids." Mom sighed, a sweet sound as though her heart filled with tender memories. "You were born and became our whole world. His Army career and responsibilities expanded, and he changed slowly into a man I no longer recognized—the man you despised, not that I blamed you then or now. He gave no reason for the harshness, but I think it had a lot to do with the demands of his work. My hope is for you to move past the disappointment. If I took my share of the blame for the failed marriage, I'd say I tried too hard. And in doing so, I looked weak in his eyes, which made his discontent worse. Your interest in books at my encouragement drove him farther away." She sniffed and Marc handed her a tissue from the nightstand.

The turmoil he'd experienced earlier rolled and slammed against his heart. "Honestly, Mom, when he left, I believed I'd let him down as a son. He wanted to make a soldier out of me, and I refused. I wanted him to love me for me. The more he criticized my reading, the more I made sure he saw me absorbed in a book. By the time he'd moved out and I discovered sports, I simply hated him more." Marc bit back another remark. "Sorry. Guess we both need to work through the past."

"You and I have always been close, more like friends than mother and son. At times I regretted my inability to seek counseling or talk to a trusted friend."

"Our relationship then and now is solid. I'm curious, though. What happened for you two to start talking again?"

"Are you sure you want to know?"

He kissed her cheek. "Yes, ma'am."

"About two years ago, he showed up at my front door and wanted to talk. Seeing him after all those years brought back tender feelings I didn't want to deal with, but his persistence won me over. From then on, we spoke or saw each other weekly. Oddly enough, I found the man I fell in love with. We laughed again, shared picnics and long walks, and he accompanied me to church."

Stunned, Marc had no knowledge of his parents' conversations. "Church? He said believers were victims of propaganda."

"Age and life experiences had mellowed him."

They sat quietly in the darkness, Marc sorting through what she'd said, and he assumed her thoughts were occupied too. Both weighed the what-ifs had his father survived.

"When did you learn about his daughter?"

"A year and a half ago. The girl was the result of an affair. After she gave birth, the mother took off and left Tessa with the grandmother. Abbott tried to find the mother, but she'd disappeared."

"Did he have contact with his daughter or the grandmother?"

"Yes. He saw the mistakes he'd made with you and didn't want a repeat."

"But she lived with her grandmother." He regretted reacting like a spiteful kid.

"Right. A long story there too. Recently Abbott completed a renovation to his home for her to live with him."

"Why did he wait so long?"

"No reason to keep it from you. The grandmother permitted visitation, but nothing else. Not joint custody and Abbott didn't want a drawn-out battle in court, especially when the grandmother loved Tessa. The woman feared losing the girl like she'd lost her own daughter. About four months ago, the grandmother was diagnosed with stage 4 cancer and changed her mind. Papers were signed for Abbott to have permanent custody. The grandmother is currently in hospice care, and Tessa chose to live with her until the end."

Poor kid. She'd received one bad break after another. "Were there plans to tell me about all this?" Guilt hit him. "That sounded immature. Let me rephrase my question. Was there a discussion about one of us meeting the girl?"

"I'd already agreed to it." She started to say more and stopped.

"You and he were getting back together, and she'd be a part of your lives. The three of you." Marc dragged his tongue across dry lips. "I want you happy, and I'd never have tried to stop you."

"That's comforting. When I talked to Abbott on Thursday, he planned to contact you today, arrange for a meetup, attempt to repair the past, and inform you about your sister."

"I see."

"A lot for your analytical mind to absorb in one sitting."

He chuckled, more nervousness than humor. "You know me well."

"Your dad said to me, 'God doesn't cause a demolition unless He's planned a renovation.'" She stood. "With those words, I'm going back to bed."

"One more question."

Mom faced him.

"Why wasn't Tessa at the funeral?"

"Her grandmother is in no shape to drive. I spoke with Tessa on the phone, and she seemed very sweet. Deeply regretted not being able to attend the service. I consoled her the best I could."

Marc heard the weariness in her voice. "I'm glad you were able to help her. Rest up."

"I will. You are a perfect therapist." She kissed the top of his head as though he were a boy again, and he didn't mind a bit. "I love you. Please, try to sleep." She closed the door behind her.

Wide-awake and his mind in investigative mode, he powered up his laptop. Through a secured FBI site, he searched for info on Tessa, including all social media platforms. Nothing surfaced on Facebook or Twitter, but he hadn't really expected a presence there at her age. Instagram seemed to be her sweet spot, and for the first time, he saw a photo. Something like an electrical shock jolted through him. He saw himself at that age in her wide smile. Her skin was fairer than Marc's olive tone, but he'd inherited a lot of Mom's Hispanic genes. Strange, he hadn't expected to see any semblance of himself in another person until he had his own child. Tessa's clean selfies and the poses with other girls gave him no indication of a teenager absorbed in herself or diving into things she had no business doing. From the green mermaid logo in many of the pics, Starbucks must have her attention for coffee drinks. Snapchat confirmed the same findings. In most of the photos, she wore her light-brown, shoulder-length hair in a ponytail. Fresh. Clean.

He approved.

Tomorrow he'd spend the day with Mom, but on Wednesday he'd drive to the office and check Tessa's school and medical records.

Marc scrolled through Instagram again to study images, reels, and stories for an indication of a relationship with their father. If he'd spoken the truth about changing his ways, Marc needed to see it. He discovered a video of his father and Tessa eating ice cream, a side of his father he'd never experienced.

The two sat at a round table with double-decker ice cream cones. He asked for a bite of her mint chocolate chip. She agreed and lifted the cone and brushed it across his nose. They laughed. The two actually laughed together. Marc had no memories to compare with what played out before him. Yet he couldn't blame Tessa either. Humiliation wound through him like a nasty virus. A grown man shouldn't feel this way, but his thirty-two-year-old heart ached like he was eight again.

7

AVERY WOKE AT SIX TUESDAY MORNING after repeatedly reliving the previous day's tragedy. Confronting Granddad would be the hardest thing she'd ever done, but she'd convinced herself to talk to him honestly. After wiggling into jeans and grabbing a T-shirt, she made her way downstairs to the kitchen. The sickness had passed, and she needed coffee to open her mind—like an alcoholic needed liquid courage.

Granddad sat at the breakfast table, a plate of poached eggs and wheat toast pushed to the side. Coffee mug in hand, he stared out the window to observe horses grazing in the distance.

"Good morning," she said.

He slowly faced her . . . his features pinched and drawn. He obviously hadn't slept well either. "Feeling better?"

"Yes. Thanks. No temp. I think the heat got to me." She poured a mug of coffee and sat across from him. The normal camaraderie between them vanished into something unspeakable.

"We need to talk." Granddad rubbed his forehead, a habit when deep in thought.

Her heart pounded against her rib cage. "Now?"

"Not here. Do you have plans this morning?"

"Just to shower and head over to the office."

"A friend is meeting me around eleven, but I'd like for us to talk before then."

She'd seen the entry on his calendar. The friend he'd called yesterday? "Did something happen last night at your meetings? Is this serious?"

"Those went fine." He set his mug on the table and folded his hands. "We both know the seriousness of a particular situation."

She captured the intensity of his clear blue eyes. "What about now? I can get cleaned up later. My appetite is zilch."

He slowly nodded. "Mine too." He scooted back his chair and stood. His broad shoulders slumped. How quickly he'd aged in one day.

They walked together to the office like most mornings. But this one was different. Neither spoke as though each sensed the burden of tragedy separating them.

Craig waved at them on his way from the stable near the office. "Mornin'." He strolled their way. "Since you're both aware of the strange goings-on yesterday, I wanted to let you know what I learned."

"Can it wait?" Granddad said. "I have an—"

"I found motorcycle tracks on Oak Valley Road entering and exiting. Looks like someone drove back to the family cemetery."

"Did you see anyone?" Granddad said.

"Nah. Must have been the rider who fired that shot." Craig shrugged. "But it could have been one of the hands. I'm thinking it's not worth looking into, except to find out who might have taken a joyride across the ranch."

"Let me know if you find out anything, and I'll handle it," Granddad said.

Granddad's familiar phrase echoed a new meaning.

At the office, Granddad pressed in the alarm and opened the door. He gestured Avery inside, and an eerie feeling shrouded her. Had she been living in a fairy tale that now had an evil side?

Granddad snatched the mail from his tray on her desk. She'd sorted it the night before, but he hadn't been here to pick it up. "Let's sit in my office," he said. "Nothing about what I have to tell you is easy." Once settled, the lines etched around his eyes seemed to deepen more. "I saw Darcy's tracks near the cemetery yesterday. You were there."

Avery nodded, sensing the barbed wire of truth about to pierce her heart. "I arrived earlier than you expected. I wanted to surprise you with lunch all set up."

"How much earlier?" He combed his fingers through thick silver hair.

She swallowed, her throat raw. "In time to see you leaning over a man's body and hear you make a call. I heard every word."

"Then I understand why you were sick. Did you see anything or anyone?"

"A motorcycle." She sighed. "A blue Yamaha Tracer 9 GT. No driver."

"I heard it too. The driver had to have arrived while I rode fence. What about the plates? Footprints? Any sounds?"

"The motorcycle was parked sideways. No one was in sight."

"You believe I killed a man." Granddad didn't ask but stated the reality of her terror.

"I'd rather you gave me an explanation. Self-defense? An accident?" She drew in a breath. "I want to believe in your innocence. But it's all confusing when I saw a gun in your hand."

"If I could share the details with you, I would. But it's impossible. Too dangerous." He captured her gaze. "You can't tell a soul about this."

She shuddered. "Why? A man's dead, right?"

"The body's been removed."

"That doesn't make him any less dead." She squeezed her fingers into her palm. "Who was he?"

"You'll find out soon enough. But not from me. Anything I say puts you in a bad place."

"Would you prefer I think you killed a man and disposed of his body? Who did you call? Who rode the motorcycle? How can I remotely consider such horror?"

"You have already come to a conclusion."

She fought a wave of sickness and summoned courage to chase it off. "But the granddad I love isn't a killer."

He rubbed his face. "If you were a member of the sheriff's department and saw me in the cemetery, what would you have done?"

"You're not being fair."

"I will do whatever it takes to protect you." His tone rose above a whisper.

"From whom? Law enforcement? Someone else? What's going on?"

"It's better this way. The less you know, the safer you are."

"Murder and a cover-up are never justified. If you're innocent, say so."

"No, Avery. We're not going there."

The burning suspicions raged, a wildfire that flamed out of control. "I know the man you met yesterday wasn't planned because you had nothing scheduled."

"Would I sink to such depravity as to note a man's murder on my calendar?"

She trembled, yesterday's ordeal repeating . . .

"Avery, pray for me to have a clear head in this mess."

"Always." Emotion rose and threatened to burst. He didn't ask for an exoneration but a clear head.

"Is this about the ranch, the construction company, politics?"

"More trouble than I've ever been in my life, and I won't drag you into the thick of it."

But he already had.

8

THE MORNING DRAGGED ON, and Avery's concentration hit the dredges of unbidden thoughts. Granddad and Frank Benton, state-house representative for their district, met behind closed doors. Granddad had two obsessions in life—Jesus and politics. He often spouted what-Jesus-would-do in relation to how he felt on a political point. She hid the humor behind his statements as though he were a country preacher conducting a revival. Love had a way of covering a multitude of quirky traits.

Except what she'd seen yesterday.

A deadline to respond on a proposal for a dam repair demanded her attention. The specs were before her, and she simply needed to type in the figures for the TCEQ—Texas Commission on Environmental Quality. If awarded the contract, Elliott Commercial Construction would complete the design and perform the work. Transferring infor-mation from Granddad's copious notes to the computer screen and going through the checklist of required documents should have been a no-brainer. *Should* ranked as Granddad's number one word to eliminate from her vocabulary.

The conversation with him from earlier this morning repeated in her mind with no more clarity than before. She prided herself in relying on facts, not half-truths. His vague comments and responses burrowed into her heart.

He neither denied nor admitted to killing the man.

He neither denied nor admitted to knowledge of the motorcycle in the cemetery. But he did appear surprised.

Without knowing the timing of the bike's arrival and departure, the number of men tramping around the cemetery fell into the unknown zone. Avery drew in a ragged breath. Did Granddad mean a clear head to avoid an arrest? For the serious trouble stalking him? Why did she need protection?

The best solution simmered in truth, and Granddad avoided it like a stubborn mule. So she wrestled with how to proceed. Take a stand and demand the truth? Ignoring it hit the impossible list. Granddad had instilled values since she tossed aside a baby bottle. Even her faith swung in the balance when the man who'd shown her Jesus could have committed the unthinkable. All of it was entwined in her love for him.

Granddad's hearty laughter rang out. When she was a little girl, he had reminded her of Santa Claus. Once she reached her preteen years, his laughter had chased away whatever worried her. At school some of the girls had given her a rough time because of his political position and outspoken mannerisms. They were brutal to the point of bullying her. After a few of them ganged up on her in a bathroom, using verbal barbs to tear her to pieces, she called Granddad to pick her up.

He refused—instructed her to face those girls with the heart and courage of an Elliott. If she didn't stand up for herself now, she'd never make it in the world. She had no choice but to stay.

The days and weeks ahead dredged up a lot of emotion, but she overcame the bullies. One thing she'd never told Granddad—she'd blackened a girl's eye for saying he only cared about himself and power. Strange to recall those times now. The girl who'd led the bullying was now her best friend.

Avery glanced at the closed door of his office. After Mr. Benton left the ranch, she'd corner Granddad and demand to know every detail of yesterday.

At twelve thirty, the men exited. "Frank and I are heading to lunch, and then I'm driving on to Austin. You need anything before I leave?"

If Granddad could read her mind, he'd not leave. "I'm good."

"Feeling okay?"

Nope, misery had swept in like a twister. "I think so. When can I expect to see your handsome face back in the office?"

Mr. Benton chuckled. "Senator, you hold that pretty granddaughter of yours in the palm of your hand."

"Hope so. She keeps me on the straight and narrow." He nodded at Avery. "Tell Mia not to hold dinner. I have no idea when I'll be back."

"Okay. Call me when you're on the road to Austin. I have a few questions to finalize a proposal."

"Sure thing. Hunker down and keep the wolves away."

Avery heard his code phrase for families protect those they love. Was he shielding her or himself?

By ten that night, Granddad hadn't called or returned home. Throughout the afternoon and evening, her attempts to contact him via text had failed, and her repeated calls went straight to voice mail. Had he turned off his phone? He hadn't recorded the appointment in Austin on his calendar either, indicating a last-minute decision.

Her cell phone rang, a number she didn't recognize. Granddad might have called her from a different phone, so she answered.

"Avery, yesterday's unfortunate incident sure made a mess of things," a distorted voice said.

"Who is this?"

"A messenger. Listen up. Do exactly as the senator tells you or your life is worth nothing."

"What are you talking about?"

"One word about this call to anyone and your grandfather is dead." The call ended in a click.

A flood of fear rushed over her. She shoved aside the nausea and grasped strength.

I'm stronger than this. I will not give in to panic.

Avery closed her eyes and prayed for strength and logic.

The dizziness subsided. Her stomach calmed. Breathing returned.

With shaking hands, she tapped the mystery number in her recent call history. A continuous ringing met her ears.

She'd keep the threat to herself. She refused to face Granddad's death or the idea of him guilty of murder.

An hour later Granddad texted. **I'm spending the night in Austin. Why haven't you returned my calls or texts?**

Don't worry. I have this handled.

Avery despised the word *handled*. She had to think through the right thing to do. Ignoring the tragedy and allowing Granddad to handle a murder simply didn't cut it. Another text landed on her phone.

In the morning, I'm sending you to a safe place until this is over. I'm afraid for you.

No. We're in this together.

Not when one of us could face a bullet.

9

AT 3:30 A.M., Avery stole down the back staircase with a suitcase, backpack, and shoulder bag. She didn't want to wake Mia, who slept in a suite near the stairway. Granddad claimed Mia woke at the sound of dust hitting the floor.

Just before midnight, Avery had deactivated the house alarm to make her exit easier. Once Mia discovered she'd left, the woman would be incredibly disappointed. But Avery would rather not face her with questions firing like a repeating rifle.

Granddad would send someone after her, but would his pursuit be focused on love or concern? Had he received a similar phone threat? How she hated the horrible conclusions rooted in her mind.

She stopped on the landing and listened. Quiet. The weight of all her belongings begged to be relieved.

Avery would internalize the tragedy and bottle up the emotions until she exploded, far beyond an upset stomach. A bit of history would repeat itself. That's what happened when at age eleven she'd left her parents' home to live with Granddad.

Mom and Dad despised him because he refused to hand over money, instead expecting them to work for it. They lacked the ability to manage their own expenses and wasted every cent, a trait she recognized even as a little girl. Avery endured their constant complaining and silently sided with Granddad, staying out of the arguments until she had a breakdown that propelled her into counseling. Midway through the sessions, Granddad talked to Mom and Dad, and they signed over custody to him.

She often thought her parents' agreement had more to do with them not having to financially support her, but she didn't want to dwell there. To this day her parents claimed no desire to see her. Abandonment issues stalked her, making it difficult to trust but a precious few people.

Granddad had loved and nurtured her more than she'd ever imagined. Unconditional love best described him and what he'd instilled in her. She learned the value of hard work, planning, and determination. While he funded her undergrad and master's education in business management, she worked for him to buy a car, to supply her basic needs and some of her wants. To her, Granddad sat atop a white steed like a fighter from the medieval Crusades. She didn't want him yanked from that pedestal. But what had she witnessed the other morning?

Inhaling deeply, she descended to the foot of the stairs. With regret for what she must do and the challenge to learn the truth, Avery wrapped her fingers around the doorknob.

She held her breath.

Turned the knob slowly.

It clicked.

She desperately needed to leave without Mia's questioning.

The light flipped on, shining a harsh ray onto her carefully laid plans.

"I thought I heard something," Mia said. "What are you doing at this hour?"

Avery released her grip on the knob and faced Mia. "I'm leaving for a few days."

"Had to leave now? Where are you going?"

"Someplace quiet to think."

"To think? You have all these acres on the Brazos River Ranch to spend time alone."

"I'm distracted here. I'm not sure where I can think best, but not here."

"I know you, Avery, and you know exactly where you're going. Which is?"

Stiffening her shoulders, she forced resolve into every inch of her being. "A quiet place to pray and contemplate the future."

"About what? You sound ridiculous. You sneak down the stairs at three thirty in the morning like a criminal with this bull of a story?"

"I was trying not to disturb you."

"Are you catching a flight?"

Avery could easily lie and stop the inquisition. "No. I'm driving. I have a lot of miles ahead of me."

"What did Senator Elliott say about this?"

She tilted her head. "He isn't aware."

"How could you do such a thing to the poor man?" Mia's eyes widened. "He'll be worried sick."

"He will understand why, and I'll be in contact with him."

"Have you two quarreled?"

"No, ma'am."

"Can't you tell me anything? I want to ease his shock when he finds out."

"He'll be back sometime today, and I left a note on his bed. Sealed."

"You're not a coward. Something has happened between you two. What is it?"

Avery set her suitcase and shoulder bag on the wooden floor and embraced Mia. Oh, how she loved the woman. "There's no need to worry. My problem is personal, and alone time will help me find answers."

"Do you have your Bible?"

Avery nodded and stepped back. "Mia, go on back to bed, and I'll see you in a few days. Tell Granddad we talked."

"Does Craig know?"

"No. This is a private matter."

"What about Leanne?"

"No one."

Mia eyed her. "Have your parents contacted you for money? Threatened you?"

"They aren't part of my dilemma." Avery hoisted her shoulder bag.

"Guess there's nothing I can do to stop you." Her shoulders drooped. "Do you have your gun?"

"Yes, I'm packing. Why?"

"No woman needs to be driving alone without protection. We never know what will happen. Bad people are out there, Avery."

10

AVERY DROVE FROM HER HOME in a mix of tears and warring emotions. For the first time in her life, she didn't want to be an Elliott.

On the dark road ahead, she'd make her way to Houston and find a hotel property to stay where she'd have a kitchenette. The threatening caller had told her to obey Granddad or face death. She shuddered. Had her decision to leave the ranch made things worse? She hoped not. She prayed not.

Before she reached her destination, she'd stop at an ATM and withdraw cash, and maybe the property she chose to stay wouldn't ask for ID. Avery audibly blew out her idiocy. Any reputable hotel would want ID, and they'd also request her license plate number. A person could track her as easily as picking up their phone. How ironic she'd armed herself with Jesus, a Sig, and no common sense.

She had over two hours of miles between the ranch and Houston to figure out something. The answers to why she'd found Granddad with a gun in his hand leaning over a dead man might come in a few hours, a few days, or longer. Patience . . . not her best virtue. Granddad had modeled how God took every problem and molded it into something beautiful. Nothing in what she'd experienced resembled a piece of art.

A vehicle's headlights sped closer and rode her bumper. Her breath slammed against her chest.

"No way," she whispered and turned off the highway. Last night's threatening phone call lingered in her mind like the smell of sour milk.

The car raced on ahead. False alarm. She'd overreacted like a panic-stricken person, a coward who jumped at the crack of trouble. She pulled back onto the highway.

At 5:32 a.m., Granddad's ringtone sounded on her phone. She responded through her car's Bluetooth. "I knew Mia would call you. Sorry she got you out of bed."

"Sweet girl, do you think I could sleep with what has happened?"

"I don't know what to say."

"Tenacity is in our blood. I understand your need to get away, pray, and think about why I've been vague about what you saw Monday. I wish you'd let me arrange a hiding place so I don't have to worry about you. I have a reservation at the hunting lodge in Canada under an alias."

"Thanks. Really. But I have to work through this myself."

"As much as I want to ensure your safety, you're probably right. Please, be careful. We can't risk anyone linking the crime to you."

More than one person hurt or killed? "You've groomed me to overcome life challenges, and now I must make my own decisions."

"I get it. A part of me is proud of your bravery while another part wants to shackle you to a ten-thousand-pound anchor. Here are the precautions for both of us—I'm trashing my phone this morning. That way no one can trace me through my calls or contacts. I'm asking you to do the same. I insist on it. Pull out the SIM card and dispose of it in a different place than your phone. Pick up a prepaid burner and pay cash. All you need the phone for is to make calls and texts. Don't install any apps and keep it turned off when not in use. Another thing, I know all your files are in the cloud, but copy everything onto a flash drive and discard your laptop. Buy another one but don't activate your cloud account. Make sure to keep your virtual private network enabled to minimize risks when connected to the Internet. I suggest not contacting anyone on your current or new devices, and that means Mia or Leanne. Their phones or laptops might lead the wrong people to you."

She and Leanne had grown up together—like sisters. "For their protection or mine?"

"Both."

"Is contacting Craig okay?"

"By email only once you've installed the VPN on the new laptop. He'll have questions about the ranch or the business. Caution is the word. I don't want you the target of a precarious situation." He hesitated. "Avery, from this moment on, we won't be talking until I'm assured you can return home safely. Not a few days but possibly weeks."

"Why? I'm afraid for you in so many ways."

"The same reason I do everything—to keep you from danger in every sense of the word and definitely away from gunfire. I made a stupid mistake, and it's caught up with me. Not sure how this will play out. Good men whom I called friends are dead. Simple as that."

She gasped. "You aren't making any sense."

"Doesn't matter. The man's name who was killed on our ranch will be announced to the media today. Rely on the values I've instilled in you. It's a situation of 'do as I say, not as I do.'"

Avery's hands trembled on the steering wheel. "You said two friends are dead. Are others? How are you and I in danger?"

"I refuse to say anything more."

"Is Mom or Dad involved?"

"Doubtful but not impossible. While I used to pray they'd change in my lifetime, now I hope they see life is about how we care for others."

How could he live with murder and pray for Mom and Dad? "Who else knows what's going on? Craig?"

"Only the people who have an interest in my circle. You don't know them for obvious reasons. Best Craig remains on the outside. He's a good man and ignorance will serve him well. I've been helping him look into vet school. Wants to specialize in equine medicine. He deserves to be free of this mess. Be honest with me, do you need money?"

"Not at all."

"You're sure? Because after we hang up, I can't personally help you. You'll need to go through my attorney."

Bewildered with the murky fog of his words, she struggled not to blurt out unwarranted accusations. "Are you disappearing?"

"If necessary."

"How will I know if you're all right?" His lack of response shattered her heart. *No, please no.* "Are you telling me I may never see you again?"

"Remember what I've always said. If your life depends on it, think bigger."

Control fled, and she sobbed.

"Don't worry about me, sweet girl. Craig can run the ranch and construction company until you return. That is, if you want the businesses." Granddad hesitated. "Avery, if something happens to me, everything I own goes to you. You also have financial power of attorney."

She ached with the grief of possibly not having him in her life. "Let's talk about a solution. What about your attorney or someone in Austin or DC?"

"At the moment I have a plan. The important thing is don't trust anyone. Be on high alert. Understand I'm not giving up."

"Giving up on what? Finding who is behind this?"

"Never mind."

"Please tell me why men are dead."

"They walked into a trap."

She swallowed acid rising in her throat. "Wouldn't it be easier to turn yourself in?"

"Admit to murder? No thanks."

She sobbed, couldn't help it. "Nothing you've taught has prepared me for this nightmare."

"I'm sorry. No matter what happens or what you do going forward, I love you. While we've been talking, I've made a decision, and it sounds like I'm contradicting myself. But I want you to contact Houston FBI Special Agent Marc Wilkins and tell him everything you saw and heard. Do so in person. Leave nothing out. That will exonerate you from those investigating me."

"He's a friend? Related to Colonel Abbott Wilkins?"

"His son. Colonel Wilkins died, and his service was Monday. Be careful and remember you're an Elliott. You are strong, wise, and God has given you a discerning mind. Watch out for danger. I've tried to protect you, but my enemy trying to get to me by harming you is a strong possibility."

"Law enforcement or evil people?"

"I'm battling the devil."

The phone clicked.

Only road noise met her ears.

She tried calling back, but he didn't pick up.

Was this where love had dropped her?

11

IF MARC COULD MOVE INTO an empty office at Houston's FBI, he'd
have tossed in a sleeping bag a long time ago. Today, his cubicle's familiar sight and smell offered a sense of normal, and he needed the order
to gain the right perspective with his personal and professional lives.

He'd given up finding information to indicate his father had met
death through any means but natural causes. Those around his father
at the grocery store said he grabbed his chest, had difficulty breathing,
and broke out into a sweat. Marc had studied the cardiologist's report,
and his father's recent physical confirmed his excellent health. That
puzzled him, and an autopsy would have provided conclusive results,
but those steps didn't happen. He needed more to indicate suspicious
death before he advised an exhumation.

His partner, Roden Clement, towered in the doorway like a football player in full pads, reminiscent of his college days at Texas A&M.
But his true muscles were his heart and mind.

Marc stood to greet him. "Hey. I was about to text you."

"I thought you were taking a few days off to be with your mother."

"I am—the reason for my text. Just in the office to wrap up the stuff on my desk."

Roden rubbed his hand over his face. "Is Ms. Donita doing okay? Really sorry for your loss."

Marc explained Mom's concerns about his father's heart attack and how Marc had been pressured to investigate his father's death with little to go on but a no-name friend's phone number who had a full voice mail box.

"You have my sympathy. A little difficult to give your mom closure."

"Right. Online links have my father connected to other people, and I plan to investigate all of them. I have a few other places to check today, then the drive back to my mother's should give me time to form a believable explanation." He tilted his head. "And I learned I have a half sister in Fort Worth."

"Whoa."

Marc nodded. "She's an A student, runs track, and is basically a decent kid."

Roden had the bloodhound look in his earth-colored eyes. "Tell me more. Did you meet her at the funeral?"

"No. I learned about her from my mother."

"Getting info from you is like interrogating a mastermind."

Marc chuckled. "I learned from the best."

"You've run an MO on her, so are you going to see her?"

"I think so."

"Think? What's holding you back?"

Marc studied his partner. "She probably found out about me when I found out about her. She's fifteen, which leads me to question how she feels about a big brother."

"Or how you feel about her?"

Marc sensed a change in his attitude. Last night the turmoil about his father's other life had a triple effect of creating hurt, anger, and regret, but now he wanted to search deeper. "My sister had a relationship with our father. Curiosity speaking here, but I'll wade into those waters to see what I find."

"Let me know if you step into a current."

Marc groaned with the pun. "You can throw me a life jacket."

"Don't I always? What's left to get you out of here? I'll give you a hand."

Marc glanced at his semiclean desk. No urgency in the remaining files and notes. "Do you have any contacts at the Army Corps of Engineers?"

"Not any more than you do."

"If my father told the truth about working with some guy on an investigation, the Fort Worth office should have record of it." Marc grinned. "I needed my partner to shake up my mind."

Roden crossed his arms over his bulging chest. "You only needed a diving board."

Marc waved his goodbye to a disappearing Roden and pressed in the number to the Army Corps of Engineers district office in Fort Worth. "This is FBI Special Agent Marc Wilkins. I'd like to speak to Colonel Abbott Wilkins's office."

"Sir, Colonel Wilkins is deceased," a woman said.

"Yes, ma'am. I'm his son."

"My apologies. I should have picked up on the name when you introduced yourself. I'll connect you with his secretary."

Marc waited a full two minutes, then a man answered. "Agent Wilkins, how can I help you?"

"I'm seeking information about my father's friends, specifically a man whom he worked with closely in corps matters."

"We are unable to relay professional or personal information."

Now the secretary was a "we." "Who is your superior?"

"That would be Colonel Wilkins."

Irritation wanted to lash out, but Marc contained it. "Who is your superior now?"

"Excuse me one moment."

Another man picked up the phone and introduced himself as Lieutenant Shipley, the officer whom Mom claimed had attended the funeral. "Agent Wilkins, we shook hands, but there was a long line at your father's service, and I don't recall any introductions. I'm sorry for your loss. Regarding your question, under no circumstances can we release information over the phone about any member of the Army Corps."

Marc stated his position with the Federal Bureau of Investigation, gave him his FBI ID, and waited. Lieutenant Shipley placed him on hold. Another five minutes elapsed before he returned. Marc learned he'd been approved and repeated his request.

"We believe the man you are looking for is Liam Zachary."

"I'd like his phone number."

Lieutenant Shipley responded.

Marc compared the number with the one Mom had given him. Same one. "Sir, do you have another contact number for Mr. Zachary? This one's voice mail box is full."

"No."

"Can you connect me to his desk?"

"He's not here today."

"I'm assuming he's a civilian?"

"Yes, the corps doesn't require enlistment to be part of the team."

"What projects were they working on together?"

"That's classified."

Never hurt to ask. "If I need a face-to-face at the Fort Worth location, would you be the contact person?"

"Yes."

"In the meantime, if you hear from Mr. Zachary, would you let him know I'm trying to reach him?"

Lieutenant Shipley agreed. "Hold on a moment. I just got an update on him. Hold on while I read this." A few moments later, Shipley sighed. "This is tragic news. Montgomery County Sheriff's Office found Liam Zachary's body. They received an anonymous call alerting them to a body dumped alongside a road. Shot in the chest. Our CID will get to the bottom of this."

The Army Criminal Investigation Division had jurisdiction, and the FBI wouldn't be involved unless CID requested it. "I'm not a man who believes in coincidences, Lieutenant. You're dealing with two men who worked together and are now dead within a few days of each other. Don't you find that more than random? Perhaps their assignments might be a good starting point."

"Colonel Wilkins suffered a heart attack. Zachary was murdered. Neither death resembles the other."

The conclusion sounded harsh to Marc. "Thank you for your time. I'm sure the Army will find the evidence needed for an arrest." Marc laid his phone on the desk and leaned back in his chair. With Zachary's death, Mom's suspicions regarding his father's passing held more weight.

What were the two men working on that might have gotten them killed?

12

MIDMORNING, AVERY STOPPED AT WALMART in northwest Houston, like she'd done for years, following Granddad's instructions. She purchased a laptop, prepaid burner phone, a case of water, box of whole-grain crackers, jar of almond butter, bananas, two microwave containers of chicken noodle soup, a pair of scissors, and a two-liter bottle of diet ginger ale. Without enough cash to purchase the needed devices, she used her credit card. No doubt the purchase would be traced, like her Mercedes's license plate. But some tasks were impossible to disguise on such short notice. An upset stomach lurked in the foreground, and she fought the queasiness with the warm soda and a few crackers.

In the restroom at a nearby gas station, she pulled out her phone, stomped on it, and wrapped what was left in wet paper towels. She buried her device's remains in the trash. The SIM card stayed intact in her purse until a later stop where she used scissors to destroy the tiny card, then tossed them both. Those action steps calmed her nerves—slightly.

By the time Avery checked into an extended-stay hotel on Highway 290, exhaustion screamed from every cell in her body. The hotel had her credit card, driver's license, and license plate numbers. She patted her shoulder bag holding her Sig.

Once unpacked, she brewed coffee and nibbled on crackers. A clock radio on the bedroom nightstand caught her attention, and she turned it to Granddad's favorite country-western station. A habit. Rascal Flatts crooned a ballad, and she let the lyrics and music distract her while she stretched out on the bed. Soon the aroma of coffee drew her to pour a mug and savor the nutty flavor. A few more songs, and news interrupted her mind's bypass. She'd not be guilty of ignoring what was going on in the world. Even if she didn't like what she heard.

A segment of national news transitioned to state, then local. A storm brewed in the Gulf and weather forecasters monitored it. She listened five minutes more, while her heart pounded in overtime.

"The Montgomery County's Sheriff's Department through an anonymous tip recovered the body of a man identified as Liam Zachary. He was found shot and killed. Mr. Zachary worked for the Army Corps of Engineers in Fort Worth as a civilian structural engineer."

Avery flipped off the radio and rubbed the chill on her arms. Granddad and Liam had been friends since she came to live at the ranch. Liam and his sweet wife had visited the ranch on several occasions. Could this be who she saw lying in a pool of blood at the family cemetery? The friend? Surely not. But the truth was often more easily denied than embraced.

God forgive me. Help me to see that Granddad would not deliberately kill a man.

Answers took time, so she set up her new laptop, connected to the hotel's Wi-Fi, and enabled the VPN. Typing the deceased man's name in the search engine, she prayed her fears were unfounded and an error had occurred. A nearly identical report on finding Liam Zachary's body appeared as local breaking news. She read through a second article—he'd left a wife, an adult daughter and son, and three grandchildren . . .

She shuddered. To suspect a guest of the ranch and a good man had been shot and killed on her beloved ranch? Why? And why remove Liam's body unless to cover up Granddad's role? His phone conversation with someone replayed. If Liam's murder occurred on the ranch, could it have been self-defense? An accident? What prevented Granddad from going to the authorities?

Who would handle the murder case? Local authorities? The FBI since the deceased was a federal employee? The Army CID? How soon before the authorities publicly confirmed where Liam's body had been found?

Avery typed in her password to remotely access her granddad's computer, but his device denied her access. She wanted to check emails for any issues between Liam and Granddad. She attempted twice more with the same results. He'd eliminated her ability to get into his computer. Avery had Liam's professional and personal information, and she wanted to contact Mrs. Zachary with her condolences. But should she? Granddad had specifically told her not to reach out to anyone. Why, when no one could trace a burner phone? But technology had the means to find out the location of where any call was made.

Despite the failed steps to cover her tracks since leaving the ranch, she still had witnessed a violent crime, and her conscience stopped her from letting Granddad handle it. What mistake had he made that put her in danger too? Real life never happened like the rapid pace of cop shows. TV producers had forty-five minutes or so to solve a crime and make an arrest. She gripped the arms of the chair. Having this mess resolved in less than an hour's time might not be a bad thing.

Granddad claimed she had wisdom and discernment. He must have been thinking about someone else, not his granddaughter, who sat paralyzed in a hotel room, struggling with fears and emotions. A man had lost his life . . . a man who had family and friends who loved him and grieved his death.

Granddad had requested she talk to Special Agent Marc Wilkins at the Houston FBI and tell the agent all she'd witnessed. Should she make contact? Was Granddad aware of her threatening call? Had he received the same? What did all this mean?

MARC ENTERED FORT WORTH'S city limits, certain he'd flushed his brains down the sewer. After a very early start, a streak of orange and yellow crossed the morning sky. Three days had passed since his father's funeral, and now he aimed his pickup toward the home of his half sister. He doubted she was even out of bed before sunup.

A peculiar eagerness filled his internal fuel tank. At Mom's insistence, he'd arranged a meeting with Tessa through the grandmother, Marnie Litton. Mrs. Litton sounded weak, coherent, but hostile. Who could blame her when life had shoved all manner of physical pain into her aging years? From what he'd learned from Mom and digging online, the grandmother had poured her life into Tessa. Mrs. Litton's mama-bear side showed when she warned Marc if he upset her granddaughter, she'd pull out her rifle and send his FBI rear to kingdom come. Her words were a little more colorful, verifying life's bitter pills often brought out the worst in people.

Marc wanted an opportunity to get to know Tessa, but he'd leave at the first unwelcome sign. Uneasiness scraped against his better judgment. Tessa might be better off without him. What did he have to offer? Career advice? College recommendations? Maybe big brother things . . . whatever those were. The grandmother claimed Tessa had expressed some reservations about meeting him too.

Like a punch in the gut, it occurred to him Tessa might not have a home once her grandmother died. Sad. Very sad. What would happen to her? Their father had no living relatives for her to turn to. Marc moaned. She had a stepmother. Why hadn't he talked to Mom about Tessa's future?

He drove courtesy of his GPS in and around streets with one right and left after another. Had Mrs. Litton purposely given him the wrong address? Two more turns and he heard the familiar "You have arrived" status. The one-story wooden houses looked like a set of dentures that hadn't seen Polident in a decade.

After parking in the driveway, he glanced at the passenger side. Yesterday while going through items Mom had kept for him over the years, he found a high school yearbook belonging to his father. Marc planned to show it to Tessa as a conversation starter, and if she showed interest, he'd give it to her. Grasping the yearbook, he exited the truck feeling like he'd exited adulthood and reverted to a pimple-faced kid on his first date.

The Litton yard cried out for help, but the weeds were all that had answered the plea. Didn't look like the type of neighborhood where the owners subscribed to a lawn service. He made his way up a cracked concrete sidewalk and knocked on a door in dire need of a paint job. A clay pot of petunias bent low as though warning him not to enter.

The door creaked open slowly.

The Tessa he'd seen online stood before him. Light-brown ponytail. Tank top. Shorts. But not too short. Large green eyes veiled in thick lashes. She nibbled on her lower lip.

"Tessa?"

"Yes."

"I'm Marc, your brother."

A shy smile met him, and she motioned him inside. "Gram is still sleeping, and a hospice nurse is with her."

"So we can't play loud music?"

She shook her head. "Or sing."

He faked a laugh, and she joined him sounding equally phony. "I'm surprised you're up."

"Gram had a bad night."

He sighed. "I'm sorry."

"This is awkward. I mean, about meeting you."

"Yeah, I'm in the awkward zone too."

In a small living room decorated in crucifixes and photos of Tessa from infancy to the present, Marc sat on a sofa, and she curled up in a brown threadbare chair.

"Thanks for agreeing to see me," he said. "Where do we begin?"

She shrugged. "You look a little like Dad, especially your jaw, except not as pale or as tall. Must be your Hispanic mother. I believe her name is Donita."

He hid his surprise that she knew more about him than he did her. "You have his eyes. My mother told me about Mrs. Litton's illness."

She studied him. "Dad said you were in the FBI, violent crime division. He said you received your undergraduate degree in law enforcement."

"Yes. I've been at the FBI about eight years."

"Do you like it?"

"Most of the time. Keeping people safe and bad guys off the streets suits me."

She glanced at her hands folded in her lap. "When did you find out about me?"

"After the funeral. My mother showed me the will, and our father's estate will help you once you're eighteen. Social Security needs to be notified about his death so those checks can start coming to your grandmother."

"If she lives long enough to receive them." She shook her head. "I'm sorry. Attitude's not so good. Dad told me about you on my tenth birthday. Said he'd been a lousy father. Didn't think you'd ever forgive him, but someday he'd get the guts to try. I guess it didn't happen." She swiped tears beneath her eyes.

So much between his father and him left unsaid. If he was honest, regret might have simmered on both sides.

"I hope Dad didn't mind I couldn't make it to the funeral," she said. "But he's in heaven now."

Marc wasn't going to debate where his father spent the afterlife. As a Christian, Marc needed a better outlook. Under different circumstances he'd have wrapped his arms around Tessa and let her cry. He'd felt more comfortable talking to an armed killer.

"You'll be in tenth grade this fall?" When she nodded, he held up the yearbook. "I brought our father's senior yearbook. Want to take a look?"

Tessa slowly stood and joined him on the sofa, keeping her distance. "I should offer you something to eat or drink."

"No need. I drank a gallon of coffee on the drive here. I know it's barely 8 a.m., but I'm in the mood for pizza."

"Must be like father, like son," she said. "Dad always ordered pizza when he visited."

"What kind?"

"Pepperoni, no anchovies, and extra mushroom and cheese."

"My favorite." And he meant it. He relaxed a little. "Thick crust?"

"The only kind, filled with cheese."

"I'll order it for ten o'clock, then I need to head back to Houston. Is that too long of a visit?"

"Perfect."

He set the yearbook on her lap. He'd never seen photos of their father as a teen. Would Marc even recognize him?

An hour later, the two had settled into conversation mode. That's what Marc called an interview when he successfully made the interviewee feel comfortable. They laughed at their father's tall, skinny frame in a track pose. Tessa said he encouraged her in sports. Marc learned he'd paid for gymnastics when she was younger and dance lessons later on. Dear old Dad even attended recitals. She'd progressed to a level of contemporary dance, which afforded her a spot on the high school drill team. Tessa chatted on, and Marc listened, experiencing a world he'd never entered before. He could do this big-brother thing.

A middle-aged woman in loose slacks and a flowered blouse entered the living area. "Mrs. Litton would like to meet you, sir."

He introduced himself to the hospice nurse and followed her and Tessa down a narrow hallway to a dimly lit bedroom. Mrs. Litton's room smelled of death, the lingering telltale odors of a failing body. The white-haired woman leaned against pillows at an incline. She peered at him like a life-size spider had crawled into the room.

He stepped forward and reached out his hand. "I'm Marc."

"I know who you are." She peered at Tessa. "Has he upset you?"

"No, Gram. We've been talking, and everything's fine." Tessa told her about the yearbook.

"He hasn't persuaded you to give him your share of your father's estate?"

"Not at all. He told me about applying for Social Security benefits." Tessa took her grandmother's hand.

The source of the woman's angst centered on the fifteen-year-old before him. "Mrs. Litton, the last thing on my mind is to cheat my sister of her inheritance."

The woman pressed her lips together. "I'm going to say this in front of my granddaughter. Promise me you'll do whatever it takes to make sure social services don't place her in a foster home."

Tessa gasped and covered her mouth. "Gram, that's inappropriate. You've embarrassed me."

"It's okay," Marc said to Tessa. "Your grandmother loves you and is rightfully concerned about your welfare." How could he reassure a dying woman and confused teen about an uncertain future? But he could do whatever possible to ensure Tessa's future held more promise than death and abandonment.

"She has no family but me," Mrs. Litton said. "Have you thought about Tessa's life when I'm gone? She has her whole life in front of her—college, a career. I know Abbott and your mother wanted to put their marriage back together, but your mother isn't real family. Not like you."

"Yes, ma'am. I drove here to meet my sister, to see if we could establish a relationship. I promise you I will do everything possible to stay active in her life."

"How?" the weak woman said.

His insides plunged to the bottom of an emotional pit. "I promise she will not be placed in a foster home."

"Thank you. I've arranged for my lawyer to draw up legal guardian papers."

Did he even have a choice? Before he responded, Mrs. Litton waved him away. "I'm very tired. The papers should be ready tomorrow, and the attorney's office will contact you. Their card is on my nightstand."

He took the card and wished her well.

Back in the living room, Marc ordered pizza from Tessa's favorite restaurant. She apologized for her grandmother's request.

"It's okay. We'll get this figured out. She has your best interest in mind, and I sincerely doubt if she leaves this earth before she's assured your future is secure. When does school start?"

"Little over two weeks." She glanced down the hall. "I have no idea how long she has. But I won't be a burden to you, and if it doesn't work out between us, I won't complain about where I live."

"I gave both of you my word." How he'd keep his promise was worse than investigating a violent crime with no leads. "We were talking earlier. Got a topic?"

"Fresh out."

"What do you want most in the world?"

She blinked. Silence wrapped a blanket over them. Finally she spoke. "You live in Houston . . . in an apartment."

He must have asked an off-limits question. "Yes. Two bedrooms."

"One for you and one for an office."

He eyed her. "That's not for you to worry about."

She held up a finger. "A girlfriend?"

"Not at the moment."

"As long as you have your kid sister living with you in a two-bedroom apartment, your love life is going to be perfect." She rolled her eyes.

He chuckled at her sarcasm. "Is there anything you haven't thought about?"

"Do you cook, clean, do laundry?"

Marc squinted. "I have a can opener and a microwave. A cleaning service comes in every other week, and I send my laundry out."

"Sounds expensive. Brother, you need to add domestic skills to your résumé."

"For what?"

"Life skills. No woman in today's world wants a guy who's helpless."

"Thanks for the marital advice."

Her delicate features darkened.

"What's wrong?"

Tessa sighed. "I know witnesses at the grocery where Dad collapsed said he clutched his chest. But I don't believe he died of a heart attack. He'd gotten an excellent report from his heart doctor. Our dad was murdered. I'm sure of it."

"Why, Tessa?" Now two women in his life suspected the worst.

"The day he died, he called me. Said after a scheduled lunch and a stop at the grocery, he'd arrange for me to have private security. He promised to tell me more when we met up again."

14

AVERY WOULD RATHER MUCK OUT stalls than battle the terror of someone wanting her dead. How did she move forward? She'd not left her hotel room for a day and a half while indecision consumed her. It was like the shooter aimed a double-barreled shotgun—at Granddad and her. No way for anyone to live.

On Thursday, she opened her eyes, resolved. She'd do exactly what Granddad had requested by talking to FBI Special Agent Marc Wilkins. Confusion and uncertainty crawled through her, but neither the emotional pain nor worries about the future altered the truth.

She touched her stomach. A queasy excuse to avoid doing the right thing. But she'd see this through to the end.

Late afternoon, she drove to the Houston FBI office. Calling first crept into her mind, but then they'd want her name and request more personal information than she wanted to give. Twice she longed to turn around, race back to the ranch, and forget the whole tragedy. But how could she live with herself? Love complicated life.

Avery tucked her Sig and phone under the car seat beneath her and walked to the FBI security gate. The guard checked her ID, scanned her purse, and asked the purpose of her visit.

"To speak to Special Agent Marc Wilkins. I don't have an appointment."

He made a call before allowing her to proceed. Again she questioned the sanity of Granddad's request. She'd rehearsed her reason for interrupting the agent's day a dozen times, still not sure if the right words were cemented in her brain.

The guard directed her to walk a long ramp from the gatehouse to the main building. At the glass entrance, someone from inside buzzed the door, and it opened into a reception area.

"How can I help you?" a woman said from behind an enclosed area, most likely bulletproof glass.

Avery slipped her driver's license from her wallet and inserted it in the tray below the glass barrier. "I'd like to talk to Agent Marc Wilkins about a violent crime."

"You witnessed the infraction?"

"I think so. Is he available?"

"Have a seat, miss, and I'll let him know he has a guest." She pointed to a printed sign. "I need you to leave any of these items with me."

Avery had read the prohibited items online, which was why she left her gun and phone in the car. Her 8½-by-11-inch purse contained a granola bar, keys, and a wallet. She eased onto a chair to wait for Agent Wilkins. Portraits of acclaimed agents and a display case depicting the history of Houston's FBI invited visitors to view, but not Avery. And definitely not today.

An interior door clicked opened, and a man called her name. She stood and met intense brown eyes. A reflection of his job or how he viewed an interruption to his day?

"I'm Special Agent Marc Wilkins. I understand you'd like to speak to me about an alleged crime?"

"Yes, sir."

He opened the door and escorted her down a hallway to the right. "We'll meet in an interview room."

She nodded, and they entered a room with a small conference table and four black chairs. Bland walls, indistinct wall hangings, and a sterile smell met her senses. "Will this be recorded?"

"Is that a problem?" His tone held the cordiality she expected.

"No. I'd prefer every word documented so I don't have to repeat any of my story."

Agent Wilkins, an attractive man with light-olive skin and a wide smile, asked for her name. He had Colonel Wilkins's wide-set eyes and square jawline but not his broad shoulders and height.

"Avery Quinn Elliott III."

He eyed her strangely. "As in past Texas senator?"

"My grandfather."

"I see." He asked for her address and confirmed she lived with her grandfather on the Brazos River Ranch. He also jotted down her temporary hotel location. "Employed?"

"Vice president of Elliott Commercial Construction and I help my granddad run the Brazos River Ranch."

"Do you hold an engineering degree like your grandfather?"

"No, sir. My degree is in business management."

"That question was for my own interest and has nothing to do with your statement. I understand you witnessed a crime?"

"An indication one occurred."

"Were you the only witness at the time?"

"I'm not sure, but it's entirely possible."

Agent Wilkins leaned back. "Start at the beginning."

Avery repeated what she'd seen but omitted a few details she found of no value. She'd do nothing to jeopardize Granddad's life. "I learned a man by the name of Liam Zachary was found dead. Could the man I saw on the ranch be the same?"

"Did you see the victim's face?"

"No. Too far away."

He shook his head. "Seems like a stretch."

"Maybe so." Avery rubbed her arms. "Trust me, I know my story sounds bizarre. But I'm not wrong about seeing a body with blood pouring from his chest."

He studied her oddly. "Could this be a misunderstanding between you and Senator Elliott? You said he requested you talk to me."

"Excuse me?" Anger simmered near Avery's boiling point. "I'm not in the habit of implicating a person in a horrendous crime because he ticked me off. Definitely not a man I love and respect."

"Miss Elliott, I'm not discounting what you saw or the turmoil of consulting with the FBI. Your grandfather is highly respected, but it's my responsibility to confirm any accusations."

She shook off her militant emotions. Agent Wilkins had a job to do. "I'm sorry, and I understand your position. Has an arrest been made in Liam's death?"

"Not to my knowledge. The crime is the Army's jurisdiction. They have their own investigative division."

Why had Granddad sent her here? "My apologies. When my grandfather requested I talk to you, I assumed you had connections due to Colonel Wilkins's position."

"Not at all. Miss Elliott, were you acquainted with my father?"

"Yes. He, Granddad, and Liam spent lots of time together, have been friends for years. Granddad told me your father passed. My condolences."

"Thank you. Had your grandfather and Mr. Zachary quarreled?"

Avery hesitated. The two men had disagreed about something, but that could have been a golf game. "I don't recall anything."

"My father's funeral was Monday. Neither Senator Elliott nor Liam Zachary attended."

Avery blinked, putting thought to the agent's words. "I have no idea why neither man attended." Confusion had once again stunned her. Why hadn't Granddad told her about Colonel Wilkins's death? An argument? Severing of their friendship? Or another reason? She shivered at the thought of the recent deaths. "Doesn't the situation seem odd to you?"

He rubbed his chin, but nothing emerged from his mouth.

"I asked you a question, Agent Wilkins."

His jaw firm, he studied her. "I wish I had answers for you. Is there anything else you can remember?"

"Only I want a reason for what I saw and why my grandfather wanted me to talk to you. I'm emotionally drained and wish I hadn't seen my grandfather bending over a body."

"In your shoes, I'd feel the same way, although I've never met Senator Elliott or Mr. Zachary." He stood. "Thank you for coming in. I'll escort you back to reception."

"I'm not finished. What caliber of bullet killed Liam?"

"The information hasn't been released."

Avery slowly rose to her feet. "I understand. By informing the public of the caliber, the guilty person could dispose of the weapon and escape arrest."

"Thank you for reporting the crime. We'll be investigating what you witnessed, and I'll relay your findings to the Army Criminal Investigation Division. If we or they have additional questions, we'll contact you."

Agent Wilkins opened the office door and reminded her to pick up any personal property before she left. She hadn't told him about the threatening phone call, but the agent obviously wouldn't have been interested.

Without a doubt, Avery had been dismissed. In every sense of the word. Granddad had misjudged Agent Marc Wilkins. Had Granddad gotten other facts wrong?

15

MARC PONDERED THE LEGITIMACY of Avery Quinn Elliott III's testimony—granddaughter of one of Texas's most renowned senators. That depiction depended on the person's political preference. She'd claimed to have witnessed her grandfather standing over a dead man, who could've been Liam Zachary, and she trembled during the entire interview. If the woman had been a political enemy, Marc would have better understood her motive to implicate the senator. But her accusation either held a strand of truth or she had some serious mental issues. Senator Elliott's record tipped beyond the stellar side. If true, her story no longer served to discredit a reputable man but to explore the roots of a violent crime. What part had Marc's father played in all of this? A true victim? Or just a casualty of an unforeseen heart attack? How could Marc trust Avery Elliott's statement?

He searched through secure sites about her background. Nothing in his findings disputed her integrity. Excellent education. Not even a speeding violation. She'd joined hands with Senator Elliott in business, community, political, and church affairs. Her deep-blue eyes had distracted him and most likely dazzled a few others. But he knew better than to allow a pretty face to derail good judgment.

Marc called his mom. "I'm working late, so don't wait dinner. But I have a question. Did my father ever mention Senator Quinn Elliott?"

"Many times. By the way, I remembered the other man's name. Not sure what was going with my memory. It's Liam Zachary. I heard it on the news. Is it true he's dead?"

"Yes. Found murdered."

Mom drew in a sharp breath. "Has something happened to the senator?"

"I don't think so."

"He needs to be warned. Something horrible is going on." Her voice rose.

"I agree circumstances look bad at this point, but the authorities are on it. Relax, and I'll leave the office as quickly as possible."

Marc dug again into connections involving the three men. They'd appeared at a fundraiser in Dallas in support of firefighters. The photo showed three smiling men seated at the same table. A golf tournament for a children's home. A charity drive associated with a horse show.

Marc pressed in Tessa's cell number. Her suspicions of their father's murder sounded like a teenage girl's overactive imagination. Maybe not. Their father had stated he'd arrange security for her. Why? This all led somewhere, and he couldn't leave it alone.

Tessa picked up on the first ring. "Hey, Brother."

He liked the sound of his title. "Hey, Sis. How's your grandmother this evening?"

"Sleeping most of the time. I wonder how much longer she can hold on. Gram has always been the strong one, but I hear her crying in pain."

"This all must be terrible for you. I'll be there on Sunday, and we can talk about the future."

"I'm sorry Gram's demands have put you in a weird situation. You're sure you don't have a girlfriend who'll be upset with me barging into your life?"

Why was she so concerned about his nonexistent love life? "No girlfriends, and if I had one and she objected, then she wouldn't be the right one. Are you alone so I can tell you something?"

"Hold on a moment. The nurse has a question."

He'd arranged for his attorney to handle the guardianship with Mrs. Litton's attorney. Finding living arrangements for them wouldn't be as easy. His two-bedroom apartment in Houston would house them for a while until he found a home in a good school district.

"I'm back," she said. "What's going on?"

"A man has been found dead—Liam Zachary."

"What happened?" she whispered.

Marc wished he knew how to form the right words. "Looks like it wasn't natural causes." Silence met him and he waited.

"Now you understand why Dad's heart attack seemed, you know, wrong."

"I'm looking into the possibility. The situation isn't the FBI's jurisdiction."

"Who then?"

"The Army has its own criminal investigation division."

"But you can do it on the side?"

"Not so sure. Have you met Senator Elliott's granddaughter?"

"No. Just heard about her. I think they're close."

"Do me a favor and forget I asked you about them. It'll be between us FBI agents."

"Marc, I'm not an eight-year-old kid who's working on a junior FBI badge. But I won't say a word. You believe me now?"

"I'm just looking into a matter for my little sister and mother.

If you see or hear anything suspicious, call the police. Keep the doors locked."

"I have nothing that belongs to Dad."

"Not everyone knows that. Promise me you'll use caution."

"Promise."

After he ended the call, Marc logged into his secure website to read the investigation reports on Liam Zachary's death. The information had already been documented. Zachary had dinner with his wife and son at six on Sunday evening. She didn't hear from him after he left the house around seven for an overnight appointment, which wasn't his normal behavior. She'd asked who, where, and when of his appointment, but he told her it wasn't important. The ME estimated time of death on Monday between 11 a.m. and noon based on his stomach contents and the high temps speeding up rigor mortis. Montgomery County Sheriff's Department located a Sig Sauer M17 about twenty feet from the body. Army CID matched the 9mm bullet removed from Zachary's body with the weapon.

Further investigation indicated Zachary's car and cell phone were missing. Authorities might never find either one. Unfortunately, the time of death matched Avery's story.

She couldn't reach the senator, which didn't look good in the man's defense.

16

MARC NEVER WANTED A REPEAT of this past week, except for meeting his sister, a blessing in disguise. His intentions to take more time off to help Mom grieve met one delay after another. Hitting delete on the memories of his father didn't make good mental health sense and dealing with emotions wasn't Marc's sweet spot.

To make matters worse, the information about Liam Zachary and Senator Elliott complicated the relationship with his mother and sister. Both expected him to provide logical answers where he didn't have jurisdiction. And he now wondered if his father's death had a little assistance. The Army Criminal Investigation Division boasted an excellent team, and even if the CID requested a task force with the FBI, Marc would be denied working the case due to a conflict of interest.

Roden was the best sounding board and brainstorming agent in the bureau. Marc texted his partner, and they met in the break room.

"How long will this take?" His partner grabbed a bottle of water from the fridge. "Two hours? Three? I'm already late for dinner, unless you're buying."

"I might need to." Marc opened the wrapper on a bag of peanut M&M'S. He dropped a handful into his black coffee and popped more into his mouth.

"You only eat those when you can't figure out a case."

Marc startled. "I like them."

Roden sat across from him. "I call 'em as I see 'em. What's happening?"

"This all goes back to the night of my father's funeral and what Mom asked me to look into . . ."

"If you went to the ASAC with this, he'd think your head took a massive hit. But with Liam Zachary's death and the additional info you've uncovered, I'm inclined to take the suspicious route."

Marc cracked a smile despite the absurdity of what he'd learned. The assistant special agent in charge might send him for a psych eval. "We've had weird cases, but this one came out of left field and into our catcher's mitt."

"Correction. It's not our case. It's CID's."

"And now the women have pulled me into it."

"Who is the pistol registered to that killed Zachary?"

"CID either isn't releasing the name, or they don't know." Marc held up a finger. "Zachary's body was moved after time of death. The ME found soil on his clothing inconsistent with where the sheriff's department found him."

"Which means he could have been killed on the Brazos River Ranch. What have you found out about the three men's relationship?"

"I confirmed they attended fundraisers together. Mom's and Tessa's claims were accurate. When we're finished, I might contact Lieutenant Shipley at the corps with a rundown of what I've learned."

"But you'd rather not. You'd rather be a rogue agent like on TV who takes the case for the love of his mother and sister, knowing the FBI isn't involved. The one thing I haven't asked is if the senator's granddaughter is drop-dead gorgeous."

"Runway material."

Roden groaned. "Who do I know in Hollywood?"

"I hope someone who can write a good ending." Marc took a sip of coffee and crunched a peanut M&M. "I've been thinking. I gave my word to Mom and Tessa, but I can't jeopardize my career by jumping into an unauthorized investigation. I've scheduled a phone meeting with the ASAC and SAC. See if Senator Elliott's implication in a crime allows the FBI to offer assistance to the corps in an unofficial partnership."

The special agent in charge could shut him down the moment Marc relayed the situation.

"Using you and me in a one-off relationship? Houston's top guns might not go along with the idea."

"Right."

"Marc, you've hitched the cart before the horse. Okay, a memorandum of understanding might be necessary but a pain." Roden slowly nodded. "By offering to investigate Zachary's murder as a favor to your family is a stretch, but the SAC and ASAC might go for it. When's the phone meeting with them?"

Marc glanced at his watch. "Seven thirty tonight."

Roden glanced at his watch. "Hmm, seven fifteen. You played me. You knew I'd go along with your wild, stupid idea."

"I gambled a little. Remember the Turner case? You neglected to tell me the woman couldn't confirm her alibi, and she ended up being the killer."

"Okay, when this is over, we're even. If we still have a job." Roden laughed. "I'd better text my wife and tell her I'll be late." He grabbed his phone. "So, Agent Wilkins, before this meeting, what does your gut tell you?"

"Several things. One, the only way to know for sure if my father died of a heart attack is to have the body exhumed. I know that's rare, but I believe it's necessary. Two, Avery Elliott showed no signs of deceit, and the idea that her grandfather pulled the trigger is eating her up. Three, the two victims had worked on projects in the past on dams and bridges, and I've seen nothing that documents the business relationship had changed."

"Are you thinking the victims learned the senator was dabbling in something illegal?"

"Hard to believe with his impeccable reputation. I'd rather think the three uncovered something incriminating and the wrong people found out, which means the senator is in danger. Maybe wishful thinking. But I believe it's worth an investigation, unless CID has it all handled." Marc recalled his original impression of Avery Elliott. "I discounted Miss Elliott's testimony and insulted her. Even if the FBI and the corps nix our idea for an MOU, I still want to talk to her again, if nothing more than to apologize."

"Let's get a feel for securing a memorandum of understanding first. Tackle your foot-in-mouth fumble later with the Elliott woman. Are you sure it's your professional image you want to protect?"

"I have my mother and my sister. Both are grieving, and I want to be there for them. Miss Elliott deserves an apology for my lousy attitude." But she did have amazing blue eyes, although the fire in them was directed his way.

17

EARLY EVENING, Avery's restless spirit sent her on a five-block walk from the hotel to a nearby church. She'd noticed the structure when she'd first arrived in the area. The nondenominational aspect didn't matter. Although she had a quiet place in her room to pray, her spirit longed for the peacefulness of a church. Granddad encouraged her to explore solitude in prayer when she needed answers, and normally she followed his advice on everything—faith, career, friends, independence.

She inwardly startled. In all her twenty-five years, she'd agreed and complied with almost every one of his suggestions and recommendations. Until now. Her struggle to pursue truth took root in his convictions. How did she handle the confusion?

Could she even think on her own?

Avery stopped on the first step leading to the church doors. She practiced Granddad's faith. Worshiped Granddad's Jesus. And treasured Granddad's favorite Bible version, verses, and songs. He'd been more than a loving grandfather but her father, hero, role model, and mentor. From the time she could walk, he'd taken her to church and Sunday school. Afterward they'd discuss the lesson and sermon over chicken-fried steak with all the fixin's. He developed a gold-star chart to encourage Bible verse memorization and placed it on his office wall. He'd quiz her, and if she could recite the verse, she added a star to the chart. Ten memorized verses meant date night with Granddad.

Two years at Columbia University for her grad work had forced her to think more for herself. She'd gotten involved on campus and formed her own opinions . . . although most of them matched Granddad's.

She'd followed his political career and respected his stands, even when his opponents attempted to shred him. The two shared an interest in math and business ventures. A kindred spirit for horses meant hours of riding the ranch. The silver-haired man with his deep-throated laugh and strong embrace filled her with pride. No matter where they went, she adored and treasured their time together.

Granddad showed her many traits to emulate about him.

His compassion for the downtrodden, often when no one was watching.

His tireless work ethic.

His wisdom.

Mia claimed Avery had lots of book smarts, but wisdom went deeper than fancy initials after her name. At the time, Avery thought the dear woman was teasing. Now . . . not so much.

Tears streaked Avery's face. From where she stood on the church steps, Granddad had shown her God in every way except what had transpired this week. The disappointments overwhelmed her, and she failed to get past it.

Avery continued to climb the steps of the gray stone church. The building reminded her of some of the church architecture she'd seen in England—with Granddad. This one had two locked heavy wooden doors. No way to get inside. Not sure why she thought the door would be unlocked.

Glancing into a gray sky filled with dripping humidity, she retraced her steps back to the hotel. How could she talk to a God she doubted when someone locked the doors to His church?

Heat rose from the sidewalk as though the depths of fire fought to engulf her. She stopped at an intersection and waited for the light to change. The rumbling of a motorcycle caught her attention. She shoved aside her disconcerting thoughts to view a blue Yamaha Tracer 9 GT, a match to the one she'd seen at the family cemetery. The rider wore a black helmet and sunglasses. When he waved and pulled alongside her, Avery's stomach threatened to erupt.

"Hey, sweet girl. What are you doing so far from the ranch?"

Hearing Granddad's nickname for her and the mention of home alarmed her. "Who are you?"

"The Messenger."

She'd heard that before. But the voice at the ranch had been distorted, and this was a distinct, younger-sounding male. "For what?"

"You were told to obey your granddad."

"I've done what he asked."

"Then make sure he knows Marc Wilkins and the FBI can't help either of you."

"Take off your helmet and show yourself." Bullies did their best work when they had the advantage. She looked for a distinguishable trait. He wasn't a large man but trim with narrow shoulders. Granddad said the details in life were what formed who we were. She glared at him. "And if I refuse?"

"Then I become an assassin." The cyclist sped away and wove into traffic.

Panic rolled through her. Again she failed to capture the license plate like at the ranch cemetery. The light changed. She quickened her pace, her mind weighing Granddad's every word. She longed to be wrong.

Back in her room, the ache in her heart matched the turmoil in her mind. The motorcycle she'd seen at the cemetery didn't belong to the dead man but to a man who'd just threatened her. Had he pulled the trigger? Who owned it? The cyclist's driver warned her to stay away from Agent Wilkins . . . which translated that the driver, aka the Messenger, was Granddad's enemy.

A man who had insight into her life.

A man who had followed her to Houston.

A man who either had murdered at the cemetery or knew who pulled the trigger.

A man who had no problem threatening her. But why? She knew nothing.

Determination seized control to face her future with caution and not fear, which meant trusting God's sovereignty.

Shoving aside the vise holding her mind and body captive, she opened the blinds to evening grayness and the parking lot. For sure the air quality made the outside a risk to breathe. Rather ironic.

She used the hotel's notepad to list her thoughts, questions, and conclusions.

God manned the control panel. No more doubts. She chose to trust Him for whatever the future held.

What caused Granddad to hide, and where was he?

Would life ever feel normal again?

Would this nightmare ever end?

He'd sent her to see Agent Wilkins, although the man infuriated her with his know-it-all attitude.

Realization twisted as though she'd swallowed a pine cone. Granddad had not killed Liam. Someone else pulled the trigger, an enemy. She didn't know why Liam was in the cemetery with

Granddad or if the man on the motorcycle who'd just threatened her had killed Liam.

But one thing she knew without a doubt—Granddad refused to state his innocence because the killer had him in his sights too, and Granddad would do anything to protect her.

She must move forward to find him and draw out the truth beginning—

The room's phone alerted her to a call, and she answered to a female voice. "Miss Elliott, a man is here in the lobby who wants to talk to you."

Her heart seemed to squeeze tight. Had the messenger-assassin shown up? "I'm not interested."

The young woman relayed the message. "He says it's important."

"What's his name?"

"FBI Special Agent Marc Wilkins."

18

A WOMAN HADN'T CAUGHT Marc's attention for a long time, but watching Avery Elliott's jean-clad figure approach him at the hotel front desk caused him to rethink his statement to Roden. The allure in her pecan-colored hair, deep-blue eyes, and curvy figure had caught him off guard.

Logic slapped him in the face. Avery Elliott III topped the list of complications he didn't need.

Marc walked her way. "Thank you for seeing me."

Her sad eyes met his gaze, then she lifted her chin and showed inner strength. "Has something happened?"

"Not at all. I'd just like to talk." Marc motioned to the dining area. "There's a small booth in the left corner away from other people."

Not a muscle moved on her smooth face. "I suppose. And I have a few things to tell you."

He gestured, and she led the way to an isolated booth. No danger of anyone hearing their conversation unless they got into an argument. A dozen people occupied the dining area, and the aroma of fried chicken wafted in from the kitchen. A young man from the waitstaff asked for a drink order, and they each ordered a Coke.

"Any appetizers?" the young man said.

Marc glanced at Avery, and she shook her head. His stomach rumbled but that took a back seat to why he needed to talk to her.

Avery turned her attention back to Marc. "Is my grandfather okay?"

"I have no idea. Have you heard from him?"

"No." She paled. "Do you have a lead? I'm afraid with your father's and Liam's deaths, he might be a suspect after what I'd told you. Or he's the next victim."

"Miss Elliott, we're working to find an explanation. However, my father passed from a heart attack. Are you rethinking what you witnessed?"

"Yes." Her tightened facial muscles relayed her determination. "I'm convinced Granddad didn't kill anyone. But I don't know who did. I only want the truth."

"A BOLO, be on the lookout, has been issued for your grandfather, and law enforcement agencies are on alert. His private jet remains parked in his hangar at the ranch, and his truck's license plates haven't been spotted by any traffic cams."

"If he can't be found, then I'm facing my worst fears. I feel like I'm in a maze and can't find my way out." She stiffened. "My apologies. You work with facts, not feelings."

"You're fine. Would your parents know how to locate him?"

"Extremely doubtful. They separated themselves from us a long time ago. They probably aren't aware of what's happened."

Rather harsh answer. Media had reported the senator and his son broke communication years ago, but Marc assumed Avery maintained some type of communication with her parents. Of course, who was he to question family relationships?

The young man returned with their Cokes.

Marc thanked him and waited until he walked away. "How long are you staying in Houston?"

"Until this is over and it's safe for me to return home." She stared at the wall behind him. "Granddad told me not to trust anyone."

"Wise man."

"Except he indicated you could be trusted, but I'm not there yet, Agent Wilkins. I'm sure you ran a background on me. Do you have questions? If need be, I can contact an attorney."

"Consulting an attorney is always your right. If you're asking if the FBI suspects criminal activity on your part, the answer is no. And please call me Marc."

"Okay. I'm Avery. What can you tell me?"

"Whether I can give you info depends on what develops and if it's something available for public knowledge."

"I made a commitment to justice and promises to Granddad. I broke one promise by texting Liam's wife and expressing my sympathy. Nothing more. Have you notified the Army's criminal investigation command?"

"I have an appointment in Fort Worth with the corps tomorrow."

She leaned forward. "I assume you ran a background on me?"

"Due diligence. You'd have done the same."

"True. Is there a way to make me a temporary special agent so I could ride along?"

He smiled and shook his head.

"That made me sound like I was twelve." She sighed. "As I explained, my emotions are scattered. I prayed and debated my statement at length before driving to the FBI. It sounds like I told you a far-fetched story, but it's true. I believe Granddad wanted to keep me ignorant of whatever is going on. My apologies for sounding vague."

"No problem."

"I've never experienced any behavior from Granddad contrary

to his convictions. He lives his stance. No gray issues or fence riding for him. All I know is what I witnessed and what he said. Or didn't say." She glanced at her hands folded on the table. "Don't you find it unusual that your father and my granddad were friends and we hadn't met? Colonel Wilkins never mentioned he had a son but obviously he did to Granddad."

"We had our differences. He abandoned my mother and me when I was eight. The man who left us when I was a kid didn't resemble the one in the casket or the man my sister calls Dad."

She nodded as though she understood. "How sad not to see him for all those years. You and I have lived through family dysfunction. Still doesn't mean I can trust you."

"Trust has to be earned, which brings me to the second reason I'm here. I owe you an apology for this afternoon. I insulted you and discounted what you witnessed."

She focused on Marc. "Apology accepted, and I've had my finer moments too."

"Do you recall anything more from what you'd told me earlier?"

"I'm worried about Granddad. My story this afternoon has nothing to do with how much I love him or what I'd do to prove his innocence."

"I understand. Have you contacted anyone else about your grandfather?"

"No. Why?"

"Any family or friends here in Houston?"

"No, and I still want to know why."

"I'd prefer you keep all details about this case to yourself unless the Army Corps needs a statement."

"I mentioned this earlier, but should I contact an attorney?"

"Up to you. I'd rather you hired a bodyguard."

She startled. "My grandfather warned me about potential danger."

"He may be aware of unsavory people."

"You might be right, and I'm taking precautions." She swallowed hard.

"What aren't you telling me? I'm not the enemy."

She clenched her fist. "Do you remember me saying I saw a blue Yamaha Tracer 9 GT at the cemetery?"

"Yes, but you were unable to get plate numbers."

"This afternoon, I walked to a church a few blocks from here. I needed time to think about our conversation."

Marc listened to her story, and his analytical mind took over. "Anything about him seem familiar?"

"No. He had a trim body and narrow shoulders. He wore a helmet and sunglasses. I didn't recognize the voice."

"You should change hotels."

She steepled her fingers. "If he found me here and knows I talked to you, then he's watching my every move." She stopped. "How did he know I talked to you?"

"Was anyone aware of your plans?"

"No one. My phone's a burner."

"The senator requested you talk to me. Perhaps his phone's bugged."

"True." Silence mounted between them before she continued. "When Granddad gave me those instructions, he still had his regular phone. Okay, if his phone was bugged, then the guy followed me and assumed I'd spoken to you. Still means he's watching my every move."

Marc made a mental note to check the security cameras around the FBI building and her hotel. Avery's theory about being tracked held ground, and if a vehicle or motorcycle matching the Yamaha's description hit the security cam's radar, he'd move one step closer to ending the case.

"Did you get the plate numbers this time?"

She shook her head. "The cyclist wove in and around traffic before I could get a single digit." She glanced away. "I'm usually good with numbers. No excuse for not paying attention."

"Avery, don't be so hard on yourself. You're upset and a crime's been committed." Marc needed to gain her trust for too many reasons to process. "We'll do our best to find him."

"Thank you."

"Have you had dinner? I know it's late."

She frowned. "Does dinner fall under FBI protocol? Because it's not listed on the website, and I read most of it."

"Nope. Personal all the way."

"Why?"

He frowned. Why did he have this attraction to a woman so different from him? "Friendship."

"You are one confusing man."

"Is that a good or a bad trait?" He knew his question skirted away from the case.

"Depends if I'm evaluating you as an agent or a guy who's coming on to me." She smirked and propped her elbow on the table and rested her chin on it. "I've told you all I can."

Marc picked up on her last word. *Can.* So there was more. "We all have to eat. Think of dinner as a rude guy's way to make up for an unprofessional interview. Name the restaurant."

"Hate to burst your balloon, but I'm not leaving the hotel."

"Sounds like a plan to me."

Now to figure out if his interest hovered over the professional side or the personal. Or both.

19

WHAT HAD DELAYED LIEUTENANT SHIPLEY? Marc and Roden had waited for him inside his Fort Worth Army Corps of Engineers office for over thirty minutes. Early this morning, Houston's FBI SAC approached the Army Corps headquarters at Quantico with Marc's request to partner in the investigation of Liam Zachary's death. The agency heads chose not to engage in a formal MOU, and Marc was relieved. By not initiating clear guidelines and responsibilities between the FBI and Army Corps, he had more flexibility. But the FBI chose to be up-front about the question of Colonel Wilkins's heart attack as the cause of death.

Marc studied a framed photo on the lieutenant's desk and recalled the balding man from his father's funeral with a fence-post frame and long arms. At the services, he displayed a solemn appearance. But posed with a wife and three kids at a lake setting, he looked friendly, approachable.

"This delay is deliberate," Marc said. "All about control, and I'm not playing the game much longer."

"Leave your sarcasm in your hip pocket," Roden said. "Neither the SAC nor ASAC are 100 percent on board with our involvement in this case."

Marc grimaced. To say he was not happy was a huge understatement. Investigating one of the most highly respected men in the state risked damaging the bureau's reputation in the public eye. "I'm already on my best behavior."

"I sense excellent cooperation in your attitude."

Lieutenant Shipley finally entered his office and closed the door behind him. The look on his face resembled having a mouthful of lemons. Wordlessly, he took a chair behind his desk and pushed aside Marc's and Roden's business cards with a shaky hand. "Agents Wilkins and Clement, I've been briefed on your outlandish suspicions regarding Senator Elliott, but my opinion appears irrelevant. Tell me what you have." He snorted. "That's what partners do."

So much for best behavior. Marc forged ahead. "I've learned a few details that may help find Liam Zachary's killer."

"I hear it involves your father's heart attack too."

"At this point, I'm not sure."

"The thought is ridiculous." Shipley frowned. "From the beginning. Please."

"After I spoke to you earlier in the week, I received a visit from the senator's granddaughter. . . ."

"Houston FBI sent me Avery's testimony. According to the document, she's staying at a hotel in Houston as a result of Senator Elliott's request. Unless we have sound evidence, the senator's attorneys will toss out the investigation and make us all look like fools." He leaned forward. "Avery already said she believes in his innocence. It's blistering hot, and the heat has a way of blurring your mind and vision. I've been a guest at the Brazos River Ranch more than once, and I find your accusations insulting."

"I understand your concerns for a man who has a stalwart reputation. Senator Elliott has our respect too. But I want to confirm that my father died of a heart attack. Last night, I started the process to have his body exhumed. The result will answer why two men involved in working on a project died within days of each other."

"I agree it's unusual—the only area of your investigation to make sense. But is an exhumation necessary when the ME stated cause of death?" Shipley appeared to carefully choose his words. "Think of what your mother will go through. She took your father's death hard."

Marc stopped himself from stating his mother wanted answers. "Good point. I'll think about it."

Shipley studied Roden. "What are your thoughts, Agent Clement? Or are you the silent type?" An unexpected smile spread over Shipley's face. "From the size of you, I assumed you were Agent Wilkins's bodyguard."

The tension broke and the three erupted into laughter. Whatever had delayed Shipley in the briefing and put him in a sour mood must have been resolved. At least Marc hoped so when they all needed to work together.

"Addicted to the gym?" the lieutenant said.

"Yes, and college ball," Roden said.

"You've kept in good shape."

"Comes with having four daughters who have hormone-overloaded teenage boys knocking on the door. Has given this forty-five-year-old more than one gray hair."

The lieutenant rubbed his balding head. "There are worse things than gray hair. Two of my three kids are girls. Other than making sure their dates see me cleaning my gun, I don't have the build to scare them off. Agent Clement, what observations about the senator's disappearance come to mind?"

"Has anyone questioned if he's been killed?"

The thought had crossed Marc's mind repeatedly. According to every report he'd read, Senator Elliott never moved an inch without a reason. The reason for his disappearance centered on his motive. As much as Marc wanted to jump into the discussion, he'd listen to Roden and the lieutenant's conversation.

"We have a serious situation if a third body is found," the lieutenant said. "I will take the lead here in investigating the senator's whereabouts and looking into all three men's financials. One of Elliott's employees claims the senator drove to a church event and didn't return. According to the pastor, the senator never made it. Neither has his truck been found. The drive to the church takes eighteen minutes on a county road. We're searching in and around the area."

"Who is the employee?"

"Craig Holcombe, foreman for the Brazos River Ranch and Elliott Construction."

"Holcombe does both jobs?" Roden said.

"Apparently he's efficient. Not married either."

Roden swung his gaze to Marc, no doubt wondering why he hadn't voiced his mind.

Marc's silence ended. "I doubt the senator is a victim when he told his granddaughter he might need to disappear. Did he leave specific instructions to any of his employees, or do things appear business as usual?"

"The latter," Shipley said. "According to our interviews, nothing prior to his leaving occurred out of the ordinary."

"If Senator Elliott planned an escape, he wouldn't have alerted anyone," Marc said.

Shipley eyed him and twitched. "Are you the devil's advocate here? Or looking to blame someone for your father's heart attack?"

"Aren't we partnering in this investigation to discover the truth? Two of the senator's friends are dead, and the senator is now missing.

Coincidences only lead to overlooking critical evidence." Marc sensed Roden's steel gaze warning him not to jump onto the caustic band-wagon. "Sir, we have too many unanswered questions to ignore any possibilities. Miss Elliott witnessed an unoccupied motorcycle before she found the body. She believes the same motorcycle followed her to Houston where she's staying. Looks to me like the CID, Agent Clement, and I have our work cut out for us."

"I agree. For the record, I'm the liaison between the FBI and CID. I worked for them years ago and have solid contacts there." Shipley powered on the monitor to his desktop. "I'll put together the inter-views from Craig Holcombe and Mia Underly, the housekeeper. I'll make sure they're sent to you."

"Thanks." Marc made a mental note to run an MO on both of them as well as Avery's parents. He also intended to find out the problems between the senator and his son. "Were those statements taken in person or by phone?"

Shipley eyed Marc as though he'd walked in from the field with dirt on his shoes. "I conducted those with a corps member."

"Agent Clement and I request permission to conduct interviews with those living and working at the Brazos River Ranch as well as those representing Elliott Commercial Construction. Perhaps their answers might change."

"Your time, Agent Wilkins."

"Have you spoken to Avery Quinn Jr. or his wife?"

"Yes, but go for it."

"Lieutenant Shipley," Roden began, "have you talked to Liam Zachary's wife and his colleagues?"

"Mrs. Zachary and Liam's secretary thus far. You'll receive those transcripts too."

"Any insight there?" Roden lifted his massive body from the chair and helped himself to the water dispenser near the door.

"Mrs. Zachary said her husband had been working long hours,

sleeping little, and was grumpy. When she questioned him, he claimed the problem would be resolved soon."

Marc digested every detail. Too many unknowns. "I'm assuming you searched his files and mirrored his devices?"

"We have."

"Results?"

"Any conclusions are pending."

Getting answers from Shipley took ingenuity, and Marc's patience ran thin. "Is a home office in the equation?"

"We have the matter under control. Any findings will be brought to your attention."

For certain Shipley preferred Roden, and Marc needed to play into it before he punched the man in the face. "Did my father leave any unfinished business, something that would help us?"

"He requested an additional inspection on a recent dam project, the Lago de Cobre Dam in Burleson County."

"Who completed it?"

"Elliott Construction."

"Was the inspection completed?"

"On my desk to arrange today."

Interesting. "Would you email me the original and the results of the new inspection?"

"There've been two previously. Both indicate the dam is in fine working order."

"Why a third? Did my father give you a reason for the third inspection?"

"Testing concerns."

More reason for Marc and Roden to have the documents. "Before we leave, I'd like to have my father's personal belongings."

"I assumed so. Have we concluded our discussion?" Shipley aimed his question at Roden.

"We will consult with you after we complete our interviews."

Roden faced Marc. "I believe we can get started with those this afternoon. Except we have one more question."

"Definitely." Marc nodded at Shipley. He'd asked this question far too many times without receiving an answer. "Who is the gun registered to that killed Liam Zachary?"

"Your father."

20

MARC'S FATHER HAD DIED before Liam's murder. Someone had taken his father's gun and used it on a good man. Had the weapon disappeared before or after his father's death?

"Lieutenant, when we talked on the phone, were you aware my father's gun was the murder weapon?"

"Yes, but the impossibility of Colonel Wilkins pulling the trigger stopped me from telling you until I further investigated the crime."

"Neither Liam nor the senator attended the funeral or acknowledged the death," Marc said.

"They were aware of the time and location of the services. A shooter killed Liam before the funeral."

"But they told no one in their families," Marc said. "As though they feared someone."

"You've taken your research into a realm that doesn't exist. Does the FBI offer counseling?"

Marc swallowed his ire. "If needed."

Shipley slowly nodded. "Good. Someone used your father's gun and committed a murder. Indications are Senator Elliott is responsible, but I refuse to believe it."

Marc recalled Avery's claim. She'd seen a gun in the senator's hand. But from a distance, she couldn't identify the weapon. "You still believe he's innocent?"

"Ask me after enough evidence has been gathered to make an arrest," Shipley said. "Follow me to your father's office."

Marc and Roden walked down a narrow hall to an office labeled *Colonel Abbott Wilkins*. The lieutenant unlocked the door and gestured the two men inside. Marc scanned his father's office, expecting to see a cold, sterile setting. Quite the contrary. This belonged to a man he didn't know. The familiar regret and resentment clouded his emotions and threatened to interfere with the investigation. Wasn't he a grown man and not an abandoned kid?

"I need to stay here until you've gone through Colonel Wilkins's personal effects. If something interests you and I can't authorize releasing it, I'll put the item aside until the case is closed." Shipley pointed to a corner where two cardboard boxes sat. "I suggest beginning with those. We've emptied his desk, closet, and placed many non-Army effects inside."

"Makes sense." Marc focused on the framed photos positioned on a glass-topped credenza and picked up one recently taken of Mom and his father. They'd been bass fishing, and both held up their catches.

Marc replaced it and studied a photo of Tessa and their father taken near a park, professionally photographed. Another one showed Tessa performing in a high school drill routine. A double frame showed Marc at around three years old on one side and the adjoining showed him receiving his high school diploma. A stranger who had displayed photos of a son he'd left behind. Upon closer examination, Marc confirmed he'd never seen the high school pic. Had his father been there?

Beneath the credenza's glass top, his father had inserted an article of Marc's twelfth FBI commendation for his work in the violent crime division. Numbness settled on him. *Where were you when I needed you?*

"Hey, let me help." Roden pointed to a plant on the desk, a very sad vine in dire need of water. "I'll begin by watering Mr. Droop."

Marc smiled. "Sure. Lieutenant Shipley, are these family photos okay to pack up?"

"All yours. I'll get you another box."

Marc nodded at the corner of his father's personal items. "Roden, after you revive Mr. Droop, want to help me tackle those?"

Twenty minutes later Marc and Roden finished examining papers, more photos, and personal memorabilia that Marc didn't recognize but intended to keep for Mom. She'd want to see every item—chronological pics of Tessa, letters from Mom written when they were still married and he was away on Army business, and more insights to Marc's growing-up years. Why had his father kept Marc's certificates of grade school perfect attendance, scholastic achievements, and sports awards? The pics taken at his college graduation were like a knife had been stabbed into his gut and twisted.

Shipley watched but said little. Perhaps he thought the moment too solemn. What did he comprehend about the father and son relationship?

"I'm sorry he's gone," Shipley said. "Colonel Wilkins was highly respected. I'm surprised you and I have never met."

Avery had expressed the same thing. "Why?"

"He talked about you a lot. Followed your FBI career and your accomplishments. Remember when you spoke at a high school commencement? He recorded every word. Had me listen to it."

"He was there?"

"That's what he told me. Are you saying you didn't know?"

Marc shook his head. "News to me. My father and I weren't close."

Shipley shrugged. "Colonel Wilkins had a few peculiar ways. This must have been one of them. One thing I've learned as a parent is once we mess up a relationship with one of our kids, restoring it is hard."

Marc placed the items back into the boxes to load into his truck. He'd never thought of his father as a coward until now.

21

IN HER HOTEL ROOM, Avery checked her email in-box for something from Granddad. She held on to hope as though it were the only life-line connecting her to him, but only emptiness met her. A flagged email from Craig caught her attention.

Hey, Avery.

Do you have any idea how I can find your grandfather? A couple of investigators from the Army Corps of Engineers were here this morning bombarding me with questions about his whereabouts.

Something is going on, and I have no clue if it's about his disappearance or Liam Zachary's murder reported on the news. This has me shook up, and I'm sure you're upset too. I tried to call the senator, but it goes directly to a filled voice mail box. In fact, I've tried calling you, and the same thing happens. I'm worried about both of you.

Why aren't you here at the ranch? When are you coming

home? Between the ranch and the business, I can't do all the work myself. In short, I need your help to keep juggling the balls.

Most importantly, are you two okay?
Craig

Craig didn't have a helpless cell in his body, and he could manage the ranch and business until the investigation cleared Granddad. *Slow down.* No point taking out her fear on Craig. If he knew the seriousness going on in Granddad's life and if she had permission, she'd fill him in. Avery reread the email and offered a prayer before she touched her laptop's keyboard.

Craig,
I'm safe, but my location and phone number are private, per Granddad's request. I have no idea where he might be. If he contacts me, I'll tell him about your concern and the investigators' visit. So very sorry the workload seems overwhelming. Payroll will be handled automatically next week with direct deposits made to all accounts.

I completed a bid for a dam repair and submitted it by certified mail. We have a couple of weeks before we hear about the contract. But the TCEQ might call.

Feel free to send questions my way, and I'll get back to you ASAP.

Give Mia a hug for me. I'll be home soon.
Avery

Craig must have been monitoring his email because his response came at lightning speed.

Avery,
You aren't making sense. Something is very wrong, and it scares me. I demand to know where you and the senator are hiding out and why.

Leanne stopped by earlier. Been here every day since
Wednesday night. She was in tears because she can't locate
you. Would you let her know you're okay?
Craig

Craig would have to deal with life by himself. But Leanne was another matter. If Avery hadn't promised Granddad not to contact her, Avery would be pouring out her heart to her best friend.

Avery answered the mound of emails from Craig regarding the construction company and ranch before she closed the lid on her laptop. Although she preferred to work alone, one more day cooped up in this hotel might cause her to check into a psychiatric hospital. For now, she must take every precaution to protect herself from the media.

Avery massaged her neck muscles. She believed Granddad's lectures and encouragement to grow into an independent woman would sustain her. But she'd waited too long to discover her own belief system, especially faith. Later this afternoon, she'd begin reading Matthew. Reputable sites were filled with Bible study guides, and she'd use them to discover what intimacy with God meant for her.

She stood and grabbed her room key. A part of her wanted a face-to-face with the messenger/assassin character to pose a few questions of her own. Deep in the pit of her stomach, she sensed it would eventually happen. Mia's urging for Avery to carry her Sig might not be that far off the logic zone.

Stress invaded her whole body, and exercise always helped. Unfortunately, Darcy grazed miles away as well as her stallion Zoom. She'd use the hotel's workout area to work out the tension while her brain fired neurons to help deal with myriad problems. Midway through tying her tennis shoes, her mind drifted to Agent Marc Wilkins. Their time together topped her curiosity list, but she had no expectations. He'd offered personal information, including the news about his half sister, and attempted to pry a few things from her. Smiling, she recalled how he probed her by asking the same questions in various ways. But she'd been taught by the best on how to avoid answering open-ended inquiries and, in Marc's case, his method of interrogation.

Marc was too cute for his own good, as Mia would say. Eyes were her go-to barometer to analyze everyone she met, and his brown pools smiled with warmth. He'd asked to see her again, but she declined. More than a curiosity, an attraction existed on her part. Why had she refused?

If not for the current circumstances, she might encourage getting to know him better.

If not for the current circumstances, Marc wouldn't show any interest in her. His motivation for friendship had everything to do with Granddad and nothing about her.

22

LATE AFTERNOON, Marc waited outside the Brazos River Ranch's iron gate for entry onto the property. The security camera had captured his pickup, and the electronic device had swallowed and spit out Roden's and his IDs. From his vantage point, no buildings were in view.

Marc palmed the steering wheel. "Does it seem to you like all we do is wait?"

"It's a prerequisite for our job, and you do it so well." Roden's attention stayed fixed on the spotted longhorn cattle and magnificent quarter horses dotting the perfectly groomed, rolling acres of white fencing. "Look at the size of the horns on that bull. Can you imagine what the animal is worth? Maybe I should have gone into pro ball instead of law enforcement."

"We're talking family money, politics, and a lucrative business."

"Check the financials of a few football players. I'm knee-deep in envy right now. Each of my girls could have a horse, which might keep them off their phones. At least some of the time."

"The key word is *might*."

Roden swung a frown at him. "Your time's coming. Just see how fun it is trying to figure out a teenage girl's mind. Toss in erratic emotions, and you're gonna need a playbook. Oh, don't forget the drama."

Marc cringed. "Not ready to think about it yet."

"You'd better be. Grandma won't last much longer."

"I know. Need to find a house in a reputable school district."

"Or a private school."

"What kind?"

"Christian."

"Not sure how I'd fit in among the churchy parents. But Tessa would get an excellent education. I spent a lot of years in parochial school." Marc's father had insisted upon his son receiving his early education from nuns, a matter in which his mother disagreed.

"Where do you think my girls go but a Christian school?"

Marc whipped his attention to his partner. "You're kidding."

"Nope, and trust me, you'll be praying the first time a boy comes knocking on the door."

"Tessa looks seventeen."

"Consider installing bars on the windows."

A canned female voice from the security cam said they'd been approved to enter, and the gate swung open. Marc pulled through and followed a winding paved road leading back into the property. Along the far right, the Brazos River flowed, lending its waters to irrigate the pastures and livestock.

Roden pointed to the Elliott mansion set on a hill resembling antebellum-style architecture. The opulent house had to be over twenty-five thousand square feet of living space. The two-story Greek columns, black shutters, and twin winding staircases in front rose to a massive second floor with a wraparound porch. Definitely a monument to Elliott money and Southern hospitality. Magnolia trees and pruned roses shaped the estate's exterior on a blanket of green that rivaled the most luxurious golf courses. In the rear of the home, a gazebo nestled between oak trees overlooking a flower garden with Texas native bushes and color.

Marc followed a sign indicating the office lay eight hundred feet ahead, a white stone building trimmed in cedar and shutters. The stables and barns were constructed of steel with stone frontage, cedar pillars, and metal roofs that spoke of wealth and prestige.

"Would you kill for this?" Marc said.

"They did over a hundred and fifty years ago."

Roden's sobering response reminded Marc that racial unity in the US was an ongoing project. "Very true."

Marc parked in an area designated for visitors. From the looks of the other trucks, his Ford model had the traits of an ugly stepchild. "We'll see what Craig Holcombe has to say. The senator took him in as a favor to an old friend who later died from cancer."

"Yep. Background disclosed Holcombe has a record from his younger days, drinking and fighting. Stole a car at seventeen. The senator cleaned him up. Now he's the senator's right-hand man."

"My guess is he's as loyal as the bloodhound running around here."

The two exited the truck and shrugged off their suit jackets in the heat. They walked to the office door, the hound sniffing at their heels and wagging his tail. The sights, sounds, and smells of a working ranch filled Marc's longing for a vacation. Hadn't taken one in five years. Must have been real hard for Avery to leave this behind, except for the fear.

Within a few feet from the truck to the office, sweat beaded on Marc's forehead, and Roden swiped at his face. A handwritten note on the office door stated the office was closed and gave a number to call. Marc obliged and introduced himself and Roden.

"Agent Wilkins, this is Craig Holcombe. I'm in the far stable at the right if you'd like to join me. You could take the golf cart parked there by the office—the key is in it. Or I'll be with you in a few." The man sounded friendly. A good sign.

Marc and Roden chose the stable route on foot. A man talked more when he stood in familiar territory.

Inside the stable, air-conditioning offered a cool change of temps. Working at the Brazos River Ranch had its perks. Marc noted the polished wood and metal stalls, stamped concrete floors, and impeccable equipment.

"Higher dollar than my apartment," Marc said. "Even the scent of horses is less than what I imagined."

"Air purification," Roden said. "But horse smells better than nail polish."

A thirtysomething man approached them. His dark hair and blue-green eyes matched the pic they'd seen online of Craig Holcombe. He held out his hand to each agent and greeted them. "I figure you're here about the senator and his granddaughter's disappearance. I'm not lying—we're worried about them. And I can't tell you if they're in the same place. Told the Army investigators the same thing."

"Can we talk privately?" Marc said.

"Sure. My office is here in the stables." He turned to three men working with an active, reddish stallion. "Go ahead and bridle 'im. Get 'im used to a lead in the arena. Nice and slow. Avery's been working him, and he responds well to her touch." The stallion snorted and reared. "Zoom, can't you pretend one of us is Avery?"

"Beautiful animal," Marc said.

"Thanks. He certainly has a mind of his own. Runs like a streak of lightning."

Roden took a few steps closer to the stallion. "Is he broken?"

"Avery's ridden him a few times. He's a handful, but she manages."

Holcombe smiled. "She has a gift when it comes to horses. She should patent her technique."

Admiration for Avery and her horsemanship sent Marc's pulse racing, one more positive for her.

He and Roden followed Holcombe to the rear left side of the building. He opened the door of an enclosed office large enough to host a dozen men. Everything was in rustic Western design—floor-to-ceiling tan-and-white stone fireplace, chandelier constructed of cow horns and candles, and a coffee bar and small fridge. Marc had stepped into a world he'd only heard about or seen in magazines. "Not what I expected in a stable."

"The senator does things right. My living quarters are connected behind my office." Holcombe grinned. "Allows me to live right next to the best horseflesh in the state. I'm a blessed man." He gestured to a leather sofa. "Have a seat. Can I get you something? Iced tea? Coke? Water?"

Marc and Roden chose water.

"How can I help you?" Holcombe removed his Stetson and placed it on a custom hat rack next to a hand-hewn oak desk that looked like a polished slab of wood. After retrieving two bottles of water, he sat across from them in a leather chair.

"Since talking to the Army investigators, have you heard from Senator Elliott?" Marc said.

"No, sir. He doesn't answer his phone either."

"What's your relationship with him?"

"I'm his friend, foreman for the ranch, and manager for the commercial construction company. He's been like a father to me for years."

"You're a busy man."

"I am. That's why I need Avery back here on the job."

"Have you heard or seen from her?"

"I've emailed her, and she responded but refused to tell me where she or they are or when they'll be home. She doesn't answer her phone either. Mia, the housekeeper, said they left separately, but that doesn't mean they aren't together now." Holcombe drew in a deep breath. "By the way, I knew Liam Zachary. Fine man and I have no idea why someone wanted him dead. Told that to the Army men too. I'm worried about the senator and Avery. Real worried." Craig stared into Marc's eyes. "Have you traced the bullet? Found the gun?"

"Working on it," Marc said. "Were you acquainted with Colonel Abbott Wilkins?"

"Yes, sir. Why? Has something happened to him?"

"He died of a heart attack."

Holcombe's face darkened. "Sorry to hear that. When did this happen?"

"Funeral was Monday."

"I had no clue. Whoa. Kin to you?"

"My father."

"Rough situation with the senator missing too. Your father was a familiar face here. Good man. I don't like any of this. Whatever you need, I'll help."

Roden walked to a window overlooking the pasture. "Who helps you with the workload?"

"I have good men and women I trust, both with the ranch and the construction company. But in just a few days, I'm behind. The senator, Avery, and I make a good team. We each have our own specialty and each other's backs. The senator compared us to the legislative, executive, and judicial branches of Texas government."

Roden smiled. "Are you surprised?"

Holcombe laughed. "It's the way he lives and breathes—everything about him is faith, family, friends, and politics."

"Have you consulted Senator Elliott's attorney?" Roden said.

"Talked to him today, and he advised me to sit tight in hopes the senator would surface soon. My guess is the attorney knows right where they are." He held up a finger and jotted down something on a piece of paper and handed it to Roden. "There's his name and number."

"Thanks." Roden returned to the sofa. "Mr. Holcombe, what's your opinion of the senator's son?"

"Buddy? A waste to mankind. Lazy. Money burns a hole in his pocket. He'd drain the senator's financials like an alcoholic drains a bottle of liquor if he has the chance." Holcombe waved his hand. "Not my position to accuse anyone of a crime, but I don't trust Buddy or his wife. They eat from the devil's Crockpot."

"You have definite opinions," Roden said.

"Sure do. Buddy and Saundra Elliott have always caused trouble, and I wouldn't put it past either of them to be up to something now."

"Are you suggesting Senator Elliott's son and wife might be responsible for the disappearances?"

"I have no idea. But I wouldn't be surprised."

"What about Avery?"

Holcombe pressed his lips together. "I care about her like family. She's smart, caring, and knows the ranch and construction business inside and out. Her faith is strong."

"Do you know any of her close friends?"

He nodded. "She's a private person but close to Leanne Archer. Would you like her number?"

Roden typed the contact into his phone. "Give me a moment here." He finished his water and eased back on the sofa. "What about Avery's weak areas?"

Marc wanted to ask more about the Archer woman, but Roden was headed somewhere in his questioning.

"Weaknesses? I've never heard her say anything against the senator or argue with his decisions. Now she may disagree with him one-on-one, but not that I've heard." He picked up a pen on his desk, glanced at it, and laid it back down. "Perhaps her nonconfrontational personality isn't a flaw but a sign of strength. If she and the senator are to offer a united front, then their differences would need to be handled privately."

Roden thanked him. "Why do you think Senator Elliott is un-available?"

"With what you've told me, I believe he's hiding out for a reason. Maybe he's in danger. Maybe Avery too. Maybe Buddy has roped himself into trouble, and the senator has to stay clear of him?"

"You're a wise man, Mr. Holcombe. Agent Wilkins and I have learned more from you than our other sources. Is there anything you can tell us that we haven't covered?"

"Call me Craig, please. Only the motorcycle tracks found by the cemetery on Monday. One of the hands saw the bike on the road but only from a distance. Could be connected or the rider was trespassing and nothing else." He startled. "Is this connected to Liam's murder?"

"We hope not."

"True. Agent Wilkins and I would like to see the Elliott family cemetery. We've heard a lot about it. Then we'll be on our way."

"Wouldn't hurt to take a few pics of those motorcycle tracks," Marc said.

Craig stood. "Let's do it. The tracks were most likely washed away in last night's rain."

23

CRAIG DROVE MARC AND RODEN to the family cemetery in Craig's truck, a Ford F-450 Limited in sleek black. Custom interior and rich leather seats that propelled air-conditioning to Marc's sweat-laden pants as soon as the engine fired to life. They took the main exit from the ranch and swung a left onto Oak Valley Road.

"How long have you worked for Senator Elliott?" Roden said.

"Since I was seventeen, coming up on eighteen years."

"Long time."

"The senator has been good to me. Helped me get a college education."

"What's your degree?"

"Ranch management and accounting. Thinking about becoming a vet."

"I thought about that too," Roden said. "One of my girls is headed in the same direction. Loves animals."

"Horses are my thing." Craig drove about a mile, then pointed to a grove of live oaks on the left. "A hidden gate and a dirt path leads to the Elliott family cemetery. Here on Oak Valley Road is where one of the hands saw a motorcycle."

"Any identifying markers?"

"I asked him, but he heard the engine and saw it from a distance. I rode my horse over here on Monday evening, but I couldn't find anything but tracks." Craig shrugged. "Sometimes if a ranch hand forgets to lock the gate, trespassers will leave beer cans, cigarette butts, or signs of drug use, but not a trace this time."

Craig stopped the truck and stepped out to clear brush and vines off an iron gate. He pulled through onto ranch property, closed the gate, and covered it with the thick brush before he climbed back into the truck.

"We would have helped you with that," Marc said.

"I'm used to it and you aren't." Craig laughed. "I'll take this any day to the heat of bad guys and smoking guns."

Maybe Craig was an all right guy.

Marc, Roden, and Craig walked the inside perimeter of the square, iron-fenced cemetery, surrounded by oaks as though keeping the occupants cool in their graves. Someone maintained the area, kept it mowed, weeded, and planted flowers. A few gravestones rose in weather-beaten marble, others smaller with the deceased and dates written in English and what looked like Gaelic. A dozen or so wooden crosses marked others buried there. The three searched outside the cemetery for footprints, but the rain had washed away any tracks.

Craig pointed to the oaks behind them. "There's where I found evidence of a motorcycle and footprints."

"Did you report this to the police?" Marc said.

"Nah. No reason."

They searched, but nothing existed but footprints beneath a shade tree.

"Those are mine," Craig said. "I mean, go ahead and take a picture of them and match 'em up to the boots I'm wearing. The ones I saw were of a sports shoe."

Marc snapped the image, and the boots and prints were the same. "Appreciate all your cooperation," he said. "Who do you suggest we talk to in finding Senator Elliott or Avery?"

"I'm fresh out of ideas. The senator has political friends, but other than the two deceased men, I have no names to offer. Except their attorney." Craig ceased his pleasant demeanor. "I will say this about the senator. He's not been himself over the past four or five months. Oh, he'd perk up when Avery was around, but I had a feelin' a huge burden weighed on his mind."

"Any reason given?" Roden said.

"I asked him, but he said everything was handled. Just getting older. The senator giving in to age is like him giving up religion. I thought he might have a health problem. No doubt about it, there's a problem out there, and it's real serious."

24

AFTER MARC AND RODEN HAD RETURNED from the ranch's family cemetery, they interviewed Mia Underly, who responded with positive comments about Senator Elliott and Avery.

"Their leaving home without notice isn't typical for either of them. And when I think about what happened to Mr. Zachary, I'm scared." She tucked her chin-length gray hair behind her ears. "Neither one is a coward but faces trouble head-on."

"What about any friends who could help us find Senator Elliott?" Marc said.

"So many, but none in particular. Craig is your better resource there."

"What about Avery's personal friends?"

She stared across an empty kitchen. "She's not dating anyone right now. Her best friend is Leanne Archer, and she might know more."

"Mr. Holcombe gave us her information, and we will follow up."

Roden complimented the mix of peppers and tomato smells coming from a huge pot on the stove. "Whatever you're cooking must bring those ranch hands in by the droves."

Her eyes widened. "Old family recipe."

"Rice and beans too?"

"Oh yes. And I use the finest cuts of beef from the ranch."

Roden closed his eyes. "Heavenly."

"If it were finished, I'd make you a plate."

"And I'd take it. I bet Buddy and his wife stop by often."

Ms. Underly snorted. "Those two wouldn't be getting any of my dishes. Doubt they'd get past the gate. They are money-hungry leeches and know better than to come by here."

"I'm sorry. Family problems are hard to manage. Looks like Mr. Holcombe has his hands full," Roden said.

"Yes, sir. He's a fine man."

Marc questioned if the dark-haired, saintly Craig might know more than he was willing to share.

★ ★ ★

Marc drove to the home of Avery Quinn Elliott II, a modest ranch of about three hundred acres. Buddy and his wife, Saundra, lived fifteen miles from the Brazos River Ranch on property deeded to them by the senator.

"I'm open for analytics about Craig," Marc said. "For the record, you're an ace in mining information."

"Strategy, which I learned viewing game recordings during my football days," Roden said. "Look for a person's vulnerability, feed on his good side, and draw out what he's really feeling."

"It works. Craig is definitely loyal to Senator Elliott and Avery. I didn't detect any cover-ups."

Roden drew in a deep breath.

"What's the hesitation?"

"He's smart. I listened to his praises for the Elliotts and candid responses about their character. But he's aware of his value to the ranch and construction business, and if he'd pull out, both would be handicapped for a season. Doesn't stop his frustration at the workload. I'm curious about how much money he makes."

"I'll talk to Avery about him. She's already shared that the relationship between her parents and the senator is rocky. Odd, I hadn't picked up on her being a yes-sir girl, but Holcombe alluded to it. Quite the opposite from my dealings with her."

"He's either underestimated her or he's allowed a green streak to rule his mouth."

"I debated telling Craig about the gun that had killed Zachary," Marc said. "I'd rather he finds out through another source."

"Me too. Let's hope he's an ally and we can count on him while we keep our eyes open." Roden held up his phone. "Want me to call the Archer woman?"

Marc swung him a chin lift.

Roden pressed in the number and placed his phone on speaker. After an introduction to Leanne Archer and the reason for his call, he eased into information mode. "We're investigating Senator Elliott's and Avery's disappearances. Can you help us?"

"No, sir. Avery and I normally talk or text every day, but I haven't heard from her since last Sunday after church. Phone calls, texts, and emails go unanswered."

"I see. Is she close to another friend, male or female?"

"Avery is a private person as far as friendships go. I mean, she has lots of acquaintances but no one to my knowledge that she confides in except me. Currently she's not dating anyone."

More confirmed information.

"Any past relationships we should know about?"

"No. Avery's picky about the guys she dates, and the last one moved to Nashville to marry another woman."

"What about her parents?" Roden said.

"They've been out of the picture for a long time. Not exactly role models for good parenting."

"Why?"

"I'd rather not say."

"When you hear from her or Senator Elliott, would you contact me? We're concerned about their safety."

She gasped. "Yes, without a doubt."

Roden gave his number and thanked her before he pocketed his phone. He pointed to a road turnoff for Marc. "Women have this thing about girlfriends, and they tell them everything. At least my wife and daughters do. Avery might not tell us where the senator is hiding out, but she might tell Leanne Archer."

Marc turned onto Buddy's property surrounded by metal fencing. He'd expected a solid home but not the sprawling stone ranch. "Not shabby."

"It's called having plenty of money."

"Remind me to check on what happens with the senator's ranch and business in the event he's out of the picture."

Roden typed into his phone. "And how much control Craig currently has."

"Right. Did you know Senator Elliott built Buddy's home, got him started raising beef cattle, and set him up financially in the home-building business?"

"Before or after the family split several years back?"

"After. Media reported the whole mess. The senator refused to comment while Buddy accused his father of holding back profits from the ranch and business." Marc grinned. "A question for you since your specialty is tackling sensitive info."

Buddy and Saundra's native, white-stoned home trimmed in cedar looked more like a lodge than a single-dwelling home. If the massive square feet measured up to the workmanship outside, the couple lived in luxury.

Buddy met Marc and Roden at the front door. Observing Avery Quinn Elliott II took Marc back to younger photos of the senator. Same thick hair turning to silver, but his gut spilled over his belt buckle. Not so with the senator. Buddy requested their IDs before he opened the door. Marc and Roden also handed him their business cards.

Buddy opened the door wide and pointed. "We can talk inside, if you're okay with it."

Marc guessed right—the Western lodge-type entrance spread to a huge two-story living area. The three took a seat on distressed leather chairs, and Marc opened the interview by thanking him for his time. "We have a few questions about your father."

Buddy eyed them suspiciously. "I've already informed the Army investigators about the family relationship. The senator and I don't speak. Neither do I hear from my daughter. Why ask me the same thing?"

"To confirm they haven't contacted you since then."

"No, and I don't expect any social visits."

Roden took over the conversation. "You have a handsome place here. It must take a lot of elbow grease to maintain the house and grounds."

"My wife and I have sacrificed for what we have. I saved to buy the land, build our home, and keep it afloat with the home construction business."

Lie number one.

"Did you design and complete the construction?"

"Yes. Took a while but was worth it. My wife and I did most of the work ourselves."

Lie number two.

"No wonder you're proud of this." Roden gestured around them. "It's a shame your daughter doesn't visit you."

"The senator has her manure-deep in his politics and religion."

A tall, attractive brunette entered the room and introduced herself as Saundra Elliott. Avery had inherited her mother's high cheekbones and slender build. Marc and Roden stood and shook her hand. "Please, sit, Agents. I heard Avery's name. Is she okay?" She eased onto a chair beside her husband.

"Various law enforcements are looking for her." Roden nodded at Marc, and the two resumed their seats.

"I'm sure she's aware of the senator's every move," Saundra said. "Avery refuses to have a relationship with us." She tilted her head and offered a thin smile. "We hope one day she'll come to her senses. Our door's open for her, but the senator had better keep his distance."

Buddy harrumphed. "She's like a wild mustang. Our daughter is capable of applying herself when the answers are in a book, but when it comes to common sense, she's clueless. Ever hear the lights are on but no one's home? When she was a girl, I tried to instill street smarts in her. Sometimes I thought I was successful and other times nothing. I'm sure the senator is dictating her every word and action."

"Family problems have a way of bringing out the worst in us," Roden said. "I have daughters too, and as much as we love them, sometimes we don't understand the way they think and act."

Buddy eyed them. "Why does the Army and FBI want to question them?"

"A good friend of the senator's, Liam Zachary, was murdered," Roden said. "Did you know him?"

"No, sir. Do you have evidence the senator is responsible? I've seen his violent streak, and I wouldn't want to be on the receiving end."

Marc had read about the senator's verbal temper but nothing about a physical problem. He listened so Roden could continue the interview.

"Tell us about his violent streak."

"When I was a kid, he talked to me with his belt. Short with the ranch hands. Physical with them too, then paid them off so they wouldn't go to the law."

"You witnessed this behavior?"

"Oh yes. One of the reasons I left. Neither my wife nor I can help you find him. He's most likely beat Avery."

"Do you have experience with how he deals with Elliott Commercial Construction's employees?"

Buddy glared. "The same. Makes me fearful about the dams and bridges with his name on the contracts."

"Why?"

"Shoddy business practices."

"How's that when the specs are approved before construction and official inspections are conducted regularly for safety?"

"You should know there are always ways to take shortcuts and make a few extra dollars."

"Can you point to a specific project for us to investigate?"

Buddy pointed a finger at Roden. "I'm staying out of it. No one would believe me anyway."

Roden glanced at Marc. "Agent Wilkins, do you have any additional questions?"

"Yes, I do. Is Craig Holcombe a man you respect?"

Buddy crossed his legs. "No dealings with him. He's the senator's yes-sir boy."

The Elliott family definitely had relationship issues. Marc and Roden stood. "Thank you for your time, Mr. and Mrs. Elliott. If you hear from Avery or Senator Elliott, please give us a call."

Outside, the sun had dropped below the horizon, but the stifling heat held like a thermostat set on high. Marc and Roden drove back to Houston.

"The Elliotts are one dysfunctional bunch," Roden said. "Avery is afraid her grandfather will be arrested for killing a man, and she might be right. Buddy and Saundra have little respect for anyone. They lied to us about the senator funding them. Did Buddy fabricate his father's temper? Because my research didn't show that."

"Argumentative but not physically or verbally abusive. All of it is info we might need. I'm in this with both feet. I intend to find out the truth behind Senator Elliott's disappearance and what happened to my father and Liam Zachary. How did the killer get my father's gun? Make a note to pull phone records on all three men and Avery. And I want everything out there about Buddy and Saundra Elliott."

The dysfunction between Elliott Junior and Senior hit too close to home. If given the opportunity, would Marc have welcomed reconciliation?

25

AVERY STARED AT THE FOUR WALLS of the hotel room. Sunday morning seemed strange without rising early for church, drinking a pot of coffee with Granddad, and discussing the previous week. They always left early to enjoy chocolate buttermilk doughnuts before greeting those attending the first service. Mia suspected Granddad's indulgence but so far hadn't said a word.

Small groups followed church, and the two joined their own classes. Avery loved choir, singing in harmony to those songs important to the rural and cowboy crowd. Granddad managed a lot of talents, but his singing would clear a pew. Over lunch, they debated sermon points. Always challenging and always fun. She trusted the one person who'd given unconditional love and spoken wisdom. And now he faced danger, and she didn't know how to resolve it.

Granddad, Mia, Craig, and Leanne had always been close by. Loneliness crept over Avery, leaving a painful void.

Today she lingered over a cup of hot coffee and wrote out a prayer for wisdom. Closing her eyes, she longed for answers. If she was the Christian she professed, shouldn't she have peace about it all?

Was she a sham believer?

Or did her worry mean she shared the fallible traits of every human?

How many times had Granddad said going to church didn't make one a Christian any more than determination to ride a bronco helped one stay in the saddle?

She dumped the coffee down the drain. She didn't want to deny her faith but to cover her heart with a quilt called relationship, purpose, meaning—and Granddad's innocence.

Oh, God, please forgive me for all the times I used Granddad as my savior instead of Your Son, Jesus.

After glancing at the time, she grabbed her purse and room key. The locked church she'd visited the other day had a service in fifteen minutes.

★ ★ ★

An hour and a half later, Avery walked back to the hotel. A miracle had met her inside the church doors. The message used the biblical accounting of David and Goliath to offer spiritual encouragement to those who battled their own giants. Her reliance on God had a long way to go, but she'd sensed His presence and that was exactly what she craved.

Still, the intersection where the cyclist had threatened her gave a moment of apprehension as though the blue motorcycle waited for her to cross the street.

A sandwich shop caught her attention, and she opened the door to walls of music memorabilia and sounds of the seventies. Only from all the times with Granddad did she recognize framed posters of the

Beatles, Creedence Clearwater Revival, and Bob Dylan. A giggle rose in her throat. Granddad and his eclectic taste in music. He wasn't fond of her favorite group, One Direction, but he did enjoy Taylor Swift.

She ordered a veggie wrap, spicy Doritos, and a Coke. Sliding into an empty lime-green booth with a red-orange table, she imagined a much younger Granddad. She'd seen the photos. His raven-colored hair, piercing blue eyes, and dimpled smile had the girls in the palm of his hand. Not unlike how Marc must affect women.

Midway through lunch, her phone signaled a call from Marc. Had she willed it? Possibly . . .

"Hi, Avery. Is this an okay time to call?"

"Sure. Have you located Granddad?"

"Not yet. I'm at my sister's and wanted to know if you'd have dinner with me tonight."

"Why?"

"Personal reasons only."

"You have a bad line, Agent Wilkins, and I recall you've used it before."

"But it worked."

"Let's see. I think you've talked to a few more people and want to question me again."

He groaned. "You've ripped my heart in two and stomped on it."

"The truth has a way of doing that."

"Dinner is more about me wanting to spend time with you than professional. Can I take you somewhere other than the hotel?"

"Oh, I hope no one is listening."

"Let me rephrase my question. Can we have dinner at a restaurant other than the hotel?"

"I haven't said yes."

"But you'd like to. Please don't tell me you have a boyfriend."

"Only a horse named Zoom."

"I saw him at the ranch, and he had my respect."

She laughed. "All right. Someplace casual. No Asian or Indian food."

"Tex-Mex? See you at seven?"

"I'll meet you there, just text me the address. Bring your questions, and I'll bring my answers. We'll wrap them in a tortilla and dip them in hot sauce."

He chuckled. "So when I ask you something you refuse to answer, you'll point to the hot sauce?"

"Count on it." Despite the circumstances, Avery looked forward to having dinner with him.

She'd not deny her attraction to him, but inching forward with thoughts of a future seemed pointless. Logic continued to tell her Marc's interest was rooted in finding Granddad. Nothing else. And if FBI responsibilities motivated his dinner plans, she'd deal with it and be a wiser woman.

26

"A GIRLFRIEND?" Tessa set two cans of Coke on the kitchen table for Marc and her. "You told me you didn't have one. But I leave you for five minutes, and you slip in a call?"

Marc had agreed to play an online version of a game called the Royal Game of Ur, supposedly five thousand years old, before hitting the road back to Houston. "And this originated in ancient Mesopotamia?"

"Yes. And you haven't answered me."

"Why would a fifteen-year-old want to play a game this old?"

"It's fun, and you still haven't answered my question."

Marc peered into her face with her button nose. Just plain cute. "She's a woman I interviewed for an open case."

She tapped her chin. "The FBI website doesn't mention taking interviewees to dinner. On a Sunday."

"Busy week ahead, and this way I get ahead of my list." He studied the rules for Ur and downloaded the game onto his iPad. "You go first. I'll take the black disk."

She took her online move, and the iPad sounded like her disk scraped over rock. Go figure.

"Brother, is she smart and pretty?"

"Haven't paid attention." He took his turn and landed on a bonus square. "I'm off to a good start."

"Not unless you change clothes before you go to dinner."

He glanced at his jeans and knit pullover. "What's wrong with what I have on?"

She shook her head. "Your jeans look like you ironed a crease in them, and you're wearing a white shirt. Not a fashion statement."

"I'll take your recommendation into consideration."

"Hard to do when I don't know what's in your closet."

"Soon you can fix me." With the game tied two to two, he reached into his reservoir of questions. "Did you play this with our father?"

"Yep."

"Ever play it with Liam Zachary or Senator Elliott?"

A dramatic breath filled the small kitchen. "Am I being recorded?"

"You are too smart for your own good." He grinned, never expecting to have this much fun with Tessa.

"Yes. Both of them. Dad got hooked on Ur." She took her move. "And I usually won."

Marc stored her response. "He was competitive?"

"Is it hot in August?"

"Ever hear a criticism about Mr. Zachary?"

"Dad said he took too many chances."

"In what way?"

Tessa shrugged. "The two were on the phone, and it was Dad's answer to something Liam said."

"What else did you hear?"

Her demeanor shadowed. "Whatever they were talking about,

Dad refused to go to you for help. He said, 'I won't put Marc into a situation that could get him killed.'"

"Why didn't you tell me this before now?" Marc couldn't mask the irritation in his voice. "I'm sorry. What's going on with you? I don't understand the concern about a girlfriend, and now I sense you're trying to protect me."

She blinked back tears filling her eyes. "Why would I want to lose you too?"

Her remarks clicked—fear in the form of teasing and lightheartedness. He scooted back his chair and walked to her side. Taking her hand, he urged her to stand. Wrapping his arms around her, he drew her close. "Tessa, I'm sorry. All of this has been so hard on you, and I let my investigative side take over." Reality wrapped around his brain. "You lost your mother, our father, your grandmother has little time left, and I think you're afraid if I find a woman, I'll abandon you too."

She trembled against him and sobbed. "Yes, I'm afraid. I know I'm almost grown up and should be able to handle junk, but it's not easy. Slowly losing Gram makes me feel like I'm being punished for something, and what happens if you find out about one of my really bad faults?"

"Not happening, Tessa. We're stuck with each other. Already told you any woman interested in me has to be interested in you and me. That's a promise."

She snuggled closer. "I don't think the awful feeling will go away easily."

"Oh, I have junk to handle too. We all do. Once we're settled in Houston, counseling is in line for both of us." He pulled back. "I need to tell you what I've learned. The gun used to kill Liam belonged to our father."

"Impossible. Dad was already gone."

"Right. I didn't want you to hear the news from anyone but me."

She reached around his waist and leaned back into his chest. "We haven't known each other for years like most brothers and sisters, but what you've shown me is a good man. Please stay safe. I'm sorry I asked you to find Dad's killer because now I'm afraid you'll get hurt."

Marc rested his chin on her head. An overwhelming surge of protectiveness rose in him, and his eyes started to blur. "I'm trained to protect others," he whispered. "I will be careful, and we must be honest with each other. I just found my little sister, and I intend to spend a lot of time with her."

"Promise?"

"Promise." Right now, he'd do anything to keep Tessa from worrying about him. She had her heart full of losing their father and facing her grandmother's final hours. Marc felt regret and a hint of jealousy that Tessa knew their father better than he did. But even more so, a longing to have experienced the man so highly respected . . . and loved.

"You asked me the first time we met what I wanted most in the world, and I didn't answer," she said. "I hadn't decided to like you or if I could trust you. But that's it—for the people I care about to stop dying."

"You're not alone. I'm right here, and you can call me day or night."

She swallowed hard. "Okay."

"One more game to beat you, then I want input on what you'd like for our house. When we're able, we can look at property together."

Tessa stepped back and swiped beneath her eyes. "You want me to help?"

"Aren't you going to live there too?"

"Yes, but I wasn't expecting that." She sniffed. "Thank you, Marc, for not shoving me aside."

"And thank you for not shoving me aside. We need to stop, or I'm going to be bawling. I think we need four bedrooms and at least two and a half baths. One story or two?"

A smile played on her lips. "Depends on the layout."

"And a big game room for your dancing."

She touched her lips. "You are the best brother any girl could have. You have blessed me when I didn't want to think about tomorrow. Forget about the game, let's look for our home. But first I need to check on Gram."

Alone with his thoughts, Marc recalled the inspection for the Lago de Cobre Dam. It had passed twice, but still his father had requested another one. Could this be part of the discussion between Liam and him? Or something else?

Marc prayed but not as often as he should. Hard for him to consider God in this chaotic world. But he asked God to keep his sister safe. Still, a twist in his gut told him a storm brewed bigger than he could imagine.

27

AVERY ADDED A DOLLOP of sour cream to her beef fajita. She'd been too generous with the hot sauce and needed to tame the fire. "This is so good," she said to Marc. "Thanks for choosing one of my favorite Tex-Mex restaurants."

"You're welcome." He cut into a second stuffed poblano.

"How is your sister?"

"Tessa's having a rough time dealing with one tragedy after another. I didn't tell you this before, but her mother abandoned her at birth, and her grandmother raised her. Now the grandmother is dying of cancer, and I'm about to become her legal guardian."

"She's scared about the future with no track record to compare it to. My guess is she's afraid you'll abandon her too. Trust will be hard for her." She lifted her gaze to him. "And she's frightened for you with good cause. Her newly found big brother and soon-to-be guardian works to solve violent crimes. Don't be surprised if anger seeps in."

Marc's gaze penetrated her very soul. "You nailed it. I don't know how to help but to spend time with her." He shared his idea about counseling.

Avery thought of the responsibility involved in raising a teenage girl and her own issues at Tessa's age. He barely knew his sister and was about to encounter her strengths and challenges. "How do you feel about it?"

"I'm all right. A little nervous." Marc told her about their starting a home search and plans next Sunday to walk through a few houses in person instead of a virtual tour.

"Tessa sounds like a survivor," Avery said. "I'd ask to see a pic, except with your investigation that might not be a good idea."

He nodded. "Yes, for now. I have a question."

She smiled to relax him. "I'm not surprised."

"What would happen to the Brazos River Ranch and Elliott Commercial Construction in the event your grandfather is not available?"

Sour way to phrase Granddad's potential future. "Everything reverts to me."

"Not your dad?"

"Granddad wrote him out of the will years ago. He's updated the document a few times in case the will is contested." Marc no doubt must have talked to Mom and Dad. "What did my parents say about our family?"

"Neither said anything unexpected."

Avery leaned closer across the table. "Marc?"

"Their comments mirrored yours."

"They despise Granddad and believe I've been brainwashed."

"Possibly."

Avery had her answer. "My parents are selfish and greedy. I'm sure the conversation went along those lines."

He lifted his phone from the table. "I want to give my partner the information you've told me." When he finished, he set the phone beside his glass.

She laced her fingers together and rested them on the table. "Tell me about your meeting with Craig."

"Cooperative. Appears capable. Cares about you. Believes you and the senator are together. He's concerned both of you are in danger, but he has no idea why or who's involved unless it stems from Liam Zachary's death."

"I got the same impression from his emails. I should be at the ranch."

"But your grandfather wants you in Houston, out of potential harm."

"Marc, anyone can be found. The guy on the motorcycle proved it."

"Why make it easy for him?" His finger traced a circle on the top of her hand. Normally she'd pull back, but not this time. His touch communicated comfort, sincerity, and a strange eeriness that they'd met for a purpose.

"In the beginning, I ran to find peace." She shook her head, mentally erecting a guarded wall not to expose too much of her thoughts. He confused her—she confused herself. "Now I want to do something—anything—to find out who killed Liam and why Granddad believes I need to be protected."

"Leave it to the professionals."

She slowly withdrew her hand from his touch. "I can't. No point going there." She took a drink of water to focus. "You had questions for me. Now is the time to ask them."

He settled back, never taking his eyes off her face. "If you are in control of the ranch and business, what would be Craig's role?"

"I hadn't thought about it. I suppose he'd remain in his current position." Curiosity crawled through her. "Why?"

"Do you two get along?"

"Fantastic. Why?"

He took a generous bite of an enchilada. "Just wading in the waters."

Or mucking stalls. "What else?"

"You'd make a great interrogator, but you've learned your techniques from a politician."

"And you seldom answer a question straight on."

"Not true. Some things aren't cleared for public knowledge. Are we keeping score on who offers the least information?"

"Maybe. What bothered you about Craig?"

He took a drink of water, no doubt to form his reply. "Nothing. How much does he earn?"

"A fair amount." When Marc frowned, she offered a slight smile. "You have the resources to find out for yourself, but I'll cooperate. Currently $150,000 a year, plus his living quarters, Mia's superb cooking, a new work truck every three years, and bonuses when the ranch or the construction business make a profit. See, I offered more than what you asked."

"And I'm grateful."

His dry tone told her to change the topic. "Why did you choose a career with the FBI?"

He dipped a chip into guacamole. "'The price good men pay for indifference to public affairs is to be ruled by evil men.'"

"I'm impressed. You quoted Plato."

"Beneath this rough exterior, I have a refined side."

He didn't have a rough exterior, and she liked his looks. He did have warm brown eyes and an adorable smile, but his ego didn't need to hear it. "Refined? As in you attended a finishing school?"

"Sam Houston. Majored in law enforcement."

"Your education grounded the rough edges. Graduated top in your class, I'll bet."

He laughed. "Not at all. In fact, a professor told me I didn't have what it took for a career in law enforcement. Said I missed the intuitive gene."

"Ouch."

"He did me a favor. I worked harder, raised my GPA." He paused long enough to dip a chip in salsa and pop it in his mouth. "Not so sure I'd have made it through Quantico without his voice drilling in my ears."

"Is the FBI your biggest time stealer, or do you have hobbies?"

"I have a few interests like swimming, watching sports, trail biking. And you?"

"Anything horse related. As a girl, I used to compete in barrel racing, calf roping, cowgirl stuff."

"Why did you quit?"

"I prefer riding to release stress than for competition. It's the one thing that relaxes me."

"Your horse's name?"

"Darcy. She's a quarter horse, and I'm in the process of training Zoom." Longing for home spread through her body. "Love his wild nature. What did you think of the horses at the ranch?"

He dipped his spoon into his black bean soup. "What I know about them could be put in this bowl of beans, but the ones at the ranch are magnificent creatures. I've ridden about five times in my life and have no style but to hang on." He abandoned his spoon in the beans. "The huge house, grounds, horses, and cattle reminded me of a vacation or movie setting. The entire operation is impressive. You, the senator, and Craig Holcombe have every reason to be proud."

"Thanks. Granddad has worked hard. Craig and I are just tagalongs. Did Old Blue sniff you and wag his tail like a terrier?"

"He did. Not much of a watchdog."

"We have security cams for those who don't belong there."

An hour later, they walked across the parking lot to her car. Marc carried her to-go box for the hotel room's fridge, and she carried a heart full of unanswered questions. Her respect for Marc grew. He maintained his loyalty to the FBI, and she admired his stand. Still, she wished he'd have revealed a few details from the ranch hands' and her parents' interviews.

"Thanks for having dinner with me," he said. "I'd like to think we could do this again."

She stopped at her car. "I had a great time. Food was amazing and the company too."

He grinned, a lopsided, little boy look. "For whatever it's worth, I wish I'd met you without this case shadowing us."

Kind words, but did he mean them? She wanted to believe so. "What would we talk about?"

"Horses. Trail bike riding. Things to do for fun." His voice lowered to a gentle whisper. "Be careful. Stay safe. Don't do anything rash until this is over."

She started to remind him of the impossibility of her assuming a role of the damsel in distress when she had to find Granddad. "I'll do my best." Marc walked away and she deactivated her car alarm. Remembering her to-go box, she called out to him. "You have my dinner for tomorrow night."

He turned and they walked to meet each other. "Do I hear an invitation?"

The moment she reached for the plastic bag, a flash of light and an explosion tossed Marc and her sprawling onto the pavement.

28

AVERY'S EYES FLUTTERED OPEN to a blaze of fire and heat straight from the pits of the earth. Stunned by the explosion, silence filled her ears and numbed her brain. She shoved aside her disorientation to focus on the arm across her back.

Marc. He didn't move.

She attempted to raise her body, but a sting in her right arm stopped her.

"Marc." She slowly turned her head and faced him, inhaling sharply. Blood trickled down the side of his face. Her gaze followed the path to a gash above his temple in his hairline. "Marc, are you okay?"

"Miss, how can I help?" She saw the huge check mark signifying the man's Nike tennis shoes, but her whole body hurt too much to lift her head. "I've called 911. But I'm afraid to touch you."

She swallowed hard and prayed for strength. Was this what trusting God meant? "Is my friend okay?"

"I can't tell. He appears unconscious."

Sirens rang in the distance . . . An ambulance? Police? Fire truck?

"Marc, answer me."

Not even a groan.

Her last thoughts before the explosion trickled in. Marc had used his body to shield hers and pull her close to him. How had she ended up on her stomach? She tried again to get up. To take care of him. She forced strength into her pain-packed body. What had happened to her, the strong and determined woman?

What if Marc had died protecting her? How could she live with the knowledge of such a sacrifice? His protective instincts might have killed him.

"I need to scoot out from under him," she whispered to the man, whose Nikes hadn't budged.

"Are you sure?"

"Yes, please." She held her breath, anticipating any broken bones or more torn flesh.

He eased her out from under Marc's monster hold. Her body burned, but she'd snapped bones in the past, and the excruciating pain nestled in her memories didn't surface. Once cleared from Marc's arm but still facedown on the pavement, she took a moment to evaluate her body.

The sirens grew closer, but not as loud as she expected with the ringing in her ears. What had triggered the blast? All the warnings from Granddad rolled across her mind. *"Don't trust anyone."* She doubted the explosion had been an accident. Was she targeted because of her search for Granddad? Because of her insistence to learn the truth, she and Marc had experienced someone's evil intent. She gritted her teeth and once again tried to lift her head and failed.

Her gaze wandered to the lower part of her car. Hers wasn't engulfed in flames but the vehicle parked next to it. Debris and shattered glass lay around Marc and her. In the gathering darkness of the summer evening, a crowd formed. A woman asked if she was okay. Another woman screamed—she owned the car erupting into more flames.

The headlights of an ambulance, then a police car whirled onto the scene. The muffled sounds confused her. When would her head clear? She had no experience to compare the sensation of being transported out of reality partnered with the inability to hear and focus. She looked for the man wearing Nikes. He'd disappeared. Maybe he stepped back into the crowd to avoid the emergency vehicles.

Paramedics poured from two ambulances.

"My friend is hurt," she whispered. "Take care of him first."

A bald man bent to Marc and felt his neck for a pulse. A young woman rushed to him with a medical kit.

"We need to move her onto her back," a third paramedic said, a male.

Strong arms lifted her onto a mat. Avery bit back the torment. Everything hurt.

The paramedic at her side asked her name and took her vitals.

"Please," Avery said. "Is . . . is my friend alive?"

★ ★ ★

Avery waited in the hospital ER for Marc to open his eyes. A piece of metal from the explosion had slammed into his head, requiring seven stitches. Machines hummed and monitored his vitals while an IV dripped healing fluids into his arm. He'd uttered a few unintelligible words, giving her hope he'd recover from the concussion.

Nurses roamed in and out, each one assuring her rest would bring his body back to normal. She'd believe them when Marc opened his eyes and spoke in a language she understood. Having him ask her something she refused to answer sounded good right now—and about three ibuprofens.

Her head pounded like someone was banging war drums, and the stitches in her right arm stung. But she and Marc lived to face whatever today and tomorrow brought.

She'd call a family member or friend of his if she knew who or how. He'd told her about a partner, mother, and sister, but without full names, she could do nothing. The hospital knew Marc worked for the FBI, but no one had shown up to check on him.

Around her everything was steeped in sterile white—the linens, walls, bandages, and cotton balls in clear jars. She'd rather smell the ranch than antiseptic. Barn odors didn't mean someone hurt or faced death. Hospitals were not a colorful place, and the only time she ever enjoyed a visit was the birth of a baby.

Earlier, a blonde female police officer in the ER had taken her statement while a doctor stitched her arm. That was, what little she remembered.

"No, I didn't see anyone lurking in the area," Avery had said. "A man helped me."

"Do you have his name?" the officer said.

"No. Never saw his face either. At the time, I lay on my stomach and couldn't move. All I can tell you is he wore Nikes. They were blue and gold with red gel soles."

The officer squinted. "The man walked away?"

"I think so. When the emergency vehicles arrived, I looked and he was gone." Avery drew in a deep breath to deal with her head. "Why did the car beside mine explode?"

"That's under investigation. Miss Elliott, you forgot to give me your phone number."

"Don't trust anyone."

The officer had displayed her ID . . . "Is my number kept in strict confidence?"

"Yes, of course."

Avery gave her the hotel number.

The officer closed her notepad and suggested Avery contact the police department if she remembered additional information.

Although the police officer didn't use the word *bomb*, something caused the car to burst into flames. Avery searched for meaning, a reason. Her fuzzy recollection bumped heads with foolishness, and she refused to discount the incident. If only she could talk to Granddad, except her new priority meant finding answers to life's problems without relying 100 percent on him.

Think for yourself.

Guilt burrowed deep. If she'd told Marc the truth about the threats made against her, chances were he'd not be in such bad shape. Trust . . . a man who'd risked his life for someone else deserved the title of trustworthy. And what she'd witnessed showed he had admirable qualities.

A huge man with shoulders the span of a sequoia stepped into the curtained area. "I'm FBI Special Agent Roden Clement. Marc's my partner."

"The hospital called you?"

"FBI notification. And you are?"

"Avery Elliott."

"I thought so." The man drew up a chair on the opposite side of the bed. "Are you all right? I read on the doctor's report you have stitches in your right arm."

She nodded. "A few bruises. I'm sure I'll feel it more tomorrow. Right now I'm worried about Marc."

"The doctor says he'll recover fine."

The agent had completed his preliminary work before he checked on Marc. Not sure how she felt about being an FBI specimen in a database of victims. "Recovery has different meanings. Marc hasn't regained full consciousness since the explosion. His doctor ordered various tests."

"His head is strong as steel. I'd have been here sooner, but I wanted to run by the crime scene. In your words, what happened?"

"Not until I see your ID."

29

MARC STARED AT RODEN AND AVERY through a pain-filled stupor. "Are you two taking bets on if I'm going to make it?"

Avery, who had a huge smudge of dirt alongside a bruised cheek, tilted her head. "I just lost."

"You put money on me being carried off to the morgue?"

Roden laughed. "She hasn't known you as long as I have." He studied Marc. "You had a close one."

Marc shut his eyes to manage a bolt of lightning to his head. Willing it away did little good. "I feel it."

Avery touched his arm. "Thank you for protecting me. I owe you."

"I'll put it on your account. Your arm's in a sling. Broken?"

She shook her head. "Stitches. The same number as yours. Seven is our lucky number."

Marc grimaced. "Ouch. How's your car?"

"It still drives. At least that's what an officer told me, but I haven't seen it. Mine didn't explode, but the car parked to my right did."

He fought the temptation to close his eyes. "Your car's at the police station?" When she confirmed it, he fought the torment in his head to move forward. "I'll make sure it's returned to your hotel. What caused the blast?"

"Good question," she said. "I tried to find out but got nowhere. Unless your partner here used his clout."

"I have the police report," Roden said. "An elderly widow owned the ten-year-old Chevy. She's retired and lives on a fixed income. Has no idea who'd do her harm."

"Agent Clement—" Avery directed a glare, icy and teasing—"I'm sure you have more details. You've been to the restaurant, read the doctor's report, and you recognized my name."

"Any evidence I might have found would be confidential."

"I believe you're fully aware of my talking to Marc about a situation at the Brazos River Ranch. Rather doubtful what happened tonight hit the coincidence list."

Marc would have slid in a few remarks about her interrogating Roden if he hadn't hurt so badly.

Not even a twitch appeared on Roden's face. "He mentioned your concern over Senator Elliott's disappearance."

She seemed to reach deep within her for control—or emotional management. "I understand your protocol and why it's in place. Maybe you can help me with a simple yes or no. Agent Clement, was a bomb planted in the car?"

"The name's Roden."

"Roden, the car was bombed?"

"I can tell you when and if it's confirmed. Which one of you is ready to tell me what you remember? Nothing personal, but you both resemble the losing end of a fight."

"Go ahead," Marc said to Avery. "My partner with the brains

and biceps might help us figure this out. Why don't you start at the beginning? I'm not going anywhere soon."

"Is this being recorded?" she said.

Roden held up his phone. "I can."

"Okay. The situation began on Monday at the ranch when the Internet went down while I was trying to resolve a discrepancy on an invoice for a dam project. I couldn't work, so I planned a surprise lunch with my grandfather. He'd left early morning to ride fence along a repair line . . ." She continued to relay what she'd witnessed at the ranch, her granddad's later request to contact Marc, and tonight's tragedy.

"Why am I just now hearing about the invoice?" Marc frowned.

"Because Liam's death took priority. It's not connected." She shook her head. "I shouldn't have mentioned it."

"We'll be the judge of that." Marc winced with an unexpected twist of fire to his back. Could the dam inspection his father requested be the same project? "What about the discrepancy raised a flag?"

"The materials supplier billed us a lesser amount for materials than the specs required." She sighed. "Craig told me we had the materials in the warehouse, and I confirmed they were picked up for the project."

Marc drew in a breath. "I see. What dam?"

"Lago de Cobre. Why?"

"Just curious."

"Marc, take a break," Roden said. "You and the sheets have this white thing going." He glanced at her. "Avery's running a close second."

Marc held up a finger to signal for them to wait until he could manage the pain.

"I'll ask questions until you're able to jump back in," Roden said. "Who signs the checks for the ranch and the business?"

"Granddad and I are the only ones authorized. That way we have no surprises." She lifted her chin. "Why?"

"We're not questioning your integrity, Avery. Just looking for more information to piece this together. What about the ranch and business credit cards? I have daughters, and I know what can happen with unauthorized credit card usage."

"Mia Underly, our cook and housekeeper, has a credit card for her expenses. Craig uses two—one for the ranch and another for the construction business. I reconcile the accounts and pay the cards when the bills come in. Tell me what this has to do with the car blast?"

"Just checking the links," Roden said. "Have you thought of any conversations or strange events leading up to you and Marc leaving the restaurant?"

"I wonder if the man in the Nikes saw anyone you could question. I wish I'd caught a glimpse of his face or asked his name. He appeared to be first on the scene."

"The police report doesn't indicate a witness." Roden stood and examined Marc's half-full IV bag. "Two thoughts here—either the man didn't want to get involved, or he planted the bomb and was admiring his handiwork."

"Mr. Nike had a gentleness about him."

"Do you think he'd give himself away?"

She glanced at Marc, then back to Roden. "I always believed my granddad didn't raise a fool, but I'm missing far too much in this puzzle. And although neither of you will mention it in my presence, there's a whole lot more going on. I wish you would tell me what you're thinking."

Marc groaned, partially out of agony and partially because of Avery's persistence to find answers.

Roden held up his palm as though he sensed Marc considered getting back into the conversation. "Why not wait until the police have finished their investigation. Yes, HPD has confirmed a bomb. Your feelings are nat—"

"Please, I know you mean well, but I've grown up with the best word master who ever walked the earth. Granddad is a politician, and he's given me lots of insight and tricks." She rubbed her temples. "I'm taking out on you and Marc the raw fear of nearly being blown to bits. But I'm not grazing in the back pasture by suspecting the car bomber targeted me."

"We have no idea until evidence surfaces," Roden said. "What if the person who planted the bomb only wanted to scare you from talking to anyone about the murder on the ranch?"

"Then he did a fine job."

Marc's eyes longed to close, but he couldn't miss anything that was said. "The restaurant's security cam could show who planted the explosive and help ID the man you talked to."

"I've requested those." Roden typed into his phone. "Do you remember any other distinguishing characteristics about the Nike man?"

"None. I've taken precautions since driving to Houston. I've replaced my phone and laptop and kept my whereabouts secret. But the man on the motorcycle must have followed me to Houston. I—"

"Whoa, guys," Roden said. "The same motorcycle you saw at the family cemetery?"

Avery pressed her lips together. "Yes. A man on the same color and type of Yamaha motorcycle stopped me outside the hotel. Told me not to talk to Marc Wilkins, and the FBI couldn't help me."

Roden turned to Marc. "Did you know about this?"

Marc nodded. "Meant to tell you. Every time I thought about it, something came up. Sorry. Avery, you cannot go back to your hotel. Whoever is responsible for the threat and tonight's explosion knows exactly where you are."

"And if I change hotels, the person will find me again. I'm not running."

"You came to me for help, and I'm giving you professional advice." The woman raised his blood pressure with her stubbornness.

"You two are pathetic," Roden said. "Listen to the voice of reason from the one who missed the invite for Mexican food. The FBI is primarily a fact-finding organization. We put together reports and send those files to who is prosecuting a case. You're in danger and witnessed a crime. Let the FBI do their job and place you in a safe house."

She massaged the back of her neck. "Marc tried to persuade me to change hotels before tonight, but I have the same answer for you as I had for him then. Tomorrow I'll think through your request. But not now."

Marc watched her tremble. The trauma from the explosion and concern for her grandfather had caught up to her. "Roden, can we arrange for surveillance at the hotel tonight and until we can get her moved?"

"Imagine so." He typed again into his phone.

Exhaustion weighed on her delicate features. "Avery, let Roden take you to the hotel. I'll be here until the IV finishes dripping. Then he can play taxi for me. Get a good night's sleep, and we'll talk in the morning."

"I'm tired and my arm is . . . uncomfortable." She peered at Marc. "In this whole mess, aren't you afraid for your mother and sister?"

Their safety had burrowed into his mind. He glanced at Roden. "On it too. I'll get someone to check on them both."

Marc pushed on. "Avery, have you been threatened more than once?"

She stood and walked to the curtained partition. After looking around her, she returned to the chair. "We should talk."

30

MARC TRUSTED HIS GUT, and his instincts told him whatever Avery had to say would irritate him. Or make him crazy worried. "Are these facts I should have had right from the beginning?"

She nodded. "Trust is hard. But after tonight, you've earned it. I'm sorry."

He thought she'd withheld information from him. "Roden, would you stand at the curtain and keep an eye out?"

"Sure thing." He took a block position from his football days.

Avery's sad blue eyes emitted relief. "Thanks." She focused on Marc. "On Tuesday night, the day after the murder, I received a call on my personal cell phone, the one I later destroyed. A distorted voice said, 'The unfortunate incident sure made a mess of things.' I asked who was calling, and the voice said, 'A messenger.' The voice told me to do exactly as the senator told me." She wrapped her arms across her chest. "And the man on the motorcycle later called himself the Messenger, but you already know about him."

"I'm listening."

"The voice said my life was worth nothing. I asked for the meaning, and the voice threatened to kill my granddad too."

Had the senator been blackmailed or coerced into something—possibly criminal? "Have you heard from the caller since you tossed your phone?" Marc didn't know whether to unload his anger or attempt to comfort her, but the agony in his body won out. "I've met with you three times since then, and you've not mentioned the first threat. Seems to me tonight he attempted to follow through with near accuracy."

Her eyes shot firebolts at him. "Would you risk the life of someone you love?"

He wanted to get out of that hospital bed and shake her. The woman dribbled facts when it suited her. "I wouldn't stand in the way of those trying to help."

"Hey," Roden said from the curtained opening. "Nothing will be solved by you two tossing acid at each other."

Marc failed to take into consideration she'd been hurt too. "You're right. Avery, I apologize. I know you're worried for yourself and your granddad, so let's talk through this." He held out his hand for her to take. She hesitated, then slipped hers into his. *Show patience. Gentleness.* But he still wanted to cuff her to a metal pole. "Have you told me everything?"

"Yes."

"Do you recall any similarities between the cyclist and the man wearing the Nikes?"

"No. Tonight all I saw were his shoes."

Roden typed with rapid-fire thumbs. "I'm taking a few notes here. Since you two are nearing invalid stage, I'm going to repeat the obvious. Sounds to me like Senator Elliott might be the victim of a blackmail scheme that included Colonel Abbott Wilkins and Liam Zachary. What we need is evidence."

Roden lifted a brow at Avery. "Number one, the senator is a person of interest. Number two, the guy who rides a blue motorcycle—

a man who knows you and Senator Elliott very well—is a suspect in the car bombing. Either he planted it or knows who did."

"He called me by my pet name, the one Granddad uses."

"What is it?"

"Sweet girl."

Roden entered the info into his phone. "If the guy contacts you again, you have to call us immediately. Number three, although we need verification, looks like the car bombing was a threat aimed at you. Or the guy messed up and placed it on the wrong car. Another assumption on my part is the person responsible is worried about what you already know."

"Meaning finding the body or the man's identity?" she said.

"Or both. Think hard, does anyone hate Senator Elliott enough to frame your granddad for murder?"

Avery touched her head. Pain or her response to Roden? "You're thinking the man on the motorcycle shot Liam and set Granddad up for it?"

"Yes, and then threatened you because you didn't see Senator Elliott pull the trigger." Roden glanced at the busy nurses' area and then back to her.

"Why tell me to do all that Granddad instructed?"

"Could be to make the senator seem guilty in your eyes and convince anyone you told." Roden paused. "I need think time on this one. The guilty person or persons has a lot to gain, and my guess it's more than vengeance and most likely rooted in money."

Avery blinked. "Right now I'm no help."

"Anyone come to mind?" Roden said.

"It's too horrible for me to say."

"Then I will for you. The investigation needs another interview with your parents. For your sake I hope they're innocent, but they have a lot to gain from the senator going to prison. I understand you're in line to inherit the ranch and the business. Who wins if you're out of the picture?"

"I imagine the estate would be tied up in court," she whispered. "No other surviving family members."

Roden's gaze softened. "Here's number four: When you're able, concentrate on Mr. Nike's traits—smells, sound of his voice, anything to help us locate him. Number five, we need a list of all the senator's enemies."

She huffed. "That would take a book. His critics are like fire ants."

"I understand. Senator Elliott has never requested protection, right?"

"Only when in office. I remember a few threats then. Can you pull those on your end?"

Roden typed. "Will do." He stared at her. "You're a brave woman to work through these questions. Tomorrow I'll make sure you have a hard copy of my notes in case something else comes to mind. One last thing, and I guess you can call it number six. I'd like the names of every person on the ranch, business, political, or church folk who just rub you the wrong way. My wife and daughters have this sixth sense about some people. I figure you have it too."

"I'll do my best."

Marc longed to get out of the hospital, off the meds, and working on the case. Too many flashes of what-ifs needed answers.

The curtain parted and Roden stepped aside for the doctor. "You're awake, Agent Wilkins."

The older doctor's church-picnic voice ground on Marc's nerves. "When the IV's finished, I'm ready to get out of here."

"I'm keeping you overnight to monitor your concussion."

"I hit my head, and now I'm good to go. I have work to do." Marc growled his words, but he had a point to make.

"That makes two of us. Then you understand why I can't let you leave."

"What time in the morning?"

"When I release you."

31

MARC NEEDED TO TALK TO RODEN without Avery in the room. She agreed to wait in the ER admission area until Roden drove her back to the hotel. The moment she disappeared, Marc posed the driving question. "What did you find out?"

"Pipe bomb. Scene was clean except for the bomb's debris. HPD is analyzing the pieces."

Marc held his breath as a shot of pain ripped across his head. "The police department works fast, so we'll see. Anyone come forward?"

"No. The security cam caught a man inserting something under the car, but he's a pro and hid his face from view. I'll look at the footage before I pick you up in the morning. Avery's scared and putting up a strong front, but she's in pain physically and emotionally. I arranged surveillance for her, Ms. Donita, and your sister."

"Good and thanks for taking charge. Appreciate you."

"You'd do the same for me and mine. The info is on your phone, but Liam Zachary has been cleared of any known criminal activity. Clean record for Leanne Archer and nothing new on Buddy and Saundra Elliott."

Marc closed his eyes. "Okay. A mistake is out there somewhere, waiting for us to find."

✯ ✯ ✯

Shortly after 2 a.m., Marc's cell phone rang with an unrecognizable number. He answered it before a nurse hushed him. "Marc Wilkins here."

"Agent Wilkins, this is Senator Elliott. I learned you and my granddaughter were injured in a car explosion tonight. Are you all right?"

"Yes, sir. Avery has a few stitches in her right arm and some bruising. But she's okay."

"Thank God. And you?"

"Stitches to my head, the hardest part of me." Marc fought to clear the fog in his brain.

"Sounds like something Abbott would say. My sympathy on his passing."

"Thank you." A part of Marc wanted to ask questions about his father, to get a grip on the real man. Maybe another time. "Why weren't you at the service?"

"A caller threatened to unload on the crowd if Liam and I showed up."

"Who?"

"If I had the answer to that, I wouldn't be in this predicament now."

"Senator, the longer you isolate yourself, the more you look guilty of murder."

"I haven't killed anyone, intentionally or accidentally. Neither do I have a suspect. Not yet, anyway."

"Then why withhold the truth from Avery and send her to me?"

"To protect her. To ensure she is safe from anyone trying to get to me. Someone shot Liam on my property, and your father's death wasn't a heart attack. Wish I had proof on that one. But until the killer is found, it's imperative Avery doesn't know who pulled the trigger."

"Didn't do much good tonight. Ready to turn yourself in? Treat your granddaughter like a mature woman?"

"You'd have a SWAT team all over me. My concern is her welfare and searching for those rear-deep in crimes."

"Looks to me like the actions of a selfish man." Marc forced back down the mix of pain and anger to continue the conversation professionally. "My apologies without due respect for your position. I understand how you care for Avery, but your methods haven't stopped whoever is responsible. Although you claim innocence of having killed Liam Zachary, and Avery believes in your innocence, you're hiding out. Did you have his body removed?"

"No. But I know who did."

"Which makes you and your accomplice guilty of unethical conduct regarding custody of a dead body and removing evidence in a murder."

"I'm well aware of the law." The senator punched every word. "And the penalty if I'm arrested and convicted."

"If? By your own admittance you assisted. Who helped you?"

"Not going there. I won't have their names tarnished for breaking the law."

"Who's on your short list for the killer?"

"You just asked me the same question. If I had a name, he'd be behind bars. Or dead."

"So why did you call?"

The senator sighed. "To check on Avery and you."

"I think you have another motive—like what did HPD or the FBI find at the crime scene."

"Marc, I need your help to find the truth. More importantly to keep Avery safe. She's in more danger than before. Can you place her in FBI protection?"

"I'm working on it, but at the moment she refuses to leave the hotel." A Plato quote marched across Marc's mind—*"We can easily forgive a child who is afraid of the dark; the real tragedy of life is when men are afraid of the light."*

"She needs to hear from me. What's her number?"

"Not going there without her permission, and I have no assurance you're Senator Elliott. Avery is one strong woman, and she's not a child you can shield from danger. She's confused and also opinionated to a fault. I wonder where she got that from," Marc said. "I'd like to help you, but I can't unless I know what initiated the murder on your property and those who are out to destroy you."

"Those in my circle are aware of your involvement—"

"Who's in the circle?"

"Friends I can trust. Good, solid people. If they agree, one of them will contact you. The crimes go back farther than Liam Zachary's death or your father's supposed heart attack—"

"Your people are also calling my father's death a murder?"

"It makes sense. I'm working my end to find the truth. I refuse to have my friends' deaths end up as notches on a killer's belt. There's been enough blackmail, extortion, and murder."

"Tell me about the extortion."

"Abbott, Liam, and I received threats about the Lago de Cobre Dam. The person wanted money, or he'd destroy the project. We didn't comply. Abbott and Liam were conducting their own investigation through the Army Corps. I imagine whatever they found got them killed."

Marc continued. "Blackmail?"

"When the extortion didn't work, threats came against us that he'd inform the corps and the public of faulty dam construction—with viable evidence if I didn't pay up. That was inconsequential to us. I had two inspection reports plus diver videos indicating no signs of stress."

"Where are those videos?"

"Locked up. Safe."

"Who's aware of those reports?"

"Liam, your father, and Craig. All sworn to secrecy."

"Why Craig?"

"Two reasons—I trust him, and he's my foreman."

"All right," Marc said. "What about those in your circle?"

"I trust them, and again, I'm not giving you names. Liam and Abbott decided the person was looking for a handout and chose to ignore him or her. The day before your dad passed, I received a call saying we'd run out of time."

"A man or a woman?"

"Distorted."

"Sir, you have enemies in your political, professional, and personal worlds. You have a list in mind. I need it for the investigation. In fact, I asked Avery to make one for us."

"I assume she agreed?"

"Of course. She'd make any sacrifice to keep you alive. What about the land acquisition to initially build the dam?"

"No problem there. The owner never complained about the eminent domain or the price."

"You and I could get a lot more done with a face-to-face. Where are you?"

"I'm in the best place I can be." The senator sighed.

"Cowards hide and put others in danger."

"Takes guts to call a man a coward."

"What would you call your actions? A wealthy, powerful man

stays in seclusion while his granddaughter and friends face multiple threats and death. Sounds like a selfish man and a coward."

"I'm protecting them!"

"Prove it. She's received at least two threats and was nearly killed in a car explosion."

"I sent her to you. Can't you rein in her stubborn streak? She seldom refuses anything I ask of her without a solid argument. But I see no logic in her holding out for a possible bullet."

"I'm not Superman, sir."

"Avery means more to me than anything in this world," he whispered, emotion evident in every word.

"Then cooperate with those who are working to end these crimes." Marc drew in a breath, sending agony throughout his body. "Who drives a blue Yamaha motorcycle?"

"No idea. I saw it from a distance when it left the cemetery. Nothing to identify the driver or bike."

"One of Avery's threats came from a rider matching the same color and model. I need someone from your circle to contact me ASAP. We're running out of time."

"I'll make known your request, but I can't guarantee a thing."

"Tell them the longer they wait, the greater the chance of another murder."

32

AVERY SANK DEEP INTO THE HOTEL BED with pain meds in her system and relief that Marc had survived the horrid blast. She'd fought filling the prescription because she didn't want to rely on meds unnecessarily, but her body constantly reminded her of hitting the pavement on her right side at the restaurant.

The uncertainty of the results of Marc's and Roden's probing the car explosion left her unsettled. Even worse, her bewildered and fearful mind failed to perform as she'd like. Her stomach churned but didn't revolt. Good. At least a minuscule of progress had occurred tonight.

Tomorrow she'd think about the reason for the bombing. To get back at Granddad, or did some jerk think she had incriminating information?

Tomorrow she'd focus on Mr. Nike's voice.

Tomorrow she'd try to remember more about the cyclist.

Tomorrow she'd check a few areas where Granddad might be hiding out.

Tomorrow she'd ask Roden about the restaurant's security cam footage.

Tomorrow she'd ask Marc how he'd handled his mother's and sister's safety.

Tomorrow she'd delve into the possibility of her parents being involved in the tragedies. They'd never resort to murder. Would they?

Tomorrow.

★ ★ ★

Avery woke on Monday to the sound of her phone ringing. Only two people had the number—Marc and the police officer. But she didn't recognize the digits. She debated answering but curiosity won.

"Avery, this is Roden. You sound groggy. Sorry to wake you."

Make it three people who had her number. "What time is it?"

"Eleven fifteen."

She blew out her exasperation. "I should have been up long before this." The meds had knocked her out cold.

"How do you feel?"

"I haven't moved." She turned to view the clock on the nightstand and moaned. "My body resembles the next day after training horses and finding myself kissing the dirt too many times."

"Or playing football with the neighborhood kids and getting my rear kicked."

She smiled and her face hurt.

"Reason number one for my call is we'd like you not to leave the hotel today."

"No problem there. Tomorrow may be a different story."

He chuckled. "I looked into the three people you mentioned who were arrested for threatening your grandfather. All came back clean."

"Thanks. That happened a few years ago. Is Marc okay?"

"The second reason for my call. Doctors kept him until ten this morning. I'm playing taxi and driving him to his mother's."

"He's with you?"

"Oh yeah, and he's crabbier than a football coach on a losing streak. I've put you on speaker. Maybe you can sweeten him up."

She closed her eyes, imagining he felt worse than she did. "Marc, take a pain pill. They work wonders for bad attitudes."

"I'm fine. Perfect. The problem is the company in the car."

"Granddad has a great saying about those who refuse to acknowledge their issues. 'If you can't find anything on your list of bad attitudes or problems, start with pride.'"

"She knows you," Roden said.

Regret wound through Avery. "Hey, I'm sorry. You saved my life, and I'm sure you have a monster of a headache."

"Plus I have to face my mother, who isn't aware of what happened. My sister's safety is a concern too. Although Roden arranged for Fort Worth PD to keep an eye on the house."

"Can't be too cautious when kids are involved," she said.

"Roden reminded me of the same thing."

"And your mother?"

"She lives in a gated community, and I could just be overreacting, but I won't ignore my gut. I need to take care of my own family."

"When you're better." She held back a stinging remark about taking care of himself.

"Something else occurred to me, and I wanted to run it by you. Your car might have a tracker."

She shivered. "How would I go about looking for it?"

"You're staying inside, remember?" Roden said. "I'll stop by later. Your car has been returned to the hotel parking lot. Stay put until I see you."

Avery's thoughts were twisting and turning like a maze.

"Avery?" Roden said. "Is there a problem?"

"I'm wondering who would be keeping tabs on me?"

"Doesn't matter. If there's a tracker, I'll find it."

"Hey," Marc said. "Your granddad called me last night."

She gasped, a sense of relief flooding her. "What did he say?"

"His biggest concern is you." Marc relayed the late-night conversation, and she hoped he hadn't purposely left anything out. "If the senator knows Roden and I are working with the corps, he has an insider helping him."

"I wish I could give you a name other than Lieutenant Shipley. Granddad says his shoes squeak, so I don't think he'd bend the law for anyone. Is he involved with your investigation?"

"He's aware of our concerns."

Marc, the vague FBI agent. "Okay. I have things to do on my end, all online or by phone. Roden, see you late afternoon. Marc, every hero has to rest."

After she hung up, Avery lay on her back and stared at the ceiling. Forcing herself to roll out of bed, she bit back the protest from every muscle and bone in her body. Poor Marc. Hard for anyone to maintain a good disposition when life tossed you into one mess after another.

After three ibuprofens, a hot shower, coffee, and much-needed prayer, she concentrated on her to-do list. Despite giving her word to Granddad not to contact anyone other than his lawyer and Marc, she made five calls to people and places where Granddad frequented. Nothing. But then she expected a negative response.

Avery longed to prove his innocence. But how? Always her thoughts swung back to the same question. Why hadn't Granddad denied the murder? Why hadn't she persisted when they first talked?

She paced the hotel room, ignoring her body's protests. *Think, Avery, what are you missing?* If she hadn't tried to surprise Granddad with lunch . . . But he could have told her not to join him. He hadn't rejected the idea but welcomed her. So the person who pulled the trigger had been the motorcycle driver? Had Liam surprised Granddad, got in the way of a bullet aimed at him?

Granddad had no reason to tell her every detail of his life. Neither did she expect it.

How sad her parents hit the top five suspects. They had so much to gain with her and Granddad out of the picture, and an unscrupulous attorney would figure out how to give them what they wanted. How awful to consider . . . yet true.

33

MARC'S MOTHER had the typical dramatic response to his accident. "You tripped on a broken piece of asphalt? An in-shape FBI agent? Maybe you should invest in a walker." She perched on the edge of a living room chair. "I could have driven to the hospital and sat with you."

"Not even necessary." He'd changed a few details. A lot of them. "I told you yesterday I'd check in with you, so I asked Roden to drive me." His inability to pass a polygraph crept into his thoughts. Roden hid Marc's stretch of the truth with a perfect poker face.

Her voice quivered. "Why look in on me when you have stitches?"

"My father and his friend's deaths have you upset. I'm being the good son." He leaned back on the sofa, willing his head to stop its incessant hammering.

Mom fumed, her typical she-was-so-mad-that-she-couldn't-talk mode. "The truth, please."

"How often have I lied to you?"

"Hard to say. It's probably a class you took at Quantico."

He grabbed a blue-and-green pillow and tucked it behind his back. The living room needed paint, the woodwork too. In fact, the entire three-bedroom ranch built in the nineties could use the touch of a paintbrush. Mom's standby pale-blue walls and green plaid sofa craved an update. She'd done well over the years. Her teaching career, purchasing a home, and paying off the mortgage were an accomplishment. With his father's inheritance, she could remodel or buy another home. Marc must be losing his mind thinking about paint and redecorating with a murder case on his hands. He blamed the meds.

Marc tried to refocus. The phone records for Avery, his father, Liam Zachary, and Senator Elliott had arrived en route here. Several calls between the men, and five calls from the same burner number hit the radar for all three men and one for Avery. Buddy and Saundra's phone records were free of any calls in question.

He needed to be at his office, where—

"Marc, have you looked in the mirror?" Mom crossed her arms over her chest. "I've been talking to you for the past three minutes, and you're out of it."

"I'm fine."

She glared at him. "You're a poor liar. Son, I will find out the truth."

Roden sipped on a tall glass of iced tea and lemonade. "He has a hard head, and the stitches improve his face."

"You are as bad as he is. I'm positive this wasn't an accident. Do you want to ask me why?"

"Sure," Roden said.

Marc gritted his teeth and waited for her to offer an explanation.

"I received a phone call from a woman looking for you."

"When?"

"About nine thirty this morning."

"What did she say?"

"She needed to talk to you about an important matter. I asked for her name and number, but she said you wouldn't recognize either. After she hung up, I had a few thoughts of my own."

"Such as?"

"Why call here instead of your cell or work phone?"

"Remember Tessa's grandmother is in hospice, and I gave the agency your number in the event she passed and couldn't reach me." The senator said someone from his circle might call, but he didn't have Mom's number. Or the need for it.

Mom eyed him suspiciously. "The woman wasn't Tessa or an older woman or a woman who represented hospice. Why wouldn't she give me a reason for wanting to talk to you?"

Marc couldn't think fast enough to answer. "Give me the number, and I'll call her back." When Mom gave it to him, he inwardly cringed. It was the same number used to contact the three men and Avery. Marc pressed in the digits to appease Mom, but the call went nowhere. He smiled at her. "I couldn't leave a message. Tells me she didn't really want to talk."

"Ms. Donita," Roden began, "hospice's guideline may not permit offering sensitive information to nonfamily members."

"Marc isn't Mrs. Litton's family."

"Hold on a minute. Let's get this figured out now." Marc phoned Tessa to see if anyone there had contacted his mother.

"Not me," Tessa said. "I'll talk to the nurse." She returned momentarily. "Nothing from hospice or their office."

Marc relayed the conversation. His mom crossed her arms again and demanded an update on his investigation.

Marc gave her the same "can't provide you with details" as he'd told Avery. "Did my father store any of his things here?"

"No. Why? Are you assuming we were keeping more than a relationship from you?"

"Not at all. I've been looking for something of his, and it wasn't in the boxes I picked up at his office."

"Marc, the Army made their statement public," Roden said. "You can tell her."

"What statement?" Mom moved deeper into stressed mode. The flush rose higher in her cheeks.

"The gun used to kill Liam Zachary . . ." He held up a palm. "Yes, the shooting happened after Father's heart attack. Apparently the gun was stolen but we don't know by whom."

"Stop dancing around the situation and tell me what's going on."

"I'm worried someone might think you have condemning information. Did you and my father have a conversation that puzzled you or meant nothing at the time?" Marc didn't want to build a wall between them about his father.

"I've shared it all with you." She closed her eyes. Her knee bounced. "If I have this straight, you're here because you're afraid I'm in danger, and the injuries from a so-called fall gave you an excuse?"

"Possibly."

"Ludicrous. I live in a gated community. There's more danger brewing at the fenced-in playground at the elementary school."

"There are always ways to gain access to people. Think about this. You were with him prior to his heart attack. If a man's ever honest, it's when he's facing death."

She shook her head. "He said he loved me, and he'd delayed calling you long enough about reconciliation. Nothing more."

She stood and walked to a window between her chair and the sofa to a full view of the street. The lines fanning from her eyes deepened, and her angst tugged at his heart. Staring out the window, she stretched her neck muscles. She'd experienced a lot of heartache, and he wanted to make it up to her.

"Mom."

She whipped her attention to him—

A whiz sounded.

A bullet grazed Mom's face.

Marc bolted from the sofa and shoved her away from the window. In his weakened condition, they toppled onto the chair. Blood trickled down her face. Not deep, but enough to alarm him. He rolled off her and tamped down a twist of fury.

"Are you all right?" He searched her face.

"Yes."

"Your cheek is scraped, but it doesn't look bad."

She touched the cut and stared in horror at the red coating her fingers. "What is going on? My worst fears about your father are true, and I've brought you into it."

"Mom, this comes with the job. Maybe Roden saw something." Marc turned to his partner. Blood gushed from his upper-left shoulder.

Mom screamed.

"Call 911." Marc grabbed a blanket and pressed hard on the wound to stop the blood flow. "Roden, stay with me."

He failed to utter a word.

34

IN THE SURGERY WAITING ROOM, Marc contacted the Dallas FBI office and requested continued surveillance for Tessa and her grandmother in Fort Worth. Once the arrangements were made, a bit of heaviness slipped from his shoulders.

Roden had been in surgery for over three hours to remove a bullet lodged in his upper-left shoulder, too close to his heart. He'd lost a lot of blood before the ambulance arrived at Mom's front door. Roden's wife, Victoria, and their four daughters huddled on a sofa in the room's cold temps. Frightened.

They all were.

Mom's face didn't require stitches . . . A relief. She held Victoria's hand.

Marc and God had this on-again, off-again relationship. God was always on, and Marc needed to get rid of the junk separating them. Right now, he needed God to put aside Marc's issues and save Roden's life.

God, I'm not always in good standing with You. But I know You're faithful when I'm not. I'm asking for Roden's healing and peace for Victoria and the girls.

His head throbbed like a sledgehammer, but his mental list demanded attention. He requested two agents from the local FBI office to pick up his truck from the restaurant and drive it to Marc's mother's, where they could get Roden's car. Within thirty minutes, an agent picked up both sets of keys and requested an update on Roden. Marc wished he had one.

His phone alerted him to a call, and Marc yanked it from his pant pocket and answered without glancing at the number.

"Agent Wilkins," a woman said. "Senator Elliott asked me to give you a few details about an investigation that he, your father, and Liam Zachary were working on."

"To whom am I speaking?"

"My name isn't important. My information, however, is critical."

A professional woman accustomed to power and control. "Is this being recorded?"

"What do you think?"

"Just confirming. I'm listening."

"Our purpose is to protect the senator from those who want him dead and to make sure justice is served."

"Who are you?"

"You already asked me, and I gave you our reasons for remaining behind the scenes. I represent the committee."

"I need names, or we're done."

"I'm authorized to give you specific facts and nothing more."

Senator Elliott had told Marc he'd receive a call from one of his friends from the circle, not the committee. And the woman had already lied about the stolen gun. "Why me out of all the federal agents and law enforcement in the state?"

"Your father recommended you."

"He's dead, and we hadn't spoken in years."

"Your stakes are higher than most people involved."

She was speaking in riddles, and he despised them. "List them. My patience is wearing thin."

"Your partner is in surgery because a shooter missed your mother."

Heat flamed Marc's face and temper. Who were these people? If they knew what had happened to Mom and Roden, then they monitored Tessa and Avery. "Is this a threat?"

"Think about it, Marc. You had no affection for your father, but a heart attack prior to Liam Zachary's murder? Are you stupid not to see a hit list? We doubt the sniper walked away from the shooting today with a satisfied grin. When will he try again? Whose name will be etched on the next bullet? Your mother's? Tessa's? Avery's? Your career isn't going anywhere with those deaths on your résumé."

"Are you resorting to blackmail?"

"We support Senator Elliott and whatever it takes to get the job done."

"Not surprised when you moved Zachary's body from the crime scene."

"We conduct our investigation according to our guidelines," she said.

"Right. If you are so plugged in to what's going on, why didn't you take the sniper out yourself? What exactly do you want from me?" Marc said.

"Buddy and Saundra Elliott stand to gain tremendous wealth if the senator is out of the picture. They believe Avery's weak, easily manipulated, and they won't have any problem gaining control of the Elliott wealth."

He'd play for a while. "Maybe they aren't guilty."

"Mia, the housekeeper, is another suspect."

"Motive?"

"She's worked for the senator over fourteen years, about the same time he took legal guardianship of Avery. Prior to her position, she supported the opposition. Politically."

He'd met Mia and her record squeaked clean. "Craig Holcombe? With the senator behind bars, he'd gain more control."

"So would Avery, and she isn't above suspicion."

"The senator named her?" Marc said.

"No. A committee member."

A huge stretch. Short of impossible. Later Marc would rethink the whole scenario. Right now, he'd maintain an unbiased facade.

Roden's doctor entered the room, his features unreadable, and approached Victoria.

"I need to go," Marc said. "How can I reach you?"

"We'll be in touch."

"I don't work with those who conceal evidence." Marc ended the call and hurried to the others surrounding the surgeon.

The tallest of Roden and Victoria's daughters wrapped her arm around her mother's shoulders. "Whatever the news, Mom, we're here for you." The other three young women cuddled in close.

Victoria bit into her lower lip and nodded. "I know." She lifted her head to the doctor. "Is my husband going to be all right?"

"Mrs. Roden, your husband is in recovery. We removed the bullet and stopped the bleeding. Once he wakens, you can see him for five minutes."

Victoria swiped at a tear on her bronzed cheek. "And the girls? They'd like to see their daddy."

"Not yet. He'll be in ICU for a while where we can carefully monitor his vitals. He needs lots of rest to heal. They will let you in for five minutes on the hour."

"Thank you. Our prayers are answered, and we are incredibly grateful."

Marc breathed his own prayer. He and Roden were closer than partners—family. Their strengths balanced each other. "Victoria," he whispered. The woman turned and fell into his arms. "I promise I'll find who is responsible for this."

"Uncle Marc, we don't want you hurt too," the youngest daughter said. "Please be careful."

Victoria briefly met with her husband, and Marc checked the number of the woman who'd called him with the phone records they'd captured.

Nothing. He needed answers.

How many people were involved with these crimes?

35

AVERY POURED A CUP OF COFFEE that was just like a political debate—hot enough to boil an egg and filled with artificial flavor. She glanced at the time: 4:30 p.m. Roden should have arrived by now, but his delay had given her time to make notes on the Lago de Cobre Dam project. The auditors were due to arrive tomorrow. She sent an email to Craig and requested he contact them to reschedule.

Slow down, Avery. One thing at a time.

Unless she successfully organized her thoughts, she'd accomplish little and make herself crazy with worry. Step by step.

Talking to Marc and Roden today about all she'd learned made a ton of sense. She'd tell them everything she knew, no matter how insignificant. That way, she'd be contributing to the conversation instead of the problem. Marc needed to rest with his concussion . . . But perhaps he'd feel like talking later on. She texted him.

Hope you're feeling better. Do you know when Roden might be here?

She checked email while she waited for Marc's response and clicked on one from Craig.

Avery,
　　Can I call you? I had to fire one of the ranch hands, and I want to tell you what happened. This week's direct deposit will be his last paycheck, and then you'll need to remove him from the system.
　　Again, where are you and where is the senator? Leanne stopped by yesterday and today. Please contact her. She's worried.
Craig

Craig,
　　Who did you fire and why? Tell Leanne I'll explain when we meet up. What else needs to be done that requires my assistance?
Avery

Avery,
　　I'm sorry I didn't mention the ranch hand's name. It's Jake Drendle, and he mistreated a horse. Warned him twice before. The phone's been ringing off the hook, and I sound like an idiot with my constant "I don't know how to contact the senator or his daughter" reply. People want to deal directly with one of you. I need you back here.
Craig

She chose not to respond. Craig's requests sounded like a leaky faucet. *Stop it.* He carried a huge burden. Taking out her frustrations on him wasn't fair.

As much as she loved Leanne, her friend would have to wait. The situation had hit code red, too dangerous to drag another person into the mess. Avery's thoughts turned to Jake Drendle, a nineteen-year-old who lived ten miles from the ranch. He wanted a full-time job for the summer and part-time when he started at the local junior college in the fall. Odd that he'd mistreat horses when he'd grown up with them. He had a quirky personality and kept to himself. She'd mention Jake to Marc just in case. What was wrong with her for suspecting a kid?

Her phone pinged with a text from Marc.

I've put off contacting you. Roden was shot at my mother's house—a shooter aimed at her. Shooter unknown. I'm with Roden's wife and daughters at the hospital. He's in recovery after a surgeon removed a bullet. Prognosis is good. Under no circumstances drive your car. I'll send an agent to check for a tracking device.

I'm so sorry. What hospital? I'll take a taxi.

Stay in your room. Don't leave the hotel.

Your mother's okay?

She'll be fine. No stitches.

I'm sorry to drag you into this, placing you, your mother, and Roden in danger.

This is my job—not yours.

Who had them all under a microscope?

36

FROM AVERY'S THIRD-FLOOR HOTEL ROOM, she watched a man inspect her battered car. He lay on his back and felt under the vehicle, then every inch of the exterior. She snapped a few pics in case he wasn't FBI. About twenty minutes later, he walked across the parking lot, but she didn't see if he carried anything or what he drove.

Marc texted that he was on his way to the hotel to see her.

Shouldn't you be resting?

I'm good. My mother is with me. Hope that's okay. We have only one vehicle here.

She's driving?

No.

Of the three injured people, Marc must have been the only one remotely able to follow the ambulance with Roden to the hospital, and he had no business being behind the wheel either time.

In the hotel lobby, Avery met Marc and an olive-skinned,

dark-haired woman who must be Mrs. Wilkins. She had the same high cheekbones and hair color as Marc. A bandage covered a good portion of her right cheek. She and Marc were quite a pair with their bandages protecting injuries. For that matter, the three of them were a wounded trio.

Marc greeted Avery. "I can't believe I brought my mother to an FBI meeting."

The woman immediately stuck out her hand to Avery. "I'm Donita Wilkins, and I won't tell anyone I was here if you don't."

"Deal." Avery grasped her hand firmly. She immediately liked the woman. "Avery Elliott. I'm so sorry for what happened to you and Agent Clement."

"Thank you." She gave a timid smile. "I've heard good things about you. You and my son need to talk, and I thought I'd have a sandwich privately."

Avery checked the dining area and announced the room had privacy. Once seated, Mrs. Wilkins in a corner booth and Avery and Marc on the opposite side of the room, she studied his battle-worn face.

"I know why you look horrible, but what about your mother? Then I want to hear about Roden."

Marc shared with her about the shooting, obviously the basics from the way he sped over it. "I followed the ambulance to the hospital and waited with Mom and Roden's family until the doctor came out of surgery."

"Praise God."

"Really? Roden nearly bled out." Marc sighed. "But he is alive."

"And he'll recover, unless you lied to me."

"I told you the truth."

She rubbed the chill on her arms, and it had nothing to do with the air-conditioning in the dining room. The reality that Roden and

Mrs. Wilkins had been targeted by a shooter alarmed and angered her. "I despise what is happening."

Marc glanced across the room to where his mother ate dinner alone. Sadness filled his gaze. "She swears my father didn't tell her a thing about what he and Liam were investigating, except they could be in danger. But her claim doesn't keep her safe. I'll arrange for tighter security, possibly a safe house."

"Your sister too. I'm sure the grandmother will agree."

He rubbed his jaw. "Been worried sick about Tessa. You should join them."

"Not until I'm convinced Granddad is okay. I'm beginning to think—" She lifted her chin.

"What?"

"I want to return to the ranch. There I can help Craig and be of some value instead of hiding in a hotel room. Staying here isn't keeping me safe or anyone I talk to."

"No way. Are you hungry?"

"Marc, changing the subject won't change my mind."

"My stomach's growling."

She shrugged. "Okay, we eat. Afterward you can digest my words."

"Won't alter what's best for you. I like the idea of all three of the females in my life safe in the same place."

A stew of annoyance simmered. "Is that who we are? Helpless females?"

"Far from it."

He secured the server's attention, and they ordered sandwiches and salads.

The more Avery pondered the idea of going home, the better she felt. Answers would be found in the familiar. "Here's a picture of a guy checking out my car. I assume he's legit. Does my car have a tracker?"

"Not any longer. The FBI will see about tracing it through the manufacturer. Will take a while. The tracker might have led someone to follow you to the FBI office, but it doesn't answer how the wrong people knew you talked to me. You were also tailed to the restaurant. I assume the person or persons already had surveillance on my mother."

"Who? Why?" She shook her head. "Sorry. What can you tell me? Doesn't take much to see your father, Liam, and Granddad are in the same pasture."

"And you, my mother, and sister are in danger by association."

Granddad had wanted her out of harm's way, but her precautions attracted evil. "I have my weapon."

"A Sig registered to you. My guess is the sniper already knows you have it. By the way, the same burner number is recorded on phone records linked to you, the senator, Liam, and my father's phones. Another reason I want you in a safe house until this is resolved. Not the Brazos River Ranch."

"Cowards run."

"Sometimes it takes more courage to run than fight a losing battle."

Definitely felt like she'd taken a loser's stand. "Here's a thought. If our sniper has my information, then why did he blow up the car beside me instead of mine?"

"Good question, and I don't have an answer—yet."

"If we had an idea of who held the winning hand, they could be stopped," she said. "I learned more about the accounting discrepancy. I'd been thinking about it since we talked earlier."

"Other than confirmation the materials for the dam had been in the warehouse and checked out?"

"Right." Avery nodded. "During the pouring of the foundation, Granddad and Liam were in Canada hunting, and Leanne and I were in Orlando. Every time our crew had scheduled to pour it, the weather didn't cooperate. Our trips had been on the calendar for months, so Craig told us to go ahead. If the weather broke, he'd oversee the project. When I returned, the work had been completed by another crew. Craig said the opportunity to get the job done opened up on a weekend, and our crew doesn't work on Sunday. I paid the invoice and thought nothing else about it, especially with the workload piled on my desk. But since all of the tragedies, my mind sped back and camped there. Seemed odd for my hands-on granddad to let Craig handle the changes. In short, I contacted the hunting lodge and learned when Granddad supposedly sent the material supplier an email letting them know we had supplies in the warehouse, he was out in the wilds with no Internet connectivity." She sighed. "Marc, it could mean Granddad gave Craig permission to use his email account. Or something else."

He leaned back. "Interesting. I'd—" The server delivered their food, and Marc waited until the woman disappeared. "It looks suspicious. Why wouldn't Craig have contacted you?"

"I don't know. Either Granddad or I take care of critical matters. Our names are on all the documentation, and we're legally responsible."

"What about your father?"

"He's done a few low things. But he'd have to change the structural designs in a convincing manner that didn't trigger an alarm for Craig. How would my dad gain access to the office? He'd need someone to help him get onto the property. The hands and the person monitoring the security cameras have been instructed not to permit my parents on-site."

"Nothing's impossible when driven by strong motive." Marc added pepper to his salad. "Money is a huge factor for most crimes."

"I assume you ran a background on my parents."

"Yes." He pointed to her food. "Eat, Avery. We're brainstorming the what-ifs whether true or not."

She stabbed a tomato with more vengeance than she intended. "Dad's like the Prodigal Son but without regrets or remorse for his actions. Mom enjoys the good life."

"His home-building company does well. A balance of pleased customers and complaints."

"I'm sure my parents gave you an earful about Granddad." She drew in a ragged breath. "I want to know what was said."

"Your dad claimed the senator did shoddy work, and he expressed a concern for other completed bridges and dams."

"He'd be cheering Granddad on if money had been deposited into his account. I don't need to get started on my parents."

"Has the senator handled any of your dad's misguided dealings?"

She set her fork on her salad plate. "You mean stupid and sometimes-illegal decisions? Granddad did bail him out of trouble until five years ago. Prior to then, he paid Mom and Dad's debts and gave them an allowance."

"What happened to stop the money flow?"

"A gambling problem."

Marc's silence told her he weighed the situation in the Elliott family. She longed to read his thoughts.

"I'm giving you a huge what-if scenario," she said. "And I imagine it's what you're thinking. My dad forged Granddad's name once to obtain money. If he managed to change the dam's specs and alter the ordered materials, he could destroy Granddad's reputation. Dad could step in, claim ignorance and apologize for Granddad's actions, and make a public announcement about starting his own construction business with integrity. Except I'm in line for the entire inheritance, unless my parents have plans to blame me."

He seemed to search her face for what? Deception?

"In my opinion, your parents wouldn't be successful. You walk a tightrope of honesty and truth. The other factor to consider is the threat against you. Buddy and Saundra might push the senator off a cliff, but their own daughter?"

"One more reason I need to be home. What if I talked to them? If they were hostile toward Granddad, I could play into their game."

"Wrong. Don't even go there. Meeting with your parents sounds dangerous. Stranger crimes have surfaced among families and friends, and Craig Holcombe already suspects them," Marc said.

"Craig is loyal and wants to honor Granddad for all he's done for him. He's not carrying any banners for my parents. My dad tried to discredit Craig during the gambling fiasco by stating Craig encouraged him."

Marc's phone alerted him to a notification, and he read it. Not a muscle moved on his face.

"Roden okay?"

He nodded. "The day Roden and I drove to the corps office, we learned my father had requested another inspection of the Lago de Cobre Dam without an explanation. Lieutenant Shipley has scheduled it for Wednesday morning." He stared into her eyes as though calculating her response.

"The reservoir filled properly, and the state inspector approved it. There's already been two inspections. Why a third?"

"They received an anonymous tip from a man who worked the project. He said the foundation hadn't been constructed according to design. Do you recall an unhappy employee or reason to contact the corps?"

"No one."

"Think about it. The inspection eliminates the accusations against the senator."

Her mind entered the analyzing zone. "You're right. Confirmation of a secure dam would add a level of peace to all our lives. There's no way the dam wouldn't meet specifications. I hate this nightmare. The idea of a family member or a friend setting up my grandfather to face murder charges and a lawsuit for not following his own specs . . . Was a crack specifically mentioned?"

"No. What causes a crack in a new construction?"

She swallowed hard to stop the anger burning her throat. "Most are simply to be monitored. They are a cause and an effect of concrete deterioration, and those have their roots in weather, seepage, chemicals, and even faulty concrete mixes. Some cracks are intentional for varying reasons. Others are indications of structural damage."

"Caused by?" Marc said.

"Structural damage cracks develop when areas of a dam are overstressed as a result of poor design, construction, incorrect foundation, or faulty materials."

"How long will the dive team take to assess the structural integrity of the dam and make a determination?"

"Hard to say. They know what to look for, but the work might take several hours. Marc, I need to be there when this happens. My name's on all the papers. Don't you see? If the dam's not up to code and Granddad's still missing, I'm responsible."

Lines deepened across Marc's forehead.

"You know it's true. I'm the fall guy just like Granddad."

"If you're permitted to be present during the inspection, I'm going with you."

She stiffened. He'd get in the way, ask too many questions. "The situation is worsening for those living in the area. Have you seen the weather report?"

"Yes, a hurricane is brewing in the Gulf and moving fast toward Galveston. Landfall could be reached as early as two days."

Vocalizing the reality of possible devastation soured her stomach. "We've had a wet spring and summer, well above the average rainfall. At this point, the Lago de Cobre Dam is on the dirty side, which means the hurricane could send torrential rains and swirling winds, and tornadoes could form. And if the dam failed, the reservoir would overflow and flood the entire community below, destroying people and property. There's more to this scenario. Should one dam fail along the Brazos, it could result in a domino effect for the others. Tell me, if that happened, how could I live with myself?"

37

MARC VACILLATED BETWEEN VARIOUS WAYS to approach his stubborn mother. He studied her across the restaurant while she scrolled through her phone and occasionally took a bite of sandwich. Convincing her to pursue safety should be easy, since she witnessed the horror of the shooter targeting her and seriously wounding Roden. Afterward Marc would tackle Tessa and finally Avery.

He compartmentalized information, a trait he needed to work violent crimes. Unfortunately, he hadn't been successful in trying to figure out where to place the women under his protection. A vacation to the Bahamas seemed the perfect solution to keep them out of danger. Of course, once they were released, they'd draw straws to see who threw the first punch.

Avery laid her knife and fork on the edge of her plate and scooted it aside. "I don't mean to sound insensitive about today. But did you or Roden have an opportunity to check the restaurant's security cameras?"

"Roden viewed the footage before he picked me up from the hospital. It showed a man inserting what's been determined as a pipe bomb on the undercarriage of the car. He wore sunglasses, a ball cap, and kept his back to the camera. Couldn't identify the shoes."

"I'd hoped for a lead." She thanked the young man who removed her plate.

"No motorcycles in sight or an accomplice. All we have is the man's approximate height and build."

"Which was?"

"Trim, narrow shoulders."

"Could be the same man," she said. "Did the camera capture the man who helped me and wore Nikes?"

"Unable to make out his features. Has to be verified. Once I hear from HPD, I'll give you more info. Have any other details come to mind?"

"The cyclist didn't have the same voice as Mr. Nike."

Two men and a woman involved in the crimes. Marc laid his napkin on the table. "Excuse me, I need to talk to Mom about taking a vacation or moving temporarily to a safe house."

"Need reinforcements?" Avery said.

Her face showed no signs of humor, just warmth from those crystal-blue eyes. Her long light-brown hair and dimples were a dangerous combination. "Not at all. She was shaken up today."

Avery scooted from the booth. "I've been threatened and nearly blown to pieces. I'm not ready for FBI protection, yet I see the value for your mother after today's rough ride."

She had no idea how persuasive he could be—or tried to be. "Suit yourself, but I don't foresee a problem with my mother agreeing to protection. Maybe she'll persuade you."

Marc and Avery walked across the room and slid into the opposite side of Mom's booth. The waitstaff had cleared the table, leaving her a glass of water with a slice of lime. In the dining room's shadows,

Mom's face darkened around the bandage on her cheek, and lines etched into the outer corners of her eyes.

"Finished?" She smiled, but the look lacked enthusiasm.

"We are," he said. "You're exhausted, and I need to get you home, but first I have a request from your favorite son."

"When you preface any conversation with 'your favorite son,' I'm in trouble. But tonight I'm too tired to do anything but agree." She reached across the table and grasped his hand. "I never fully understood how dangerous your job is until today. I'm ready for you to change careers, like a librarian or an accountant. I'm so sorry I pressured you to look into Abbott's death."

He placed his other hand over top hers. "Mom, I'm trained in defending those who are victimized and stopping bad guys."

"The danger got really personal today."

"No need to worry, Mom. This is a part of my life."

"It doesn't have to be. Tell me about the stitches in your head and Avery's arm."

"I already did. Avery fell at the ranch. First thing in the morning, I want to arrange either a vacation for you, in which I'll foot the bill, or a safe house. I'd like to include Tessa. It's difficult for me to work the case—"

"And I'm in the way like your sister?" Mom said.

Marc sighed. "I need to be assured you two have armed bodyguards 24-7."

Mom massaged the back of her neck. "I'm not going to be a tax burden."

"Would you rather be fitted for a casket?"

She startled. "That's no way to speak to your mother."

"I'm sorry, and you're right. But as you've experienced today, these people are serious."

She lowered her hand. "I'd rather you take off more time and work from my home."

"Impossible. I have people to see and situations where you wouldn't be permitted."

She shrugged. "I'll deal with what happens. If the good Lord says it's my time, no armed guards will stop it."

"Mrs. Wilkins," Avery said, her voice gentle. "I'm driving home tomorrow to the Brazos River Ranch. Why don't you join me? We could drive to Fort Worth and pick up Tessa, then backtrack to the ranch."

"Absolutely not!" Marc stood.

"Sit down, Son." Mom pointed as though he were five. "Senator Elliott's property?"

"Yes, ma'am. There's plenty of room. The ranch hands know how to use firearms and are capable of keeping us safe. And I'm a good shot. The other perk is the area is gorgeous and peaceful, a vacation for you and Tessa."

"Out of the question," Marc said. "You make the ranch sound like a resort, and a man was killed there."

Mom's eyes widened.

Avery leaned toward Marc. "That's no different than what Mrs. Wilkins and I have witnessed."

"Right," Mom said. "It would be a wonderful opportunity to spend time with Tessa and Avery. Can't you join us and work from there?"

Marc had opened the door to the Alamo—a disaster in the making.

"Great idea," Avery said. "Besides, the Lago de Cobre Dam is much closer to the ranch than here. Plus you mentioned following up on interviews there. In actuality, you'd be our bodyguard."

He didn't feel good about the three camping out at the ranch. Not at all. But enlisting the help of the local sheriff's department would increase security. Mom would want her time with him. He and Tessa needed to house shop. And Avery . . . the attraction grew deeper. He'd be an emotional mess, but at least he'd know the three were okay. When this was over, he'd be ready for the psych ward.

"I think the time together would be fun," Mom said.

"We'll make sure it is—all that and more."

Mom nodded at Avery. "You didn't fall at the ranch any more than Marc tripped, right?"

Avery's glance darted to Marc and back to Mom. "No, ma'am."

"Thank you for the honesty, and I appreciate your generous invitation."

Marc humphed. "Sounds more like a nightmare." He needed to say a few things before the two conspirators ganged up on him again. "I'll confirm someone will keep an eye on you when I'm not at the ranch." He glanced at his watch. "In the morning I'll contact Tessa's grandmother. I imagine she'll be fine with the little vacation."

"One more thing," Mom said. "What is the status of exhuming Abbott's body and performing an autopsy?"

"Earlier today I checked in since more than one person has questioned my father's death. The procedure takes two to four hours, and it's scheduled for Wednesday." He didn't want to think about a lengthy toxicology report requiring weeks for the results. Great, the dam inspection and the exhumation were occurring on the same day. The lingering threat of bad weather on the horizon and forcing the Army Corps to postpone the inspection picked at him.

Mom narrowed her gaze to study him. "If Abbott was killed, Liam's death, your and Avery's wounds, and today's shooting are all connected."

"As we spoke on the way to the hospital, someone is serious about eliminating those who might have vital information. The problem is, we're piecing it together without all the facts. Like who's responsible and why." A motive had started to percolate with the announcement of the dam's inspection. For now, he'd keep his thoughts to himself.

Buddy, Saundra, and Craig all had strong motives, and he'd thought so before the unidentified woman's call earlier.

"Son, you're the perfect agent to keep us company. You have multiple reasons to end the scare. Yes, I'm afraid for you, and I'll be on my knees until arrests are made. But you are . . . What are the words? Locked and loaded?"

Any other time, he'd have laughed.

Marc drove his sleepy mother to her home. He hoped no one attempted to break into her house tonight because staying awake hit the impossible zone. He'd asked her repeatedly to install an alarm system, especially when she rarely locked the door. She claimed her gated community negated a need for an alarm.

"Tomorrow, before we leave for the ranch, I'm arranging a police-monitored alarm system."

"What good will that do when the shot came through a window?"

Yeah, he needed sleep to get his mojo back. One day soon, the interlocking pieces would slide into place. Until then, he'd chase down every clue, even the ones from a female caller who had lied.

38

AFTER A RESTLESS NIGHT, Marc formed the right words to convince Tessa's grandmother to allow Tessa to stay a few days at the Brazos River Ranch to form a strong bond with his sister. The request should have been face-to-face, yet time played a critical role.

"Maybe you can get the fool thought out of her head about her father not dying of a heart attack," Mrs. Litton said. "It sinks her deeper into depression, and my condition doesn't help either. She's afraid of being alone. I appreciate that she no longer has to worry about a foster home when she has you. I admit I was leery of you in the beginning, but you're a good man. Just like your father."

Her final statements cut to his heart, a glimpse of the man who'd fathered him. Something he'd never experienced. What would it have been like to have a father-son relationship? "Mrs. Litton, I'll do my best for Tessa."

"What she needs is your love, and lots of it."

"She has it. My mother will be at the ranch too."

"I'm pleased. She needs a motherly influence. I don't want Tessa to see me breathe my last. I'd rather her memories be happy ones. In fact, keep her with you until I pass. Has she been told about the trip?"

"Not yet. I wanted your permission first."

"I'll tell her. She'll object if you ask. Let me know when you'll be here, and I'll make sure she's packed and ready. Have you considered school beginning in two weeks?"

"Yes, ma'am. I'm researching Christian schools. If necessary, she can begin online."

"You're blessing me before I see heaven." Her last words trickled out in a hush. Marc hadn't thought about Mrs. Litton preferring Tessa not to witness her death.

"I'll call when I'm close to Fort Worth."

He laid the phone on the kitchen counter and rubbed the area of his head around the stitches. A funeral might tempt the killer with his targets caught off guard.

"Does your head hurt?" Mom entered the room as though she wore moccasins.

"A little." He relayed Mrs. Litton's agreement for Tessa to visit the ranch.

"I've finished packing." She glanced around her. "My indoor plants will die without water." She stiffened. "My neighbor next door has a key. I'll ask her to check on them. I'm sorry. You're doing your best."

He wished he could believe her. "Mom, you can't tell your neighbor why you're leaving."

"I understand. The problem is, how long will we be away?"

"I suggest taking enough for a week and remember you can always wash clothes there."

"True. At least you have a few things already here," Mom said.

What to wear hadn't hit the radar of importance. "I'd like to leave before lunch. We have miles to go today."

"How can you drive with your head stitched and hurting? The doctor told you not to get behind the wheel."

"And you're in better shape than I am?"

"I think Avery should pick us up."

He shook his head. The next few days with the women in his life called for all the patience he could muster. "I've got this. You're about to see an agent in action. It's called autopilot."

Mom failed to find humor in his response.

★ ★ ★

Tessa had the fifteen-year-old attitude going. No hugs when Marc picked her up and plenty of tears when she told her grandmother good-bye. Yet compassion spilled over him when he viewed Tessa's reluctance to release her grandmother's paper-thin, heavily veined hand.

Outside the front door, he took her suitcase and set it on the sidewalk.

"What happened to your head?" she said.

"Stitches. I got too close to an explosion. Look, Tessa, I'm not the enemy."

Her lips quivered. "I'm afraid something will happen to her while I'm gone."

"She's stronger than you give her credit for." Marc hoped he wasn't filling her with unreasonable explanations.

"Was the trip to the senator's ranch her idea?"

He refused to lie, although the idea tempted him. "No. It originated with the senator's granddaughter, Avery. And Mrs. Litton agreed."

She slipped her hair behind one ear. No ponytail today. "She doesn't want me with her when she dies."

Again he wanted to spare her the truth. "My mother will be with you too, and I'll be at the ranch a good bit of the time. When I'm gone, an off-duty deputy will take my place."

Tessa's gaze flew to the truck. With the tinted windows, Mom wasn't visible. "Is she with you now?"

"Yes."

She bit hard into her lower lip. "Dad said she's a saint."

"She is an amazing woman."

Tessa turned back to him. "Tell me what's going on."

The truth. "A shooter tried to hurt my mother. She moved and the bullet hit my partner. He'll be okay. Obviously a bad guy believes my mother is aware of privileged information from our father. That potentially puts you directly into the line of fire."

"Marc, it sounds like a bad movie."

"I wish it were. But you need to be aware of the danger until this is over."

"Will you always tell me the truth when I ask questions?"

He stared into the face of innocence, his little sister who'd seen too much of the harsh realities of life. "As long as it's not confidential information. But I need you to trust me."

39

AVERY DROVE THE WINDING ROAD leading along her beloved rolling acres to home. She swiped a wandering tear. Leaving had been a mistake. Like a child, she'd run instead of facing the challenges.

Marc planned to arrive with Mrs. Wilkins and Tessa close to dinnertime. Avery had called Mia earlier and explained the arriving guests. The older woman laughed, her excitement spilling into her voice. "Barbecue. We will have a fantastic dinner. Will the senator be with you?"

"Not this time, but soon."

A sense of normalcy from the phone conversation offered peace surely to come.

What had happened to her resolve to face life with determination? Shaking off the fears, she gripped the steering wheel as though the padded metal could offer courage.

She stopped at the security gate and pressed in her private code.

It opened wide to welcome her. With the house, stables, and office up ahead, Avery reached deep for the faith and wisdom Granddad had instilled in her.

Heat rose from her feet to her legs, chest, arms, hands, and up her neck and face. Fear and a strange awareness of something supernatural enveloped her. She tingled while a soothing peace filled her. God walked with Granddad and her through this storm. They weren't alone.

The tragedy separating her from Granddad had an explanation. He'd face a firing squad before he put her and innocent people in danger, and he'd sacrifice himself first. That's how men of integrity lived.

And that's how women of integrity lived.

Pulling off on the shoulder, she exited her car and inhaled the comfort of home. The air smelled of freshly mowed grass, sweet, but gray clouds moved in fast.

She walked to the white fence and grasped it for strength. In the distance, Granddad's prized beef cattle and longhorns grazed with the finest horses in the state. When he and Grandma set up housekeeping, they'd bought a hundred acres with borrowed money to add to what he'd inherited from his father. They worked night and day to build the stock and nurture the land. Granddad purchased more acreage and started the commercial construction business, then developed an interest in politics. Many had tried to discredit his name, but none succeeded. *Justice and Jesus* mixed with courage to face his opposition.

Avery pushed back from the fence and glanced up at the sun behind the storm clouds. She'd step back into her role at the ranch until Granddad returned.

And he would. She'd fight for him, and he'd fight for her.

At the ranch office, Avery parked in her spot. She longed to see Granddad's massive pickup. Oh, to fling open the office door and rush into his arms. The memory of his deep voice embraced her heart's void.

Craig must have seen her approach because he came running to her car. She couldn't release the seat belt fast enough. She hurried into his arms.

"Are those tears?" Craig said. "Avery Quinn Elliott never cries."

"Unless I'm a reservoir of emotion."

He pulled a clean handkerchief from his pocket and dabbed at her eyes. "Are you home for good?"

She nodded. "You and I can handle all of this until Granddad returns."

He stepped back and frowned. "What happened to you and your car?"

"I had it parked too close to an explosion." She shrugged. "I fell getting out of the way."

"I think you're skipping over the facts."

"Later. I'm okay."

A familiar voice called her name. Leanne!

Her dear friend pulled Avery from Craig's arms. Her waist-length auburn hair swept over Avery's arms. "You and the senator had us scared to death. I'm so very glad to see you."

Avery hugged her and stepped back to take in Leanne. Craig wrapped his arm around her waist, and she snuggled against him.

That's when Avery saw a special light in their eyes not evident in the past.

"Oh, my goodness. Are you two . . . together?" Avery's gaze darted from one to the other.

Craig kissed the tip of Leanne's nose. "The most beautiful gal inside and out was right here in front of me, and I didn't have the sense to see her."

Leanne blushed. "I'd wanted him to notice me for years. It finally happened."

"You never said a word," Avery said.

Leanne grinned, her eyes glistening with tears. "I thought Craig wouldn't give me a second look when he's—"

"Say it. I'm an old man, eight years older."

"Not true."

"For sure when you bounced around here at sixteen, and I was twenty-four."

Avery crossed her arms and shook her head at them. "My two favorite people have found a real gift. I'm incredibly happy for you both."

"Yep." Craig nodded. "We've been blessed despite the tragedies going on around here."

"We are survivors," Avery said.

40

DURING DINNER AT THE RANCH, Marc directed the flow of conversation to those seated around a table on a massive stone patio. He studied an outdoor kitchen that rivaled a decorator's magazine and inhaled the tantalizing smells of barbecue and the trimmings. Senator Elliott's Olympic-size pool complete with a small waterfall caught his eye. Lots of white stone and exquisite landscaping, a luxurious lifestyle Avery had grown accustomed to. Made him question if his crazy attraction to her headed toward disaster. He could never provide for her in the way she'd grown up.

Marc shifted his thoughts to the safety precautions for his mother, Tessa, and Avery. "It's critical to keep me informed of unusual happenings or conversations. Craig, Leanne, and Mia need to heed all I'm requesting."

"How would Tessa and I recognize anything unusual?" Mom said.

He noted the telltale pain lines of a headache creasing her

forehead. "I see you're not doing well, Mom. Have you taken your prescription?"

She gave him a timid smile. "After we've eaten so as not to upset my stomach."

Back to business. Marc trusted Craig as a man who valued responsibility and cared about those on the ranch. He received the truth in private before dinner, and Marc hoped he'd made a good decision.

"We need to discuss protective measures," Marc said. "Later on tonight, I'll share with the ranch hands what's necessary. The sheriff's department has deputies stationed at the main gate to keep anyone from entering."

"But the gate's locked and monitored by a security system," Mia said.

"Right, but that doesn't stop anyone from climbing over or hacking into it. We have no idea who could be part of the threats, and there's the extreme likelihood of a mole among the ranch hands. All of you must be the eyes and ears to keep danger from marching through the front gate."

"You're our bodyguard, right?" Tessa removed her earbuds and tucked them into her jeans pocket.

"Yes, while I'm here. In the meantime, I need everyone's cooperation." He captured the gaze of each person there. "Mom, Avery, and Tessa, none of you leave the ranch without me or another agent. Mia is included, and I'll share this with her. Neither do you roam the ranch without an escort. Solo exploration is limited to no farther than the gazebo."

"Why am I included?" Avery said. "My Sig is with me all the time. I'll be back and forth to the office, and I don't want to be a burden. It's less than twelve hundred and fifty feet from the house."

"An escort is for your own good." Craig leaned in closer to her. "We don't know who is threatening you."

Avery glanced at the pool, but Marc doubted she concentrated on the still blue water. "You've both made your point. This is an inconvenience, but at least I'm home. Mrs. Wilkins, Tessa, I apologize for sounding selfish."

"It's okay," the other two said as if choreographed, and the tension eased.

Marc gave Craig his attention. "Let me know when you plan to run errands away from the ranch. Make sure someone goes with you, either me or a deputy."

"Got it," Craig said. "The deputies won't let anyone through without proper ID verification, but that doesn't stop someone on foot or driving in on the back road near the family cemetery."

Marc pulled his phone from his shirt pocket and typed in his thoughts. He missed Roden, who kept him grounded. "I'll order a security cam on the road and request a deputy park a squad car there. If the sheriff's department is limited on manpower, we'll acquire law enforcement from another area." He analyzed what a few men could accomplish on foot. "We might need to hire a few law enforcement types to ride the fence line. Not ranch hands. We don't want anyone hurt or overreacting." He swung his attention to Avery and Craig, who agreed.

"I have a registered handgun," Craig said. "When possible, I can escort the women. If I need to be sworn in as a volunteer deputy, bring it on."

"I appreciate the offer, but I've already told Avery she needs to stay put. If anything changes, I'll be knocking on your door. A few other instructions here. I've picked up burner phones for all of you, which means I want your cell phones. It's too easy to trace any of you. Avery is already using one." He held out his hand, and the three handed him their phones—with frowns.

"What about business?" Craig said. "Can't work without communication."

"I'll be in the office checking those calls on the landline," Avery said. "We'll make it work."

Marc continued. "Do not give the burner numbers to anyone. I don't care how much the person begs. If you need to make an important call, use mine or the office landline.

"I want to reinforce what I said earlier. Be aware of what is going on around you at all times. If someone seems suspicious, get help. Don't answer the door. Sleep with your bedroom doors locked." Marc slid a sideways glance at Avery. "Don't investigate anything—you or Craig. These people play for keeps. You and Tessa jog, and it's a great way to manage the stress. But don't go alone."

"How long will we be in FBI jail?"

Marc took his sister's hand. She had legitimate fears about her grandmother and leaving her friends behind in Fort Worth. "For as long as it takes."

"What about school?"

"My mom's a teacher and there are online options." He despised frightening her. "Note you are the only one of the three musketeers who hasn't been wounded. I intend for that situation to stay intact."

Tessa paled. "I wonder where this all would have led if I hadn't told you I thought Dad had been killed."

"I told him the same thing, and I doubt our situation would be any different," Mom said.

Tessa touched her lips. "Someone wants all three of us dead? I mean, I heard you, but it didn't hit me until now."

Marc thought Tessa understood the risk. He'd not done a good job of explaining to her the real danger. "We think so. Our father and Liam Zachary might have stumbled onto a crime. If so, the guilty person is out to eliminate anyone who has potential information."

"Is that why Senator Elliott is missing?"

"He's keeping a low profile until this is sorted out." Marc weighed how much he could tell her. "My partner and I are working with the Army Corps of Engineers in an informal investigation about the two deaths."

"Is your partner coming to the ranch, the one who was shot?"

"He's still in the hospital."

Her young eyes widened. "What a nightmare."

"Yes, Tessa. Your grandmother wanted you protected at all costs."

Tears filled her eyes. "What else haven't you told me?"

Marc had said far too much for a kid to comprehend. "I'm here to keep you from danger."

"I don't know anything," she whispered, as though the wrong person listened. "Why do those close to me get hurt or killed? Is it my fault?"

Avery left her chair and bent to Tessa's level. "Bad people pick on the innocent. None of us here have any intention of cowering to a criminal, but we have to be smart. Do exactly as Marc says. Nothing about what we're experiencing is your fault. Never has been. When things bother you, we'll talk, pray, do whatever it takes."

One more reason Marc liked Avery. Her compassion for others tugged at his heart.

41

MARC HELPED THE WOMEN clean up the table, a reprieve from the burden of the situation. The summer temps had cooled, and the overhead patio fans had made for a pleasant dinner. Craig needed to follow Leanne home, so Marc reiterated the caution. He didn't like Craig leaving the ranch alone, but until tomorrow and arrangements were made for additional security, Marc would have to let this one slide. No surprise Leanne and Craig carried firearms.

The barbecue and fixings, right along with freshly churned ice cream and strawberries, had filled his belly fuller than usual. Eating like this headed him for disaster the next time he had to chase down a bad guy on foot or pass his FBI fitness quals.

"What would you like to do?" Avery said. "We could swim, tour the stables, ride, or do nothing."

"I need to unpack," Mom said. "I think it will be a short evening for me."

"Whenever you're ready for time alone, feel free to escape to your room," Avery said. "No schedules here. Marc and I are going to inspect a dam in the morning. Craig will be here, and deputies will be in place. You and Tessa are welcome to come along."

"I'd rather play it by ear." Mom needed sleep as her weakened voice indicated.

"I'm not sure." Tessa lifted a tray of dirty dishes. "If I'm up, I'll join you."

"Right," Marc said. "I won't hold my breath. I remember how much I slept at your age."

"What about a walk through the stables when we've finished here?" Tessa said. "I'd like to see the horses."

Avery tossed them an amused look. "Go ahead."

"You're not coming?" Tessa said.

"I'll walk with you to the office, and you can stop for me on your way back. I need to check in on business things. If you have questions, the hands are close by. We'll have plenty of time to tour the stables and ride."

"I've never ridden."

"Now you have a teacher. We'll begin tomorrow afternoon if you like. I'll make a cowgirl out of you."

Tessa's face brightened. "And how to shoot too?"

"Only if your brother is available to supervise." Avery slid her gaze to Marc.

"Right. But you don't need me for riding lessons. I know zilch about horses except to admire them."

"Got it," Tessa said. "I can go with you and Marc in the morning if you need me."

"Sweetie, sleep in. My guess is you'd be bored."

Marc smiled at the interaction. He wanted to believe tonight's conversation paved the way for Tessa to get along fine with Avery and Mom.

"Thank you so much for letting me stay here with you and Mrs. Wilkins," Tessa said. "This house is incredible." She walked the tray into the kitchen and Mom followed.

"Mom, have a good night's rest, and don't forget your pain meds."

"Who's the matriarch here?" Mom tossed him a mom-frown. "Oh, all of you, except Marc, call me Donita." Mom and Tessa disappeared into the house.

Marc stared after them, relief easing his stress. "Thanks for helping me make Tessa fully aware of why she's here. I thought for sure we were headed for dramatics."

"She's a sweetheart. From the teens I've been around at church, she's typical. I work with high school girls, even do summer camp."

"Now I understand how well you relate to her."

Avery tilted her head. "When I came to live with Granddad at age eleven, I experienced the power of unconditional love and faith. I believe in paying it forward."

Another reason he liked this woman. "You've got compassion tattooed on your heart."

She blinked. "How kind. If you only knew my struggles in allowing you and Craig to manage me. I've given stubbornness a run for its money."

"I'm not immune to what's happened either. I'm in the same zone. My emotions have gone from resenting my father's choices to investigating his murder. And discovering he wasn't the man I remember."

Avery glanced at the doorway. "I hope you'll help me prove Granddad's innocence."

"You're not walking a thousand feet from this house without me."

"Marc, please, I have a business and a ranch to run . . . and people to question."

He stepped closer and gently grasped her shoulders. "You're not trained, and you've experienced how serious these people are. Let me work the investigation and keep you safe."

She touched his face. "I'm not afraid."

"You should be." Her touch heated him from head to toe. Everything about her he liked. Yet keeping her, Mom, and Tessa safe meant sacrificing his growing feelings. For now.

★ ★ ★

Marc wished the time at the ranch could have been relaxing instead of requiring a safe-house solution. With Tessa beside him, they walked through the stables. He thought of Roden and how his friend appreciated all the ranch had to offer. Marc needed to check on him before going to bed tonight—after talking to the ranch hands.

"I love the smell of fresh hay," he said. "Seems like I can taste it, and I mean that in a good way."

She glanced around them. "All I can say is it's amazing. I can't imagine growing up here."

"Me either." He reached into his back pocket. "I have an idea to help you stay in contact with your grandmother," he said.

"What do you mean?"

He handed her a small recorder. "A little archaic, but it works. Record messages for her, and I'll make sure they're sent to hospice."

Her eyes widened. "Thank you." She tilted her head and studied him.

"What's going on?"

"I was thinking about how God's helping me deal with Dad's death and Gram's sickness. But what about you? How do you handle the bad things in life?"

"I process. Analyze. If that doesn't work, I figure God had a reason for whatever happened."

"Dad said the same thing. I mean, God always has a reason for what's going on. You're more like him than you think."

Marc wanted to probe deeper with her claim, but his priority was her safety.

She inhaled deeply. "So you're Christian?"

Where was this conversation going? "I made a decision at a junior high church camp. My mother is a believer, and I know you are. Why? Is there something going on, and you need to talk about it?"

"Just asking." Tessa peered inside a stall. "Our dad became a Christian five years ago."

Marc wasn't going there about his father when he needed to think through past assumptions and facts. "My faith has its ups and downs."

"Because of your control-freak personality and job?"

Oh, the bluntness of youth. "Are you analyzing me, little sister?" He sighed for her benefit. "I always have questions about faith and where God fits in the whole scheme of life."

"But you believe in Jesus?"

Why did this feel like an interrogation? "Yes. Without a doubt."

"Just checking to be sure. Ready for another question?" He lifted his chin and she continued. "What would you ask Jesus if you had one-on-one time with Him?"

"Hard to wrap my brain around that. I could have a huge list or nothing at all."

"Jesus can handle all your questions. Are you mad at Him?"

Mad? "And this is all about faith, or are you headed in a particular direction? If this is about my job, I believe faith and my commitment to the FBI walk hand in hand."

"So do I." She held up her palm. "I've frustrated you. I can tell by the lines crinkling across your forehead."

He laughed. "You'd do well in law enforcement."

"Dad said I'd do well in the military. But I'm not interested in either. Talking about Dad and God puts you in a nasty mood."

For good reasons. "I suppose you're right."

"Which is why he didn't want you to know he went to your football games and—"

Marc startled. "What?"

"He went to your middle school and high school football games."

"Little sister, you've dropped me into the deep end." But Marc had seen evidence of his father keeping up with Marc's life after he'd abandoned him and Mom.

The boxes of his father's personal belongings from his office sat in the corner of Marc's apartment. He'd sorted through them for an idea of what he and Liam had been investigating, but the personal memorabilia had to wait for his attention.

"Have I run you off?" While her tone was upbeat, her eyes told another story.

"Not at all." His cell rang, giving him a moment of reprieve.

"Agent Wilkins," a distorted voice said.

"Yes."

"You only think your mother, Tessa, and Avery are safe."

Marc took several steps from his sister. She studied him in obvious confusion, but he nodded and increased the distance between them.

"Don't you have anything to say?" the voice said.

"What kind of scum threatens an innocent kid and women?"

"I'm a smart man who deals in business."

"A messenger or an assassin?"

The man snorted. "You've heard of me."

"Only by reputation. I understand you have a fast motorcycle."

"I do."

"What do you want?" Marc said.

"Back off on the investigation. All of it."

"We could meet, talk about the problem. Work out something amiable for both of us."

"Why?"

"Stop any more bloodshed. Give you what you want."

"I want money. More than you have. But not impossible for you to get."

"We'll do it. Name a time and place, and I'll be there."

"Wilkins, your negotiation skills need a refresher. I'm not a fool. Watch what happens next. The senator will be destroyed."

The call ended, and he walked to Tessa—forcing a smile when anger surged through his veins. The caller examined the four of them under a microscope until he rolled his plan into place, and he had firsthand knowledge of the targets. The caller's arrogance paved the way for him to make a mistake.

"Everything okay?" Tessa said.

"Sure. Work stuff."

Avery burst into the stables and fast-walked to them. "Marc." Her frantic voice added to the alarm of his call. "Someone broke into the office."

42

AVERY FOUGHT THE URGE to rush into Marc's arms. Although they'd known each other a short time, the danger they'd shared had drawn her closer to him. Yet Tessa had voiced her confusion about the apparent danger, and seeing Avery reach out to find comfort from Marc would increase the poor girl's uncertainty.

Avery drew in a cleansing breath and slowed her pace before she reached them.

Each time Avery vowed to claim courage to trek through the fire roaring against Granddad, the flames stole her breath. Her fear played straight into the person's plan who'd ransacked the office. Granddad had raised her not to run from danger or show fear. He'd instructed her to weigh each incident and word before responding. Sometimes true courage meant backing off, and that's what she chose now.

"Ready to help me sort this out?" she said.

"Let's take a look." Marc swung an arm around Tessa's waist. "Are you ready to play investigator, Sis?"

She nodded. "Great way to tell me I'm going with you because you don't want me alone."

He smiled. "Smart girl."

Avery listened more to what the two weren't saying that spoke louder than the audible words. Both feared for the safety of the other, and she so understood.

The three walked to the office. She sensed Marc wanted to ask a truckload of questions but not with Tessa present.

"Hey," he said. "Did you see anyone?"

"No. The door's always locked. I hesitated going in . . . Just wanted to enjoy the familiar and pretend life hadn't taken a U-turn." She shot up a prayer for strength. "I walked into a mess, and I didn't touch a thing."

"Since I'm the trained agent here, I'll check out the damage before I call the sheriff's office."

"Why call them when you're FBI?" Tessa's voice held a slight tremble.

"The sheriff's department has a team to do an evidence sweep. For the FBI to come from another location would take too long. Not a wise use of money and manpower."

"I didn't realize the cops, the FBI, and the Army Corps work together."

"The movies don't always get it right, Sis. We have our specialty, and we help each other."

Marc stopped in front of the office. "Wait in the doorway while I go inside."

No need to caution them further. Avery had attempted to show a warrior side with the car bombing, but the break-in had violated her home, tossing her into a mix of fear and anger.

"The blinds are always closed," she said. "That prevented anyone from seeing the destruction, but I don't understand why no one heard it. Had to have happened during the night or today because Craig said he'd been here yesterday morning."

She viewed the ransacked area with a different purpose, the motive. Her desk in the receptionist area teetered precariously on its side, the drawers removed, and contents dumped on the floor.

Marc bent to the desk where someone had removed the legs. A crushed plant mixed its dirt with glass from a photo frame containing Granddad in his Western gear. Closer scrutiny showed the backing had been ripped from the frame. File cabinets had been taken apart with a screwdriver that still lay on the floor. The destruction from wall hangings and floor-to-ceiling bookcases resembled a demolition zone.

Marc angled his phone to take pics. He appeared to study two open office doors—both had been removed from their hinges. He turned to her. "Which one belongs to the senator?"

"The one on the left is a conference room, and the other is Granddad's office. Craig has his own office in the stables."

He stepped over papers and debris to the conference room. A black credenza looked in better shape than the files strewn over the floor.

Whoever was responsible had searched for an item important enough to risk detection. Avery had given Marc all the details she could remember. Marc scrutinized corners, ceilings, overturned furniture, and broken remains of antique pieces, always snapping pics.

What had the person or persons been looking for? Proof of Granddad's involvement in a crime? Evidence Granddad had found about a crime or illegal activity?

The events surrounding the three friends were connected to what they had in common—the last dam project or possibly the last few projects?

The office phone in the receptionist area rang. Marc joined Avery and Tessa. The phone rang again, and he glanced at Avery. "Answer it, please, but don't let the caller know anyone is with you."

She picked up the receiver and pushed Speaker. "Brazos River Ranch."

"Have you discovered my surprise?" a distorted voice said.

"Yes, rather low, don't you think?" She craved calmness to hold her own in the call.

"I'd call it thorough. A real Texas twister."

"Did you find what you were searching for? Or was this just a cleanup project left for me?"

"Avery, you're too smart to play stupid."

She dug her fingernails into her palms. "Guess I'm clueless. Explain it to me."

"Either you, your granddad, Donita Wilkins, or sweet Tessa have an item that belongs to me. I want it before I dive deeper into an assassin's role."

"I'm still clueless."

"I'm running out of patience. Who dies next to prove I'm serious?"

She shivered. "The problem is you kill us off, and you'll never find what is so important to you."

"Yeah, but I'll leave a string of bodies behind."

Avery huffed. "I suggest you take a closer look at who you're dealing with."

43

LONG AFTER THE SHERIFF and his team finished sweeping the office, Marc reflected on Avery's quick thinking and reaction to the threatening phone call. Once she'd ended the conversation, she shook like a fall leaf, but she'd also been furious. Could he ever learn all the ways Avery's mind worked? She gave so much to others, like a bubbling well of goodness. The more time he spent with her, the more his resolve to hold back from sharing his heart weakened.

A list of questions and things to do taller than his six-foot frame dumped into his mind. If the sun were up, he'd be pushing ahead on the dam inspection—Avery's evaluation and the dive team's findings. From there he could analyze the outcome with the FBI and the corps to put the case together and bring Senator Elliott out of his temporary cave.

If only Marc had an idea what the intruder demanded.

No one hid from law enforcement on short notice without help.

Meaning the senator either had a plan in place before Marc's father and Liam Zachary's deaths, or he'd secured the right connections to keep him out of the public eye. For certain, the latter. The senator had personal, professional, and political relationships across the globe.

Who did the senator trust with his life?

Logic pointed to someone who had clout with law enforcement, government contacts, and believed Senator Elliott had legitimate reasons to stay incognito. Avery should have this type of confidential information, but she wouldn't spin her wheels trying to find him.

Earlier Marc had phoned the hospital for a status report on Roden, who'd been placed in a private room and responded well to treatment. Good news for a change.

Marc glanced at the time. After 2 a.m. Avery needed sleep to heal, and any self-respecting gentleman would leave her alone. But stopping a killer went beyond creature comforts. He texted her.

Are you awake? I could use your input.

The dots on his phone showed she was typing her response.
Awake now. Want to talk in the upstairs living room?

Marc pulled on jeans and a T-shirt before meeting with her. Avery's droopy eyelids gave him pause. They'd already decided to get a head start to the dam in a few hours, and he'd interrupted her sleep.

"Have we been threatened again? Another death?" She slid onto a recliner.

If she wouldn't punch him, he'd take her into his arms. Another time. "Not at all. I have a few ideas to run by you."

"Aren't you exhausted?"

"I should be." He eased onto a matching chair across from her. "When working a case, I survive on pure adrenaline. When it's over, I'll sleep for three days." He drew in a breath to slow his thoughts. "I'm sorry to wake you."

She leaned her head back and closed her eyes. "You wouldn't have texted me if it wasn't important, and the churning in my stomach says the danger gets worse with every passing minute. Two people are dead and by all rights, the number should be higher." Her shoulders slumped. "I'd give the caller what he wants if I thought the crimes would stop and if I knew what he wanted."

"Something valuable enough to kill for." Marc's mind swept back over the possibilities. "Money or power. Toss in hate and/or revenge."

"The issue with the dam's repeated inspections make me crazy. We've all been lucky. No, not lucky. God is watching over us. And I worry Granddad might be in the killer's sights. I hope you have fresh ideas because I don't."

"Who does the senator trust the most? Those who are his insiders?"

She opened her eyes, the confusion in them as murky as flood-waters. "Marc, I've already contacted everyone I could think of. No one has seen him or offered where to look. I contacted resorts, hunting lodges, and areas outside the country."

"Do you think any of those people would go against his wishes? He could have been right there listening to your conversation."

Her features fell as though contemplating his questions. "Anything is possible. Haven't you done your FBI thing with the list?"

"Yes. With the FIG."

"The what?"

"FBI's Field Intelligence Group. Includes special agents, linguists, intelligence analysts, and surveillance specialists."

"I learned something new."

He smiled. "Is there a woman in the senator's picture?"

"Not since Grandma died when I was a little girl. He's married to the ranch, the business, church, and politics. He occasionally has dinner with a congresswoman from Oklahoma, but that's rare. And her name is on the list."

"Jeannie Blackford? You've talked to her?"

Avery's eyes flashed. "I told you I had." She held up her bandaged arm, minus the sling. "My apologies. No reason for me to take out my lack of sleep on you."

"Yes, there is. I woke you." He studied her. "We need our rest. The drive to the dam will be early. I assume you want to start your inspection before the dive team gets there."

She nodded. "I hope the Army Corps doesn't turn me away."

"They won't. I received permission through the FBI—as long as I'm with you."

She shook her head. "You're stuck with me."

"Do I hear excitement about spending time with me?"

"I feel like you're my babysitter."

If the pangs of longing in Marc's heart were the real thing, he had no desire to babysit. "What about a man who cares about your safety?"

"He should have learned his lesson."

Marc captured her blue gaze, warmth sliding through his chest. "Maybe he likes your company."

"Maybe she likes his company." She bit her lip, holding his gaze, as though looking away might end the moment.

"Where are we going?" he whispered.

"I wish I had an answer." Avery stood. "You're right. We need our rest for later today. I'll ride and you drive."

"You're going to sleep the forty minutes it takes to get there?"

"Absolutely." Her breathing quickened.

He joined her, fighting the urge to taste her lips. "See you at six."

A pink blush spread over her face. "I'll be ready."

Did she feel as attracted to him as he was to her? Back to business. "One more thing. Shortly after midnight, the weather report issued an update. Hurricane Braxton is gathering strength in the Gulf. The dam and lake are still on the path of the dirty side."

She stiffened her shoulders. "Any more good news?"

"You're tired. In the morning we'll talk about the worst-case scenario."

She shook her head. "The dam is fine. My grandfather is a man of integrity."

"But you don't know the capabilities of who might have plotted against him."

44

AVERY COULDN'T SLEEP. An hour after she and Marc had ended their conversation, she stared up at a dark ceiling. In the shadows, the fan whirled in rhythm to her roiling thoughts. At 4:03, she dressed in jeans and a T-shirt that read *Stress Is a State of Mind*. The phrase should boost her troubled attitude.

Should.

Downstairs Avery crept to a storage area near the utility room. She stuffed the items needed for the day into her backpack—sunscreen, bug repellant, mini first aid kit, binoculars, flapping tape, small notebook, pen—and added her phone to the outer pocket.

"Avery, do you ever sleep?" Mia's soft voice oddly enough comforted her.

She faced the woman who'd dressed for the day in capris and tennis shoes. "I could ask you the same thing. Why are you up?"

"To brew coffee and make breakfast sandwiches for you and Agent Wilkins."

"You are so sweet, but I have plenty of time to do those things."

"Of course you do." Mia's teasing tone shoved a shade of normal Avery's way. "The coffee might be okay, but the sandwiches would be worse than dog food."

Avery laughed and opened her arms. "I've missed that snarky wit."

Mia stepped into the embrace. "I am the voice of reason and common sense." She separated herself from Avery. "You finish your packing, and I'll work my magic in the kitchen."

A nagging question persisted. "When I left for Houston, why did you ask me if I had my handgun?"

Mia sighed. "You were upset, and I had no clue why. Your grandfather had asked me to keep an eye on you and deter you from leaving the ranch. I assumed the worst, and unfortunately my instincts were right."

"We haven't had an argument."

"I'd rather you two were in a shouting match than this."

At five forty-five, Marc joined them at the coffeepot. "I followed my nose." His eyes held the glint of a little boy ready for adventure.

Mia handed him an insulated mug. "Avery has breakfast sandwiches and fruit for the trip."

He grinned and thanked her, then fixed his attention on a huge bowl of packaged candy. After grabbing a snack bag of M&M'S, he ripped them open and dumped the candies into his black coffee. "Are you married, Mia?"

"No, sir. My husband died nineteen years ago."

"I'm in the market for a wife who's pretty and cooks."

That leaves me out.

Mia pointed to sugar and creamer for him. "Eliminate Avery from your search then. She doesn't know which end of a frying pan to use."

"I'm good with numbers," Avery said. "That must count for something."

"Right. You think pie is the sixteenth letter in the Greek alphabet."

Avery groaned and grabbed her backpack with the breakfast bag. On the way to the truck, two deputies from the sheriff's department offered a good morning. Their presence eased her concern for those left behind.

No way could she sleep on the road when Marc needed instructions to help her with the inspection. She gambled on the Army Corps of Engineers to allow her admittance. Marc claimed she had permission, but the military had a way of changing their minds. She stared up at the sky, noting the colors of peach and blue ushering in dawn. Granddad said sunrises always brought a promise of God watching out for us.

"We might need a shovel, hard hats, rock hammer, watertight boots, and snake leggings," she said. "We can get those in the storage shed behind the office."

"Diving equipment?"

"Not for us. The job needs trained divers who know the dangers. I'm glad the team has us on the schedule before Hurricane Braxton delivers heavy rain."

"How many on the team?"

"Usually five. Two divers, a top-sider, spotter, and a dive master who monitors the adherence to the dive plan onshore."

"I have zero background in dam construction. This guy needs help."

She laughed. "The diver uses an underwater camera to record the inspection. We'll know something when the divers surface."

They loaded up his truck bed, and Marc opened the passenger door. "Gorgeous premorning. I never want to take a new day for granted."

He sounded like a younger version of Granddad, who always tried to have an attitude of gratitude. She hoisted her backpack onto the floorboard and buckled up. Once on the road and after a few sips of coffee, she turned to business. "I'll need your help today, if you don't mind. I'll be snapping pics and making notes, but anything you see that is questionable, please let me know. We have about twenty surface inspection points and a few instruments to check. I might need you to record details on your phone."

"Hey, I'm ready to do whatever is needed. But this is your wheelhouse."

"You'd know a crack or leak if you saw one?"

"Yep."

"And if a spillway was overgrown?"

"Sure."

"Low spots where water flow could condense and erode the dam?"

"Yep."

"Wet ground that should be dry? Sinkholes?"

"Yep."

"Since this is a new concrete construction and we've passed Texas inspections twice, none of those things I mentioned should appear. My biggest concern is the structural foundation below the surface that can cause cracks invisible to surface inspection." Her thoughts swept back over Texas's safety standards for engineers. "We use various computer programs in the preconstruction and construction phases to avoid a critical failure. We also employ unmanned aerial vehicles or UAVs to develop 3D models of the project. The technology provides information to avoid and prevent accidents."

"If a structural crack is found, how long does it take to repair?"

Avery reached for the bag of breakfast sandwiches. "Longer than we have with the storm coming in. Pray the hurricane makes a turn and heads back out into the Gulf." She handed him an egg, bacon, cheese, and jalapeño sandwich, still warm, and a napkin.

"Where do we begin this morning?"

"By walking and observing. Probably boring to you, and it will get sticky hot."

He took a bite, then grabbed his coffee. "I hadn't expected this to be spicy. Definitely woke me up. My stomach might have an acid leak."

"Better your stomach than the dam."

His demeanor sobered. "Thousands of people are in the floodplain. Could mean a mandatory evacuation."

She stared out at the highway. "It's impossible to stop thinking about how many people could be affected. Innocent kids and adults. Imagine the property and home damage. Marc, we must find answers this morning."

"Have you been on-site when an Army Corps dive team is working?"

"Yes. Their job isn't easy—demanding and takes time. Many are volunteers. I talked to a man who'd been diving for the Army Corps about six years. He claimed the divers depended on each other and were like family. The work underwater is dark, making it unpredictable."

"I'd think the risk of head pressure could take a life, not discounting the other mechanical aspects that could go wrong." Marc shrugged. "The whole underwater setting is dangerous."

"The man I talked to said divers could identify each other by their breath sounds. The calling fits the personality, like what you do for the FBI."

✵ ✵ ✵

At the Lago de Cobre Dam, the sun rose at half-mast and glistened like glass over cerulean waters. Even the riprap sparkled in the sunrise. Recreation enthusiasts already gathered with their water toys to enjoy the lake within the appropriate zone. Avery took a mental snapshot of nature's beauty in hopes it promised a good omen for the day. Already temps soared toward a midmorning prediction of triple digits and dripping humidity. But Hurricane Braxton moving closer to Galveston's shores stalked those in its path, and rainstorms upstream were unrelenting. Should the two combine forces, the outcome bordered on the unthinkable.

Near the diver's crew boat, the Army Corps assisted the team into wet suits. Already in place, they checked gear, equipment, and offered last-minute instructions. One diver had a camera for the video inspection. Each diver had a transducer attached to his face mask, a device that converted the diver's voice into an ultrasound signal. Avery had no clue how it allowed the divers and those aboveground to communicate. Except it did.

She dug her fingers into her palms. *Calm, down. God is in control.*

She walked alongside Marc to Lieutenant Shipley, dressed in a soldier's uniform. Most likely he didn't intend to stay, or he'd have worn cooler clothes.

"Morning, Lieutenant Shipley," Marc said. "You're here early."

"I wanted to be on-site when the divers entered the water before I drove back to Fort Worth." He glanced at her. "Hi, Avery. I saw you were coming. Wish it was under better circumstances."

"Yes, sir."

"We all want answers, but right now those are in the dive team's hands. May be a long day. Add to it the storm strengthening in the Gulf."

"My concern is confirming the dam's structure is secure." She wasn't the only one caught up in fear of the weather and what it meant to those living in the reservoir area. "A third dive team inspection is costly when we have solid evidence of no issues in two previous videos."

"I understand. We think it's unnecessary, but we need to follow up on the construction worker's claim."

Long after Lieutenant Shipley had left the site, she and Marc walked the spillway.

Long after she and Marc repeated the outer inspection and noted nothing structurally wrong.

And long after those on land grew tired of waiting in the Texas inferno, the divers surfaced.

"I want to hear their first words," Marc said. "We need good news for a change."

Avery and Marc approached the water's edge. The divers climbed from the water with less enthusiasm than when they'd jumped in.

The dive master helped a diver who had photographed the dam remove his gear. The two men talked in private. The dive master approached a corps member. No smiles or head nods. Avery held her breath. *Please . . .*

Marc and Avery joined the diver and dive master.

The dive master glanced at Avery and Marc. "What they spotted isn't in the senator's favor. The dam's foundation elements fail to meet the standards for soft soil. The construction should have included additional rock expanding the footprint with a footer and other foundation elements that aren't evident." He pressed his lips together. "The repairs will take time and money."

"Sir, Braxton is a category 5," a diver said. "On target to reach landfall in Galveston Thursday morning. This area will get hit hard."

The dive master frowned. "The dam might not hold."

45

MARC SENSED AVERY'S ANGST in the stillness of the afternoon heat. The dive team's inspection and video evidence nailed the senator's responsibility in altering the dam's structure. It also implicated Craig due to his position as foreman. Two men whom Avery trusted faced arrest . . . and as an officer of the company, she faced legal action too. How had the two previous inspections passed?

The dive master wiped the sweat from his forehead. "Hard for me to believe Senator Elliott deliberately put thousands of people in danger."

"You're wrong," Avery spat out. "There's been a terrible mistake. A dive team previously inspected it, and the dam passed."

The dive master blew out a heavy sigh. "Since I wasn't the dive master for the other inspections, I don't have an answer for you. But it's clear someone made alterations to the specs. My team saw the shortcuts, and I'll send you a link to the video once it's uploaded. Like you, I'd rather believe Senator Elliott overcompensated on the side of safety instead of what the team found."

A corps officer called for the team's attention. "The TCEQ has been notified. And the EAP will alert the residents with recommendations to evacuate. The hurricane headed this way increases the risk of structural failure."

Marc glanced out at the peaceful reservoir and the magnificent dam. The Texas Commission on Environmental Quality and Emergency Assistance Program would alert first responders and local law enforcement of the potential problem.

"Am I under arrest?" Avery said.

"No." Unless incriminating evidence caused him to take her or Craig into custody. "There's nothing more we can do here. We'll talk about our next steps on the drive back."

Grief-stricken blue eyes met him. Wordlessly, she took the concrete path to his truck. Marc watched her until she was beyond earshot. He contacted the sheriff's office handling protection at the ranch and requested Craig Holcombe be held for questioning.

At the truck, Avery slid into the passenger seat. Still, she said nothing. Her lips quivered against a pale face.

Once on the road, he broached the problem. "I wish I could take away those findings."

"Me too." She failed to look at him.

"What are you thinking?"

"You called the ranch and requested Craig stay put?"

"Yes. I'll talk to him there."

"I assume you need to question me."

"I've interviewed both of you, but I will need to do so again. You have the right to an attorney." He palmed the steering wheel. "I sounded cold when I'd do anything to spare you this heartache."

"Marc, the faulty dam is reality. I have nothing to hide. Neither do I want an attorney, but Granddad would drag me through manure for not taking advantage of my rights." She swiped beneath an eye. "Have I become the enemy? Your mother and Tessa won't want to stay at the ranch when they hear the inspector's report."

"You three are still victims."

"Am I, Marc? Or am I a fool?"

Marc reached across the seat and grasped her hand. What could he say? His logic guided him toward FBI protocol, but his heart softened for her. "I understand you believe the senator is innocent of wrongdoing, and I admit it doesn't fit his stellar reputation. That leaves someone at the helm who is desperate and willing to do whatever it takes for—"

"What is so valuable? I want your professional evaluation, then I'll share mine."

Marc chose honesty with a bent toward his feelings for her. "I see more pros for your grandfather's innocence than cons. For every accusation shoved his way, I see evidence of blackmail."

"But Craig? No one could be more loyal to Granddad." She stared out the side window. "Why didn't I see this coming? Has the good life tainted my mind?"

"No. You were just blindsided."

"No excuse to jeopardize people's lives and property." She nodded at the radio. "The weather. What are the updates?"

The strong woman had slipped into an emotional overload. Marc understood, although her mental state solved nothing. He pressed on the radio.

"The National Weather Service has issued a mandatory evacuation for Galveston and the surrounding area. Hurricane Braxton, now a category 5 storm, will make landfall on Thursday at 11 a.m. The time to leave is coming to an end. For those who haven't chosen to leave, you must shelter in place. The causeway will close at 7 p.m. tonight."

A live audio report from Galveston showed bumper-to-bumper

traffic over the I-45 causeway bridge. "Vehicles attempting to get out of the hurricane's path are creating long lines of traffic and short tempers."

Avery checked her phone, as though she expected a better report. "Thunderstorms and high winds will spark tornadoes. But my fear is Braxton will stall, dumping heavy rainfall." She laid her phone in the console. "I'm repeating what we already know."

"Processing information provides an opportunity to look at the situation from different angles."

"Sounds like a quote from the FBI handbook."

He chuckled. "You might be right."

The station switched to a local news update that added another level of anxiety to the situation. Local authorities warned that with the predicted rainfall from the hurricane combined with the rapid filling of the reservoir due to incessant rains upstream, the Lago de Cobre Dam might not handle the stress. "Earlier the Army Corps of Engineers tested the dam, and the Texas EAP advised those in the low-lying areas below the dam to evacuate. Quinn Elliott Sr., owner of Elliott Commercial Construction, completed the dam approximately six months ago. Elliott was not available for comment."

Unlike residents near the Gulf, these people weren't accustomed to enacting a disaster plan. Panic . . . Marc despised what he had seen from otherwise law-abiding citizens during emergencies.

Avery stared at him. "This isn't about me. Never has been. But I'm saying it. Can this situation get any worse?" She turned to face him. "No need to answer. My mind's cluttered right now, but once I think through what we've learned, I'll be able to speak more clearly to it."

At the turnoff onto the ranch property, Marc's cell phone alerted him to a call from Burleson County's sheriff. He pressed the Bluetooth to respond.

"Agent Wilkins, I'm here at the Brazos River Ranch. Craig Holcombe hasn't been located, and he's not answering his phone.

We contacted the woman he's been dating, Leanne Archer, and she claims not to have heard from him since he left her home around midnight last night. Doesn't appear he made it back to the ranch or contacted anyone here."

"Would you send a couple of deputies to scout outside the ranch's perimeters?"

"Already on it. Also doing a search on the property."

Another murder or a man on the run?

46

DISTRESS FOR CRAIG ENFLAMED Avery's face. She refused to believe this tragedy had dug another trench, but his disappearance lent itself to another murder. Or his involvement . . . Craig had filled the big-brother role to Avery for years, and to think of him gone or behind the crimes made her physically ill. She'd be a stronger woman for having gone through this and would one day help others who faced life's challenges. But not today.

She breathed in sharply and prayed for strength. "Ask the sheriff if his deputies or the ranch hands have searched the property." A peculiar calmness settled within her. "Craig could be anywhere on a stretch of thirty-five thousand acres. Is his truck on the property? Are any of the horses missing? Has one of the ranch hands been hurt? Have they talked to Mia?"

Marc relayed Avery's questions to the sheriff. Her mind raced as though she were riding Darcy. No, more like Zoom.

She gathered her phone from the console and pressed in a text to Craig. **Please call or text me. I'm worried about you.**

Leanne . . . Avery texted her. **Have you heard from Craig?**

Not since last night around 12. I tried calling him earlier, but he didn't pick up.

Would you let me know if he reaches out?

Sure. I'm sick about this, Avery. Please find Craig.

Craig, Granddad, where are you? Her anguish moved her to prayer again. She craved answers, solid ones about what he, Colonel Wilkins, and Liam had discovered—if anything. But if they hadn't uncovered a crime, then why all the secrets? She recalled the threatening call from last night. Had Craig met up with the assassin?

She glanced at Marc, who captured her gaze, then pored his attention into his phone. "Yes, sir. We're within five minutes of the ranch. If I understand correctly, Craig hasn't responded to phone call attempts. Deputies and ranch hands are combing the ranch. No one's been hurt, and neither Mia nor any of the others have seen him since last evening. His truck is gone. In short, we have no idea where he might be. Yes, sir. You're right." Marc concluded his call.

"We need to face the facts," she said. "I'm not sure I can do it."

Marc pulled up to the secured gate entrance. "Hold on until we're inside the property." A deputy waved them ahead, and Marc continued. "Any places on the ranch without cell coverage?"

"Yes. The ranch hands know those spots too."

"The deputies and some of the hands have been looking for him for over an hour. Searching the acreage will take much longer."

She swallowed a sob. "What if he's hurt badly?"

"Avery, force yourself to get a grip. I'm sure there's a logical explanation."

She nodded, embarrassed about her breakdown. Marc's scenario in no way reflected Craig's habits. "How do you work day after day with such horrendous crimes? My emotions are shot."

"That's because you care deeply for those who've been hurt, killed, or wrongfully accused of crimes. I have compassion for victims and a commitment to protect and keep people safe. If I added a heart connection, I'd be a candidate for sedation. My work is a calling, and God gives me what I need when I need it."

She studied his brown eyes, an intensity of warmth and intelligence. "I haven't heard you talk about faith, except your actions reflect godly character."

He shook his head. "Not always. A lot of not always. Someday I might tell you about a few of my failures. Until then—" he took her hand—"we have to find out who's behind the killings and why the dam wasn't constructed according to design."

She stared at the hand firmly holding hers. Friendship, reassurance, or something more? "Before this is over, we might go our separate ways. I—"

"I hope not." He offered a tender smile. "Do we have the beginnings of a relationship? More than just two people caught in the middle of a series of crimes?" Staring back at the road, he inhaled deeply. "Bad timing. I apologize."

"Why?"

"Why the beginnings of a relationship, or why my timing is bad?"

"Both." The hand around hers tightened, taking her heart for a wild ride. Wasn't this what she wanted?

"Not sure how you feel about me, us. And I could jeopardize the case by getting emotionally involved. Can't happen on any level."

She saw how innocent people could get hurt or a bad decision made if his heart ruled his head. "I'm interested in us, but I agree this needs to be over before we . . . go any further. Marc, I must defend my grandfather. Granddad told me years ago that truth is first believed in the heart. Now I have to prove it."

"I expect no less, and I hope you're right."

At that moment, she felt closer to Marc than any man she'd ever known, other than Granddad. Even then, not in the same way. But they were headed down the same path with a huge fork in the road. One led to life as she'd known it, and the other led to uncertainty.

47

MARC LISTENED TO THE DEPUTY repeat the same information he'd just been given over the phone. No one knew where Craig might be, and the search spread over the ranch and community.

Seated inside Craig's office with two deputies and Avery, Marc's phone rang. He stared at the *Possible Spam* on the screen and stepped out to answer the call.

"Marc. This is Quinn Elliott. Are you at the ranch?"

He recognized the senator's deep voice. "Yes, sir."

"Your sister is with her grandmother?"

"She's with me."

"That would have pleased Abbott." The senator's voice lacked his hearty rumble. "Your mother and partner?"

"Mom's with me and Tessa. Roden is recovering in Houston. He went home from the hospital earlier today."

The senator coughed. "I sent Avery to you for her protection. Abbott said you were the best, and then I learn she's in the thick of—"

"Avery has a mind of her own, and I can't force her to think your way or mine." Over the next ten minutes, Marc brought him up to date on what had transpired, including the office break-in and the sheriff's department watching the house and property. If the senator had a hand in the crimes, he might let something slip. "Today we've uncovered two more issues."

"I heard about the condition of the Lago de Cobre Dam."

Marc clicked his pen. "I need details."

"Check the dates when the foundation was poured against my calendar. I happened to be in Canada. Normally I'm on the site. But rain had delayed pouring it, and I had a hunting trip scheduled with Liam."

"Who did you leave in charge?"

"Craig. Who else? Avery and Leanne were in Orlando. The weather . . ."

Marc had learned an identical story from Avery. "I need all the specifics about your trip, including witnesses, flight numbers, times, phone numbers, and what you brought down in the hunt. Avery told me you sent an email to the material supplier during the time you were hunting in an area with no connectivity."

"I gave Craig permission to act in my authority while I was gone. He had access to my email account. I'll put together the trip's itinerary and text you."

"The sooner, the better."

"The idea of accusing Craig Holcombe . . . I don't see how or why."

"Then who?"

The senator let several seconds of dead space ensue before he responded. "Craig is like a son to me, more so than my own flesh and blood. If this leads back to him, he's proved I'm an old fool. And if he's guilty, he's made a handful of cash. But murder doesn't fit him."

"What about Buddy?" Marc said. "Is he capable of murder and working with Craig for control of the ranch and the construction business?"

"I'd like to think neither of them would let greed rule their actions."

"Buddy has accused you of murder. Craig suspects Buddy."

"I'm not surprised. You're investigating both men while aiming both barrels at me?"

"I'm investigating a violent crime. Who else has motive to alter the dam's design?"

"No idea and then too many to name. Folks either side with me or hate me. I'm curious about Craig's explanation after the dive team's inspection."

"I'm sure you and I are tracking the same way. Craig's either taken off in the heat of things or lying somewhere with a bullet in him. I can't help you unless you fill me in on the background. I don't believe any of this took you by surprise."

"Threats have always been a part of my life. But not murders and the intricate plan I see unfolding."

"Who informed you of the faulty construction?" Marc said.

When the senator's lack of response hit dead air, Marc repeated the question.

"Lieutenant Shipley, a good friend."

"He's in your circle?"

"Yes."

"What else?"

"All right. About eight months ago, I received a call from a computer-altered voice that said I needed to part with some of my money. The caller threatened Avery and demanded ten million dollars. I refused, thinking it meant nothing, and hung up. I hired a private investigator to handle the threat, but nothing surfaced. Not the first time someone has tried to squeeze money out of me. I finished the dam and received another call. This time the voice said the dam wouldn't hold. Impossible when we'd received a valid inspection. I talked to Abbott and Liam, and we hired the original diver to inspect the dam and take another video. He said the project had been completed according to spec. I have both videos of the inspections."

"Where are they?"

"In my possession."

"Was Craig aware?"

"Yes."

"I need the diver's name, and how I can get in touch with him."

"He's dead. Bruce Ingles."

Marc clenched his jaw. "Three verified deaths, and you kept the information from the Army Corps or the Feds? Sounds suspicious to me."

"Ingles died in a one-car accident. Fell asleep at the wheel."

"Imagine that." The possibility of his father being murdered rose several points. But in Marc's opinion, his father had done his best to protect Mom and Tessa.

"I see your point," the senator said. "I should have gone to the right people when Abbott and Liam died, but we had no names or groups to offer. No wonder I'm a suspect."

"Like connecting dots." Marc bit back sarcasm as thick as tar. "Ready to turn yourself in?"

"I'm not guilty."

"Then why are you hiding?"

"You already said it, to connect the dots. I can't find who is responsible when I'm in jail."

"There are trained investigators who know more about solving crimes."

"Where has your experience gotten you on this one?" The senator's voice rose.

"You called me, so what's your agenda?"

"Are you willing to help me find who is behind this?"

"My job has always been to investigate the truth and protect the innocent."

"You're so much like your father. Makes me question who I'm talking to."

Not exactly a compliment from Marc's point of view. "Look, I need proof, and you refuse to see me face-to-face. Your granddaughter deserves more than threats and attempts on her life."

"We've both failed."

Marc wanted to hang up, but those thoughts were his pride speaking. "I'm tired of empty words. A question here—who is the committee?"

"What?"

"A woman called me representing you as part of the committee." When the senator didn't respond, Marc moved ahead. "Give me something I can use, or leave me alone."

"Committee? There is no committee. If you remember, I used the word *circle*, and I asked one of them to contact you, but he dragged his feet. Concerned he didn't have enough evidence. That call wasn't from anyone authorized by me. Shipley has a few answers. I'll give him permission to talk to you about what's been discovered. Keep it to yourself. You'll understand when he's finished."

Marc would determine the confidentiality of the information after he reviewed it.

"I'm contacting Shipley now. Just keep the information from him private. He's risked his career in this."

"I'll give you thirty minutes, then I phone him. What's the name of the crew who poured the foundation?"

"Avery has the name, address, and number in her records."

"And you doubt Craig's guilt?" Marc sensed someone had joined him. He turned to Avery.

"You're talking to my grandfather?" Not even a hint of emotion on her face.

He nodded.

"Marc," the senator said. "I hear Avery."

"She's here."

Avery reached out her hand. "I want to talk to him."

Marc pressed Speaker and handed her his phone. The senator had avoided her long enough.

"Where are you?" She gripped her fingers around the phone.

"Can't tell you."

"And why not? Shutting me out while I face threats?"

"I'm protecting you," the senator said.

"Really? Where were you when the doctor stitched up my arm? Nearly killed Marc, his partner, and Mrs. Wilkins?"

"I'm doing my best, Avery. I'm innocent of the killings, constructing a faulty dam, and the crimes surrounding it all."

She closed her eyes, and a tear slipped down her cheek. "I know you're innocent, but I don't know why you wouldn't tell me the truth in the beginning. Are you in danger?"

"Yes."

"Are my parents or Craig responsible?"

"Maybe. I haven't heard or seen Craig. I told Marc I'd cooperate with what we've uncovered. He needs information from the files. If you'd get it for him, I'd appreciate it. Listen to him. He and I differ about how to proceed, but you and I need his logic and contacts. I'm ending the call now. I love you."

Avery blinked and returned Marc's phone. She trembled, and he interpreted her reaction as anger and helplessness. "Are you okay?"

She nodded. "Whatever you need, I'll get it for you."

48

MARC AND AVERY NEEDED to form a response to the dam's failed inspection. He didn't hold out on Shipley contacting him, but they'd stay in Craig's office and wait it out.

"Media will be all over this," he said. "Those who oppose the senator will tear him to pieces. Even those who are reporting the facts will see him as the responsible party. Yes, you and Craig are in the line of fire. I suggest contacting your attorney for legal advice but refrain from making a statement."

"I agree with all you've said. You may want to document my response." Avery gave a sad smile. "No point in making a statement that could worsen the situation." She completed a call to the attorney, and they reached the same conclusion.

She massaged her neck. "I have no idea where to go from here except to steer clear of reporters."

"I'd like more info about the construction crew who poured the dam's foundation."

A few moments later, she lifted her gaze from her laptop screen. "I have the company's name. Expert Commercial Concrete Specialists goes by ECCS. Headquarters in Oklahoma City. I have a phone number, email address, a website, and a contact of W. S. Wiseman. Want me to call?"

Marc nodded. "Let's find out what Craig arranged."

Avery pressed in a phone number. Moments later she frowned. "Either I pressed in the wrong number, or the company is no longer in operation." She tried again, then turned to her laptop. Within moments she blew out obvious frustration. "What now, Marc? There's no such company, email, or person. Nothing."

"I'll work my end." He contacted the Field Intelligence Group with the information available. "FIG will fill in the blanks. A bogus operation seals Craig's involvement."

She lifted her chin. "I hate the sound of it. I have a bill from a Best Western near Brenham for the crew. Looks like meals were at different restaurants. I'll check to see what I can find."

While Marc checked email and spoke to Victoria about Roden's continued recovery, Avery spent time on the phone. She finished and buried her face in her hands. "I don't know what to think. The hotel reservations were under Expert Commercial Concrete Specialists and paid for by Craig's business credit card. The same with the meals. He must have joined them for every meal. I never even thought to verify the company. How stupid of me."

"You were lied to." He stared out over the stables but not really seeing. "If anyone is stupid in this mess, it's me for not reading Craig."

"Can we get Granddad back on the phone?"

"I already tried."

"When I asked Craig about the materials used for the foundation, he said they came from the warehouse. I confirmed the supplies were pulled by a crew member under Craig's authorization."

Marc thought through the new info. "I believe in your and Senator Elliott's innocence. This took more than Craig to pull it all together."

"Who else?"

"Someone the senator trusts implicitly."

She shrugged. "Who? Do you suspect someone?"

"Yes and no. Without the senator and Craig, we can only keep digging with the tools we have."

49

MARC CHECKED THE TIME. Thirty-five minutes had passed, and Lieutenant Shipley hadn't called. Avery curled up in a huge leather chair that made her look frail, too pale for his liking—not because she suffered physically but due to the mental stress. He'd never reveal his thoughts when she'd demonstrated repeatedly her amazing strength. But everyone had a breaking point.

She stood and walked to a window and stared out at the shadowed acres of quiet beauty, horses and cattle—her life. She processed silently, and yet he ached for her suffering and fought the need to wrap her in his arms.

Murders. Accusations. An unstable dam. Hurricane Braxton. Craig's disappearance.

Lieutenant Shipley's claim of ignorance about Liam Zachary's and his father's investigation hadn't been true. Liars always placed their agenda as a priority, usually self-serving. Shipley had provided just enough information to lead the FBI on a wild chase. He'd played a game all along, observing Marc and Roden while they went through his father's office and offering pleasant conversation. Marc understood the Army would have removed secure information, but Shipley's denying the FBI true leads added to Marc's ire. The more he dwelled on the man holding back the truth, the more anger mounted. If Roden were here, he'd talk Marc off the ledge.

The manner and motive of Shipley's involvement confounded Marc. Could he be trusted when he'd lied to Roden and him at their first meeting? Whoever was responsible for the crimes had pocketed thousands of dollars, and they intended to keep it at the expense of lies and lives.

Where did the supplies go that Craig supposedly used to build the dam's foundation?

Marc checked his email for an update on his father's autopsy. The procedure had been completed. Nothing yet to report.

"It's time," Avery said from the window. "Talking to Granddad let me know he's safe, but he still refused to tell me where he's hiding. Maybe Lieutenant Shipley will be more cooperative."

"I don't trust anyone in the senator's so-called circle."

She faced him. "I understand what you're saying. It's hard for me to accept Granddad's vague responses and the excuse of keeping me protected when all of us have been threatened." She tilted her head. "Has your personal involvement affected your judgment?"

Avery had hit the target. "I'm all right." Marc punched in Shipley's number. The man answered on the first ring.

"Senator Elliott told me to expect your call," Shipley said, his tone cold.

"He told me you could be trusted, but from what I've experienced, I'm not so sure."

"This is bigger than your FBI suit."

Marc caught Avery's attention and smiled. He'd calm down for no other reason than the woman before him. "Really? Why agree to a partnership when you intended to lie and mislead Agent Clement and me? The FBI doesn't appreciate deceit. Are you aware my partner took a bullet meant for my mother in these crimes?"

"This conversation needs to be face-to-face," Shipley said.

"I agree. I'm at the Brazos River Ranch, and I'll let security at the gate know to expect you."

"Agent Wilkins, you're hot, and I don't blame you. I'm on the road and will be there in less than an hour. I'll only talk to you."

"Why not Avery?"

"She's too close to the situation."

★ ★ ★

Lieutenant Shipley sat across from Marc in Craig's closed office sipping coffee. Their brief cordial communication had hit the end.

"We'll talk in my truck." Marc stood and grabbed his mug. "I'm not taking any chances of a recording device hidden anywhere on this ranch. Neither do I think taking a walk makes sense with the way sound carries."

"The senator never took these extreme precautions."

"And look where he's at now."

Shipley grasped his mug and his hand jerked. "I get it."

In his truck, Marc turned on the AC to cool the cab from the grueling heat. When Shipley gazed out at the night surroundings, Marc pressed Record on his phone . . . just in case.

Shipley rubbed his face. Dramatics? Geared up to lie?

"I need the whole story," Marc said.

"What has the senator told you?"

"I want to hear your version."

Shipley repeated almost word for word what the senator had said earlier. "He is safe and working through various channels to bring closure to the problems."

"He's not working through the FBI, so is CID on this?"

"Somewhat."

"I see, which means this is your game. You're the 'various channels to bring closure to the problems'? Three men are dead, possibly four if Craig Holcombe has been killed."

Shipley's placid features showed a man in control. "I'm not the only person involved. The senator has requested you be given information. I'm complying, but I think it's a bad idea."

"Why? Are you any closer to finding the killer? Proving who's responsible for the faulty dam construction?" Marc took a sip of coffee before he fired with both barrels. Nothing pointed to Shipley, but it was his word against Marc's. "Is Representative Frank Benton a part of this?" Shipley's silence confirmed Marc's suspicions. "Give me what the senator has approved."

"Abbott, Liam, and the senator came to me for help six weeks ago. They were worried about their families and themselves. Their investigation hadn't gotten them anywhere. In my opinion, Craig Holcombe is a person of interest in the blackmail and extortion. The cover-up in the dam's defective structure leads back to him too. The senator couldn't reconcile himself to Holcombe being rear-deep in it, but since then he's reconsidered. Especially since Craig's disappearance. The senator isn't an idiot when it comes to Buddy and Saundra. The three could be working together, but we have nothing to go on. Surveillance and phone taps are inconclusive."

Marc set his mug on the dash. "If Senator Elliott is in prison, everything reverts to Avery. Is she viewed as easy to manipulate?"

"That's where the case goes foggy again. Hard to believe Buddy and Saundra would stoop to murdering their own daughter, but if they're already complicit in the other murders, Avery may be considered collateral damage. On the other hand, Craig has had a spotless record since his teen years before the senator took him in. But greed can change a person's priorities."

"There's no bequest for him in the senator's will. Craig is better off with the senator free of any accusations, and he appears smarter than to cut a deal with Buddy and Saundra. If Craig planned to end up on top, he'd get rid of Avery and stay in the senator's good graces."

Shipley gripped his fist. "With both of them out of the picture, Buddy and Saundra would contest the will and have the potential to gain it all. But we need evidence, and believe me, we've looked."

"Who is 'we'?"

"I'm not authorized to give you names. Just what I've told you."

Marc tapped his finger on the steering wheel to keep from punching Shipley. "This is a sophisticated plan, and framing someone is a central part of it. The obvious culprits are the senator, Craig, Buddy and Saundra, and Avery. The dam's construction and the murders point to all of them. Every one of them is incredibly intelligent. They'd not implicate themselves."

"Looking beyond them, who has the most to gain and the most to lose?" Shipley said.

"For sure the owner of a blue Yamaha Tracer 9 GT—the man who wears blue, gold, and red Nikes. A woman who phoned my mother looking for me and the woman who called me claiming to represent the senator's allies. Add the person who stole my father's gun, used a computer-generated voice to make threatening calls, and placed a GPS tracker on Avery's car."

"Vengeance. Someone who felt the senator cheated him." Shipley huffed. "The motive could be political or business. And we've gone through a list already."

"I'd like to see it."

"Not without permission."

"I suggest getting permission. Now. I want to talk to the senator's pastor and a recently fired ranch hand. I need the senator's whereabouts."

Shipley glanced at his watch. "He'll be at the ranch's main gate in about fifteen minutes."

50

THE TIME NEARED 9 P.M., still early, but Avery longed to go to bed. Donita Wilkins had bid them good night thirty minutes before. Tough day in view of all that had happened.

Tessa sat with her in the media room engrossed in a Netflix documentary on the FBI. Avery liked her. A typical teen, like the ones Avery worked with at church. Tessa had a bit of old-soul wisdom. Strikingly beautiful too with incredibly smooth skin, and thick honey-colored hair. Avery smiled. Marc already had the protection gene going, and keeping the boys away from Tessa might be a bigger challenge than he faced with any FBI case.

The sound of heavy feet in the hallway caught her attention. Marc and Lieutenant Shipley must need to speak to her. Avery drew in a cleansing breath. For a few moments her mind had wandered to a calmer place than reality.

"Hey, sweet girl." The man in the doorway startled her.

She flew into Granddad's strong arms, fighting tears but not fighting love. The smell of the man who'd always loved her, guided her, and shared his insight ushered strength into her weary body. Bigger than life but still a man. She hesitated to let him go.

Thank You.

Stepping back, she saw the wetness in his blue eyes and swiped beneath her own. "I was afraid I'd never see you again."

He touched her stitched arm, where she'd abandoned the sling earlier today. "My efforts to keep you safe failed."

"I'm okay." She scanned him from head to toe. He'd lost weight, and his weathered face offered a glimpse of the turmoil he'd suffered. "I have so many questions, but not now. Let me feast on having you home."

She glanced behind him to see Lieutenant Shipley. Marc nodded. The lieutenant maintained a grim demeanor. Granddad's arrival must not have his approval. But why?

"Gentlemen, I'd like a few minutes with my granddaughter before we talk business."

"I'll go to my room," Tessa said.

Granddad made his way to the girl's side. "No way. We'll talk in the library." He stuck out his hand, and she grasped it. "I'm Quinn Elliott."

"I'm Tessa Wilkins." She bit into her lower lip. "Your ranch is amazing."

"Thank you." Granddad turned his head slightly. "You favor your dad more than Marc, and you're a whole lot prettier than either of them. Your dad thought you and Marc hung the moon. Wish you were here under better circumstances."

"Me too."

"When this mess is handled, you'll need to head back and relax. So far have you been treated well?"

"Yes, sir. Avery's going to show me how to ride and shoot."

Granddad chuckled. "She's the best teacher I know." He glanced back at Avery. "I've hugged Mia, and I'll meet Mrs. Wilkins in the morning. The bags under your eyes tell me you're tuckered out. Would you rather talk in the morning?"

"Not at all."

"Okay. Marc, Shipley, join us in the library downstairs in about twenty minutes. Text me if you need something."

What she needed was concrete evidence to prove Granddad's innocence.

★ ★ ★

Avery and her granddad entered the massive library, and he shut the door. This was his favorite room and no wonder. He'd filled the floor-to-ceiling shelves with books on US and Texas history, politics, religion, philosophy, and biographies. Looking at him standing in the middle of wall-to-wall knowledge reminded her of the photo shoots done here and the countless renowned guests who've visited him here.

They sat on the leather sofa, and she held back her many questions for him to begin.

"You believe I'm innocent of Liam's death?"

"Without a doubt, but I can't figure out why you wouldn't tell me the truth. Or why I wasn't told about Colonel Wilkins's death." She paused. "Or should I ask who you're protecting me from?"

"I'm no closer to the who or the why than before. Liam and I were threatened if we attended Abbott's funeral, and I chose to spare you the tragic news. Not one of my smarter decisions because you'd still have learned about his death. Now I hear the dam is substandard. Have you ever mistrusted Craig?"

"Never."

"The diver provided two video logs showing the dam was constructed according to specs."

"I know. I saw them. Could Craig have falsified the videos?"

"Anything's possible. Can't bring myself to say he's guilty. Neither do I want to add him to the death list."

"Dad and Mom?"

He clenched his jaw. "I pray not. But someone is determined to ruin me . . . us."

"Are you staying?"

"Yes, even if it means an arrest." He took her hand. "During two separate phone calls, Marc called me a coward for subjecting everyone to the tragedies while I hid. The first time made me furious. The second time knocked some sense into this thick head. He's a good man, Avery. Every bit as fine as his father, and so much like him."

"They didn't have a relationship."

He nodded. "Abbott and I shared lots of hours discussing our regrets about our kids."

She glanced at the strong hand wrapped around hers. "I want to be a part of the discussion with Marc and Lieutenant Shipley."

He rubbed his face. "It could get heated."

"I'm already in the middle of the storm. The hurricane makes landfall tomorrow morning. Projected at eleven o'clock. Not sure why I'm not out there volunteering with first responders urging people to evacuate."

"I'm right with you. The dirty side of a hurricane is a powerful enemy. I've ordered several cases of water, food, and blankets to be delivered to either Galveston or shelters near the dam as soon as I get an address. Anonymous donation."

"Thank you. Text Marc and Shipley so we can get started. This will be a long night."

51

AVERY CHECKED THE PROGRESS of Hurricane Braxton on her phone while Marc and Lieutenant Shipley made their way to the library. The violent, slow-moving storm was forecast to dump an inordinate amount of rain well inland. Local news urged people below Lago de Cobre Dam to evacuate in the event of flooding. The same message she'd heard repeatedly since the dive report.

Granddad welcomed the men and gestured for them to be seated. "Marc, I'd like for you to facilitate this discussion. If not, we'll end up arguing and accomplish nothing."

"I'd be honored, sir. I'm laying out facts that aren't what any of us want to hear. But necessary to get to the bottom of how the Lago de Cobre Dam's structural problem occurred and the link to the murders. Bottom line is the senator and Avery are legally responsible and are suspects in both criminal activities. Craig's actions put him at the top of the list with them. Evidence stacks against him if money is his motive. Until we talk to him, we have lots of unanswered questions. Buddy and Saundra have motive and are persons of interest, which leads us back to at least three deaths, and I don't believe in coincidences." Marc turned to Granddad. "I'd like you to tell us what happened prior to Liam's death."

Granddad relayed threats to him and his deceased friends. He continued with the threats made against Avery if money wasn't paid that also included a public release of information about the faulty dam. "We met with Lieutenant Shipley at the corps office and told him everything. We knew about his previous work with CID and asked him to help find the blackmailer. The four of us wanted the dam inspected again to ensure the report and video matched the originals. Ingles seemed like the perfect choice given he'd already completed the dive the first time."

"Did Craig object to the additional inspection?" Marc said.

"He wanted to know why, and I told him to appease an old man's heart. We both are over-the-top diligent with safety. Ingles took the video and gave us a thorough inspection report that raised no red flags. I have both. Two days later Ingles died in a car accident. The police report stated he fell asleep at the wheel."

Marc sat back in his chair. "My father died three weeks after Ingles died. Liam the day of his funeral. Since then, a shooter has gone after my mother, Avery's been threatened more than once, my partner's in the hospital, and Craig's missing. I've also received distorted calls. One occurred last night."

He hadn't told Avery about the latest threat, but she'd been preoccupied with the office break-in. Like Granddad, Marc wanted to protect her, no matter how frustrating.

Avery's phone alerted her to a news update. "The media has their ammunition." She managed to remain calm when she'd like to scream at the unfairness. "Quinn Elliott Sr., past Texas senator and CEO of Elliott Construction, was responsible for constructing the Lago de

Cobre Dam on the Brazos River. Elliott Senior is reportedly under investigation for the dam's faulty construction, which has resulted in evacuating thousands of people in the surrounding area. The Army Corps of Engineers earlier today publicly released results of a dive team's inspection that confirmed issues with the dam's foundation that could result in a failure. Elliott hasn't been located for comment."

"We expected this," Granddad said. "I'm surprised it hasn't hit the news front sooner, and some of it has. We will handle this mess. The one or ones responsible can't hide forever."

"In the meantime, we look guilty," Avery said.

Lieutenant Shipley spoke up. "Why are we wasting time talking when it's obvious Craig Holcombe is behind the crimes? I suspect he's working with Buddy and Saundra. I—"

"Who rides a blue Yamaha motorcycle?" Avery said. "Who placed a tracer on my car? Wears blue, gold, and red Nikes?" She paused and punched the truth. "I saw the cyclist in Houston and heard his voice. He bore no resemblance to Craig."

Granddad stared at her like she'd grown horns. Her assertiveness surprised her too.

Shipley huffed. "You—"

"I'm not finished," she said. "The man you want to take the blame stayed with me at the hospital last winter when Granddad had pneumonia." Avery stood from the sofa and faced Shipley. "The man you want to blame is researching vet school. The man you want to blame talks to high school kids about staying away from crime. I'm not buying your know-it-all stance."

"You're protecting Craig just like your grandfather. He's a killer!"

Avery tamped down her fury. "Prove it. But not by accusing an innocent man because you don't know who's guilty."

Granddad added, "I think this is about more than money. Craig, Buddy, and Saundra have plenty of it. None of them are hurtin'. This is about hate and vengeance."

"As if your son and daughter-in-law don't hate you for cutting them off?" Shipley said. "Or Craig resent your interference in his life? He thinks this place couldn't run without him. That's motive for all three of them to frame you. Right along with Avery."

"Enough." Granddad reddened from the neck up. "You are a lousy judge of character. When I called you about Liam's murder, you dumped his body on a back road. Said he didn't know the difference—he was dead. His cell phone's missing, and what happened to his BMW?"

"I have both," Shipley said.

"And you call yourself a man who respects the law?" Granddad said. "Taking the easy way out? Wrap this up so your résumé sparkles? You don't deserve the uniform."

Avery stole a glance at Marc. Why didn't he intervene?

Granddad joined Avery, who stood facing Shipley. "We're here to make a plan. Not toss convictions or make inappropriate accusations. We have the same goal but different opinions. Only by calming down will we figure out who's responsible."

"Let's review the facts," Marc said. "Buddy and Saundra have been informed of their person-of-interest status. Can't question Craig until he's found. Who are the members of the circle?"

Shipley glanced at Granddad.

"We need those names." Marc's voice sounded calm, but she heard the firmness.

Granddad cleared his throat and aimed his words at Shipley. "By not providing Marc with names, he's handicapped working the case."

"Not a good idea." Shipley's face flushed. "Remember two of the members are dead. Our trusted friends need to be informed before we hand over their names and contact numbers to the FBI."

"Then I'll call them and make sure Marc has all he needs to work this case."

"Thank you," Marc said. "Lieutenant, are you still maintaining a behind-the-scenes approach on this investigation?"

"I am."

"All right. In the morning, I'll have an agent from Houston accompany me to interview a few people on my list."

"Who's the agent?" the lieutenant said. "I have a right to know."

"I'm not sure yet."

"Yes, you do. Wilkins, you're off the case."

"You have no authority." Marc maintained a stoic demeanor. "The governor requested the FBI work the investigation. You don't want me on the case? Take it up with him."

52

MARC SAT IN THE SENATOR'S LIBRARY long after everyone had left. The senator requested a private conversation with Shipley and walked him to his truck before he drove back to Fort Worth. The two men's discussion wasn't against the law, but that didn't mean Marc approved. In view of their earlier disagreement, perhaps they discussed how the two might cooperate.

Marc weighed each person's words and delivery from tonight to discern truth and lies. He'd always believed motivation led to the killer. Other investigators swore finding the killer determined the purpose of a murder. Perhaps both.

The guilty person or persons had gone to a lot of trouble to set up the senator, Avery, Craig, Buddy, and Saundra. Craig surfaced in the money equation . . . But if guilty, he'd been reckless. Unless Marc had totally misjudged character, he wasn't convinced any of them were guilty. But he'd been wrong in the past, and successful crimes demanded brilliant minds.

The woman who'd phoned Marc while Roden underwent surgery called the senator's insiders the "committee," but the senator referred to them as the circle. The Elliotts had a long list of enemies. No secrets there. What secret was buried so deep that to keep it hidden dictated murder and placed thousands of people at risk? The motive always swung back to the senator, Marc's father, and Liam Zachary. Two of those men were dead, and the third feared for his granddaughter. Who had the agenda and tools to cover up one crime after another?

The senator entered the library and closed the door. He walked slower and his drawn features showed his stress. "I've contacted those in the circle, and I'm ready to give you names."

Marc pulled out his phone to take notes. "Okay. Let's do it."

"Shipley, Congresswoman Jeannine Blackford, Congressman Frank Benton, the railroad commissioner, and the Texas attorney general. All are aware of the investigation. We've been friends for years, mostly to support each other and provide a person each could trust. We are a full circle of friendship."

Marc's mind exploded with the political fervor about to erupt. No surprise Shipley objected. "Okay. I'll contact them tomorrow. If Houston can't send an agent, I'll talk to the sheriff about helping out." He studied the senator. "Have you told me everything?"

He nodded. "Fresh out of ideas."

"Where did you go when you left the ranch the night of Liam's death?"

"Austin. Late that night, the circle met." He started for the door, then turned to Marc. "See you in the morning. Me and the Lord have some serious talking to do. Good night, Marc. Abbott would be proud to see you digging for truth."

"Thank you. I wish we'd stayed in contact." For the first time, Marc wished he'd experienced what others had witnessed.

The door closed and weariness settled on him. He missed Roden.

They'd been partners too long for Marc to work on a critical case without his input. The clock read 11:20 p.m. He tapped his finger on the arm of the chair. Roden played the night-owl game. Unless sedated, he'd be awake reading a sport biography or watching TV.

He pressed in Roden's number. If he didn't answer on the second ring, Marc would end the call. One ring.

"Hey, Marc. Are you breaking broncs and fishing at the ranch?"

The familiar upbeat voice sounded good. Real good. "I wish. Checking on you."

"Doing much better. Bored out of my mind. How's the case?"

"Complicated. Do you feel up to advising your partner?"

"Bring it on. Victoria's waiting on me hand and foot, and the girls hover over me like helicopters. Driving me nuts."

Marc took the next several minutes to detail what had transpired since Roden's hospitalization.

"And you're running down each of the circle members in the morning?"

"Right."

"Like you, my take is Senator Elliott and Avery have been framed. Craig Holcombe doesn't seem a likely suspect, especially since he's probably dead. Buddy and Saundra aren't smart enough to pull this off. My guess is they're sitting back hoping the family business reverts to them. Now, they might have hired someone to do their dirty work."

"True. Both are a little squirrelly," Marc said. "The evening Senator Elliott disappeared, Buddy drove to Austin. That's in my notes. I have a request in to check traffic cams. I want to know where he went and who he saw. I've ordered a background and the ME report on Bruce Ingles, the diver who conducted two video inspections of the dam. Another thing is Craig fired a ranch hand, and I'll talk to him in the morning."

"I'm curious about Shipley withholding information from our

first meeting with him. He knew about the threats and the investigation. The man's a control freak."

Marc laughed. "A pain in the rear too. I could have used you tonight to deal with him. But I managed."

"Do you suspect his involvement?"

"Not really. He wants to lead the investigation and dictate the path forward. I put in a request to see his military records and financials. Everything else is clean."

"See? You can run this investigation without me."

"Not really, Roden. We're a team."

"What's the ASAC saying about your working alone?"

"Another call for in the morning," Marc said.

Roden chuckled. "Keep me posted. One more observation. It's impossible for every foot of the ranch's perimeter to have security cams. Too much going on for you to run offense by yourself, and the sheriff's department is already running thin."

"Yeah. I'll remind the ASAC of the same thing when I plead for help."

A light outside flickered. The dog barked. "Hey, gotta go." Marc laid his phone on the library desk and doused the lights. He crept to the window. Only still darkness. Glancing around the room, he spotted a red light . . . probing.

Someone had a laser scope looking for a target.

He snatched his phone and group-texted Avery, Tessa, his mother, Mia, and the senator. **Prowler outside with laser. Stay put and don't turn on any lights.**

The second text went to the deputy leading up security at the front gate. **Prowler with laser on west side of house. Headed to check out.**

He rushed up the stairs to his room, flipping off lights as he went. After retrieving his Glock with a vow not to breathe without it again, he returned to the library for signs of the shooter. The dog no longer barked, but that didn't mean the shooter hadn't eliminated the animal, especially if he had a silencer.

Or the dog knew the shooter.

Marc slipped out the rear of the house and stole his way to the west side. Red dots appeared to the right of him. He crouched low and made his way in the opposite direction of the laser's pinpoint. Behind a hundred-year-old oak tree, a shadowed figure aimed what looked like a rifle at the library window.

Marc circled the area to the rear of the shooter, on alert for a change in the red laser. He wanted this guy alive, but he'd not hesitate to blow him away.

Lights and sirens made their way closer from the security gate. Twenty-five feet behind the figure, Marc took cover behind a tree. "FBI. Drop your weapon."

The shooter turned, firing repeatedly in and around the tree. Marc returned gunfire. A grunt of pain met Marc's ears, and he bolted forward, tackling a slender but muscular body.

The man fought back with a punch to Marc's face, sending his head into pounding spasms of pain. The man's wound didn't deter his fighting back, and he refused to release the rifle.

Marc seized the man's right hand and shoved the rifle barrel into the dirt. He grabbed the man's thumb, bending it back until his hand broke free of the weapon. Marc tossed it aside and flipped the man, pulling his arms behind him.

"Agent Wilkins," someone called. "Are you all right?"

"Yeah. Could use some cuffs. Call an ambulance too. This guy's shot." Marc stuck his knee into the shooter's back and reached for his LED flashlight to show his location. He then aimed it on the man facedown in the dirt. Blood poured from the man's left side.

A deputy handed Marc cuffs and the other offered an assist.

The man yelled, "Don't touch me."

"I know this guy," the same deputy said. "I thought he worked here at the ranch. Jake Drendle."

Marc noted his smooth features and ear-length blond hair. A kid.

"Marc?" Avery's voice carried across the night air.

"Follow the flashing lights."

She crashed through to the scene and joined them. "Are you okay? I heard the gunfire, so I grabbed my Sig."

"I'm fine. What happened to staying in your room?"

She huffed. "I deleted it."

"Spoken like a true Elliott," the deputy said.

The senator stepped into the scene. "Thanks, Deputy." He peered down at Drendle. "How did you get mixed up in this, Jake?"

"None of your business. You're going down, old man. Just watch what happens."

"If you didn't already have a bullet—" The senator stopped mid-sentence. No doubt thinking about the repercussion of finishing those words in front of law enforcement.

Drendle sneered. "Keep talkin', old man." He spit at Avery. "I should have let you die."

53

MARC WOKE WHEN HIS PHONE'S ALARM alerted him to 5:30 a.m. Three and a half hours of sleep should give him enough rest to push through the day. Maybe ten years ago. Between the throbbing headache and his body screaming out for rest, he'd pose as a candidate for Pathetic FBI Special Agent of the Year. He tossed off the blanket and headed for the shower before a one-on-one with Mia.

Hot water soothed his aching body. The idea of spending the rest of the day there sounded good—until he remembered yesterday his father's body had been autopsied. Another reason to stop whining and get out of the shower.

He slowly descended the stairway leading to the kitchen and smelled the fixings of sausage, jalapeños, and spices that would tickle the taste buds of the dead. Probably a bad metaphor with the case but undeniably true.

"Mornin', good-lookin'," he said to Mia, who stirred together corn bread batter. Dressed in jeans, sandals, and a button-down shirt, she appeared outfitted for the day.

She glanced up and frowned. "Morning to you. Why are you up so early? Expected you to sleep in after last night." She anchored one hand on her hip. "You look like the bad side of a beating."

"Feel like it too."

She nodded at the coffee station. "Just finished."

"You're a saint." He poured a mug decorated with a motif of the Brazos River Ranch. "Bet you'll be glad when we're all gone."

She handed him a package of M&M'S, then poured corn bread batter into a huge cast-iron skillet. "Depends on how I look at it. I love cooking for guests, but I hate what's brought y'all here. The senator is the finest man I've ever met. Oh, he had his faults and made me angry plenty of times, but his heart is one of a true gentleman who loves Jesus and wants the best for everyone."

Marc had contemplated Mia's possible involvement in the crimes. He'd observed her verbal and nonverbal communication, and she'd demonstrated admiration for the senator. "I want this ended too." He took a drink of the coffee. The first sip of the day was always the best. "How well were you acquainted with the Drendle kid?"

"Ah, you're up early to question me?"

Marc heard the teasing in her voice. "And if I am? Besides drinking the best coffee in the state and basking in the company of the most beautiful woman in Texas."

"My youngest son thought sweet-talking me would get him whatever he wanted too."

"Did it work?"

She shook a wooden spoon at him. "I wised up to him real fast." She shook her head. "Okay, Jake Drendle stayed to himself. A loner you'd call him. A little odd. Far as I know, he did his job until Craig fired him for abusing a horse."

"He has a clean police record and lives not far from here with his parents. You said odd?"

"More like peculiar. Can't put my finger on it. Could just be his way."

"What can you tell me about his folks?"

"They've been a part of the community their whole lives, but I don't know them well. What will happen to Jake?"

"After the doctor releases him from the hospital, he'll be in jail. Pulling a weapon on a federal officer with the intent to kill is a serious charge." Would a scared nineteen-year-old give him the information to stop the killing?

"Did he tell you much last night?"

Marc laughed and took another huge drink of the coffee. "Now who's interrogating whom?"

She grinned. "I'm a curious cook."

"He asked to see his dad. Refused to talk. But today he faces questioning."

"Hard to understand people and their wild behavior. I listened to the news earlier, and the hurricane's predicted landfall hasn't changed." She scraped the bowl ensuring every last drop of batter made it into the pan. "Most people near the dam have evacuated the area."

"The ones who stay behind risk their lives. Do you have friends or family near there?"

"A few friends who have abandoned their homes for higher ground." She trembled. "Whoever thinks those here at the ranch could be responsible need to look at what the senator, Avery, and Craig have done by donating thousands of dollars to take care of those in need. Makes me furious."

"I understand. Wish we could find Craig."

Mia swung to him. "Alive."

"I need to ask you something private." When she agreed, he continued. "Have you ever seen or heard anything from Craig that tainted his integrity? Or heard him argue with the senator or another person about an unusual topic?"

"He's rough on the hands when they are out of line or make mistakes. But he also delivers praises and encourages them. They respect him."

"Does he have feelings for Avery?"

"More like a big brother. Now he has Leanne, and they seem very happy." She sighed. "The idea of him hurt or worse tears me apart."

"Does he have family?" Marc's background check showed a half sister in Montana who hadn't heard from him in over twenty years.

"His father passed, and his mother is in a nearby dementia care facility. He visits her on Sunday afternoons." Mia tilted her head. "Ask the senator or Avery. He might have other family in the area. Before you ask about his friends, he works all the time, and his friendships are with the other hands and at church."

Marc gave her a thumbs-up. "Thanks." He sniffed. "When's breakfast? My stomach's growling."

"The corn bread's got to bake. For the record, your father loved my corn bread."

"Did you know him well?"

Mia tilted her head. "I've heard the talk about his younger years, but the man who visited the senator impressed me with his quiet mannerisms and wisdom."

"Thanks. Appreciate that." Something about his father, the man others knew, was drawing Marc closer to him.

"But the corn bread still needs to bake before breakfast."

"All right. I'll survive. Think I'll see what's happening at the stables."

"Refill your mug and take it with you. Maybe Craig's back."

Marc refused to tell her he'd be the first to know. Each hour ticking by lessened the chances of Craig turning up alive.

Last night, Drendle carried a military-grade scope rifle. Registered to his father, who claimed he didn't know the rifle was missing.

"I smell coffee."

Marc whirled to see Avery dressed in jeans that hugged her curves just right. "You're up way too early after our midnight party."

She gave Mia a kiss on the cheek and reached for a mug with an aerial view of the ranch. "And good morning to you too. Are you headed somewhere?"

"The stables, Miss Perky."

"I'll join you."

He wanted her company. Very much. Outside in the hours of predawn, the air hadn't taken on the extreme temps sure to come later in the day.

"Is it my company you want or—?"

Avery stepped in front of him and kissed him. She tasted of toothpaste and tenderness. Sweet and sassy.

And he wanted more.

In the pale light coming from the stables in the distance, Marc held her with one hand and drank in a long kiss that tasted better than the first sip of coffee any day.

54

AVERY HAD NEVER BEEN SO BOLD WITH A MAN. But after last night and fearing Marc might be hurt or worse, she'd shaken off more of her introverted, cautious self.

"I don't want to talk about this. Something I had to do." She stepped back. "You scared me to death last night."

"I'd have scared you sooner if I'd known this would happen."

She blinked for control. "Why didn't you ask me to help?"

"Because you're not trained law enforcement."

"I'm volunteering to protect my home and those I care about."

"The FBI looks at protection differently." The glimmer of a smile emerged.

"Marc, I realized something early this morning."

"You can't resist me?"

"No. Well, maybe. Seriously, Jake might be the man I saw on the motorcycle in Houston. Noting his body build make me think so.

But I don't recall any hair sticking out from under his helmet. Is there a way he might confess?"

"Possibly. If he pulled the trigger on Liam, he knows who else is involved. Cutting a deal for the name of the kingpin goes a long way in ending the crimes." Marc held her hand and stared toward the stables. "Craig fired him and because he'd allegedly abused a horse. But since Craig is missing, he might have stumbled onto the answers we need, and Drendle eliminated him. After breakfast, I'll pay him a visit."

"I'd like to come too. Confirming his voice takes this all farther down the road."

"Okay. A deputy will be with him at the hospital."

They walked on to the stables, and he released her hand. Good idea when gossip might put him in bad light with the FBI. The closer they moved to the ranch hands, the harder she tried to paste an everything-will-be-okay smile on her face. Her heart told her she failed.

Marc greeted four men readying for the day. "Do any of you have family or friends who are in the path of Hurricane Braxton?"

"Yes, sir, but they've taken to higher ground." JC drank coffee from a metal cup and leaned his lanky frame against a horse stall like a cowboy from the 1800s.

"Good. This could be serious and better safe than trapped by floodwaters."

"The senator's truck is here," JC said with a nod of his wide-brimmed hat. "Is he back at the ranch?"

"For now. I'm keeping him inside as much as I can."

"Don't hold your breath. Like lassoing a twister, but we'll do our best." He nodded his point. "What about Craig?"

"Hasn't turned up yet." Marc panned his gaze over the small group. "Anyone seen him?" They responded in the negative. "I'm sure you want to know about the excitement last night." Marc relayed spotting a shooter with a laser, bringing him down, and the identity.

"Jake? You've got to be kidding." Will's dark hair spilled over his ears, and his voice held a Spanish accent. "Has he been charged with the killings? Messin' with the dam?"

"He's in custody. I'm headed there this morning."

"Somebody ought to put a bullet in him." Will huffed.

"I did." Marc paused. "Make sure you men ride in pairs. This isn't over yet."

Will glanced around him. "We're okay. For the record, you have the best shot on the ranch standing beside you."

Marc tossed Avery a grin. "Then I'm in good hands. Do you men have any questions? If you need to talk, especially if the matter's private, text, call, or come looking for me."

"I have a question for Miss Avery." JC hung his empty cup on a stall latch. "What can I do for Zoom? We've been training him in the arena."

"How's he taking to the bridle?"

"Depends on his mood. I could check his temperament, and if I think he's ready, I'll toss on a blanket. But when I've tried before, he wouldn't cooperate. He prefers you."

She gave him a thumbs-up. "Go ahead. He might have changed his mind. I miss not riding him. Maybe later today."

Avery and Marc moved toward the house. Once clear of earshot of the ranch hands, he pointed to the sunrise. "Gorgeous. You carry a Sig. I'd think you'd prefer a smaller handgun."

"It's not too clunky."

"What kind of shot are you? You have earned the ranch hands' respect."

How was she to answer? "Oh . . . better than their mamas but not as good as their daddies."

Marc chuckled. "One day I've got to see for myself."

Avery and Marc entered the kitchen, and she watched Tessa busying herself with breakfast. She'd been frightened last night—the second female to fly into Marc's arms. His mother rushed in as number three. Marc greeted his mom and Tessa.

"Couldn't sleep, Sis?" Marc headed for the coffee. "Barely seven o'clock."

"Not really. You can make up for last night by pouring me a cup of coffee."

"Sugar and half-and-half?"

"Lots of both."

Avery wrapped her arm around Tessa's thin shoulders. Too much for one girl who had experienced more than many adults. "It's okay," she whispered. "He frightened all of us."

"Is the guy from last night in jail?"

"He's still in the hospital but from there, he'll head to jail."

"We're safe now? No one's going to hurt us?"

Another question Avery couldn't answer. She glanced at Marc.

"Sis, we came a long way last night in ending the crimes. Avery and I are talking to him this morning. Hopefully to settle this."

"Okay. And what about the dam holding?"

"The Army Corps of Engineers have their eye on it."

Tessa gave Avery her attention. "Could we celebrate after lunch and give me a riding lesson?"

"I'd love it."

Avery prayed they had reason to celebrate.

Tessa gave Marc a side hug. "Would you check on Gram before you leave?"

He held up his phone. "Checking now." He pressed in the number and informed hospice the reason for the call. After tossing a glance in Avery's direction, he walked to the kitchen patio door and outside. Not a good sign.

Avery sensed Tessa's growing anxiousness. She paced the kitchen floor. Not good either. She stopped and stared after Marc outside. "Tessa, give Marc a minute to get specifics about your grandmother."

The girl's shoulders lifted and fell. Slowly she faced Avery with tears streaming down her face. "I'm afraid Gram is gone, and I wasn't there to hold her hand while she breathed her last."

"I understand. I really do."

Tessa melted in Avery's embrace. "She's done everything for me. Always has. Been my mom and gram. Can't imagine her not in my life."

"When I think of something happening to Granddad, I can't breathe. But their passing will come, and there's nothing we can do about it."

Avery felt the strong arms of Granddad surround Tessa and her. "You two sweet girls need to accept the truth. None of us have any control of when the good Lord takes us home. What we do control is how much we love and show our love. You two are diamonds, God's diamonds."

"Thank you, Granddad."

"Me too," Tessa's tearful voice said.

"And we make mistakes too," he said. "Don't hold those against us."

Avery snuggled closer to him, and so did Tessa.

"We will get through the tragedies, the threats, and all the what-ifs, but only if we let God carry the burden."

"You have no idea what it's like." Tessa sobbed. "My mom dumped me with Gram. Didn't want a kid."

Avery sensed a burning in her spirit. "Yes, I do know what it's like. As soon as Marc gives you the latest report, we'll have our breakfast outside, and I'll tell you my story."

55

AVERY OBSERVED MARC through the glass patio doors, noting his FBI facade had vanished to one of concern . . . Big brother cared. He slid open the sliding-glass door, and his gaze leveled on Tessa.

"Is she still alive?" Tessa said.

"At the moment, yes. She had a bad night but is better this morning."

"The timeline?"

"At the most a week."

Tessa bit into her lower lip. "Have you sent her my messages?"

"I have. Maybe you'd like to do more today."

"I will. Can I record a video from your phone?"

"Sure."

"Breakfast is ready," Mia said. "Warm food made with love will help soothe the soul."

"That's our Mia," Granddad said. "Bacon, eggs, hash browns, corn bread, cinnamon rolls."

"Ah, I have a separate plate for you," she said. "Egg-white omelet with spinach and peppers. And a slice of whole wheat toast without butter or honey."

Granddad moaned, taking the edge off the visceral moment.

Avery turned to Tessa. "Breakfast on the patio?"

"I think so."

Marc lifted a brow at Avery.

"Just between girls," Avery said. "No guys allowed."

Outside, Avery and Tessa sat where the morning sounds of nature sang like a choir. How many times had she taken this incredible beauty for granted? She'd been blessed, and now it was time to help the teen work through her pain.

Tessa took a long drink of orange juice. "What did you have to tell me?"

"First, I want to say something about your mother."

"She didn't want me."

Empathy threaded through Avery's heart. "She left you with your grandmother, and abandonment hurts. But maybe she knew your grandmother would take better care of you than she ever could. And think about how much your dad loved you."

"A counselor said the same thing. So did Gram. I forgave my mother, but not without tons of help from Jesus and Gram." She swallowed hard. "Gram told me forgiveness was a gift to myself. Without it, I'd be eaten up with hate."

"She's right."

"I really miss Dad, and I see so much in Marc that reminds me of him. But you're right, I hurt, and I'm afraid something will happen to him."

"I'm here whenever you want to talk. Nothing will be repeated unless you give me permission."

"Thanks. Do you like my brother?"

"Yes. He's a fine man, and we're becoming good friends."

"Anything more?"

Marc had warned Avery about Tessa's fear of losing him. "I have no idea. We need to resolve the danger, and for now we're working side by side. Why?"

"He likes you. So do I. You two look good together."

Heat rose up Avery's neck and face. "Are you playing matchmaker?"

Tessa shrugged. "Maybe."

"Thought so. Have you asked him the same thing?"

"Not yet. I'm kinda worried a girlfriend would think I was in the way."

"Looks to me like you two are a great package together."

Tessa blinked. "Is that what you really think?"

"I do."

"Thanks. Makes me feel better. Marc said we came as a package deal, but hearing you say it means more. You wanted to talk to me, and I'm taking up the conversation."

"Not true. You and I have much in common. My parents always told me I'd been a mistake. If it hadn't been for Granddad, I'd have starved as a little girl, physically and emotionally. They let him keep me whenever he wanted, and I loved every minute with him."

Tessa placed her fork at her plate and tilted her head.

"When I was eleven, I had a breakdown, and my parents signed over custody to Granddad. While what my parents did sounds horrible, God had a much better plan for my life. My parents' abandonment was the best thing that ever happened to me. Granddad showed me Jesus and how to live life with goals and instilled in me the value of an education."

"Gram and Dad did the same for me."

"Tessa, you and I are survivors. We'll get through this and be stronger women for it. You can talk to me anytime because I've been where you are. Rejection and abandonment tell us we're no good, when we are diamonds, just like Granddad said." Avery touched Tessa's hand. "If we let our food get cold, Mia will be upset."

They finished in silence. Avery sank into her own thoughts, and she believed Tessa sorted out her own. Precious girl, filled with love and so much potential. They had much in common, including an irresistible FBI agent.

Avery and Tessa carried their empty plates inside. If not for the ugliness raging through them all, the kitchen scene would have resembled family and friends enjoying each other's company.

The doorbell rang and Granddad disappeared down the hall to answer it. A few moments later, footsteps sounded, but no voices indicated the visitor's name or purpose. Avery assumed it was one of the deputies—ranch hands used the back door so Mia could load them up with food.

Marc startled and scooted back from the table. "You've got to be kidding."

"What's wrong?" Avery said.

Roden Clement stood in the brick archway facing the breakfast area. He looked a little weak but bigger than life. "Mornin', Marc."

Marc drew him into a right-sided bear hug like they hadn't seen each other in weeks. "Tell me you didn't drive here."

"Okay, I won't." Roden's booming laughter filled the kitchen. "I heard you requested an agent. Hurt my feelings."

"What did Victoria say?"

Roden leaned on his left leg. His whole side must hurt. "The First Lady of the Clement household gave the devil a run for his money. If I come back with so much as a mosquito bite, I'm sleeping on the couch for a month."

"Oh, where does she put me?"

"There isn't a hole deep enough for you to hide."

Avery listened to the two men toss back and forth the banter of friendship. But she couldn't eliminate the worry of the storm, not just the hurricane but where the crimes were headed. Someone she and Granddad trusted had committed multiple murders to cover up a loathsome scheme. God help her if the guilty ones were her parents. Time to confront them.

56

SERVING A SEARCH WARRANT on an unsuspecting party always worked best, and Marc had secured a warrant from a local judge to search Jake Drendle's home. But first things first. At 10 a.m., Marc arrived at the hospital with Roden and Avery to interview Jake. They made their way to his guarded room. No doubt Jake's dad or an attorney awaited them, and Marc had no intention of informing Jake or anyone in his room about the legal document.

After displaying their FBI credentials and Avery presenting her driver's license to the guard, they entered the hospital room. Jake leaned back against propped pillows, and an IV ran healing fluids into his body. As expected, two men in their late forties sat on the far side of the bed. One man wore jeans and a button-down shirt, and the second man was dressed in a lightweight sport jacket over jeans. Both wore boots—standard gear for this community.

"Good morning, Jake," Marc said.

The kid sneered, must be his favorite response.

Marc extended his hand to the two seated men. "I'm FBI Special Agent Marc Wilkins, and this is my partner, Special Agent Roden Clement."

Mr. Sport Jacket stood and shook their hands. "Dale Morrow, the Drendles' attorney."

The second man reluctantly rose and lightly grasped Marc's hand, then Roden's. "Drendle. Jake's dad." He nodded at Avery. "Miss Elliott."

She returned the greeting and sat in a far corner, a prearranged position where she would observe Jake.

Morrow smiled. "You men must have taken a beating."

Marc forced a slim-lipped smile in return. "That's what happens when someone is trying to stop you from ending a crime spree. Are you aware of the charges against Jake?"

"We are," Morrow said. "Seems to me like they're trumped up since he gave you a beating."

Marc swallowed his retort. "Last night Jake refused to talk. I'm hoping he'll cooperate this morning."

The elder Drendle rose to his feet. "I don't like your implications. Last night was a misunderstanding. A kid's retaliation against the man who fired him."

"The foreman who fired him is missing."

"Jake couldn't see in the dark."

"That means shooting a man is all right?"

"Depends on who the man is."

"Sir, Jake entered private property clearly marked No Trespassing. The entrance gates are guarded by the sheriff's department and monitored with security cams. He jumped a fence where he knew the security cams were beyond range and used a rifle equipped with a laser scope and aimed at those inside the Elliott home. He attacked a federal officer and got himself shot. He's also a person of interest in the deaths of three men and attempted murder in two other cases."

Drendle shook a beefy finger at Marc. "You're just out to build your reputation by laying false accusations on my boy."

"Drendle, sit down," Morrow said. "Best allow me to manage the discussion."

Red-faced and with the look of an enraged bulldog, the elder Drendle eased onto the chair. "Earn your money or I'll find someone else to represent Jake."

Morrow stared at the senior Drendle. "You're making matters worse. Calm down, and let's continue the conversation, then you can decide if my representation is appropriate. Agent Wilkins and Agent Clement, you may question my client. Jake has the right to refuse to answer or consult with me before responding."

Marc understood those instructions were to remind Jake of his legal rights and to pacify Drendle, who'd be footing the bill. "We're ready, and I'm recording the interview."

"No problem," Morrow said. "Figured as much."

Marc selected Record on his phone. After confirming Jake's legal name, address, and birth date, he dove in. "Were you fired from the Brazos River Ranch by the foreman, Craig Holcombe?"

"Yes. False charges of mistreating a horse. He lied to get rid of me."

"Why? Is there something we need to know?"

"'Cause I'm smarter than he is. He's unorganized, an idiot, and I told him so."

"I need evidence and a witness to back up your statement."

"Like anyone would go against the all-important Elliotts or their people."

"The FBI doesn't care about status. If someone breaks the law, he or she faces charges. Do you know where Craig Holcombe is now?"

"How would I know? I'm not the scum's keeper."

"Jake, did you shoot Liam Zachary on the Brazos River Ranch?"

"No." Jake shook his head. "Never heard of him."

Marc wanted to say a killer didn't have to know his victim. "Have you made threatening phone calls to Avery Quinn Elliott Sr., Colonel Abbott Wilkins, Liam Zachary, Avery Elliott III, and myself?"

"Nope. Search my phone records."

"Do you own a Yamaha Tracer 9 GT?"

"No."

"Have you ever ridden one?"

"No."

"Did you threaten Avery Elliott III last week on Thursday night?"

"How could I when she was in Houston?"

"I never said where Miss Elliott was at the time."

Jake huffed. "News travels fast when the uber rich are rear-deep in crime."

Mr. Drendle chuckled.

"Where were you Sunday afternoon and night?" Marc said.

"With friends."

"I'll need names and contact info to validate your whereabouts. You can give them to your lawyer. Someone placed a pipe bomb in a car in Houston parked next to Avery Elliott's Mercedes. Was that you?"

"Not hardly."

"What kind of tennis shoes do you wear?"

Jake huffed again. "None of your business."

"Do you own a pair of Nikes?"

"I own lots of tennis shoes. No clue of the brands."

"Do you have any information regarding the disappearance of Craig Holcombe, the deaths of Bruce Ingles or Colonel Abbott Wilkins, the attempt on Donita Wilkins's or Miss Elliott's lives, the shooting of Special Agent Roden Clement, or the threats to any of these people including Avery Quinn Elliott Sr.?"

"I told you, no. How many times are you going to ask the same questions?"

"As many as it takes." Marc stared into the face of the young man hardened by his attitude and behavior.

"There you are," Drendle said. "My son's ignorant of any of these crimes."

Roden slowly stood, his enormous frame filling the room. "Looks like your son will have time to think about his answers while he's in jail for attacking a federal officer." He turned to Marc. "Agent Wilkins, you can stop the recording." Roden leaned over Jake's bed. "The bullet fired from the rifle and dug out of my shoulder matches the one you used last night." He turned and nodded at Marc and Avery. "I think we're done here. A little time might jar Jake's poor memory."

The three left the room.

At the end of the hall, Marc's curiosity got the best of him. "We haven't had time to compare the bullets."

Roden grinned. "The three back there don't know what we've done."

"Priceless," Avery said. "Jake has a solid role model in his daddy. Surprised he hasn't been in trouble before now. Guys, I made an observation back there. Jake isn't the one who threatened me in Houston or the man who wore Nikes when the car bomb exploded."

"You saw the guy in the Nikes after the explosion, right?" Roden said.

"No, I was facedown on the pavement."

"While your head and ears were ringing?"

She gasped. "I wouldn't have recognized his voice."

"Right, and once Jake figures that out, he's in deeper trouble than he thought. From his answers, he owns the Nikes."

Marc pressed the down arrow on the elevator. "Roden, would you mind checking his financials on the drive to the Drendle property? If he took on the kill orders, someone paid him."

"And before you two serve your warrant, would you take me back to the ranch? I want to keep Tessa company."

★ ★ ★

After returning Avery to the ranch, Marc drove to the Drendle farm with the search warrant. The element of their unexpected arrival could be their ace, but only if Jake's mother answered the door. Marc admired a well-maintained farmhouse, and a beagle barked and sniffed at them. Marc rang the doorbell while Roden stood back.

"How about taking over the interview with Mrs. Drendle?" Marc stepped back for Roden to take the lead.

"I'll turn on the charm."

"Thanks." Marc noted his drawn features. "Are you feeling okay?"

"I'll nap when we're done here."

The door opened, and a round-faced woman appeared wearing a kind smile.

"Mrs. Drendle?" Roden said. She nodded, and he continued. "I'm FBI Special Agent Roden Clement, and this is Special Agent Marc Wilkins. We have a search warrant for Jake's room and any areas where he stores his vehicle."

"He's in the hospital."

"Yes, ma'am. We just came from there." He offered his creds, and Marc followed suit.

She looked at both IDs and returned them. "I have no idea if these are real or fake. Let's see the search warrant."

Marc showed her the signed document. She read through it and pointed to a signature. "I recognize the judge's name. Says this is for Jake's room and garage, specifically for a motorcycle, which he doesn't have. I'll show you his room." She gestured them inside. "I'd better call my husband."

"Yes, ma'am. The search warrant gives us legal permission to conduct our work without the presence of Mr. Drendle or Attorney Morrow. Shouldn't take long."

"Go on ahead. If you're breaking the law, you'll go to jail. Our attorney will see to it." She held a hardened glint in her eyes.

Inside a room that took cleanliness to a power level, Marc and Roden snapped on nitrile gloves. They opened drawers in which every sock, T-shirt, and boxer lay perfectly folded and color coordinated.

Mrs. Drendle pulled a cell phone away from her ear. "Jake gets real upset if anything's out of place."

"We'll be careful," Roden said.

Nothing came to their attention in the chest of clothes. Roden moved to the closet, as pristine as the drawers—shirts arranged according to button-down, short-sleeved, long-sleeved, color, and three inches apart. Pants and jeans hung in the same orderly distinction. Shoes were stacked in plastic boxes with blue lids and labeled alphabetically according to type and color. A form of OCD rolled into Marc's mind. Mia had noted Jake was odd, peculiar. No wonder he considered Craig disorganized.

Roden pointed to a shoebox—Nikes. Blue. Gold. With red gel soles.

57

CONTRARY TO AVERY'S PRAYERS for Hurricane Braxton to blow itself out in the Gulf, the storm had made landfall on Galveston Island right on time. The dirty side headed straight for their area and the dam. Avery refused to show her concern in front of Tessa. Instead, during their time together, she'd look for every opportunity to reassure the girl that Marc and Roden had the skills to protect her and the others.

Tessa jogged into the stables and to Zoom's stall, where Avery brushed down her stallion. The teen wore a helmet and boots from Avery's stash.

"Where's Marc?" Tessa's eyes opened wide and . . . innocent.

"He dropped me off so you and I could spend time together."

"Did the man in the hospital confess? Is the trouble over?"

"The shooter will be released to the custody of the sheriff's department. He'll be held in jail without bond. Marc believes the man's responsible for some of the crimes. Maybe all of them."

"That's good news, right?"

Avery laid the brush aside and studied Tessa. "It's the best news we've learned in days. Your brother and Roden are experts."

"I'm not stupid. Someone hired the guy. What about a plea bargain?"

Tessa and her FBI documentaries. Add in her desire to be more a part of Marc's world. His work intrigued Avery and his ability to work through logic without letting emotions interfere. What would it be like for him to kiss her again . . . feel his arms around her—?

"Avery, I asked you a question."

Tessa's voice broke through her thoughts.

"I'm sorry. What did you say?"

"You must have been thinking about my brother because your face is red." She giggled. "I'm right. Anyway, I wanted to know about a plea bargain."

Avery regained her composure. "Oh yes. It's a possibility. We're hoping the man thinks about the charges against him and reconsiders his original statements of innocence."

Tessa chewed on her lip and nodded.

"Ready to get started?"

"Yes. I've wanted to learn how to ride all my life. What's the first thing I should do?"

"We begin with the basics. Don't walk behind the horse or the animal could get spooked. When that happens, the horse might kick out or twist. While the behavior is not the norm for most horses, it's a possibility. I'm putting you with a gelding by the name of Cozy. Like his name, he's incredibly gentle." Avery walked to his stall, and Tessa followed.

"What's a gelding?" Tessa said.

"He's been castrated, and the procedure removes the wildness of a stallion. Geldings are calmer, even-tempered." Avery picked up a bridle in her left hand and opened the stall door. She demonstrated how to place the halter over Cozy's nose and ears. "Slip the bit over his nose and into his mouth. Cozy doesn't mind the bit, but some horses need a little coaxing. The bit doesn't hurt them." Avery pointed out the noseband, browband, crownpiece, and throatlatch. "I think we're ready to make friends." She led Cozy from the stall.

"He's amazing. I love his gray color and black tail and mane." Tessa breathed in deeply. "Thanks for not making me feel stupid about my questions."

"We can't learn unless we ask questions." Avery patted Cozy. "Hey, handsome."

"Can I pet him?"

"Of course."

The girl stroked his neck and smiled. Wouldn't be the first time a horse succeeded as therapy for those under stress. "Tessa, watch his ears. They tilt in the direction of where he's paying attention. If they lay back, be cautious. By using a confident posture and filling him with sweet words, you can draw a horse in to make him feel safe with you."

"Are you listening, Cozy? We'll be good friends. I bet I can talk to you about anything. What's next, Avery?"

"The best approach to riding a horse is caring for the animal first." Avery pointed to a tack box. "Inside you'll find a comb and brush." Avery showed her how to groom the animal and Tessa obliged.

"Have you taught others to ride?"

"Many times. Are you ready for me to saddle him?" Tessa agreed and Avery picked up a saddle pad. She brushed off the dirt and placed the pad on his back. She then lifted the saddle onto Cozy's back. "This is a western saddle."

"Is that the kind most people use?"

"It is on our ranch." Avery ensured the girth strap and right stirrup were clear before she laid the saddle on the pad and lined up the horn. "Watch how I tighten the saddle. No one wants a saddle to slip. Now I'll finish securing the strap like a man ties a tie."

"Dad showed me. He said every woman should know how to do it."

Avery smiled. "The next time, you'll bridle and saddle him, and I'll watch. I think Cozy is ready for me to lead him into the arena." She pointed to the stable door. "We're heading to the indoor, air-conditioned arena to avoid the heat."

Once they met the sunlight streaming in through high windows, Avery showed Tessa how to lead him. "Before mounting him, be aware Cozy senses your confidence, which I mentioned before. Some horses don't mind if you mount from one side or the other, but some get skittish if approached from a different side. Cozy prefers mounting from the left. Reach up and grab the saddle horn to stabilize yourself. Put your left foot in the stirrup and swing your right leg over the saddle. Relax and sit back against it."

Tessa took a deep breath before she anchored her foot in the stirrup and swung her right leg over the saddle.

"Congratulations. You made it."

Tessa grinned. "So far. So good."

"Keep your weight in the stirrups. Hold the reins firm yet gentle, allowing them to rest. Don't pull back unless you want to stop. If you pull too tight, the horse believes he's in charge and will likely rear up."

Avery led Cozy around the arena, encouraging horse and rider. What a grand way to shake off the weight of the tragedies. Horses had been Avery's haven for years.

For a few hours, Avery had forgotten about the storms invading their lives. If Jake committed the murders, who ordered them?

Thunder cracked in the distance.

58

THE PLASTIC SHOEBOX CONTAINING Jake's Nikes matched Avery's description of the young man who'd helped her after the car explosion. Marc and Roden searched under the bed, between the mattresses, in the pillows, and the bookshelf. Nothing else surfaced in Jake's bedroom.

Mrs. Drendle blocked the doorway of Jake's room with her five-foot-four body. "Where are you taking my son's shoes?"

"Evidence," Marc said. "Shoes matching these were identified at a crime scene. We need to have any dirt or debris from the soles analyzed. If nothing matches our crime scene, it's to Jake's benefit."

"That's crazy. My son paid a hefty price for those."

Roden took over. "Ma'am, your son's shoes are amazing. Wish I could afford them. I assure you, once we're finished with our investigation, they will be returned."

"He'll be furious."

"We need to check Jake's garage before we leave you for the day. Does he share the space with you and Mr. Drendle?"

"Jake has his own garage. My husband and our lawyer should be here any minute."

"Yes, ma'am."

They followed her outside to a shedlike side door. "No one goes in there but Jake. He loves to tinker and values his privacy." She turned the knob. Locked.

"Do you have a key?" Roden said.

"No, I don't. Not sure my husband has one either. Really sorry, but it looks like y'all are finished here."

Roden twisted the knob but had no luck either. "Stand back, Mrs. Drendle."

"You're going to break the door?" The woman paled.

"Yes, ma'am, unless you have a key."

"What about your injury?" Marc said. "You could break the stitches."

"I'm smarter than that. And you're one to talk." Roden pushed with his right side, all defensive line of him. The door splintered on its hinges. "Thank You, God, for particleboard." He reached through a hole and unlocked the door.

Marc snapped on a light.

Rows of identical metal shelving in color-coded, labeled containers lined the walls. Not a speck of dirt anywhere. Even the shed window was spotless. An older-model black Ford truck glistened like a showroom special. Engine parts were stacked nearby on a workbench. But no motorcycle. How had Jake gotten to the Brazos River Ranch last night?

"See, nothing here," Mrs. Drendle said. "You gentlemen are free to go."

"Not just yet," Marc said. "Since this is Jake's space, we need to search for any indication of criminal activity." Outside a car door slammed, then another one. "That must be your husband and attorney. Agent Clement and I will be right here."

She left them alone in the garage. Roden whistled. "Would you look at this? Alphabetical too. This kid's OCD would make me crazy."

Marc walked to the shelf labeled *A* and read the contents of large and small containers. "Here's one tagged *Ammo*. He flipped over the lid to boxes of 9mm and rifle shells. "We'll take this with us." He moved on to the *B* section. "Nothing here shows the items needed to construct a bomb."

Roden examined a row midway in the shelving. "We got it, Marc."

"Got what?"

The elder Drendle barreled through the broken door. Morrow followed on his heels. "Slow down, Drendle. I verified their search warrant on the way here."

Roden placed a large plastic bin on a pristine table. In red lettering, the label read *Boom*. He pried open the lid, and Marc joined him to examine the contents. "This is exactly what we need to identify the makings of the pipe bomb in Houston."

Drendle spluttered. "Wait a minute. Just because Jake has a collection—"

"Collection?" Roden pulled a stapled booklet from the plastic bin. "Maybe you could explain why Jake has directions how to build a pipe bomb?"

"Just curious. A man has a right to study."

Roden's jaw tightened. This time Marc intervened. "Study this, Mr. Drendle. Jake had forty thousand dollars in cash recently deposited into his bank account in amounts of ten thousand dollars each. Where did a nineteen-year-old get that much money?"

59

THE DEPUTIES AT THE SECURITY GATE had no legal jurisdiction to stop Avery from leaving the ranch. Neither could they force her to tell them where she was going. No doubt as soon as she pulled away, they'd be on the phone to Marc and Granddad.

Avery took the long way to Mom and Dad's. She laughed aloud at the irony. Six months ago, she would have thought long and hard about confronting them. Their past and latest tricks would have poured through her mind, but she'd never conceivably moved forward. Six months ago, she had opinions but rarely voiced them. Six months ago, Jesus was a common trait between Granddad and her, but now she personally experienced His love and guidance. The horror of all the crimes had grown her as a woman . . . A difficult journey and yet worth every step.

Marc, where did he fit in with the new Avery? Not really new but more mature with years of learning ahead. She respected his leadership qualities, his gentle mannerisms, his take-charge personality—although she often balked at it. He invited her views on things, and when she caught him studying her . . . she sensed intense emotions that frightened her.

She just had friendships with guys in the past. Nothing serious. The truth was, when the right guy came along, she'd recognize him as the one. Could he be Marc?

Thinking for herself, making choices, and discovering the insights of faith came with responsibility. Like knocking on the door of the two people who'd given her life but also made it clear they wanted her out of theirs. Hard to accept. Harder yet to forgive. And she couldn't have taken the hurdle without Jesus . . . just like Tessa.

She slowed at the driveway and turned, leading to their home. Granddad hadn't spared any expense in providing for her parents, and although she'd never stepped inside it, she'd seen the blueprints and the invoices.

Right on cue, her cell phone rang—Granddad. "Yes, sir."

"Where are you?"

"Parked in front of Mom and Dad's."

He groaned. "Why? Never mind, I know the answer."

"I'm a grown woman, and I need to confront them on a few things. Where is Craig? If he's dead, where's his body? If he's alive, is he behind the murders and crimes?"

"Trained people are handling those questions." His voice softened. "I'm afraid for you."

She dug deep for courage. "I've discovered a few things about myself since the Monday I mistook you bending over a body for something inconceivable. I made a commitment to learn the truth. Your love and support have made me a survivor. Now I have to stand up for what I believe is right and face the consequences for my mistakes."

"You have big heartache, and I helped cause it. Because I wanted to protect you, always have. I interfered with your decisions, fought your battles, told you what to believe. When trouble hit, you weren't prepared. I'm sorry. Along the years, you grew up, and all I could see was the little girl who ached for someone to love her."

Avery swallowed the lump in her throat. "You showed me love when Mom and Dad told me I had no place in their lives. My indecision over so many things was my choice. I wanted you to take care of me. My education and position at the ranch and company masked my insecurity. My grad work and living away from home helped, but as a grown woman, I failed you."

"I was the adult first, so let me take the blame where it's due. I saw a difference the moment I laid eyes on you yesterday. You exhibited a strength I'd not seen before, and I'm proud of you. Please forgive this foolish old man."

"There's nothing to forgive. I love you. I'll always treasure you."

"But it doesn't stop me from being afraid. What you're doing right now isn't wise. Come on back home. Marc and Roden found proof to nail at least one of the crimes on Jake Drendle. He's also in line for the threats."

"Has Jake offered who's behind it?"

"Not yet. Marc thinks Jake will open up. He won't make it living in jail conditions with his OCD."

"Really great news. Doesn't change why I'm at Mom and Dad's. I'll call you on the way home." Avery dropped the phone into her shoulder bag and stretched her neck. Her stomach churned, the age-old response to stress. She prayed it faded fast.

Lightning streaked the sky.

Thunder cracked.

Weather forecasters expected to receive up to two inches of rain per hour in the Lago de Cobre Dam area. That could mean up to four feet in twenty-four hours.

Tomorrow's rainfall forecast claimed more of the same.

Flood management officials had issued a stage 2 flash flood warning.

Stepping from her battered car, she counted the steps to the front door. There was immaculate landscape, and any other time she'd take greater note of the flowers and bushes. Willing her heart to slow, she rang the doorbell.

The door opened and Dad eyed her from head to foot. His hair had grayed, and he looked so much like Granddad that the resemblance startled her.

"What brings you here? I'm busy."

"Good to see you too, Dad. Is Mom around? I'd like to talk to both of you."

"She's getting her nails done. Whatever you have to say, I'll relay to her." He glanced behind him. "I suppose you want to come in?"

"No. We can talk right here."

"Good, 'cause you're not welcome in my home." His eyes held anger, and she softened. Dad lived with misery, self-imposed but still misery.

"First thing on my list is to find out if you've heard or seen Craig."

"Nope. Told the FBI agents the same thing. I guess you and the senator might avoid arrest if you can nail Craig with the murders and faulty dam?"

Dad's resentment added jealousy to his vendetta. "The killer has been arrested. My concern is Craig."

"What about your mother and me? The FBI referred to us as persons of interest in the dam's poor structure."

"I care about you both, which brings me to my second point. I've held a grudge against you for too long. No point in going over any of it, but I forgive you."

Dad huffed. "Big of you. Did the senator send you on this mission trip?"

"No."

"You've said your piece, so get going. I have things to do." He walked out and pointed to her car. "What happened to your Mercedes?"

"Someone tried to kill me."

Dad startled. "Are you all right? Is that why your arm's bandaged?"

"Yes. A few stitches."

"Is the person under arrest?"

"I think so."

His gaze held a spark of what? Remorse? "What have you and the senator done to upset the wrong people?"

"I wish I had the answers. My last question, then I'll leave you alone. If you have the name of who's behind the crimes, I'm asking—no, I'm begging—for your help."

He shook his head. "Not a clue. Got my own concerns without getting involved."

"Okay." She walked to her car. Thunder rumbled.

"Avery."

She faced her dad, hoping like a child for a sign of any affection.

"Get him to change the will in my favor, and I might be able to help."

60

MARC RUBBED THE BACK of his neck and stared out an upstairs wall of windows. The rain beat the ground like a jackhammer boring through concrete. He'd hit the same concrete trying to obtain information from the circle members.

Shipley kept information locked inside his head. Marc suspected he deep-sixed evidence critical to the case.

Congressman Jeannine Blackford maintained that Craig Holcombe had the resources to blackmail the senator and sabotage the dam. "He's missing because he's hiding out," she said.

Congressman Frank Benton had been friends with the senator longer than Marc's father or Liam Zachary. "I haven't any developments that you aren't already aware of," Benton said. "But I'll tell you this. The kingpin has either installed a bug in the senator's office or phone. How else would the person have inside info to every facet of his life?"

The railroad commissioner had conducted the most research.

"When I learned about a separate crew pouring the dam's foundation, I ran a background check. The crew Craig used doesn't exist. Where did he find them, and where does that put him? Good luck telling Senator Elliott. He has a blind spot when it comes to his granddaughter and foreman."

"You suspect Avery played a role in this?"

"Wouldn't surprise me in the least. Look, I'm no fool, Agent Wilkins. Senator Elliott harbors a lot of guilt for the way his son and daughter-in-law mistreated her. But Avery has bad blood flowing through her veins."

Avery entered the room just as he ended the call and stood beside him, staring at the same rain, her arms folded across her chest. He could smell the light scent of her, like citrus and spring. Or maybe she reminded him of spring because of the fresh beauty she'd brought into his life.

"You look like life has kicked you in the gut," she said. "Guess it has."

"Phone conversations have me in analyzation mode."

"Here I thought you were mad because of my trip to see my parents."

He hadn't forgotten. "Very dangerous, Avery."

"Doesn't do any good to rake me over the coals when the deed is done."

"You scared me and your granddad."

"I'm sorry. We've all been frightened out of our wits, but talking to my parents face-to-face had solo stamped all over it."

"I'd have taken you."

"No, Marc. I needed to show Dad strength, courage, and say I'd forgiven him and Mom."

"You didn't talk to your mother?"

"She had a nail appointment."

"Is there a reunion in the future or hope of one?"

She shook her head. "He laughed at me. But I stayed in control. For . . . a moment I thought he might mellow." She blinked. "He'd give me a name of who might be behind the crimes if I convince Granddad to put him back in the will."

Marc had arrested a few lowlifes in his career, but animals cared more for their young than Avery's parents. "Good thing you went alone. I'd have leveled him."

"He'd have sued the FBI." Avery wrung her hands. "I don't hate them. Just feel sorry for their selfishness."

"Is it one parent more than the other?"

"Not really. My dad has the most issues with writing bad checks and gambling. Mom enjoys spending money."

They looked out on the flower garden and gazebo, where Tessa must have gotten caught in the rain. She wore earbuds and had anchored her phone into cutoffs. Her lithe body moved to a dance, the rhythm playing in her ears.

"My talented and beautiful little sister." The moment seemed reverent, as though peering inside Tessa's heart. Odd for him to think with such sentimentality.

"Each move is precise, graceful," Avery said.

"She told me our father paid for her dance lessons. I hope she wants to continue once we're in Houston."

"Artistic expression helps work through grief."

"I'll encourage it. Add counseling to the mix. She's been through tough times, and I'm not equipped to ask the right questions."

"Smart man."

"A timid man when I think about the responsibility. Tessa and I barely know each other." He smiled at her battling the rain to run to the house. "I may come begging for your help. You have experience with teen girls."

She tossed him a dimpled grin. "You have it. I like Tessa. We have much in common."

"I'm sure Tessa and I will have our ups and downs, but I'm committed to making it work. She brings out a powerful protective instinct." So did the woman beside him, but unlike the new relationship with Tessa, he wanted the one with Avery to develop slowly. Danger had brought them together, but a strong friendship and love would make sure they lasted. He'd held off long enough and turned to her. Fighting the effect she had over him neared impossible. He grasped her shoulders. "Avery, do you have a clue how much you mean to me?"

Her lips quivered. "Do you have a clue how much you mean to me?"

Marc sheltered her in his arms and kissed her tenderly, then deeper as they embraced.

"About time." Tessa stood in the doorway. "Thought you two were blind to what the rest of us had figured out."

He stepped back. Little sister had lousy timing. "I've been working on a case."

"I see." Tessa's voice was laced with humor.

Avery glanced up at him and grinned before she turned to Tessa.

"Your face is red, Avery. Tell you what, I'll leave you two alone. Dinner is ready, but I'll tell Mia you're working on a case."

"We're coming," Avery said. "No need to slow down progress."

"Right." His phone rang, and the ME's office displayed on the screen. "You two go on. I need to take this call. It's the medical examiner's office."

Tessa touched her mouth. "Dad's autopsy?"

He nodded and answered the phone. Neither Tessa nor Avery budged.

"Agent Wilkins, we've conducted the autopsy on your father. The complete toxicology report will take a few more days, but we found toxic levels of cyanide in his system."

Poisoned. "The symptoms masquerade as a heart attack?"

"Yes, sir. You'll be notified when the full report is available."

"Thank you." Marc always believed the truth set a person free. He lived by it, but how could he tell his sister and mother that the man they loved had been murdered? The explanation of his father's death angered him. No one deserved to take the life of another.

"Marc," Tessa whispered. "Dad didn't die of a heart attack? I mean, with all the stuff going on, I'm even more sure his death wasn't natural."

He opened his arms, and she crossed the room to let him hold her. Soft sobs caused her body to tremble against him. He glanced up at Avery, who offered a slight smile before she left the room. Then he'd break the news to his mother.

"Tessa, I believe our father and the others discovered a massive crime, and those behind it will do whatever it takes to cover their tracks. We believe the killer is in custody, but we don't have a name for who hired him."

"This is so scary."

Scary needed to be eliminated from Tessa, Avery, and Mom's vocabulary. "I'm working with trained people who will stop the killer and end the crimes."

"Soon? I know you can't promise because none of us are insiders to God's plan."

"I promise not to turn my back on any piece of evidence." But Marc feared the kingpin was hiding in plain sight.

AVERY WOKE WITH A JOLT. Her phone buzzed again, and she snatched it through sleep-laden eyes. Craig!

"Are you okay?" she said.

"No. Shot. Just . . . just found my phone. Help me. Near the Old River Gate."

The call ended. She hadn't been dreaming, and she knew Craig's location. Myriad questions bombarded her mind—why hadn't the deputies or ranch hands found him?

It was close to six thirty. She tossed back the blanket and texted Marc. **Craig called. He's hurt and I know where he is.**

He fired back a text. **Where?**

I'll show you. Meet me downstairs.

Be there in 5.

The two headed out the back door to a utility vehicle. They took a bumpy ride across the pasture with rain beating against the vehicle's roof. Gray skies. Waterlogged earth. Turmoil all around them. Avery hoped they didn't get stuck. She explained how Craig sometimes took a back road to the ranch through the Old River Gate.

"Years ago that was the main gate, but it flooded too many times. So Granddad installed the new one. If Craig's there—"

"Sounds like he's in bad shape," Marc said. "Can you deal with the state he's in?"

Her stomach rolled at the thought of Craig hurt . . . and the blood. "I'll be fine. He's alive, and I'm holding out for his survival. The area by the Old River Gate was searched . . . more than once."

"Right. We all have questions, and we'll figure it out later."

"I'm glad you're with me, Marc. You help me stay calm."

"In a short time we've been through a lot. I think we're a good team."

"Maybe so. Time will tell."

"As we get closer, stop the UTV and point me in the right direction."

"Won't you need me?" she said.

"Both of us have wounds, and I'm the trained agent."

"Really, Marc? And to think I just agreed we're a good team. I'd punch you, but I don't want to assault a federal officer." She drew in a breath. "Was Jake transferred to a cell?"

"Late last night. Roden and I hope a combination of a night in jail and his OCD will persuade him to talk."

Anger swirled where moments before she'd fought sickness. "Are you saying he might be released if he talks?"

"No, Avery. He's guilty of attempted murder. Talking could render a lesser sentence."

"I don't like the idea of a man dying, even for murder. But I hate the thought of him back on the streets more."

"Not a chance."

"Is your mother all right? She went straight to her room after dinner."

"Like Tessa, Mom believed our father was murdered, but the reality shook her up. The news also confirmed her as a target."

"I'm sorry. I'll make sure to spend some time with her today and Tessa."

"At the ranch. Promise me."

"Not going anywhere in this rain. Have you checked on the dam? The weather report says the storm's one of the slowest on record, dumping inches per hour as it creeps inland and now over us."

"Your granddad texted me before 5 a.m. with an update. He can't sleep with the chaos and the water's rising."

Jake's arrest for murder released the burden of guilt for those crimes but not the dam's poor construction. She pointed to a grove of oak and pine trees ahead. "The gate's in there. Not visible from the road, and you have to know where to look from this side."

"I'll walk the rest of the way."

"It's pouring, Marc."

"I need to search the area, and I have my phone."

Avery stopped the UTV to let him out. Lightning flashed. Thunder roared, and the wind whipped the rain horizontal. "I'm going with you."

He turned to her, his face granite. "Stay put." He jogged toward the trees, sloshing through mud and standing water. He wanted to spare her finding a body, and she appreciated it. Despite the suspicions against Craig, he was family, like one of Granddad's sons. She struggled with learning the truth, and the waiting tormented her soul.

Another flash of lightning. Closer. Thunder cracked the sound barrier. Several feet away, Marc circled the area, each time closing in on the perimeter. He slowed, then rushed toward something. What had he found? He bent to the wet ground and waved in her direction.

She pressed the gas pedal and raced toward him, the tires spinning in the mud, while she hoped and prayed he hadn't found a dead man. Marc battled the rain to tend to someone. He pulled his shirt over his head. To bandage a wound?

She pulled the UTV next to him. A pair of jeans and boots extended above a puddle.

"He's alive." Marc scooped him up and carried him to the vehicle's rear seat. "He has a bullet wound on his right side, and he's lost blood. I'll stay back here with him. He's unconscious."

She called 911 and alerted Granddad. While attempting to turn the UTV toward the ranch, she spun the wheels. They were stuck in mud.

"I'll push," Marc said. "Can you keep an eye on Craig while steering?"

Craig's blood- and rain-soaked clothes caught her attention, but his unconsciousness alarmed her the most. "Craig," she whispered. "Can you hear me?"

No response.

Marc shoved on the UTV.

Nothing.

He repeated.

Nothing.

"I'll walk back," he said. "No other choice."

Through the fog of pouring rain, Avery studied the water and mud-laden path to the house. "Looks like riders are headed this way."

Marc whirled around, water dripping from every inch of him. "I think you're right."

Within minutes JC and Will dismounted and hurried to the truck bed. "When the senator told us where you'd gone, we had a feelin' you needed help," JC said.

"You're an answer to prayer," Marc said. "Craig needs medical attention."

JC and Will helped Marc push the UTV out of the mud and back onto the path. The two ranch hands glanced at Craig before they mounted their horses and rode back to the house.

No matter how carefully Avery drove, she hit mudholes and low spots. Why hadn't anyone found Craig during the previous searches? He'd lain in the heat and storm, bleeding and hurt.

At the house, Granddad and Roden helped Marc carry Craig to the side enclosed porch. "You called for an ambulance?"

"Yes," Avery said.

Marc had wrapped his rain-soaked shirt around an open wound on Craig's right side. Blood seeped through and dripped down his arm.

"Craig," Granddad said. "If you hear me, move your head."

His eyelids fluttered.

Avery held her breath.

"Good." Granddad took his left hand. "Can you squeeze my hand?"

Craig obliged.

Marc leaned in. "Do you know who shot you?"

He didn't respond.

Avery stared at Marc. She wanted answers too.

Sirens sounded in the distance, reminding her of the car explosion and Marc's encounter with death.

"The ambulance is nearly here," Marc said. "Roden, want to ride with me, and we can run by the jail afterward? Could Jake have pulled the trigger before we arrested him?"

Roden held his bandaged arm. He must have hurt it when he helped to lift Craig. "I'm ready."

"Let me grab a clean shirt. Once Jake knows Craig survived, I'm betting he'll be ready to talk."

Avery wanted to believe he'd confess. Where did all this lead? Could the end be in sight?

She sensed Marc's attention on her. Had the crimes drawn the two together—to end the violent streak? Or something else?

62

MARC PACED THE FLOOR of the ER while a doctor examined Craig. A balding man in scrubs exited the treatment area and called for Agent Wilkins.

"Mr. Holcombe is in stable condition," the man said. "The doctor is admitting him."

"Can we talk to the patient?" Marc said.

The balding man pointed to the double ER doors. "He's the third patient on the right."

Marc and Roden found Craig awake, his bandaged side exposed. An IV sent life-sustaining fluids into his battered body. Marc had seen enough IVs from this case.

"I'm going to make it," Craig said.

"Of course you are," Marc said. "How are you feeling?"

"Like I've been shot and left to die in a wet pasture."

"Ranch hands looked there for you."

"I never heard or saw anyone, but I was out of it."

Marc gestured to Roden. "Do you remember my partner, Agent Clement?"

"I do. You look like you met the same shooter I did."

Roden nodded. "Appears so. Our shooter might be in jail." He told Craig about the incident at the ranch with Jake, the search warrant, and subsequent arrest.

Craig closed his eyes. "I'm a little weak. Hard to keep my brain working. What about the problem with the dam?"

"Marc and I are interviewing Jake after we leave here. He probably has the name of who's behind the crimes."

"He's a peculiar guy."

Marc picked up the conversation. "Obsessed with order and cleanliness. What happened when you were shot?"

"I was driving to the ranch and took the shortcut at the Old River Gate, where you found me. I parked my truck to open it. That's when someone shot me." He took a labored breath. "I stumbled through the gate and fell. Heard someone drive my truck away." Talking weakened Craig even more.

"Thanks. Get some rest. Looks like two people were involved since your truck's missing."

Craig nodded.

Outside in the hall, Marc caught Roden's attention. "If Jake is responsible, we need to investigate his friends."

"We'll toss it in the mix. Explain how Craig laid there all that time, didn't bleed out, and no one found him?"

"Doesn't make sense."

Leanne arrived as the agents left the ER. Her reddened eyes showed her care and concern.

Marc and Roden headed to the parking lot. "The mystery of where Craig found the separate crew to lay the dam's foundation is critical," Marc said.

"His background is clean since his teen years. And you requested the FIG to dig deep into his financials?"

"Yes. As well as the senator, Liam Zachary, and my father. They haven't found a thing we could use. Wish we had the ME's report on Bruce Ingles."

At the jail, a female deputy reported Jake refused to talk to them without his lawyer. No surprise there. They waited in wooden chairs at the sheriff's office for Dale Morrow. The game of keeping the FBI agents on their rears continued.

"You're not hiding a thing," Roden said, his voice low.

"Hiding what?"

"You and Avery. You're doing a lousy job of acting like nothing's going on between you two."

Marc maintained a placid demeanor, but that wouldn't last long with Roden. "We're just friends."

"I told Victoria's brother the same thing."

"I'll do a better job of hiding it."

Roden blew out a frustrated breath. "For a smart man, your actions are stupid. Do I need to remind you how an agent's emotions affect his judgment?"

"I'd never put her or anyone else in jeopardy."

"You already have by not admitting your feelings. Trust me, Senator Elliott sees everything. Is this lust or the real thing?"

Marc hesitated while he formed his words. If his attraction was only desire, he wouldn't be keeping a mental checklist of her compassion for others, intelligence, and the way she listened to others.

"Don't tell me you don't know."

"The real thing."

"That's worse in my opinion. What if I ask her?"

"Ask her what?"

"Look, Marc. If Avery is the woman for you, I'm glad. But use your head and hold off until we nail this case."

Marc digested his words. "You're right, and I will."

"Have you . . . ?"

"We've kissed. But what do I have to offer her, Roden?"

"Takes a whole lot more than a fat bank account to make a relationship work. It's in the sacrifices that Victoria and I have grown closer."

Dale Morrow entered the office, wearing a crisp white shirt and jeans. "Gentlemen. Let me have five minutes with my client. Sorry to keep you Feds sitting here." He greeted the deputy, and she led him behind closed doors.

Marc's phone alerted him to an update. Traffic cams in Austin showed Buddy had driven to the Four Seasons hotel as an invited guest of a private party. According to hotel waitstaff, the group played cards most of the night. Buddy left the hotel at eleven o'clock the following morning. Marc relayed the info to Roden.

"Gambling has ruined many a man. Makes sense since he left Saundra at home."

Five minutes moved into twenty before they were admitted to an interview room. Jake's gaunt and pale features indicated a bad jail experience compounded with his wound.

Marc and Roden seated themselves at a table across from Morrow and Jake, who rested his cuffed hands in his lap.

"How are you faring at the city's hotel?" Marc said.

Jake's nostrils flared. "Why?"

"You look like you haven't slept."

"I'm done with the—" Jake swore. "What do you want?"

"Agent Clement and I have a bit of news for you. We found Craig Holcombe."

"You gonna pin his murder on me too?"

"He's alive."

Jake frowned. "How sad."

"Easy," Morrow said.

Marc leaned in closer. "Did you shoot him and leave him for dead?"

"Not just no, but—"

Morrow touched his arm. "Don't say another word."

He wrestled with his handcuffs. "I hate this guy."

Roden took over. "Jake, my partner can be a pain. I get it. And here he is aggravating you after a night in jail. I bet the noise, the smells, and the filth kept you awake. Would me."

Jake shuddered. "I've got to get out of here."

"That's why I want to help. Let's talk about you giving us information, and I'll speak on your behalf to the judge."

Jake turned to Morrow. When the lawyer gave verbal permission, Jake agreed to hear Roden out.

"You're a smart man. You're organized, and I bet you know where everything is. Someone used you to murder because that person knew you'd do a good job and clean up the messes. The person paid you more money than you'd ever dreamed, but the stipulation was that you and possibly your parents would be killed if the information leaked."

The cuffed man paled.

"I'd feel the same way if my family was threatened," Roden said. "Whoever hired you set you up to take the blame for all the murders. We found the proof in your garage. Without your help, this guy goes free. You, on the other hand, could face the death penalty. At the very least, life imprisonment, which is worse conditions than what you've gone through in here. We learned you deposited ten thousand dollars cash into your account on four separate occasions. So, Jake, what crimes were committed for you to receive the exact amount of money each time? Strange how the deposits coincide with Bruce Ingles's and Liam Zachary's deaths, the car bombing in Houston, the supplies and instructions to build a bomb found in your garage, and right after Craig Holcombe went missing."

"Jake, you don't have to tell these men a thing," Morrow said. "We can talk first."

Jake moaned. "Doesn't matter. I have no clue who hired me. All arranged by phone in a weird voice. I ignored it at first, but then the guy told me where to pick up the ten grand—"

"Where?" Roden's gentle tone caused Jake to blink.

"A spot on our property. In a brown paper bag."

"What did you do when you found it?"

"Deposited the money into my account. Stupid thing to do."

"The person called me four days later. I told him I wasn't going to kill anybody, but he threatened to kill Mom and Dad if I refused. I had no choice. The first person was the Ingles guy." He shrugged. "Found where he drank, joined him, and slipped a sleeping pill into his drink. The voice would give me a name, and when I carried it out, the voice let me know when and where to pick up the cash."

"Always the same spot?"

"No. Different places on our land."

Marc stepped in. "Now you know how upset I am about my father's death, my mother as a target, and my partner getting shot."

Fear streaked across Jake's face. "Look, I had a list. Ingles, Zachary, Avery, and your mother were on it."

"Did you plant a bomb beside Avery's car?"

"Yes." He stole a glance at his attorney. "Avery's always been good to me, and I couldn't bring myself to kill her. Afterward, I wanted to make sure she hadn't been hurt too badly. Not sure why I got paid on that one."

"You took off when the police and ambulances arrived?"

He nodded. "Wait, what's your father's name?"

"Colonel Abbott Wilkins of the Army Corps of Engineers. Worked out of the Fort Worth office. Originally thought he died of a heart attack but later learned he'd been poisoned by cyanide." Marc heard a level of pride in his voice at stating his father's name. Strange.

Jake closed his eyes and leaned his head back. "I'd give you a name if I had one. But I had nothing to do with your father, and I didn't pull the trigger on Holcombe."

63

FRIDAY EVENING, Marc viewed a press conference online conducted by District Commander Colonel Knowles of the Army Corps of Engineers in Fort Worth. Senator Elliott, Roden, and Avery viewed the colonel on a big screen in the senator's library. Colonel Knowles shared the emergency measures to help those affected by the flooding and offered a website with a list of FAQs. He announced the arrest of Jake Drendle in a series of murders tied to the construction of the Lago de Cobre Dam.

"Senator Elliott is the contractor for the dam," a female reporter said. "Why hasn't he been charged?"

"The situation is under investigation."

"What about the inspections?" another reporter said. "Aren't those supposed to catch and prevent construction issues? Elliott constructed a faulty dam, and innocent people are impacted."

"Their safety is foremost in mind, and many have been evacuated as a precaution. Those responsible for the dam's foundation problems will face charges once we have concluded our investigation."

Questions mounted, but Colonel Knowles ended the press conference.

"I spoke to Knowles yesterday," the senator said. "I updated him on the investigation."

"Does he know about the threats?" Marc said.

"Yes, which is why I'm not in jail."

"What about Shipley?"

"He's done his best to help end the crimes. But he doesn't have any more answers than we do."

"With the sophistication of these crimes, someone laid the groundwork for Drendle to take the fall." Marc glanced at the time. "The ranch hands are ending the day, and Roden and I need a word with them."

He sensed Avery's gaze. "I want to talk to Craig again tonight."

The senator stood. "Ask him why the dam's foundation doesn't meet specs."

"Roden, are you feeling up to a hospital trip?" Marc said.

The big man joined the senator. "I'm not missing out on any of this. Senator, we'll pose your questions, but we insist you remain here. It's for your own protection."

"What about my granddaughter? Her—"

"She stays here too." Marc picked up his phone. "I'll call security at the gate to arrange a deputy is with you once we're ready to leave."

"That's not fair." Avery's voice rose over Marc's.

"Too dangerous," Marc said, "and we're not taking any unnecessary risks. Isn't Shipley driving here tonight?"

The senator nodded. "With all the rain, he wanted to monitor the low-lying areas."

"Why here?" Avery said. "Can't he find a hotel?"

The senator eyed her curiously. "What happened to my complacent granddaughter?"

Avery crossed her arms over her chest. "She's an Elliott."

★ ★ ★

Marc and Roden gathered the ranch hands at the stable before many of them drove home. They'd spent a long day driving cattle and horses to higher ground. Tired, mud-covered men faced them.

"This won't take five minutes," Marc said. "Many of you know Craig was found early this morning on the northwest corner of the ranch near the Old River Gate. He'd been shot and is now hospitalized. He doesn't know who pulled the trigger. JC and Will followed their guts and rode out to help us. Without them, not sure Craig would be alive."

"Agent Wilkins," JC said. "We searched the area where you found Craig. He wasn't there."

Marc scanned the crowd of exhausted men. "How many of you rode the fence line near that gate?"

Four men raised their fingers. "Twice," Will said. "Maybe he stumbled through the fence from the other side and doesn't remember it."

"We searched there too," JC said.

That contradicted Craig's story.

"JC and I rode out there after the ambulance picked him up." Will rubbed his jaw. "I'm telling you, we'd have seen him."

★ ★ ★

Roden remained strangely quiet while Marc drove to the hospital. "Marc, I have a few suspicions about Craig. I believed he ran with the winning team, but I made a critical error in my evaluation. He's hiding something or is afraid to speak up. The timing's all wrong, and by all rights, he should be dead."

"The rain washed away tracks of those riding out to look for him. Let's get the doctor on the phone. It's late but the answering service might alert him."

"I'm on it." Roden left an urgent message and added his position at the FBI.

Within five minutes, Craig's doctor called and Roden pressed Speaker. "Yes, sir. We're looking for the time Mr. Holcombe was shot. With the rain, it's hard to tell."

"Approximately five to six hours before being transported to the hospital."

"You're sure?"

"I am."

"Thanks, Doctor. Appreciate your returning the call," Roden said.

Marc shoved pieces around in his head. "Craig lied to us. His whole story is a lie. Jake couldn't have shot him. And the call to Avery? Looks like another detail of covering this up. Craig had his phone in his hand when I found him."

"I'll get a warrant for his previous and present cell phone records. Those might give us a clue to what's going on." Roden sent the request. "I'd like to give the questioning a rest and not let on that we talked to the doctor."

"Sounds good to me. He might give us more info if he thinks we swallowed his story." Marc's thoughts did another kick at the doors of his mind. "Someone still shot him. Jake denied pulling the trigger, but he didn't say a word about the other shootings. Is Craig afraid to give the shooter's name? Or would he have shot himself and tossed the weapon to make us think he was a victim?"

"He'd risk hitting an internal organ. But when I leverage Craig's lies concerning the dam's foundation, I wonder what else he's lied about."

Marc turned to his partner. "Don't let me forget to post a deputy outside his room for his protection until we figure out his role."

At the hospital, Marc and Roden flashed their creds to the deputy and gained access to Craig's room. The injured man lay propped in bed with the TV on and the remote in his hand.

Craig greeted them and pressed off the TV. "Didn't expect you two on a Friday night. But I'm glad you're here. Leanne left about thirty minutes ago, and I'm bored out of my mind."

Roden clicked better with Craig, and Marc wanted to study him, so he took the farthest chair.

"Are they taking good care of you?" Roden seated himself closer to Craig.

"Okay, but I'm ready to leave. My own bed sounds real inviting."

"The doctor needed to get a few bags of IVs in you after the shooting."

"Right." Craig sobered. "Glad my fingers found the right buttons to call Avery."

"Had you tried Leanne?"

"Nah. She'd have been too emotional. Avery has the logical gene." Craig shuddered. "Lying there in the rain was the worst night of my life."

"You mean nights?"

"No. I'd been gone a couple of days, and I took the Old River Gate entrance. Someone shot me when I closed it."

"Why there and not the front gate?"

"Long story."

"Where were you all this time and why didn't you tell anyone you were leaving?"

Craig worried his lip. "Stuff, Agents. Not illegal but nothing I'm proud of."

Marc inwardly startled. Later he'd piece together what it all meant. "We're having a hard time figuring out the truth behind the crew who poured the dam's foundation. Unable to locate them, and evidence points to a bogus crew."

Craig frowned. "You're kidding."

"We'll get it straightened out," Roden said. "Is the doctor releasing you in the morning?"

"That's what he said. With all this rain, I'm worried about the livestock."

"They've been moved to higher ground."

Craig appeared to fight sleep. "Those guys do just fine without me."

"You scared them."

"I'll apologize." He studied Marc. "You're not talking much, which tells me you think I'm rear-deep in crimes."

Marc couldn't figure this guy out. One minute he wanted to cuff him, and the next he hesitated. "Your actions make you look guilty of sabotaging the dam."

"I swear, I'm on the side of the good guys."

"Until we hear your long story, you're in protective custody. And a person of interest. Deputies will be posted outside your door."

"I understand, and I don't blame you. The nurse gave me a sleep med or I'd unload now."

Marc and Roden stood. "We need to get back to the ranch. Lieutenant Shipley is driving in," Marc said.

"He doesn't sleep much."

"You know from experience?"

"Just observation."

Did Craig purposely allude to Shipley's stellar reputation? He glanced at Roden. "Is there anything else you'd like to ask Craig, or should it wait until the morning?"

"Don't think so. We'll request the sheriff's department to escort you back to the ranch."

"Leanne asked to pick me up." Craig covered his mouth to stifle a yawn. "She'll find out I'm in custody soon enough. Guess it's best she hear it from me. The deputies outside my door will stay?"

Roden nodded. "We want the person who planned these crimes in cuffs."

"I still believe it's Buddy and Saundra. They've caused the senator and Avery a lot of headaches. I have no idea who shot me, but I wouldn't put it past one of them."

Craig thought he'd pulled off whatever he tried to hide. He had between now and at the ranch tomorrow to concoct a story or make a confession. Which would it be?

64

AVERY HAD LONGED TO TALK to Granddad, one-on-one, for hours.
But Shipley's ETA gave them about twenty minutes. She walked onto
the massive second-floor balcony where he stared into the darkness
toward the cemetery.

"It's time, Granddad. Time these attacks against you, me, and
innocent people ended."

"I've been praying for the same thing."

They'd always shared an uncanny sense of perception for each
other . . . A need to talk. Deep pain. Sickness. Celebrations. Knowing
one was at the other end of a phone call without a ring.

He drew her to him with a hug around the waist. "I do like the
spunky gal standing in front of me right now. Reminds me even more
of her grandmother."

Avery smiled and leaned into his shoulder. "I'm working on it."

"But I know a secret about you." He eyed her curiously. "You beat
the tar out of the girl in junior high who bullied you."

She covered her mouth to stifle a giggle. "I'm ashamed of it. How did you find out?"

"The janitor."

"Now Leanne and I are best friends. And I've apologized to her countless times. Glad to see she and Craig are together."

"Life is full of surprises."

"Honestly, are Mom and Dad behind this?"

"I wish I had an answer. Truth is, I have a lot of enemies."

"The kind who kill. Who want both of us destroyed and don't care who gets in their way." Avery shuddered. "Right now, I can't suspect Craig. He could pull it off, but he'd need motive, and now he's a victim. I'm back to Mom and Dad. When you, Liam, and Abbott discussed the threats, who came to mind?"

"Political opposition." He shook his head. "Buddy and Saundra."

She heard the angst in his tone. "Granddad, we've weathered storms before, and we will again."

"You're right, sweet girl. Let's promise each other to move forward with a more mature relationship."

She kissed his scruffy cheek. "Deal."

"Tell me, where does Marc fit?" He faced her. "Neither of you are fooling me."

Avery hoped no one else had picked up on their growing . . . attraction. "We've been through a lot together in a short time."

He chuckled. "I detect more than an FBI agent working on a case. Yes, his father is a victim in the murders and his mother faced a near assassination, but the way he looks at you is a man smitten. And the way you look at him says you feel the same way."

She let the joy of thinking about Marc flow through her. "When we're together, he backs off."

"He has to keep his emotions grazing in the back pasture or his judgment could be impaired. When he and Roden make arrests, then you'll know I'm right."

In the distance, headlights of a car stopped at the gate. Granddad immediately received a phone call. "Yes, let Lieutenant Shipley in. Thanks." He pocketed his phone and watched the headlights approach. "Maybe he has good news for a change."

65

THE RAIN FELL in miserable gray sheets, causing a curtain of low spirits and concern for those caught in flooding. Heavy drops splattered the balcony outside Avery's bedroom in a cadence of gloom.

She glanced at the time—barely 8 a.m., and already she wished the day were over.

Or the rain stopped.

Or arrests were made beyond Jake.

Or proof her parents weren't behind the crimes.

Or she'd wake up and discover this had been a nightmare.

Or Craig hadn't betrayed Granddad's love and trust.

She reflected on the latter thought. Last night's discussion with Granddad brought them back together in honesty and strength. They'd confessed their mistakes from the past and committed to a better future. Couldn't those character growths have happened without deaths? Times like these, she didn't understand God's hand. But that's why He was God, and she wasn't.

Granddad and Shipley had taken residence in the library last night, and they stayed behind closed doors long after Marc and Roden returned. Earlier she'd gone for coffee and heard muffled voices inside the library. Had Marc and Roden joined them? Marc had announced last night that the two planned to delve into reports and consult with Granddad and Shipley.

Staying in her room until the world changed for the better tempted her. Although the idea made her seem incredibly selfish, and she detested the trait. Instead, she'd spend time today with Donita and Tessa.

Now to shower and dress. Not her typical Saturday of running errands.

She'd plaster on a friendly face and think about someone other than herself.

God, help me. I want to crumble. So many concerns, and I need You to help me stay strong.

★ ★ ★

In the kitchen, Tessa sipped on coffee. Avery had never seen one teenager inhale so much coffee. But with what Tessa placed in it, the taste must resemble a candy bar. This morning she sat at the counter staring at her phone with a tall glass mug of some sugary delight and a huge mound of whipped cream. A straw perched from the top like a flagpole on a snowy mountain peak. Avery kissed the top of the teen's head. A pair of green eyes smiled back at her.

Donita stared out the breakfast area patio, no doubt feeling similar angst. Avery poured another cup and stood beside the woman.

"Good morning," Avery said.

Sad eyes stared back at her. Had she been crying? "Morning."

"Need coffee?"

"No thanks. I've had plenty. I saw where people living in low areas faced evacuation by boat."

"I pray the dam holds."

"I pray that too."

Avery studied the identical gloom from earlier in her bedroom. "We all are filled with too many fears."

Donita tilted her head, a lovely woman who had given Marc his gorgeous brown eyes and olive-colored skin. "I'm glad my son has a good friend like you. This is difficult for all of us—the deaths, the threats, and unpredictable weather."

Avery gestured around her. "This house feels like a prison. I long to ride, and I thought you, Tessa, and I could have some girl-time. So far, we're stuck inside because of the rain, wishing we were ducks."

"Rather than sitting ducks?"

Avery moaned. "Good one."

"Is there more between you and my son?"

Sounded like a question repeated from last night with Granddad. "We're good friends."

"A solid relationship begins with friendship. Is that why he kissed you?" A smile played on Donita's lips.

"Tessa tell you?"

"Yes. We're getting to know each other quite nicely. She's precious."

"Smart and very typical." Avery swung her gaze to Tessa, oblivious to the world except on her device. "Marc's a good big brother. He's looking forward to building a home for Tessa and him."

"They were to search tomorrow, but another day will do."

"Marc and I are still friends."

"Uh-huh. Let's see where that goes after this nasty business is over."

Another phrase echoing from Granddad.

"He has lots of hurt inside him for the way his father abandoned us. When Abbott found the courage to ask Marc for forgiveness, he was killed."

"Don't you think he's viewing his dad through Tessa's eyes? I mean, in a healthy way? He told me about chats with her, and those were positive. He also told me about finding evidence of his dad keeping up with his growing-up years."

"I agree, and time with prayer is the best prescription for both of them."

Tessa stood from the kitchen counter. "Hey, can we do something? Even if it's with umbrellas? I'm so bored."

Or had Tessa changed the subject because talking about Marc and their father was uncomfortable? "Sure," Avery said. "Any suggestions?"

Mia entered the kitchen. "I heard your question. Here are two ideas for you lovely ladies. A visit to the stables and riding in the enclosed arena. The second is a cookie bake."

Tessa's eyes widened. "Gram said cookies were the next best thing to an angel's kiss."

Mia glanced at Avery and Donita. "Are you up for whipping up something gooey and chocolate?" When they chimed in, Mia reached into the fridge's freezer and pulled out a pound of butter quarters. "I'll go ahead and soften these."

Maybe today would have a happy ending.

Maybe today would shower them with answers and relief.

Maybe today would end in the same depression they felt but refused to discuss.

A whirling sensation in the pit of Avery's stomach edged toward uneasiness. No point in fooling herself. Nothing changed unless the guilty person knocked on their front door and showed up in cuffs.

66

MARC GREW TIRED OF LISTENING to the senator and Shipley say the same things—backward, forward, and arguing all the way. No way would these two figure out the end of someone's vile game.

When a text flew into Marc's and Roden's phones from one of the deputies stationed at the hospital about Craig's release, they excused themselves and made their way up a flight of stairs to the balcony off a massive sitting area.

Roden phoned Craig for details and placed his phone on speaker. Although the rain continued, they could still hear.

"Heard you were getting dismissed around three," Roden said. "Need us to pick you up, or are you fine with a deputy?"

"I'm good with a deputy. Leanne is here, and she's having a prescription filled and will follow us to the ranch. She wanted me to stay with her for a couple of days, but that looks bad and people talk." He hesitated. "I told her about the person-of-interest thing."

"Craig, it's safer here for you. The flip side is how would you feel if Leanne got in the way of a stray bullet at her home? It's happened here more than once."

"You're right. Thanks for looking out for us."

Marc wrestled with Craig's innocence or guilt. But he'd been fooled before.

"You got it. See you and Leanne soon." Roden pocketed his phone. "He thinks he pulled a good play."

"I'd like more info on Leanne," Marc said. "Mind if I talk to Avery?"

"She might open up more to you about Leanne if I'm not there." He grinned. "Gives you time alone."

Marc nodded. "Never could pull anything over on you. Hey, did you hear anything new last night or today with the senator and Shipley?"

"Shipley insists Jake Drendle pulled this all off himself and refuses to listen to Senator Elliott's arguments about the impossibility of a single person at the helm. Can't figure out why unless he just wants it over. I'm going to rest in my room. Text me when you know something."

Marc found the women in the stable arena. He shook the rain from an umbrella, and Mom waved from the sidelines. Tessa rode and Avery gave instructions. Marc pulled his phone from his pocket and videoed the two. Even if Mrs. Litton didn't survive to view it, he wanted it for himself.

"You're doing great," Avery said. "Sit tall and don't hold with your knees."

"Thanks. When can I go faster?"

"Trotting and cantering come when you've mastered balance and coordination."

Tessa nodded. "What else?"

"Always stay alert and be aware of your surroundings. Here in the arena, there's nothing to distract Cozy, but the pasture is another matter. Horses have what I call horse-talk, and it takes time to learn their language." Avery turned and waved at Marc and his mother. "Be right with you." She gave Tessa instructions to keep riding the circle.

Avery walked his way. She had her hair in a ponytail, wore jeans, boots—a fresh beauty he could never get enough of. When could he tell her more than . . . wait, until this was over? "How's the riding lesson?"

"Tessa catches on fast, and she's not afraid of Cozy."

"Might need you to give me lessons."

She smiled, and her blue eyes filled with warmth. "Whenever you're ready."

"I'd like to ask a few questions when you're finished."

"Give me about thirty minutes. We're wrapping this up, and Tessa needs to brush down Cozy."

"How about in the library?"

A flicker of hesitation crossed her face. "Okay. See you then. A deputy will walk us back. If we aren't all carried off by the rain."

He gave Mom a kiss on the cheek and headed out of the stables. He whirled Avery's way. "Craig's on his way, and Leanne will be joining us."

"Good. She and Craig are part of our family." She paused. "I hope their innocent status remains the same."

Marc wasn't so sure Avery wanted to call either of them family, not with the lies Craig had told.

☆ ☆ ☆

Inside the library, Marc and Avery seated themselves in leather chairs. She smelled of horse and hay. How could one woman look like a runway model and fit into ranch life?

"What did you want to ask me?" she said.

"Tell me about Leanne."

"We've been friends for years." She told him about the bullying incident in junior high and how the two had been best friends ever since. "She's funny. Brilliant. Nothing gets by her."

"College degree?"

"Yes. In accounting. Granddad wanted to hire Leanne and finance her master's degree, but her dad threatened to disown her if she accepted."

"Her dad's at odds with the senator?"

"Politics. They ran against each other for the Texas senate, and Mr. Archer lost—twice. He also belongs to a different church denomination."

"Ouch."

"Right. Granddad tried to talk to him about leaving the past behind so Leanne could work for him and take advantage of continuing her education."

"Must not have gone well."

Avery huffed. "That's putting it mildly. Until about six months ago, Leanne still lived at home. Then her dad learned about her many visits to the ranch and exploded. She moved out and bought her own place. Wants to have a couple of horses and run a few cows."

"Where is she employed?"

"An accounting firm in Brenham."

Marc put together a few facts. The threatening calls to the senator and his friends started about six months ago . . . the same time Leanne moved out of her parents' home. Would her father have put together a plan to destroy the senator? Political rivalry? "What's your relationship with Leanne's father?"

Avery held up a palm. "I stay as far away from Ross Archer as possible. He has an extreme dislike for anything Elliott. But to others, he's solid and an asset to his party."

"Has he ever threatened the senator or you?"

"Yes."

"Why wasn't he on the enemies' list?"

"He's more bark than bite." She drew in a quick breath. "Are you thinking about talking to him?"

He nodded. "I have time before Craig and Leanne arrive."

"Take Roden with you. Might need backup with your questions."

He grinned. "Yes, ma'am. If Mr. Archer is behind the crimes, he'll get a kick out of seeing the shape Roden and I are in."

"I never understood how a person's political and church affiliation set the stage for friendship. Granddad gets it, but not me."

"Some people's roles define them, the way they think and act. While others value life lessons and experiences to define who they are."

"Sounds like you've been around Granddad."

Marc had experienced motivation to destroy lives for a whole lot less. Ross Archer's vendetta could be the catalyst for the crimes.

67

MARC AND RODEN TOOK A CHANCE on an unscheduled meeting with Leanne's father. Arranging appointments with those who had volatile personalities often went south before a word was spoken. But the opportunity to read the man could lead to the crime's kingpin.

Roden held up his phone while Marc drove through pouring rain. "I have Archer's background including financials. Here's a pic."

Marc took a glance and returned the phone. "Let's hear it. I'm in the mood to put this case to rest."

"Congressman. Impressive work for his political party. Retired from a lucrative law practice. Married for forty-five years. Three adult children. Leanne is in the middle. Nothing flagged in his financials. He's done well and made solid investments."

"Run him through the FIG."

Roden typed. "Figured we'd need the report."

"The best we have is his dislike for the Elliotts and Leanne's friendship with them. Which might be all we need."

Marc's GPS gave him directions to the Archers' five hundred acres. A large two-story brick home set back on a hill, stately but not the caliber of the Brazos River Ranch.

Once parked, the two men made their way to the front door. Roden rang the doorbell, and a trim-built man in his sixties answered. "Mr. Archer, I'm FBI Special Agent Marc Wilkins and this is my partner, Special Agent Roden Clement. We'd like to ask you a few questions."

The man stood square in the doorway. "First off, I need identification." After examining the agents' creds, he continued. "I'd let you in, but you're dripping, and the wife keeps a clean house. What's this about?"

"We're investigating a series of murders possibly connected to the construction of the Lago de Cobre Dam."

"Gentlemen, Quinn Elliott is a criminal in his own right. The media reports say he's rear-deep in taking shortcuts in that dam's foundation. If you want my opinion, he had those people killed to cover his rear."

"We need evidence, Mr. Archer," Marc said.

He shrugged. "He's too smart to cross my path."

"We understand there's animosity between you two."

"An understatement. What are you driving at?" Archer said.

"Is it true you broke contact with your daughter Leanne because of her friendship with the Elliotts?"

"You got a lot of nerve." He tried to shut the door, but Roden stuck his size fourteen foot in the way.

"Sir—" Roden used a calm tone for a gentle giant—"we're not interested in family squabbles unless differences lead to murder, sabotaging a dam, or both."

"If you're asking me if I took part in any crimes, the answer is no. I can't stand the Elliotts, but I'm not a killer. Show me a search warrant, and I'll provide you with my calendar and whereabouts." He looked dead center into Roden's brown eyes. "Now, if you will kindly remove your foot from my door and be on your way."

"One more thing, sir. If you're innocent, why not cooperate with the FBI?"

"I'm an attorney, and I know my rights."

"True." Roden handed him a business card and the folded piece of paper. "These are the dates in question if you change your mind. We'll make sure a search warrant is issued within twenty-four hours."

"A judge around here won't sign a warrant until Monday. If I had evidence that would send Elliott and his cohorts to prison, I'd gladly hand it over. Might want to consider bringing your umbrella next time."

Roden removed his foot, and the two returned to Marc's truck. Their wet clothes soaked the seats.

"I should have taken a boat," Marc said. "Or had sense enough to bring towels."

"When's this rain supposed to end?"

"The storm's stalled, so who knows?" Marc started the engine and headed back to the ranch. "The senator has done tremendous good for the state by using his influence to lower taxes, create more jobs, and provide generous donations to colleges for scholarships, but his opponents are after blood. I'd rather deal with those carrying a gun than politics."

"Just different weapons. In my opinion, Ross Archer isn't our man. He'd have invited us inside and made small talk instead of lashing out at Senator Elliott. Archer's too smart to point a finger at him. Those on the senator's list of enemies are dwindling. Agent interviews and backgrounds haven't given us a thing. The only person who has intel is my pal Craig."

"Can you work on him?" Marc said.

"I'll tell him I'm in the market to buy my girls a horse. Ask for advice."

"Good."

"On another topic, how are you doing in investigating the potential murder of your father?"

Marc hadn't worked through his emotions like he wanted—or needed. "I wish the past had been different." He paused. "I think I might have respected him."

"Forgiveness is a tough tackle."

"Not there yet."

"I get it." Roden nodded. "Any updates on the dam's condition?"

"Still holding, and the reservoir isn't overflowing," Marc said. "But for how long?"

68

THE LINGERING SMELL of chocolate chip, ginger, cinnamon, and lemon bars swirled sweetness around Avery. After the baking extravaganza, she finished the kitchen cleanup with Donita and Tessa. Avery and Tessa had eaten far too much cookie dough but had enough sense to stop before they were sick. They talked and laughed, momentarily forgetting the upheaval ready to erupt again.

The deputy hadn't arrived with Craig and Leanne yet, causing Avery to cast a cautious eye at the time. She texted Leanne. No answer.

Marc and Roden entered the kitchen from the side of the house.

"Do I smell cookies?" Roden said. "Or have I died and gone to heaven?"

"This isn't paradise, but we have plenty of cookies," Avery said.

"We'd love to have a dozen or two, but we're soaked."

Donita huffed. "There's a bathroom on your right with towels to dry off. You're not helpless."

Marc chuckled. "Really? Guess it depends on how badly we want those cookies. Any fresh coffee?"

Donita shook her head at Tessa and Avery. "Men are just little boys in big bodies."

Tessa bolted off a stool. "I'll make a pot."

Donita feigned a frown. "Don't placate him or he'll have you waiting on him hand and foot."

"We hear every word," Marc said from the bathroom.

Avery loved the bantering. Normal. Memory makers. Treasured gems to hold in her heart when life dealt a vicious blow.

Less than five minutes later, Marc grabbed a healthy handful of all the cookies and a huge mug of coffee. "Gotta few minutes for me?" he said to Avery with his mouth full.

"Of course she does," Tessa sang her words.

Roden and Donita shared a laugh at Avery's expense. She ignored them and poured coffee. "I could spare a few."

She followed him to the garden room off the formal dining room. He and Roden had talked to Leanne's dad, and she was more than interested in the conversation.

"Great cookies," he said.

"We did the woman-bonding thing in the kitchen while Mia escaped for a little downtime." A dab of chocolate stained his lip. "You're wearing a chocolate chip."

"Why not kiss it off?"

"How old are you?"

"Old enough to ask for a kiss."

"Okay." Temptation got the best of her, and she accepted his challenge, then stepped back, unsure, insecure, and wanting more.

"Whoa, you're not getting away that easily." He placed the cookies and mug on a table, took her mug and placed it beside his, then drew her into his arms.

He seemed to drink deep from her heart's well, and she struggled whether to stop him or encourage more. Somehow her arms had encircled his neck, her fingers winding through his thick hair. He ended the kiss yet kept her close. His labored breathing cautioned her, and again she moved back from his embrace.

She sensed his gaze and met his warm pools of growing emotion. She felt it too, longed for his touch. The sound of his voice calmed and thrilled her at the same time . . . She could taste his lips on hers.

He swallowed hard while holding her at arm's length. "This is where I need to keep you until the case is over."

"I understand, but it's hard."

"The problem is, the more I'm around you, the deeper my feelings." His hands trailed down her arms until he grasped both of her hands in his. "If I focus too much on you, on us, I could make a mistake and get someone killed. My head's got to be in the game." He smiled. "Now I sound like Roden."

"But he's right. We both know it." She gazed into his mesmerizing brown eyes. "You must wear professionalism to bring logic and experience to the table. Soon it will be over."

"There's another problem." Marc hesitated. "Avery, I can't give you what you have here."

Such a dear man. "I don't need these things to be happy. Contentment and joy come from God and family." She waved her hand. "I have clothes and stuff I never use."

He rubbed her arms. "Are you sure?"

"Without a doubt." She pointed to the cookies and coffee. "We need something to hold on to besides each other."

He handed her the mug and took his own. "I'd much prefer you."

She refused to respond because she didn't like keeping her distance either. Instead, she handed him a lemon bar. "You wanted to talk to me?"

"I did, but I got distracted."

"Eat your lemon bar and drink your coffee, Agent Wilkins."

He groaned and grabbed the sweet treat. "We talked to Ross Archer. As expected, he's not a fan of the Elliotts, but to suspect him of murder or putting lives in danger seems a far stretch. Opinionated, yes. A killer? Don't think so. He didn't hide his animosity, which wouldn't make sense if he were guilty."

"Have you done a background?"

"Waiting on a detailed report, but initially he's clean."

"Where are we in ending this?"

He blew out obvious frustration. "We? Oh, Avery, I have a strong suspicion, but I can't talk about it just yet. What I will say is those who've spent a lot of time framing the senator have done a good job of cleaning up their tracks."

Marc's phone buzzed, and he answered. "Yes, let them inside. Thanks."

"Leanne and Craig?"

"Yes."

She studied Marc's frown. The violent crimes had worn on him, and each passing moment increased the chances of one more death. Did he suspect Craig too?

69

RAIN BATTERED against the game room windows, reminding Marc of Hurricane Braxton's stalling over the area. Craig's prescriptions had put him to sleep without dinner, and Leanne's hospital vigil sent her home to bed. But none of the rest of the household was ready to call it a night.

Marc groaned as Tessa slid her last tile into the winning square, taking the lead on their ongoing game of Ur. "One more time, you beat me. But barely."

"Ready to play again?" Tessa said.

"Not yet. I need to develop my strategy." Marc glanced at Avery, who bit back a grin. Tessa had beat her too. The senator and Shipley were engrossed in a conversation. At least they weren't arguing. "Lieutenant Shipley, have you ever played the Royal Game of Ur?"

He shook his head. "Is that what you're doing over there? Sounds like stone scraping across stone."

"Close. Tessa introduced me to the ancient game from Mesopotamia, which is over four thousand years old. Want to give it a try?"

"Whoa. An ancient game I can play on my iPad? Why not. My kids might like it too. What are the preliminaries? I catch on fast."

"I'll give the game a whirl afterward," Roden said.

Marc showed them the board. "Touch the throw button and move ahead that many squares. A rosette means another throw, but if you stay there, you can get kicked off and sent back to the starting point." He pointed out the safe areas. "The object is to move all your tile pieces off the playing board before your opponent." He moved aside for Shipley to take his seat.

The first game, Tessa beat him. "A practice game," she said. "I hate to take advantage of the Army."

Shipley didn't laugh. Competitive?

The second game, Tessa sent his pieces back off the board twice resulting in a win.

"Had enough?" Marc studied him.

Shipley's eyes darkened. "Don't think so."

The third game, he lost and clenched his fists. "Do you have this rigged?" he said to Tessa.

"No, sir. It's a mix of chance and skill."

"I never like losing." His voice was deadly calm. "I'd think a young woman of your age would respect a man of my caliber."

"You're out of line," Marc said. "I don't appreciate your talking to my sister like she's done something wrong. This is a game. If you don't like it, quit."

"I'll quit when I'm ready." When the lieutenant lost the fourth time, he wordlessly stomped from the room. Marc caught the senator's eye. An unspoken realization passed between them.

"What did I do?" Tessa said.

"Nothing," the senator said. "We just saw a side of Shipley we haven't seen before. A little unexpected." He rose to his feet. "He's my guest, and he needs to apologize."

Tessa held up both palms. "No. It's not necessary. I—"

"Young lady, if you'd insulted him, I'd have demanded an apology from you."

Marc expected an experienced Army officer to accept defeats, no matter how insignificant.

The reaction to Tessa winning shoved Marc into probing mode. Shipley's record with the Army Corps was squeaky-clean. "Senator, can you talk to me and Roden privately before meeting with Shipley?"

The senator said without hesitation, "The library all right?"

"Perfect." Marc nodded. "We may be a while."

They entered the library, and the senator locked the door behind them. Marc and Roden chose the leather sofa, and the senator faced them in a matching chair.

"Gentlemen, Shipley's behavior tonight hit the inappropriate list. We're all stressed and worried, but we're also adults. I'm embarrassed and a little angry. Please accept my apologies."

"No problem, sir." Marc waved away the remark. "Have you ever seen Shipley respond to losing a game like he did a few minutes ago?"

The senator folded his hands across his trim middle over an over-size belt buckle. "He lost a game of golf with Abbott, Liam, and me. Once. Never played again. I remember he stayed strangely quiet and excused himself. Didn't answer his phone for a week. We chalked it up as a sore loser. He refused any future invitations for golf."

"Senator," Roden said, "do you want Avery in on this conversation?"

"Can we record it for her to hear later? I'm not leaving her out of any information."

"On it." Roden pressed Record on his phone. "How long have you known Shipley?"

"Ten years, professionally. He and I met occasionally for dinner and sometimes with Abbott and Liam. We approached him with the threats about four months ago."

"Have you ever questioned his behavior or if his head wasn't in the game during the investigation?"

"Not really. Just because he has a few issues with losing doesn't mean he's a killer."

"I agree," Roden continued. "We need to examine everyone and weigh facts against motive. Marc has spent more time with him than I have." He gestured to Marc. "What's your take?"

"A question rolling through my head is if the lieutenant's former position in the CID meant working undercover, and how would that affect assisting in this case? How much power does he have?"

The senator gripped his hands over his knee. Was he processing past and present? "When we shared the threats with him, he assured us the guilty person didn't have long on the streets. He also insisted no one be told. We assumed Shipley went to his bosses about our problem. As far as his past work with the CID, I imagine it depends on the situation."

"Who recommended confiding in him four months ago?"

"Liam. He trusted Shipley for discretion."

"Any suspects other than Craig?"

"None mentioned."

Marc's and Roden's phones buzzed with an update. Marc scanned the report to learn the FIG had found nothing incriminating against Archer. Marc pocketed his phone. "If Shipley was the one who masterminded the dam's structural damage and paid Jake to murder those who got into his way, what would motivate him?"

The senator peered into Marc's face, but his eyes were distant. Long moments passed before he spoke. "What a stretch. He's a by-the-book man. Loyal to his country. Solid friend. Like me, he'd do anything for those he loves. Unless . . ."

70

FROM THE SENATOR'S REDDENED FACE, Marc feared the man's health headed for a nosedive. He brought the senator a bottle of water from the library fridge before they talked further.

The senator took a long drink and thanked him. "I'm all right, really. Appreciate your concern. I've got a minor heart problem, and stress makes it act up."

Marc doubted it was minor. "Are you sure you've told me everything about Lieutenant Shipley?"

The senator's shoulders lifted and fell. "He has a personal burden in the care of his middle daughter. She has a rare type of Huntington's disease that requires a hefty output of cash each month."

"It's not covered under his medical insurance?"

"There's a co-pay. His wife confided in me over dinner one night about the situation. Shipley had excused himself to take a call, and she opened up. She said the disease is hereditary from the paternal side, and the other two kids had a 50 percent chance of inheriting it. Shipley blamed himself, and I understood why. I promised her I'd do whatever I could to support him."

Roden grimaced. "I'd be a wreck. Pride, guilt, and the inability to provide for your family are strong motivators. If I faced his challenges, I'd do about anything to find a cure."

The senator ran his fingers through his silver hair. "I approached him privately, offering my resources. He said a few things, but the gist of it was he told me to mind my own business. He might not have money like I did, but he could take care of his family. He accused me of trying to lure his wife into an affair. I dropped the whole matter. I hadn't seen him angry before, and his reaction took me back a bit. Later he apologized."

The senator drew in a ragged breath. "I should have asked for details. Have we all been fools? But his hand in the murders and faulty dam construction make no sense."

More reason for Shipley to restore his family and pride by planning murders and an unsafe dam. "Have you witnessed Shipley and Craig in private conversations?"

"Plenty of times. Shipley admired Craig's horsemanship and leadership abilities. Why?"

"If not for Craig getting shot, I'd suspect the two men were working together." Marc glanced at Roden. "We've noted a few discrepancies."

The senator anchored both hands on the arms of his chair. "Shipley's a victim, as loyal as a man can be. Craig's family."

Roden stood. "Senator, are you all right? Do you need an ambulance?"

Marc yanked his phone from his jeans pocket to make the 911 call.

The senator held up his hand. "Please don't. I'm okay. Shocked. Upset. Once we're finished here, I'll take my meds."

Roden pointed to the door. "Go get them now. We'll wait."

The senator stood. "Are you suggesting Shipley and Craig linked up to destroy me?"

Marc studied him to ensure a heart attack wasn't in the making. "Sir, we'll talk about it after you've taken your meds. Do you want one of us to join you?"

"No thanks, Marc. Remember everything in this room is recorded, so don't talk about me." The senator forced a smile.

Roden opened the library door. "Not a word."

Marc took the few moments of waiting to reflect on Shipley's state of mind—the overwhelming guilt and lack of control over his responsibilities. How far would a man go to protect his family? The senator had worked and failed to keep Avery safe. Roden would give his life for his family. And Marc held the same convictions about Tessa and his mother. Still, neither money nor vengeance would reverse his daughter's disease.

The senator returned and eased onto the chair. "I've been thinking. I've never been a man to call another man's wife, but if Hope Shipley opened up to me before, perhaps she will again. Do you mind if I call her?"

Marc glanced at Roden, and they agreed.

The senator pressed in a number, then the Speaker button, and set the phone on the table before them. "Hope, this is Quinn Elliott. How are you?"

"Okay. If you're trying to find Nick, I haven't seen or talked to him, but I've followed the news stories about the problems with the dam. I'm so sorry. You might as well know the truth. I left Nick six weeks ago and filed for divorce."

That coincided with the time the senator, Liam, and his father met with Shipley regarding the blackmail and threats.

The senator's eyes flashed a mix of surprise and concern. "Why?"

"I'll tell you if time isn't an issue."

"I have plenty of time and a good ear. Colonel Abbott Wilkins's son is with me and an FBI agent. Does their presence pose a problem?"

She inhaled sharply. "Has Nick broken the law?"

"Not that we know of. He seems distracted."

"Nick's not the man I married. Something about him has changed, and it may be the Huntington's affecting his behavior."

"Your daughter?"

"Yes, but Nick was diagnosed five months ago. He hasn't told you?"

"Right. I'm sorry to hear the bad news. You wanted to tell me a story?"

"You deserve to know what's going on. From the time Nick and I were newlyweds, we dreamed of one day retiring on a small ranch. We scrimped and saved to one day have our little spot of heaven. In Nick's Army career, he aligned himself with successful men who offered sound advice on everything he faced. After he took the position with the Army Corps, he and Liam Zachary became good friends. Liam introduced him to Colonel Wilkins and later to you.

"Nick sincerely admired all of you. When you invited him into a small circle of friends who shared common beliefs about faith, family, politics, and golf, he was thrilled. He learned from you and emulated your ways. About a year ago, he overhead the three of you discuss the possibility of a lucrative investment. Nick interpreted the conversation as a sign from God. Without telling me, he invested all our retirement into the same company.

"When our daughter was diagnosed with Huntington's, we discovered—because Nick is adopted—he carried the gene. I researched for any medication or treatment to help. I found an experimental drug developed in Europe and highly effective in treating the disease, but the drug hadn't been approved in the US. I went to Nick with the idea of pulling money out of our savings. He told me he'd poured our life savings into a company that folded. He lost everything. Nick blamed Liam, Abbott, and you. His bitterness built a wall in our marriage. I couldn't talk to him about anything without him exploding. He accused me of horrible things. I had little choice but to move out with the kids."

"Hope, again I'm sorry for the tragedy in your family. None of us recommended he make an investment, and I had no idea of the loss. Now I understand his irrational behavior. Are you seeing a counselor?"

"Yes, and so are the kids. I appreciate your listening."

The call ended, and the senator shook his head as though denying Hope Shipley's words. "I despise what's happened. Shipley's and Craig's involvement seemed incredulous, but unfortunately the theory makes sense."

Marc forged ahead. "We're speculating here, but we need to examine all possibilities. Shipley's motivation could be a personal issue related to passing Huntington's disease to his children and the lack of funds to pay for medical expenses. Craig, I'm not sure. We have questions for him in the morning." He nodded at Roden. "What do you think?"

"Shipley's carrying a huge load. His daughter may have at the most ten to fifteen years. I know because a friend from college was diagnosed with Huntington's. The downhill side of the disease is the complete helplessness prior to death."

Marc raised a finger. "I noticed his involuntary jerking and thought nothing of it."

"Those symptoms started in the last few weeks," the senator said. "If he's guilty, nothing justifies what he's done. No one deserved to die or face the dam failure, but his actions show his desperation."

Another thought begged for an explanation. "Shipley wouldn't have the money to finance such an operation, but Craig might have had access to the funds."

The senator's face paled. "Anything is possible. Have you researched their financials?"

Roden leaned forward, his massive frame like a bulldozer, but his countenance was one of compassion. "Shipley's finances are in lousy shape. But Craig has saved money for years, and no high-dollar withdrawals have been reported. Ever. He and Buddy spent time at the gambling casinos in Oklahoma. Even then, Craig's bank account stayed the same, which tells me he gambled with money from another source."

The senator spoke up. "Bonuses and earned profits have amounted to quite a fistful of cash. What else?"

"Up until nine months ago, Craig frequented a few gambling spots in Louisiana. He did well at the blackjack table. No record of gambling since then."

"Buddy told me Craig gambled, but my son has lied about so much that I blew it off." The senator scrubbed his hand over his face. "If you're right, I've been played. Two people I trusted might have turned against me. Jake goes down for the murders, and I end up in prison for changing the specs on the dam." His attention darted to Roden and then Marc. "Avery has been a target all along. Jake had her on his list, not just to frighten me but to follow through on his contracts. I might kill whoever is responsible myself."

"Slow down, sir," Marc said. "Letting anger take over doesn't solve a thing. If we are to tackle this head-on, we need to talk it through with logic."

"True. We men have a protective instinct when it comes to those we love."

"I've felt the same way with Mom and Tessa." He'd not mention Avery. "We still need level heads."

"I'm trying to force my anger aside. What else have you speculated?"

"Avery assumes control of everything in your absence. But if prosecution can prove she covered up the faulty foundation, she'd face a ruined reputation and possibly jail time. Her signature is on all legal documentation. The assets from the ranch and construction business would be frozen and tied up in court for years. But Craig wouldn't have a job. Shipley collects on his vengeance but still doesn't have money for medical expenses. With you and Avery out of the picture, Buddy has an opportunity to hire legal help to possibly gain control of the ranch and company. We ran a background on Ross Archer, but nothing surfaced."

The senator kept a stoic expression. "All four men have intelligence in their wheelhouse."

"Have you ever suspected Craig might be padding the books?" Marc said.

"He would have been caught. Meticulousness is one trait Avery and I share."

"Sir," Roden said. "Marc has experienced a woman caller who used the same burner number as the threatening calls. Who would you suspect?"

"You lost me there. More than one woman opposes me, especially those who object to my political stands. Have you discovered a potential problem in the list I provided? There are women on it."

"Nothing at present."

The senator sighed. "Why would Craig conceive such a plan? I've paid him well, offered every conceivable compensation."

"Except a stake in the ranch and company," Roden said. "Unlike Marc, I haven't checked Archer off the list. He and Craig might seem like an unlikely pair, but Archer is Leanne's father." He rose and stretched his tree-trunk legs. "The reason Craig wouldn't betray you may be the reason he has."

Marc's and Roden's phones buzzed with an alert.

Marc scrolled down the message and clenched his fist.

The dam had broken.

71

SHORTLY AFTER MIDNIGHT, Avery authorized water, blankets, and food to be sent to a centralized emergency shelter. She'd slept fitfully with the news of the dam's breach, dozing and then startling awake. Repeatedly. The people and property in the path of the massive flooding filled her mind. First responders and volunteers worked furiously to find those who had refused to evacuate earlier, and she longed to help. Once daylight hit, perhaps she'd drive to one of the shelters and offer aid. Marc and Granddad would object—actually they'd pitch a fit—but she'd deal with them.

At 6 a.m., Leanne texted her.

Craig has left the ranch to help people stranded with the flooding.

Avery typed, her fingers shaking. He's in no shape to help anyone. And he's a person of interest and was told not to leave.

I tried to stop him or pleaded with him to take me along. He said it was too dangerous for anyone looking for him and many of the roads were impassable. He isn't guilty of any crime. I'm sure of it.

But Avery had her doubts. **I'll see if I can contact him. Don't worry.**

Avery checked with security, and Craig had left the ranch at five thirty. The deputies' instructions were to stop those coming in and out. Hadn't Marc alerted them to Craig's person-of-interest status?

She dressed and grabbed her keys. Craig hadn't answered her calls or texts. The man's brains must have dripped out with the blood lost from his wound.

Avery hated to neglect Leanne, and sneaking off from the ranch to console her might not be her best decision. But she'd text Marc and Granddad once she was on the road. Not the first time she'd upset them with a bit of impulsive behavior.

After leaving a sleeping household, she waved at a deputy manning the gate and drove to Leanne's. Her best friend had recently bought a home and fifty acres, thanks to grandparents who'd left her a sizable inheritance. The property hadn't cost half what she'd inherited, allowing her to bank the extra dollars. Leanne had the levelheaded thing going, and she wanted to one day invest in her own accounting firm.

Although rain had slackened under cloudy skies, Avery's windshield wipers still moved at a steady cadence. She flipped on the radio for weather-related updates. The stalled storm poured water into low-lying areas, but the worst damage came from the compromised dam. So far, the storm contributed to three deaths. A twinge of guilt assaulted her for the high ground of their home, barns, and stables. One section of beloved acreage rested on the family cemetery high above the flood zone.

The rising waters blocked the shortest way to Leanne's, making the drive twice as long. Leanne remodeled the one-hundred-year-old farmhouse in her spare hours.

At a stop sign, she sent an audio text to Marc and Granddad. "Gone to see Leanne. She's upset because Craig left the ranch earlier to help with the flooding emergencies. Not sure how he got past the deputies."

At Leanne's home, Avery parked in the driveway and dashed to the front porch. She rang the doorbell. Waited. Knocked. And repeated. Leanne kept her Jeep parked in the small barn, and Avery hurried there in the mounting rain. The barn stood empty except for a corner where Leanne stored hand tools, a ladder, and a tool chest.

Rain attacked the barn roof like soldiers in action on a battlefront. She moaned. Why hadn't she grabbed her umbrella? Glancing about for something to shield her head from the downpour, she searched through the assortment of equipment. Nothing caught her eye to protect her from the rain.

She walked through the barn to see if a rag or towel lay in one of the two stalls. Inside the one on her right, a tarp covered something, perhaps a piece of equipment or building supplies. A ratty towel caught her attention. She bent to retrieve it, and a patch of blue metal behind the far end of the tarp sparked her curiosity.

Avery lifted the tarp—a blue Yamaha Tracer 9 GT motorcycle.

She trembled, fury and suspicion tumbling through her. She pulled her phone from her jeans pocket and pressed in Marc's number.

He answered on the first ring. "Have you lost your mind?"

"Maybe so. I'm at Leanne's, and she's not here or answering her phone."

"And I get it you're worried about her taking off after Craig in this weather, but—"

"Marc, I'm in her barn, and I think I've found Jake's motorcycle."

"Why would it be there?"

"Not sure. Leanne and Jake are cousins, and he must have needed a place to store it. I feel horrible even thinking she's involved."

"I'm on my way. Are you in your car?"

"No. Still in the barn."

"Take a pic of the bike and head back here."

"I'm staying until you arrive. If Leanne returns, I'll ask her about it."

"Avery, listen to me. Get your rear back to the ranch."

"No, Marc. I can't. Leanne is my dearest friend, and she'll give me a truthful explanation for this. You can't get through on the main road, so take an alternate route. It will take a few minutes longer." She ended the call. Rain pelted her car like the devil throwing rocks.

72

MARC'S FIRST THOUGHTS leaned toward wringing Avery's neck. She'd allowed goodwill and compassion to alter her judgment and put herself in danger. He slid into jeans, T-shirt, and shoes before he tucked his Glock in his back waistband and took the stairway to the first floor. The senator met him at the foot of the stairs.

"Security gate claims Craig left around five thirty this mornin'," the older man said. "He wakened a deputy who, in a sleep stupor, let him through. The same man told me Shipley left the ranch at 3:05 this morning, claiming he had a family medical emergency. The deputy knows how I feel about incompetence. Now both our suspects are gone."

Marc's face flushed. "The deputy allowed two persons of interest to leave the ranch. The man doesn't deserve his badge."

"The sheriff will get an earful. I'll drive to Leanne's."

No reason to argue when Marc had his weapon. "I'm texting

Roden." He yanked his phone from his pocket and put his thumbs to work. "I'll call him once we're on the road."

"We need him to protect our girls here at the ranch and keep an eye out in case Shipley shows up."

"One more thing, Leanne's not at home."

The senator pressed a button to open a door of the triple-car garage. The downpour sounded like a waterfall. They climbed into his truck, and the senator backed out. "Should we wait to see if we pass Avery on the road?"

"Don't think so. She's staying in case Leanne returns. One more thing, Avery found Jake's motorcycle, the missing piece to his guilt."

The senator palmed the steering wheel. "Are you serious? If Leanne is working with Craig, another murder won't mean a thing."

"Senator, I tried to get Avery to leave. I have no idea why she was in the barn or how she found the motorcycle."

"My granddaughter, until life erupted, rarely did anything unexpected. Oh, she'd break horses and outshoot me most of the time, but I never saw this wild, spontaneous side that could get her killed."

The windshield wipers flew at lightning speed, but the commotion didn't stop the senator from pressing on the gas and potentially hydroplaning. Marc couldn't get to Avery fast enough either.

At Leanne's home, the senator whipped into the driveway, bouncing his truck in the water-filled ruts. He swung in next to Avery's car.

"You'd think Leanne would get those holes handled," the senator said.

Marc chose not to respond. No point.

Avery stepped out of her battered car with an umbrella that the wind popped upside down and hurried into the barn. Marc and the senator rushed after her.

"If you were five, I'd turn you over my knee," the senator said. "Have your brains turned into chicken feed?"

"I'm fine." She stood dripping wet, like most of them had been the past few days. "I need to talk to Leanne." She led the way to the stall where she'd uncovered the blue Yamaha motorcycle.

Marc snapped more pics before he contacted the sheriff's department to confiscate the evidence. He studied Avery, a little pale to his liking. "Is Leanne in the habit of not answering texts and phone calls?"

"Never. I'm worried she's gotten trapped in high water. Or Craig is not who we think he is, especially after I listened to y'all's library conversation on my phone while driving here."

Marc heard the near panic in her voice. How much more could she take? "I'll try to reach her again."

"No, she's my friend." Avery pressed in a number. "I've got this on speaker." She stared back at Marc, her lips quivering.

"It will be all right. Take a deep breath."

She lifted her chin. "Leanne, where are you? I'm at your place."

"I'm with Craig helping people get to a shelter. I was on the road when I called you earlier. You've tried to reach me, and I'm sorry. Been incredibly busy. Look, I've got to go. We're about to transport a family by motorboat to a shelter."

"We're on our way. What's the location?" Avery repeated it, and Marc typed the address into his phone before she ended the call.

"Marc, why don't you go with Avery, and I'll follow," the senator said.

"Really?" She slapped the keys into Marc's hand. "Am I about to get a lecture?"

Marc winked. "We're good. I'll update Roden on the way."

Roden picked up on the first ring, and Marc explained where they were headed. "If Shipley returns, keep him at the ranch. Cuff him if necessary. Are Mom and Tessa all right?"

"Yeah. The latest weather report says the rain should be moving out by noon."

"Best news we've had for a while."

In thirty-five minutes, they arrived at a large church campus hosting emergency supplies and shelter for flood victims. Bunk beds lined the church's recreation building. Tables held water and snacks, and signs indicated the cafeteria offered hot meals.

Marc experienced an unexpected surge of compassion and appreciation for all those who sacrificed time and resources to help the victims. His mother and Tessa wanted to help too, but not with the danger.

God. You have good people serving You. Thanks. And, God, I need help in ending this case. These people needed to know those responsible would be held accountable for their actions. *Help me with insight and wisdom. Thanks again.*

"You're quiet," Avery said.

"Thinking. I want the guilty people in cuffs."

"I know, and as much as I don't want to believe Leanne, Craig, and Shipley have instigated this, evidence points to them."

The senator approached and pointed to Leanne and Craig, who were assisting a young family to the registration desk. Leanne wrapped her arm around a pregnant woman's waist, and Craig carried a toddler opposite his wounded side. How could these two be behind the murders?

Or was this a way to ease their consciences?

Avery faced the senator and Marc. "I want to ask Leanne the hard question. We've been friends for too many years to allow one of you to confront her."

"Sweet girl, are you sure?" Love laced the senator's tone.

She reached up and kissed his weathered cheek. "Yes. Let's do this."

The three joined Leanne and Craig, and Marc led out. "Craig, you were told not to leave the ranch, even to help these people. You broke the law."

Craig held his side where blood had seeped through the bandage. "I couldn't ignore the suffering. Yes, it was wrong, but I don't regret giving these folks a hand."

"Why didn't you contact me?"

"You'd have stopped me before I got started."

True. "You're not blind to the serious evidence stacked against you."

"No, I'm not. And I will tell you the truth once we're back."

Avery turned to her friend. "Leanne, while at your house, I looked for your truck in the barn, and the rain started to pour again. I searched for something to cover my head and found a motorcycle in one of the stalls."

"My cousin asked me to store it for him. Why?"

"Jake?" Avery said.

"Yes. Not sure why he didn't have room at his parents' place. Why?"

"It's been seen with a suspect during the commission of a few crimes, namely murder."

She gasped. "That's why he's in jail?" When Avery nodded, Leanne touched her mouth. "I had no idea. He brought the bike over while I was at work. In fact, I've never seen it. I owe you a huge apology. I knew he'd been arrested, but I've been so consumed with all of this, and I didn't follow up on what he'd done."

Craig startled. "Finding the motorcycle seems like Leanne and I are part of these crimes." He turned to Marc. "I assure you. We are innocent of any murders or the stressed dam."

The senator cleared his throat. "We need proof to exonerate both of you."

"I understand." Craig's features fell. "I've committed to serving meals for the next hour. I'd like to finish."

"Impossible." The senator lifted his chin. "No argument. On the way back, you'll ride with Marc, and Avery will drive your truck."

Craig squared off with the senator. "Then I guess I'm under arrest until you and the agents confirm my story."

73

MARC HAD WAITED LONG ENOUGH to question Craig. The deaths, flooding from the dam, and the overwhelming evidence should have him behind bars. Volunteering to help victims didn't erase murder charges or patch a leaky dam.

Marc glanced at the senator, Roden, and Avery seated in the ranch's library. "Craig and Leanne will be here in a few minutes. They're changing into dry clothes. We need answers. If they want to make a deal by naming someone as an accomplice, Roden and I will listen."

Roden's lined face indicated his wound bothered him. "Shipley hasn't been located. Neither has he returned my calls or texts. He's lied to us, but why? Where is he now? Hightailing it out of the country? Trying to figure out his next move before we get to the truth?"

"Let's hope Craig has an idea of his location. I'll see if Shipley answers a text from me." Marc typed and read the message aloud. "'Are you close by? We have new information and need your input.'" He pressed Send.

Marc read Shipley's response to the group. "'I'm home. Call or text.'"

Marc typed, **This is too sensitive. We'd rather see you. I'll check back later.**

"I'm requesting a BOLO," Marc said. "Tired of playing games."

"Back to Craig," the senator said. "He denied the crimes earlier, but he's also had time to reconsider. I'd like to give him the opportunity to confess and name who else is involved."

"It would look better on his record." Marc hid his distaste for anyone involved in murder. "Leanne too if she agrees."

Avery frowned. "You don't believe Jake stored the motorcycle there, and she had no idea it was used in crimes?"

Marc understood her friendship and loyalty to Leanne and the heartache of Craig's vicious crimes. "It's odd she wasn't aware of why he'd been arrested, but I must follow the law. There's a chance Jake might exonerate her."

"What about their willingness to talk?" Avery said.

"It's a plus." Marc understood their emotions dictated their thoughts and behavior.

"No need to say the obvious," she said. "His noble actions might be viewed as another means of covering up his crimes."

The senator's phone alerted him to a text. The older man sighed. "Craig and Leanne are on their way down."

★　★　★

Avery longed for the suspicions about Craig and Leanne to be wrong. Families didn't pin murders on each other.

Unless they were guilty.

Craig and Leanne entered the library. She'd changed into a pair of jeans and a T-shirt of Avery's, but Craig still wore his wet clothes.

He shook Granddad's hand. "Senator, I need to talk to all of you. I've asked Leanne to support me with what I'm calling a confession. She knows the whole story."

Granddad gestured to chairs. "Sit down. You two are worn-out."

"I'd rather stand. I'm soaked. Forming my words, the truth, to you seemed more important than dry clothes." Craig focused on Granddad. "This may take a little while, so I'd appreciate patience. I'm embarrassed to admit I had an addiction to gambling. Started in my twenties, but I stopped nine months ago. Senator, I couldn't tell you and face the shame of disappointing you.

"When Lieutenant Shipley visited, he often joined me in the stables. We talked about ranch life, the horses, the construction business, and our admiration for you. I felt like I could trust him, so I told him about trying to get rid of the gambling problem. He encouraged me to make sure my life wouldn't ever get tangled up in an addiction again by getting counseling. I told him I should tell you, but he believed if you ever learned about my addiction, you'd lose respect for me. Fire me on the spot. He offered to help with my responsibilities regarding the dam construction so I could spend a little time off in counseling. When I asked him why, he said he believed every man deserved a second chance." Craig dragged his tongue across dry lips.

"Last night, the accumulation of murders, the compromised dam, and the question of who shot me came together." He swallowed hard. "Sir, I know you're friends with Shipley. But I need to tell you a few things about him."

"Why?" Granddad set his jaw. "You said he helped you find the tools you needed to overcome your gambling issues."

"Look at when the problems started. Six months ago, he came to me with dates for an addiction recovery facility. I paid cash to avoid filing with insurance and you and Avery learning the truth. Later I saw it coincided with your hunting trip, and we needed to pour the dam's foundation. We were already behind. I thanked Shipley but told him I needed to wait until the next time the extended counseling was offered. He persuaded me to let him take care of the dam project. He requested the specs, and he'd ensure the work met all guidelines.

"I turned them over to him, and he arranged the crew. When I asked the reason for not using our standard crew, he said the new team had a higher rating and worked on Sundays. We'd been looking for a break in the weather to pour the foundation, so I agreed and arranged for the crew's hotel and food. Aside from deceiving you, the recovery program really helped me continue to fight my gambling addiction."

The idea of Craig struggling with a gambling problem surprised her. "The last inspection showed the foundation materials weren't used. But they were picked up at the warehouse. Where are they?"

"I have no idea." Craig dug his fingers into his palms. "Why did I fall for such a stupid idea?"

Granddad moaned. "I would have canceled my trip to help you, Craig. You're like a son to me."

"Thank you, sir, but there's more. When I disappeared a few days ago, I returned to the same facility. Shipley said with all the problems here, I could use a break to reinforce the counseling. He feared I might start gambling again, and Leanne deserved a strong man. I refused because of all the trouble we were having with the dam and the murders. Again, I let Shipley talk me into going. He claimed he'd tell you in confidence that I had a personal situation and I'd be back this past Thursday night. I wanted to tell Leanne, but he claimed I'd lose her. What I didn't say earlier is cell phones are not permitted at the facility, so I never saw anyone's calls or texts."

"Craig," Marc said. "You really have no idea who shot you?"

"None. On the way back from the facility, I read the texts and listened to the voice mails. I immediately called Shipley, but he didn't answer. Then I called Leanne, who was hysterical. Feared I'd been killed. Rather than call the senator, I chose to use the Old River Gate and tell him the whole story the following morning. But a bullet stopped me. I fell and was knocked unconscious. I woke and called Avery. Honestly, I don't remember much except at the hospital Shipley called and recommended I hold back telling you the story about my gambling, because you had too much on your mind." He glanced at Marc. "My cell phone records have the numbers for both facilities."

Marc shook his head. "Craig, you're wrong. There's nothing on your phone records linking you to any facilities or calls to Shipley."

Craig stepped back as though he'd been punched. "Is it possible to have numbers deleted on my phone without my knowledge?"

Marc nodded. "Technology can accomplish far more than you or I can imagine. Your online calendar doesn't show any info either."

"I have no idea who erased my cell phone calls and calendar dates. I also don't know who hired Jake Drendle to murder those men or who compromised the dam, but I am—" Craig swallowed hard, and Leanne took his hand. "I'm sure Shipley is part of the scheme. Why would he befriend me except to set me up for a string of crimes?"

Granddad rubbed his forehead. "Whoever shot you tried to kill you. That means you're still a threat and a target."

"I think surviving a bullet still stacks the cards against me." Craig waved his hand. "I apologize for the pun."

"It's okay," Granddad said.

"But you're right, sir. A doctor could tell when the shooting happened, maybe pinpoint the time. And a good prosecuting attorney could take in the time aspect and still have a valid claim to my involvement."

Avery digested Craig's words. "How do we go about proving or disproving Shipley's role?"

Marc picked up the conversation. "We have a possible motive. Senator, would you share what you told Roden and me earlier?"

Granddad explained Shipley's daughter's illness, the guilt, the cost of the medicine, the likelihood of his other children developing Huntington's, and his wife filing for divorce. "I assumed he felt inadequate to take care of his family, but murder and sabotaging a dam? Hard for me to conceive a friend planned such evil, a man I poured out my guts to when I feared for Avery, Liam, and Abbott." He paused. "Murdering Judas."

Avery touched Granddad's arm. She hadn't seen him so upset since he cried openly at Grandma's funeral.

He patted her hand. "Somewhere in all of this, he's slipped on a big pile of manure. Marc, what are your thoughts?"

"We can easily prove Craig attended the rehab facilities. The conversations with Shipley could be tossed out of court, but if Jake offers to cooperate and names him, we're on more solid ground for building a case that would hold up in court."

"The problem is," Roden said, "Jake stated the murder contracts were made via phone. I reviewed Jake's phone records while you were gone earlier, and the number belongs to a burner. In fact, the same phone used to call Avery and the two calls to Marc, one a man and another a woman."

Avery weighed their words, wishing she had more skills to help. "Is there software that changes a man's voice to a woman's?"

Roden huffed. "Sure. Shipley's prior job with Army investigation would have alerted him to his own mistakes and the high probability of finding those flaws in his plan."

"Then why deliberately plan a crime?" she said.

"Huntington's disease affects the mind too."

She nodded. "Makes sense."

"Until this is sorted out," Craig said, "am I permitted to work the ranch?"

Avery studied Marc and Roden. Hesitation stared back at her.

"What guarantee do we have you won't attempt to leave?" Marc said.

"You don't. Just my word, I'll—"

"I'd like for Craig to go about business as usual," Granddad said.

Marc glanced at Roden, and the two slowly nodded. "We'll take it one day at a time. Any slips, and he's behind bars."

Craig's phone sounded, the bugle battle cry. "Would you believe it's Shipley?"

Roden crossed his muscular arms over a broad chest. "Put it on speaker."

Craig obliged and answered the phone. "Hey, did you drive home?"

"Yes. Needed to check in on the family."

"Everything okay?"

"Yeah. I needed to make an appearance. By the way, have you told the senator about your gambling and the trips to rehab weekends?"

Avery wanted to scream, but instead she kept her contempt of Shipley quiet.

"I took your advice and chose not to. He's stressed to the point I'm afraid he'll have a heart attack. Jake's in jail for the murders, which is a comfort, but the senator needs a few days to get past the murders and the compromised dam."

"Good decision. I'll be back there in the morning. Media has torn him to pieces, and he needs our support. Marc said he had an update. Do you know anything about it?"

"They don't include me on those discussions."

"Maybe leaving you out is for the best. Take care of yourself."

Craig ended the call and peered at Marc. "What are you thinking?"

"Shipley is lying, and we need to find out his role. I want to see the three dam inspection videos. Why do the first two show a well-constructed dam?"

74

MONDAY MORNING MARC WOKE to the reminder of how a life storm had shaken his world in the last two weeks. He'd attended his father's funeral and learned he had a sister, a beautiful and intelligent young woman who'd opened his eyes to their father's change of heart. The man Marc had referred to as contemptible mended his past mistakes by claiming a spot in Tessa's life and repairing his relationship with Mom. Time for Marc to put aside his pride and forgive his father . . . his dad. The change would take time, perhaps, the rest of his life. But Marc had to begin somewhere.

As a kid at church camp, he'd asked Jesus to take away his sins. A pastor at the same camp said to be forgiven, one must forgive, but Marc couldn't bring himself to reconcile with God the Father and his earthly father. Over the years, loving God had been easy, but not Abbott Wilkins. But now God needed every part of Marc's life, with-holding nothing.

In the bed of an estate home that whispered grandeur in every corner, Marc ended the feelings of bitterness toward the man and asked Jesus to help him. Holding a grudge against anyone only hurt the person refusing to accept that humans made mistakes. He refused to allow bitterness to destroy his life.

So many matters marched across his mind. Unsolved murders. A hurricane. A stress fracture in a dam that poured a reservoir full of water into thousands of acres. Attacks on Avery, Roden, and his mother. Suspects who were innocent. People who believed they'd gotten away with death and destruction.

All tragedies in their own right. But good things journeyed into his mind too. Mom survived a sniper's shot. He enjoyed his new role as a big brother to Tessa. And a growing attraction to Avery, one both of them felt.

Marc strained to hear rain splattering against the outside balcony. Not one drop. The amazing sound of silence. While water continued to rise in some areas as it flowed down to the Gulf, the cleanup could begin. He longed to begin the cleanup on the case, but the likelihood of it happening today had risen like floodwaters. This morning, he and Roden would serve Ross Archer's search warrant. A step further in the investigation.

Grabbing his phone, he checked texts and emails. Last night he'd viewed the three dam inspection videos and sent them to the FIG for their expertise. He also requested more information about his father's death. This morning, a response provided much-needed answers. On the day Dad supposedly died of natural causes, he and Shipley had lunch at a popular restaurant in Fort Worth. Further investigation indicated Dad had paid the bill. How clever of the killer to drop cyanide into whatever Dad was drinking. From there, Dad drove to a grocery where he exhibited signs of a massive coronary. Marc forwarded the findings to Roden and asked to meet him in the media room.

Roden joined Marc on the balcony in jeans and bare feet. The isolated spot had become their safe place to discuss the case.

"I requested a search warrant for Shipley's phone records and to mirror his devices," Marc said. "Should have it after we see Archer."

"Shipley could have followed your father to the grocery and snatched his phone and gun then." Roden leaned on the balcony railing. "Has anyone fingerprinted your father's car?"

Marc shook his head. "No need until now." He typed the request to Fort Worth's police department.

"You know, chances are Shipley wore gloves to break into the car. But we can hope for a fumble."

Marc glanced up. "The grocery store has security cams. I'll make the request." After typing, he looked at the time. "It's seven forty-five. He could arrive now, and I'd be fine."

"I wonder where he's been hanging out?"

"Good questions. I don't want him out of our sight."

Marc's phone alerted him to another text. "This is from the FIG." He read enough to capture Roden's attention. "The first two videos done by Bruce Ingles are identical. Looks like he faked the second video log by developing it before the dive, then switched it with the one he videoed during the first dive. My guess he used a microSD card. And duplicated the original."

"And now Ingles is dead." Roden appeared to ponder the findings. "He was the one man who knew the truth. According to the specs filed in Senator Elliott's office, Shipley didn't alter them. He had to duplicate them with changes prior to the crew laying the foundation. We need to question those men. They'd have recognized shortcuts, and yet they didn't do a thing about it." He held up a finger. "Shipley said one of the crew members contacted the corps about the faulty construction."

"Sorta falling into place. In the meantime, let's keep the info to ourselves."

The French doors opened, and Tessa appeared, light-brown hair ruffled and dressed in boxers and a Beatles T-shirt. "Got a minute, Marc?"

"Always." He reached for her, and she stepped into a side hug.

"Am I interrupting?"

"Nope." Roden grinned. "I'm heading for coffee and then a shower." He left them alone in the morning light, a wonderful diversion from the gray and rain.

"What's up?" Marc said.

"School starts on Thursday. Not sure what I should do. So much to think about. I mean with Gram and when this will be over."

"I called your grandmother's yesterday and spoke to a hospice nurse. She's weakening, but she's also a fighter." He pulled her closer. "Can't imagine how much you miss her or the grief you're experiencing. Talk to me, Tessa."

"You've got tons on your mind already."

"Not too much for you. We were supposed to look for a house in Houston yesterday. Didn't happen but it will. There are two school districts not far from the FBI office, and I also wondered about a private Christian school. Do you have a preference?"

"I have no idea. Does a Christian school have sports and after-school stuff?"

"The one I researched does. We wouldn't know how large the program is until we visited." He rested his head atop hers, and they stared out at the front manicured yet waterlogged lawn. "I have no guarantees when this will be over."

"I've heard a few things when y'all thought I was on my phone or not paying attention. I don't like Lieutenant Shipley. He's one sketchy guy. No need to say anything 'cause you can't."

"Right. Since he's not your favorite, stay clear of him." Best they avoid the topic of Shipley.

"Yes, Brother. When will you and Avery have your stitches removed?"

"A doctor is coming by tomorrow."

"Good. Every time you or Avery hug me, I'm afraid I'll hurt you."

He squeezed her. "With the school dilemma, my mom has offered to temporarily homeschool or set you up in a virtual classroom."

"We talked about it, and I'd like the virtual classroom. Done it before." She peered up at him, her green eyes trusting and innocent. If only he could keep her safe from the world's battering ram.

"The idea of getting behind in your education bothers me."

"Me too."

"You and I will find counseling once we're back in Houston. I want you mentally healthy after all you've been through, and I want us to have a solid plan on how to move forward."

"Like when we argue? I mean, we haven't really yet, except when I had to leave Gram. But we will."

He laughed. "Yes, conflict management is good."

Marc's gut told him the worst conflict crept forward, and he feared those he loved would be in the thick of it.

75

MARC HAD POURED HIS SECOND CUP of coffee after breakfast when Craig burst into the side kitchen entrance and called for the senator.

Senator Elliott met him across the room. The older man hadn't shaved, and his shoulders sagged. "What's wrong?"

"Water's rising in the east pasture. We're doing our best to round up the livestock and move them to even higher ground."

"Let's do it." The senator moved to the outside door.

Avery set her dishes in the sink. "I'll saddle up."

Marc needed to stay until Shipley arrived. Still he wanted to help. "I'll head your way as soon as we deal with Shipley."

"Appreciate it, but no need," the senator said from the doorway. "You'd be in the way. When Shipley arrives, keep him here until I get back. Hog-tie him if you have to." He walked back into the kitchen. "Didn't mean to order you around. I'm just angry."

Doors slammed, leaving Marc with Roden, Mia, Mom, and Tessa. Outside, the sun perched in the sky with the promise of a gorgeous day. Maybe.

"They already moved the cows and horses once." Tessa carried her empty plate to the sink of what once held pecan pancakes and thick maple syrup. When Marc agreed, she continued. "If I were a better rider, I'd help."

"We'd be in the way, like the senator said. Sis, Lieutenant Shipley will be here soon. When he arrives, I'd like for you, Mom, and Mia to stay in your rooms. Locked. Make sure you have your phones, and they're charged up. Don't hesitate to contact the deputies at the security gate or call 911 if you suspect danger."

Tessa dropped her silverware. "Really?"

"The situation's serious."

She studied Mom and turned to Roden. "Is Marc overreacting?"

Roden shook his head. "Do exactly as he and I ask. We will let you know when it's safe."

Mia paused from wiping the table and touched Tessa's shoulder. "Better idea. We have a safe room with loaded weapons inside."

Marc captured his mother's attention. She stood immovable, fear apparent in her brown eyes. "It will be okay, Mom. Mia knows what she's doing. This should be over today."

Nearing 11 a.m., Shipley pulled through the security gate onto the Brazos River Ranch. Marc and Roden met Shipley at the door and explained the whereabouts of the senator, Craig, and Avery.

Shipley snorted. "Why isn't Craig in jail? Once they're back, I'll make sure he's arrested. Makes me wonder if you've gone soft." A bulge in his navy sports coat indicated a firearm.

"Craig's a person of interest, and he could face arrest before the day's over. Right now, the ranch hands need him." Marc pointed to the jacket. "Hot day for a coat."

"Early morning appointment and never took it off."

Marc gestured to the library off the foyer to talk. "I think you can help us make a solid arrest today."

Roden entered the room last and shut the door. He took a chair on the opposite side of Marc forming a triangle with the three men. "We'd all like for this to be over so we can rejoin our families. My wife and girls think I still need to live in my recliner."

"You bet." Shipley took a seat. "Mine is tired of my coming and going. I kissed my wife goodbye this morning and told her I hoped to see her this evening. Receding water will speed up the dam repairs. Doesn't help the loss of life or downstream flooding."

"Last toll indicated eight people dead," Roden said.

"Sad situation. How's the senator handling the bad press?"

"As best as can be expected. Sir, we have a few questions."

"Certainly. Has Drendle confessed to more crimes?"

"Not yet. The matter of who poisoned Colonel Wilkins is a concern."

Shipley twisted his head as though he hadn't heard correctly. "He died of a heart attack. Marc, you went ahead with exhumation?"

Marc took over. "Yes. Cyanide. Looks like he ingested it during lunch."

"Technology always surprises me," Shipley said. "Makes sense the ME actually could pinpoint the time."

"I never asked about the last time you saw my father."

"A few days before his death."

"Odd, security cams show you had lunch with him the day of his death. He ordered a Dr Pepper. Is that where you dropped the cyanide?"

Shipley jerked. "Are you out of your mind? Yes, I had lunch with Abbott, but it was to discuss a personal matter. Not poison my friend."

Marc probed the man's features. "Did the conversation have anything to do with your diagnosis of Huntington's disease?"

"The senator must have told you about the medical problems."

"He's concerned about you. Another interesting point is the security cams at the grocery show you broke into my dad's car. Is that when you stole his gun and phone?"

Shipley bolted to his feet and whipped out a pistol from inside his jacket. He aimed at Marc. "I can't get both of you, but I can eliminate one."

"Did Dad have incriminating evidence on his phone?"

"Doesn't matter, does it?"

"Did he accuse you of altering the dam inspection video?"

Shipley glared.

Marc inched forward. "Or is that what you were looking for when you broke into the senator's office?"

"Changing my copy of the specs from Craig proved easy. But you're right—I need the video, and I'll get it before the day is over." He extended his arm with the pistol. "Stop where you are."

"Are you sure this is how you want things to go down?" Marc obliged and kept his tone calm. "We can talk and figure out a solution."

Shipley waved his gun at Marc. "Move to your buddy. I've been through many negotiations, and you're wasting words on me."

When Marc didn't move, Shipley aimed at his face. "Now."

Marc moved to stand beside Roden.

"Using your left hands, place your guns on the floor, and kick them my way. Wilkins, I despise you as much as I did your father."

Both obliged. Marc calculated how fast he could slam his body into Shipley, but risking Roden's life wasn't in the equation.

Roden spoke. "Bruce Ingles on your payroll since he put together a fake video log?"

"Does it matter since he's dead?"

"Why the murders and sabotage the dam?"

He swore. "They set me up to lose my life's savings in a bogus investment, like I was a joke."

"They ridiculed you," Roden said. "I understand prejudice."

"Yeah, bet you do. Comes a time when a man must take charge of his own self-respect. I tried to get them to pay up, but they were ignorant of what I could do. The idiots actually came to me for help."

Roden congratulated him. "We know how you manipulated Craig, changed the dam specs, paid off Bruce Ingles, and hired Jake for the murders. Brilliant. I assume you sold the unused materials pulled from the warehouse?"

Shipley snickered. "Made a few dollars to pay Jake. Made quite a bit from Liam's BMW too. Sold Craig's truck too. Ingles was collateral damage—got too greedy. Having a crew member call the Army Corps with a guilt-ridden conscience hit the bonus button. Enough said." He pointed at Roden. "Get into the closet behind you, and Marc will lock it."

"Why Roden?" Marc said.

"You and I have plans. Now."

Marc made eye contact with Roden, hoping his friend could predict Shipley's actions. Marc locked the closet door and faced Shipley. "Now what?"

"Step away."

The moment he cleared the closet, Shipley fired four bullets into the door.

76

AVERY'S PHONE VIBRATED in her jeans pocket—Tessa. A shiver in the heat whispered not good.

"Hey, Tessa."

"Lieutenant Shipley is here. Four shots were fired, and Marc told us to stay locked in the safe room." Tessa struggled for breath. "Marc's not answering his phone either."

Avery dug her heels into Zoom. "Mia and Mrs. Wilkins are with you?"

"Yes. There aren't any windows in here, but a security monitor shows the outside cameras. I don't see anyone, and I'm scared."

"I'm on my way. Are you okay to contact the deputies at the gate?"

"Mia is calling them. Wait. Lieutenant Shipley and Marc are walking to the lieutenant's truck. Real close. Mr. Roden isn't with them."

"Stay put, and don't leave."

"He has a gun pointed at the back of my brother's head. Looks like he's forcing him to drive." Her panic-stricken voice broke.

"Pray, Tessa. Help is on the way."

Avery called her granddad, who rode closer to the house than her location, and quickly relayed what was happening. He might beat her there, which could be in Shipley's plan. Her Sig rested in the small of her back. Fear shoved adrenaline through her body.

Help me, Lord.

Patrol cars sounded, which indicated the deputies ensured the security gate held. Where else could Shipley go with the rising river sweeping away everything in its path? Except if he used Marc as a hostage or—

Shipley's tan-colored truck appeared ahead to her left as though heading to the Old River Gate, where Craig had been found. Not smart. Had he panicked? Water continued to rise in the low area, and the truck couldn't possibly make it. Granddad raced his stallion behind the truck. How had he gotten there so quickly? A patrol car bumped over the ground closing the distance to Granddad.

Shipley aimed out the truck's sliding rear window and fired. Before Avery could scream a warning, Granddad fell from his horse. Firing with her left hand, she sent a bullet into the rear left tire, but the truck failed to stop. She urged Zoom faster.

The patrol car arrived to where Granddad lay in the mud. Both deputies rushed to his side.

"Avery, I'm good," Granddad shouted. "Keep the wolves away."

His code phrase for "families protect those they love" spurred her on to stop Shipley and help Marc. The deputies had the first aid training to help Granddad, and their car could no longer follow the truck without getting stuck.

Lord, I need You. Take care of Granddad and help me.

The truck turned directly toward the Brazos River, and water rose over the truck wheels. She peered closer. Marc had the driver's window down. On purpose? Shipley's order? She dug her heels into Zoom's side after them.

The closer she rode, the slower the going. She needed the truck to stall before Zoom was unable to swim against the water's powerful force.

Shipley opened the sliding rear window again. The bullet went wild.

Avery took careful aim at Shipley's right arm, the one holding the gun. She squeezed the trigger with her left hand and Shipley slumped.

The truck entered the edge of the water, and the current took hold. Why didn't Marc take control of the situation? Or had Shipley switched hands with his gun and demanded Marc drive into the rough waters?

Shipley opened the passenger door, holding his upper-right shoulder. He swam into the brown churning water and headed in the direction of the Old River Gate. What was he thinking? The bridge near there had washed out. He'd drown.

The truck sank deeper, and Marc pulled himself onto the roof. He dove into the raging river and grabbed a tree branch.

Zoom stood firm, unwilling to fight the swirling mud-filled river. She had no choice but to watch the men struggle and stay in the saddle. She swung a lasso with her left hand at Marc, but he held on to a tree limb.

She glanced at Shipley. He went under. Then back up. Despite what he'd done, she didn't want him to drown. He swam toward a fallen tree, reached out, and missed. He attempted to grab it again. She twirled her lasso ready to throw his direction, but a massive current pulled him under and he disappeared. If only her right shoulder didn't have stitches.

Marc released the tree branch and battled the water's power to swim to the riverbank. But how long would he survive in the raging water?

She turned Zoom his direction and again swung her lasso into the raging water.

77

EXHAUSTION AND THROBBING ARMS attempted to steal Marc's strength. Each stroke felt like his last. He lunged for Avery's rope in the muddy water as though his life depended on it. And it did.

He missed, and he gulped a mouthful of water. She threw the rope again, and it landed about six feet from where Marc struggled to stay afloat.

He fought the water to wrap his hand around the rope. This time he grasped it firmly, and the stallion leaped ahead, pulling Marc to safety.

At the river's edge, he crawled through mud until he could catch a painful breath. Avery jumped from Zoom's side and helped Marc to his feet.

"Are you wounded?" she said.

He shook his head and coughed, his lungs ready to explode.

"Take your time." Her voice was gentle, caring.

He bent over and willed his body to cooperate. "Any . . . any idea how badly the senator's hurt?"

"No, but he was conscious when two deputies stopped to help him."

"I saw Shipley go under."

"So did I."

"You risked your life to save me. Thanking you will never be enough."

"Thank Zoom. Without him, you'd be swimming." At the mention of his name, the stallion nudged her. "You're a rock star." She patted his wet neck.

"Your marksmanship is incredible with your left hand."

"I've practiced with both hands but never knew lives depended on it."

"Without Shipley's wound, we'd be dead. He intended to kill you and me."

Up ahead the sound of emergency vehicles approaching met her ears. No doubt more deputies had arrived on the scene. The idea of Shipley shooting the senator dug at Marc. Good men had died in Shipley's quest for vengeance. Good men . . . like his dad. How sad Marc found respect for his father in his death. Closure would have sealed the father-son relationship, but heaven offered the biggest reconciliation of all. Facing his own mortality shoved gratefulness into every breath.

"Avery, thank you for all you've done in this tragedy."

"What I did was small in comparison to how you and Roden fought for the truth."

He gasped, remembering his partner might be badly wounded—or worse. "Shipley forced Roden into the library closet and fired four shots."

"No," she whispered, but it sounded more like a whimper. "Roden and Granddad need us."

He stared at the faint outline of the house and barns. Lights flashed. "We've got to walk back. Slow going, but we can do it."

She took Zoom's reins and wrapped another arm around Marc's waist. "We're a team."

He studied an approaching vehicle in the distance. "Help's coming."

Avery drew in a quick breath. "It's the UTV."

Within minutes, JC, the lean man with the wide-brimmed hat, pulled alongside them. "You two are always needin' my help."

"I'd kiss you, but I have a mouth full of mud," Avery said.

JC grinned and helped them board the UTV, then tied Zoom to the rear.

"Have you seen Roden or Granddad?" Avery said.

"I saw paramedics treating the senator, and he was hollering like a mad bull. But no signs of the agent."

At the house, Avery and Marc rushed inside and to the library in search of Roden. Marc swung open the bullet-riddled closet door. Empty. No blood.

"Roden?" He rushed into the foyer. "Roden?"

"Maybe he's with a paramedic?" Avery said.

"I'm coming." The big man ambled down the hallway.

Marc grabbed him into a bear hug. "I thought Shipley got you for sure." He drew back for confirmation of no blood.

"Figured he planned to drill me with holes. I squatted down the best I could and hoped he fired for my head and stomach." He pointed toward the library. "I was spot-on."

"Who let you out?"

"Bro, does this man look like he needs help eliminating a door? I've been trained to block. The women are out in Craig's office. Afraid to stay in the safe room or house."

Marc sobered. "I lost my phone. I'd appreciate it if you'd let them know Avery and I are okay."

Roden yanked his phone from his pocket and texted them. Once finished, he glanced up, obviously needing information.

"We think Shipley drowned," Marc said. "From what Avery and I saw, the current pulled him under."

"Sorry to hear, but I'm tellin' you, I'm glad this is over."

"You know it. I need to check on the senator. He took a bullet, and the ordeal could—"

"Shove him into a heart attack," Avery said.

"Just spoke with him outside. The bullet grazed his left arm, but he broke it when he fell. Refused to be transported to the hospital until Avery showed up."

She bolted to the front door.

"The senator would do anything for Avery," Marc said. "Nearly gave his life."

"So would you," Roden said.

"In more ways than I ever thought possible."

78

AVERY HELD GRANDDAD'S UNINJURED HAND while the paramedic inserted an IV before transporting him to the hospital. She swallowed one lump after another, refusing to cry. Even if she did give in, were they tears of relief and sorrow?

"You're doing it again, sweet girl."

"What?"

"Stuffing your emotions. Time to stop." His eyes watered, and she questioned if the broken arm and bullet had raised his blood pressure to a dangerous level.

"Granddad, we need to get you to the hospital. I'll follow the ambulance."

"In a minute. I have a few things to say first."

Horror pierced her heart. "Are you having a heart attack?"

"My heart's fine. It's my dad-blasted arm that hurts. Hush, so I can say my piece. We weathered a horrible storm, and it nearly destroyed us. Now you know the truth, and it does set us free."

Sobs rose in her throat and spilled out onto her cheeks. "I wanted to be strong for you, and stuffing my emotions keeps me from crying."

A tear slipped down his cheek. "Tears are not a sign of weakness but love."

"I love you, Granddad." She tried to smile but the gesture seemed impossible. "To the moon and back."

He drew his hand from hers and reached up to hug her. "We Elliotts ride together."

A hand encircled her waist, and she sensed Marc's presence. Strong. Supportive.

"What can I do?" he said.

"Never let her go." Granddad closed his eyes. "Avery is the most precious gift this old man ever was given."

"I can't think of anything better." Marc kissed her forehead. "And I won't ever let her go."

★　★　★

Later that evening, the group shared dinner on the patio, although Avery had no appetite and neither did the others. She glimpsed Granddad in a wrist-to-shoulder cast, reminding herself of how she'd nearly lost him. Marc, Tessa, Donita, Roden, Craig, Leanne, and Mia had faced insurmountable dangers. Answers to the horrible crimes should have brought a celebration, but instead they all mourned reality. Good people were dead, while Jake would be the one facing a judge and jury for the murder of Bruce Ingles, Liam Zachary, and attempted murder of three other people. Lieutenant Shipley's body had been recovered farther downstream. Granddad had relayed the news to Shipley's wife, who now had a heavy burden to bear.

"I'm establishing a trust for the Shipley family's medical needs," Granddad said to the group. "Makes sense to help where I can.

Tomorrow I'll talk to the Army Corps of Engineers about repairing the dam."

Marc and Roden had pulled together the evidence to prove Craig had nothing to do with the crimes. He and Leanne snuggled close together.

Donita and Tessa sat on each side of Marc like guards protecting a fearless leader. In the midst of today's turmoil, Tessa's grandmother had passed through heaven's gates. Tomorrow Marc and Donita would help the girl plan a memorial service. Tessa would move in with Marc in his two-bedroom apartment until he purchased a home. The girl had so much of life ahead of her, and the ordeal of the past few weeks would strengthen her if she allowed it. Donita had remained quiet, and Avery assumed relief and exhaustion had drawn her inward.

Roden sat at the end of the table, the space reserved for lefties. He'd been on the phone to his family for nearly an hour. In the morning, he'd drive home.

The FBI in conjunction with the Army Corps of Engineers planned a press release for eight o'clock this evening to exonerate Granddad and Craig for the crimes. She hoped the corps showed compassion for Lieutenant Shipley and the tragedy of Huntington's disease.

Avery caught Marc's attention. Unspoken words passed between them. They had yet to talk, but for now their feelings for each other were sealed.

79

SIX MONTHS LATER

AVERY FINISHED UNLOADING the last box of dishes into Marc and Tessa's new home. The three had worked all day putting the two-story house together. She admired the choice of a traditional style, open floor plan, and huge kitchen.

Marc set the last box on the counter. "Where's Tessa?"

"Organizing her bathroom."

"She'll be another two hours." He grinned. "But she's my favorite sis. What's the senator up to?"

"Spending the day teaching fatherless boys how to ride."

"He's smiling more since the dam's been repaired. Can't say I blame him."

"What a nightmare."

"What about your dad? Are the two talking at all?"

Avery shook her head. "Granddad tried but my loving father said

387

he wasn't interested in a relationship until he and Saundra were back in the will."

"Hey, I'm sorry."

"Nothing we can do. Granddad and Craig are planning a hunting trip in Canada."

"They invited me, but I have a case to work on."

She whirled and frowned. "You need to take time for yourself."

"I'm saving up vacation days for our honeymoon."

Oh, she loved this man. "We aren't going hunting."

He feigned shock. "I've already bought you a new rifle."

She tossed a wet rag at him. "Save it. What do you plan to put into your thirty-four-hundred-square-foot home?"

"A family." He walked across the kitchen and drew her to him.

"The last few months have been amazing. So happy for you and Tessa. Counseling going okay?"

"Yes. So much for me to learn about teenage girls. Her abandonment issues are better, but the therapist says the healing will take time. You have been a lifesaver." He planted a kiss on her lips. "I respect her choice to attend a public high school."

"The decision took a lot of guts, especially when her name hit the news all over the state."

"She wants to live her faith where the opposition could be huge, and she's making friends. One invited her to a Bible study. And the dance lessons are good for her."

"You mean the creativity helps her deal with emotions?"

He sighed. "I love you."

"To the moon and back?"

"Yep. I'm having a hard time waiting until Valentine's Day. Can't we slip off and get married quietly and then have a ceremony for family and friends?"

"Would we tell anyone?"

His eyes held a little-boy sparkle, and he rubbed his thumbs alongside her cheeks. "We might have to. Roden would kill me since he's best man."

"And Tessa is so looking forward to her big brother's wedding. We should wait. Note, I said should. We'd disappoint Granddad too, since he's giving me away and footing the bill." She refused to dwell on her parents' refusal to attend the wedding.

"Doesn't stop a man from wishing." He stared beyond her, and she knew the refrigerator at her back wasn't that exciting.

"Your mind's spinning," she said. "What are you thinking?"

"About us."

"Scared?"

"In a good way."

She studied him. "How?"

"I have no clue how to step into the role of a husband any more than looking out for Tessa or you working remotely for your grand-dad. Might take me a lifetime to figure out the family man stuff. But we can do it together."

"How about a January wedding?"

A NOTE FROM THE AUTHOR

Dear reader,

Life's challenges always catch us off guard and we're afraid. The means we've used to deal with life no longer work, and the need to change becomes a struggle. I've been there and so have you.

Only by trusting God through the floodwaters can we avoid drowning.

Only by holding His hand can we swim upstream against a ferocious current.

Only then do we understand when we are weak, He is strong.

I hope you've enjoyed Avery and Marc's story. They saw through pain and adversity that their faith grew stronger and were blessed with the gift of love.

How amazing is that?

DiAnn

PROLOGUE

SHELBY

Would I ever learn? I'd spent too many years looking out for someone else, and here I was doing the same thing again. Holly had disappeared after I sent her to the rear pantry for potatoes. She'd been gone long enough to plant and dig them up. I needed to get those potatoes boiling to feed hungry stomachs.

I left the kitchen to find her. The hallway to the pantry needed better lighting or maybe fewer corners. In any event, uneasiness swirled around me like a dust storm.

A plea to stop met my ears. I raced to the rear pantry fearing what I'd find.

Four women circled Holly. One held her arms behind her back, and the other three took turns punching her small body. My stomach tightened. I'd been in her shoes, and I'd do anything to stop the women from beating her.

"Please, stop," Holly said through a raspy breath. For one who was eighteen years old, she looked fifteen.

"Hey, what's going on?" I forced my voice to rise above my fear of them.

"Stay out of it, freak."

I'd run into this woman before, and she had a mean streak.

"What's she done to you?" I eyed the woman.

"None of your business unless you want the same."

"It's okay, Shelby. I can handle this." Holly's courageous words would only earn her another fist to her battered face.

And it did.

"Enough!" I drew my fists and stepped nose to nose with the leader.

The four turned on me. I'd lived through their beatings before, and I would again. I fell and the kicks to my ribs told me a few would be broken.

A whistle blew, and prison guards stopped the gang from delivering any more blows to Holly or me. They clamped cuffs on the four and left Holly and me on the floor with reassurance help was on its way.

I'd been her age once and forced to grow up fast. No one had counseled me but hard knocks, securing an education, and letting Jesus pave the way. I'd vowed to keep my eyes and ears open for others less fortunate.

Holly's lip dripped blood and a huge lump formed on the side of her head. I crawled to her. "Are you okay?"

"Not sure. Thank you for standing up for me. I thought they would kill me. Why do they do this? I've never done a thing to them."

"Because they can. They want to exert power, control. Stick by me, and I'll do my best to keep you safe."

1

I tightened my grip on the black trash bag slung over my shoulder containing my personal belongings—parole papers, a denim shoulder bag from high school, a ragged backpack, fifty dollars gate money, my driver's license at age sixteen, and the clothes I'd worn to prison fifteen years ago.

The bus slowed to pick me up outside the prison gates, its windshield wipers keeping pace with the downpour. The rain splattered the flat ground in a steady cadence like a drum leading a prisoner to execution. I stepped back to avoid the splash of muddy water from the front tires dipping into a pothole. Air brakes breathed in and out, a massive beast taking respite from its life labors.

The door hissed open. At the top of the steps, a balding driver took my ticket, no doubt recognizing the prison's release of a former inmate. He must have been accustomed to weary souls who'd paid their debts to society. The coldness glaring from his graphite eyes told me he wagered I'd be locked up again within a year. Maybe less. I couldn't blame him. The reoffend stats for female convicts like me soared high.

For too many years, I imagined the day I left prison would be bathed in sunlight. I'd be enveloped in welcoming arms and hear encouraging words from my family.

Reality hosted neither.

I moved to the rear of the bus, past a handful of people, and found a seat by myself. All around me were those engrossed in their devices. My life had been frozen in time, and now that I had permission to thaw, the world had changed. Was I ready for the fear digging its claws into my heart?

The cloudy view through the water-streaked window added to my doubts about the future. I'd memorized the prison rules, even prayed through them, and now I feared breaking one unknowingly.

The last time I'd breathed free air, riding the bus was a social gathering—in my case, a school bus. Kids chatted and laughter rose above the hum of tires. Now an eerie silence had descended.

I hadn't been alone then.

My mind drifted back to high school days, when the future rested on maintaining a 4.0 average and planning the next party. Maintaining my grades took a fraction of time, while my mind schemed forbidden fun. I'd dreamed of attending college and exploring the world on my terms.

Rebellion held bold colors, like a kaleidoscope shrouded in black light. The more I shocked others, the more I plotted something darker. My choices often seemed a means of expressing my creativity. While in my youth I viewed life as a cynic. By the time I was able to see a reflection of my brokenness and vowed to change, no one trusted me.

All that happened . . .

Before I took the blame for murdering my brother-in-law.

Before I traded my high school diploma and a career in interior design for a locked cell.

Before I spent years searching for answers.

Before I found new meaning and purpose.

How easy it would be to give in to a dismal, gray future when I longed for blue skies. I had to prove the odds against me were wrong.

DISCUSSION QUESTIONS

1. Avery Elliott sees her grandfather as a man of integrity and faith . . . until the day she finds him standing with a gun over the body of a dead man and begins to doubt all she knows about him. Is she right to wonder about his innocence? If you were able to counsel Avery, what advice would you give her in the first few hours after the incident? Would your advice change later?

2. Uncertain where to go, Avery seeks out a church, only to be turned away by a locked door. Has God ever felt distant to you? What can you do to feel closer to Him?

3. As Avery searches for the truth, she's hit hard with fear and questions. She even wonders why, if she is a true Christian, she doesn't have more peace. Does an absence of peace indicate unbelief or reveal the weakness of human nature? What does the Bible say about peace? (Look up Isaiah 26:3 and Philippians 4:6-7, for starters.)

4. Having grown up without his father, Marc Wilkins is surprised to learn how involved Colonel Abbott Wilkins was in Marc's half sister's life. For what reasons might Abbott have engaged

more with his daughter? Does Marc give his dad enough chances to be involved in his life?

5. Marc recognizes that in his "on-again, off-again" relationship with God, "God was always on, and Marc needed to get rid of the junk separating them." What is holding Marc back from being fully engaged in relationship with God? What does he do to address those things? Are there areas in your life that are keeping you from being "always on" with God?

6. Avery, Marc, and Tessa all face rejection and abandonment from their parents. But Avery reminds Tessa that God sees them as diamonds. What does she mean by this? Where do you place your self-worth?

7. Marc observes that sometimes people's roles shape the way they think and act, but other people are defined more by life lessons and experiences. Which category do you tend to fall into?

8. Marc wrestles with forgiving his father. What does this mean for his relationship with both God the Father and his earthly father? What can make forgiveness so challenging sometimes? How do you move past hurts and forgive others?

ACKNOWLEDGMENTS

Ryan A. Cook—Thank you for sharing your wisdom for dam and bridge concrete.

Linda Goldfarb—Thank you for helping me teach Tessa about horses.

Larry and Lori Johnson—"One friend can change your whole life."

Heather Kreke—Thank you for brainstorming!

Edie Melson—How do I thank a friend who knows me all too well and still loves me!

Edwina Perkins—Thank you, dear friend, you are my cheerleader.

Karynthia Phillips—I appreciate your friendship and support.

Leilani Squires—Your inspiration is a priceless gift.

Tammy Karasek—Thank you for all your encouragement.

ABOUT THE AUTHOR

DIANN MILLS is a bestselling author who believes her readers should expect an adventure. She weaves memorable characters with unpredictable plots to create action-packed suspense-filled novels. DiAnn believes every breath of life is someone's story, so why not capture those moments and create a thrilling adventure?

Her titles have appeared on the CBA and ECPA bestseller lists and won two Christy Awards, the Golden Scroll, Inspirational Reader's Choice, and Carol Award contests.

DiAnn is a founding board member of the American Christian Fiction Writers and a member of Blue Ridge Mountains Christian Writers, Advanced Writers and Speakers Association, Mystery Writers of America, the Jerry Jenkins Writers Guild, Sisters in Crime, and International Thriller Writers. DiAnn continues her passion of helping other writers be successful. She speaks to various groups and teaches writing workshops around the country.

DiAnn has been termed a coffee snob and roasts her own coffee beans. She's an avid reader, loves to cook, and believes her grand-children are the smartest kids in the universe. She and her husband live in sunny Houston, Texas.

DiAnn is very active online and would love to connect with readers through her website at diannmills.com.

CONNECT WITH DIANN ONLINE AT

diannmills.com

By purchasing this book, you're making a difference.

For over 50 years, Tyndale has supported ministry and humanitarian causes around the world through the work of its foundation. Proceeds from every book sold benefit the foundation's charitable giving. Thank you for helping us meet the physical, spiritual, and educational needs of people everywhere!

 Tyndale | Trusted. For Life.   **tyndale.com/our-mission**